HJFORD

Tales of the Arabian Nights

Tales of the Arabian Nights

ANDREW LANG

ILLUSTRATIONS BY
H. J. FORD

SIRIUS

Disclaimer
Throughout the text readers may find that some of the language used and sentiments expressed are offensive and unacceptable by today's standards. These reflect the attitudes and usage common at the time the book was written. In no way do they reflect the attitude of the publishers.

SIRIUS

This edition published in 2025 by Sirius Publishing, a division of Arcturus Publishing Limited,
26/27 Bickels Yard, 151–153 Bermondsey Street,
London SE1 3HA

ISBN: 978-1-3988-5857-2
AD012330UK

Printed in China

Contents

Preface

The stories in the Fairy Books have generally been such as old women in country places tell to their grandchildren. Nobody knows how old they are, or who told them first. The children of Ham, Shem and Japhet may have listened to them in the Ark, on wet days. Hector's little boy may have heard them in Troy Town, for it is certain that Homer knew them, and that some of them were written down in Egypt about the time of Moses.

People in different countries tell them differently, but they are always the same stories. The changes are only in matters of manners and customs; such as wearing clothes or not, meeting lions who talk in the warm countries, or talking bears in the cold countries. There are plenty of kings and queens in the fairy tales, just because long ago there *were* plenty of kings in the country. A gentleman who would be a squire now was a kind of king in Scotland in very old times, and the same in other places. These old stories, never forgotten, were taken down in writing in different ages, but mostly in this century, in all sorts of languages. These ancient stories are the contents of the Fairy Books.

Now "The Arabian Nights", some of which, but not nearly all, are given in this volume, are only fairy tales of the East. The people of Asia, Arabia and Persia told them in their own way, not for children, but for grown-up people. There were no novels then, nor any printed books, of course; but there were people whose profession it was to amuse men and women by telling tales. They dressed the fairy stories up, and the characters lived in Bagdad or India. The events were often supposed to happen in the reign of the great Caliph, or ruler of the Faithful, Haroun-al-Raschid, who lived in Bagdad in 786–808AD. The vizir who accompanies the Caliph was also a real person of the great family of the Barmecides. He was put to death by the Caliph in a very cruel way, nobody ever knew why. The stories must have been told in their present shape a good long while after the Caliph died, when nobody knew exactly what had really happened. At last, some storyteller thought of writing down the tales, and fixing them into a kind of framework, as if they had all been narrated to a cruel Sultan by his wife. Probably the tales were written down about the time when Edward I was fighting Robert Bruce. But changes were made in them at different times, and a great deal that is very dull and stupid was put in, and plenty of verses. Neither the verses nor the dull pieces are given in this book.

People in France and England knew almost nothing about "The Arabian Nights" till the reigns of Queen Anne and George I, when they were translated into French by Monsieur Galland. Grown-up people were then very fond of fairy tales, and they thought these Arab stories the best that they had ever read. They were delighted with Ghouls (who lived among the tombs) and geni, who seemed to be a kind of ogre, and with princesses who work magic spells, and with peris, who are Arab fairies. Sindbad had adventures which perhaps came out of the *Odyssey* of Homer; in fact, all the East had contributed its wonders, and sent them to Europe in one parcel. Young men once made a noise at Monsieur Galland's windows in the dead of night, and asked him to tell them one of his marvellous tales. Nobody talked of anything but dervishes and vizirs, rocs and peris. The stories were translated from French into all languages, and only Bishop Atterbury complained that the tales were not likely to be true, and had no moral. The bishop was presently banished for being on the side of Prince Charlie's father, and had leisure to repent of being so solemn.

In this book "The Arabian Nights" are translated from the French version of Monsieur Galland, who dropped out the poetry and a great deal of what the Arabian authors thought funny, though it seems wearisome to us. In this book the stories are shortened here and there, and some omissions are made. The translations are by the writers of the tales in the Fairy Books, and the pictures are by Mr Ford.

I can remember reading "The Arabian Nights" when I was six years old, in dirty yellow old volumes of small type with no pictures, and I hope children who read them with Mr Ford's pictures will be as happy as I was then in the company of Aladdin and Sindbad the Sailor.

The Arabian Nights

In the chronicles of the ancient dynasty of the Sassanidae, who reigned for about four hundred years, from Persia to the borders of China, beyond the great river Ganges itself, we read the praises of one of the kings of this race, who was said to be the best monarch of his time. His subjects loved him, and his neighbours feared him, and when he died he left his kingdom in a more prosperous and powerful condition than any king had done before him.

The two sons who survived him loved each other tenderly, and it was a real grief to the elder, Schahriar, that the laws of the empire forbade him to share his dominions with his brother Schahzeman. Indeed, after ten years, during which this state of things had not ceased to trouble him, Schahriar cut off the country of Great Tartary from the Persian Empire and made his brother king.

Now the Sultan Schahriar had a wife whom he loved more than all the world, and his greatest happiness was to surround her with splendour, and to give her the finest dresses and the most beautiful jewels. It was therefore with the deepest shame and sorrow that he accidentally discovered, after several years, that she had deceived him completely, and her whole conduct turned out to have been so bad, that he felt himself obliged to carry out the law of the land, and order the grand-vizir to put her to death. The blow was so heavy that his mind almost gave way, and he declared that he was quite sure that at bottom all women were as wicked as the Sultana, if you could only find them out, and that the fewer the world contained the better. So every evening he married a fresh wife and had her strangled the following morning before the grand-vizir, whose duty it was to provide these unhappy brides for the Sultan. The poor man fulfilled his task with reluctance, but there was no escape, and every day saw a girl married and a wife dead.

This behaviour caused the greatest horror in the town, where nothing was heard but cries and lamentations. In one house was a father weeping for the loss of his daughter, in another perhaps a mother trembling for the fate of her child; and instead of the blessings that had formerly been heaped on the Sultan's head, the air was now full of curses.

The grand-vizir himself was the father of two daughters, of whom the elder was called Scheherazade, and the younger Dinarzade. Dinarzade had no particular gifts to distinguish her from other girls, but her sister was clever and courageous in the highest degree. Her father had given her the best masters in philosophy, medicine, history and the fine arts, and besides all this, her beauty excelled that of any girl in the kingdom of Persia.

One day, when the grand-vizir was talking to his eldest daughter, who was his delight and pride, Scheherazade said to him, "Father, I have a favour to ask of you. Will you grant it to me?"

"I can refuse you nothing," replied he, "that is just and reasonable."

"Then listen," said Scheherazade. "I am determined to stop this barbarous practice of the Sultan's, and to deliver the girls and mothers from the awful fate that hangs over them."

"It would be an excellent thing to do," returned the grand-vizir, "but how do you propose to accomplish it?"

"My father," answered Scheherazade, "it is you who have to provide the Sultan daily with a fresh wife, and I implore you, by all the affection you bear me, to allow the honour to fall upon me."

"Have you lost your senses?" cried the grand-vizir, starting back in horror. "What has put such a thing into your head? You ought to know by this time what it means to be the Sultan's bride!"

"Yes, my father, I know it well," replied she, "and I am not afraid to think of it. If I fail, my death will be a glorious one, and if I succeed I shall have done a great service to my country."

"It is of no use," said the grand-vizir, "I shall never consent. If the Sultan was to order me to plunge a dagger in your heart, I should have to obey. What a task for a father! Ah, if you do not fear death, fear at any rate the anguish you would cause me."

"Once again, my father," said Scheherazade, "will you grant me what I ask?"

"What, are you still so obstinate?" exclaimed the grand-vizir. "Why are you so resolved upon your own ruin?"

But the maiden absolutely refused to attend to her father's words, and at length, in despair, the grand-vizir was obliged to give way, and went sadly to the palace to tell the Sultan that the following evening he would bring him Scheherazade.

The Sultan received this news with the greatest astonishment.

"How have you made up your mind," he asked, "to sacrifice your own daughter to me?"

"Sire," answered the grand-vizir, "it is her own wish. Even the sad fate that awaits her could not hold her back."

"Let there be no mistake, vizir," said the Sultan. "Remember you will have to take her life yourself. If you refuse, I swear that your head shall pay forfeit."

"Sire," returned the vizir. "Whatever the cost, I will obey you. Though a father, I am also your subject." So the Sultan told the grand-vizir he might bring his daughter as soon as he liked.

The vizir took back this news to Scheherazade, who received it as if it had been the most pleasant thing in the world. She thanked her father warmly for yielding to her wishes, and, seeing him still bowed down with grief, told him that she hoped he would never repent having allowed her to marry the Sultan. Then she went to prepare herself for the marriage, and begged that her sister Dinarzade should be sent for to speak to her.

When they were alone, Scheherazade addressed her thus:

"My dear sister; I want your help in a very important affair. My father is going to take me to the palace to celebrate my marriage with the Sultan. When his Highness receives me, I shall beg him, as a last favour, to let you sleep in our chamber, so that I may have your company during the last night I am alive. If, as I hope, he grants me my wish, be sure that you wake me an hour before the dawn, and speak to me in these words: 'My sister, if you are not asleep, I beg you, before the sun rises, to tell me one of your charming stories.' Then I shall begin, and I hope by this means to deliver the people from the terror that reigns over them." Dinarzade replied that she would do with pleasure what her sister wished.

When the usual hour arrived the grand-vizir conducted Scheherazade to the palace, and left her alone with the Sultan, who bade her raise her veil and was amazed at her beauty. But seeing her eyes full of tears, he asked what was the matter. "Sire," replied Scheherazade, "I have a sister who loves me as tenderly as I love her. Grant me the favour of allowing her to sleep this night in the same room, as it is the last we shall be together." Schahriar consented to Scheherazade's petition and Dinarzade was sent for.

An hour before daybreak Dinarzade awoke, and exclaimed, as she had promised, "My dear sister, if you are not asleep, tell me I pray you, before the sun rises, one of your charming stories. It is the last time that I shall have the pleasure of hearing you."

Scheherazade did not answer her sister, but turned to the Sultan. "Will your Highness permit me to do as my sister asks?" said she.

"Willingly," he answered. So Scheherazade began.

The Story of the Merchant and the Genius

Sire, there was once upon a time a merchant who possessed great wealth, in land and merchandise, as well as in ready money. He was obliged from time to time to take journeys to arrange his affairs. One day, having to go a long way from home, he mounted his horse, taking with him a small wallet in which he had put a few biscuits and dates, because he had to pass through the desert where no food was to be got. He arrived without any mishap, and, having finished his business, set out on his return. On the fourth day of his journey, the heat of the sun being very great, he turned out of his road to rest under some trees. He found at the foot of a large walnut-tree a fountain of clear and running water. He dismounted, fastened his horse to a branch of the tree, and sat by the fountain, after having taken from his wallet some of his dates and biscuits. When he had finished this frugal meal he washed his face and hands in the fountain.

Whilst he was thus employed he saw an enormous genius, white with rage, coming towards him, with a scimitar in his hand.

"Arise," he cried in a terrible voice, "and let me kill you as you have killed my son!"

As he uttered these words he gave a frightful yell. The merchant, quite as much terrified at the hideous face of the monster as at his words, answered him tremblingly, "Alas, good sir, what can I have done to you to deserve death?"

"I shall kill you," repeated the genius, "as you have killed my son."

"But," said the merchant, "how can I have killed your son? I do not know him, and I have never even seen him."

"When you arrived here did you not sit down on the ground?" asked the genius, "and did you not take some dates from your wallet, and whilst eating them did not you throw the stones about?"

"Yes," said the merchant, "I certainly did so."

"Then," said the genius, "I tell you you have killed my son, for whilst you were throwing about the stones, my son passed by, and one of them struck him in the eye and killed him. So I shall kill you."

"Ah, sir, forgive me!" cried the merchant.

"I will have no mercy on you," answered the genius.

"But I killed your son quite unintentionally, so I implore you to spare my life."

"No," said the genius, "I shall kill you as you killed my son," and so saying, he seized the merchant by the arm, threw him on the ground, and lifted his sabre to cut off his head.

The merchant, protesting his innocence, bewailed his wife and children, and tried pitifully to avert his fate. The genius, with his raised scimitar, waited till he had finished, but was not in the least touched.

Scheherazade, at this point, seeing that it was day, and knowing that the Sultan always rose very early to attend the council, stopped speaking.

"Indeed, sister," said Dinarzade, "this is a wonderful story."

"The rest is still more wonderful," replied Scheherazade, "and you would say so, if the Sultan would allow me to live another day, and would give me leave to tell it to you the next night."

Schahriar, who had been listening to Scheherazade with pleasure, said to himself, "I will wait till tomorrow; I can always have her killed when I have heard the end of her story."

All this time the grand-vizir was in a terrible state of anxiety. But he was much delighted when he saw the Sultan enter the council-chamber without giving the terrible command that he was expecting.

The next morning, before the day broke, Dinarzade said to her sister, "Dear sister, if you are awake I pray you to go on with your story."

The Sultan did not wait for Scheherazade to ask his leave. "Finish," said he, "the story of the genius and the merchant. I am curious to hear the end."

So Scheherazade went on with the story. This happened every morning. The Sultana told a story, and the Sultan let her live to finish it.

When the merchant saw that the genius was determined to cut off his head, he said: "One word more, I entreat you. Grant me a little delay; just a short time to go home and bid my wife and children farewell, and to make my will. When I have done this I will come back here, and you shall kill me."

"But," said the genius, "if I grant you the delay you ask, I am afraid that you will not come back."

"I give you my word of honour," answered the merchant, "that I will come back without fail."

"How long do you require?" asked the genius.

"I ask you for a year's grace," replied the merchant. "I promise you that tomorrow twelvemonth, I shall be waiting under these trees to give myself up to you."

On this the genius left him near the fountain and disappeared.

The merchant, having recovered from his fright, mounted his horse and went on his road.

When he arrived home his wife and children received him with the greatest joy. But instead of embracing them he began to weep so bitterly that they soon guessed that something terrible was the matter.

"Tell us, I pray you," said his wife, "what has happened."

"Alas!" answered her husband, "I have only a year to live."

Then he told them what had passed between him and the genius, and how he had given his word to return at the end of a year to be killed. When they heard this sad news they were in despair, and wept much.

The next day the merchant began to settle his affairs, and first of all to pay his debts. He gave presents to his friends, and large alms to the poor. He set his slaves at liberty, and provided for his wife and children. The year soon passed away, and he was obliged to depart. When he tried to say good-bye he was quite overcome with grief, and with difficulty tore himself away. At length he reached the place where he had first seen the genius, on the very day that he had appointed. He dismounted, and sat down at the edge of the fountain, where he awaited the genius in terrible suspense.

Whilst he was thus waiting an old man leading a hind came towards him. They greeted one another, and then the old man said to him, "May I ask, brother, what brought you to this desert place, where there are so many evil genii about? To see these beautiful trees one would imagine it was inhabited, but it is a dangerous place to stop long in."

The merchant told the old man why he was obliged to come there. He listened in astonishment.

"This is a most marvellous affair. I should like to be a witness of your interview with the genius." So saying he sat down by the merchant.

While they were talking another old man came up, followed by two black dogs. He greeted them, and asked what they were doing in this place. The old man who was leading the hind told him the adventure of the merchant and the genius. The second old man had not sooner heard the story than he, too, decided to stay there to see what would happen. He sat down by the others, and was talking, when a third old man arrived. He asked why the merchant who was with them looked so sad. They told him the story, and he also resolved to see what would pass between the genius and the merchant, so waited with the rest.

They soon saw in the distance a thick smoke, like a cloud of dust. This smoke came nearer and nearer, and then, all at once, it vanished, and they saw the genius, who, without speaking to them, approached the merchant, sword in hand, and, taking him by the arm, said, "Get up and let me kill you as you killed my son."

The merchant and the three old men began to weep and groan.

Then the old man leading the hind threw himself at the monster's feet and said, "O Prince of the Genii, I beg of you to stay your fury and to listen to me. I am going to tell you my story and that of the hind I have with me, and if you find it more marvellous than that of the merchant whom you are about to kill, I hope that you will do away with a third part of his punishment?"

The genius considered some time, and then he said, "Very well, I agree to this."

The Story of the First Old Man and of the Hind

I am now going to begin my story (said the old man), so please attend.

This hind that you see with me is my wife. We have no children of our own, therefore I adopted the son of a favourite slave, and determined to make him my heir.

My wife, however, took a great dislike to both mother and child, which she concealed from me till too late. When my adopted son was about ten years old I was obliged to go on a journey. Before I went I entrusted to my wife's keeping both the mother and child, and begged her to take care of them during my absence, which lasted a whole year. During this time she studied magic in order to carry out her wicked scheme. When she had learnt enough she took my son into a distant place and changed him into a calf. Then she gave him to my steward, and told him to look after a calf she had bought. She also changed the slave into a cow, which she sent to my steward.

When I returned I inquired after my slave and the child. "Your slave is dead," she said, "and as for your son, I have not seen him for two months, and I do not know where he is."

I was grieved to hear of my slave's death, but as my son had only disappeared, I thought I should soon find him. Eight months, however, passed, and still no tidings of him; then the feast of Bairam came.

To celebrate it I ordered my steward to bring me a very fat cow to sacrifice. He did so. The cow that he brought was my unfortunate slave. I bound her, but just as I was about to kill her she began to low most piteously, and I saw that her eyes were streaming with tears. It seemed to me most extraordinary, and, feeling a movement of pity, I ordered the steward to lead her away and bring another. My wife, who was present, scoffed at my compassion, which made her malice of no avail. "What are you doing?" she cried. "Kill this cow. It is the best we have to sacrifice."

To please her, I tried again, but again the animal's lows and tears disarmed me.

"Take her away," I said to the steward, "and kill her; I cannot."

The steward killed her, but on skinning her found that she was nothing but bones, although she appeared so fat. I was vexed.

"Keep her for yourself," I said to the steward, "and if you have a fat calf, bring that in her stead."

In a short time he brought a very fat calf, which, although I did not know it, was my son. It tried hard to break its cord and come to me. It threw itself at my feet, with its head on the ground, as if it wished to excite my pity, and to beg me not to take away its life.

I was even more surprised and touched at this action than I had been at the tears of the cow.

"Go," I said to the steward, "take back this calf, take great care of it, and bring me another in its place instantly."

As soon as my wife heard me speak this she at once cried out, "What are you doing, husband? Do not sacrifice any calf but this."

"Wife," I answered, "I will not sacrifice this calf," and in spite of all her remonstrances, I remained firm.

I had another calf killed; this one was led away. The next day the steward asked to speak to me in private.

"I have come," he said, "to tell you some news which I think you will like to hear. I have a daughter who knows magic. Yesterday, when I was leading back the calf which you refused to sacrifice, I noticed that she smiled, and then directly afterwards began to cry. I asked her why she did so."

"Father," she answered, "this calf is the son of our master. I smile with joy at seeing him still alive, and I weep to think of his mother, who was sacrificed yesterday as a cow. These changes have been wrought by our master's wife, who hated the mother and son."

"At these words, of Genius," continued the old man, "I leave you to imagine my astonishment. I went immediately with the steward to speak with his daughter myself. First of all I went to the stable to see my son, and he replied in his dumb way to all my caresses. When the steward's daughter came I asked her if she could change my son back to his proper shape."

"Yes, I can," she replied, "on two conditions. One is that you will give him to me for a husband, and the other is that you will let me punish the woman who changed him into a calf."

"To the first condition," I answered, "I agree with all my heart, and I will give you an ample dowry. To the second I also agree, I only beg you to spare her life."

"That I will do," she replied; "I will treat her as she treated your son."

Then she took a vessel of water and pronounced over it some words I did not understand;

H.J. Ford

then, on throwing the water over him, he became immediately a young man once more.

"My son, my dear son," I exclaimed, kissing him in a transport of joy. "This kind maiden has rescued you from a terrible enchantment, and I am sure that out of gratitude you will marry her."

He consented joyfully, but before they were married, the young girl changed my wife into a hind, and it is she whom you see before you. I wished her to have this form rather than a stranger one, so that we could see her in the family without repugnance.

Since then my son has become a widower and has gone travelling. I am now going in search of him, and not wishing to confide my wife to the care of other people, I am taking her with me. Is this not a most marvellous tale?

"It is indeed," said the genius, "and because of it I grant to you the third part of the punishment of this merchant."

When the first old man had finished his story, the second, who was leading the two black dogs, said to the genius, "I am going to tell you what happened to me, and I am sure that you will find my story even more astonishing than the one to which you have just been listening. But when I have related it, will you grant me also the third part of the merchant's punishment?"

"Yes," replied the genius, "provided that your story surpasses that of the hind."

With this agreement the second old man began in this way.

The Story of the Second Old Man, and of the Two Black Dogs

Great prince of the genii, you must know that we are three brothers – these two black dogs and myself. Our father died, leaving us each a thousand sequins. With this sum we all three took up the same profession, and became merchants. A short time after we had opened our shops, my eldest brother, one of these two dogs, resolved to travel in foreign countries for the sake of merchandise. With this intention he sold all he had and bought merchandise suitable to the voyages he was about to make. He set out, and was away a whole year. At the end of this time a beggar came to my shop. "Good-day," I said. "Good-day," he answered; "is it possible that you do not recognise me?" Then I looked at him closely and saw he was my brother. I made him come into my house, and asked him how he had fared in his enterprise.

"Do not question me," he replied, "see me, you see all I have. It would but renew my trouble to tell of all the misfortunes that have befallen me in a year, and have brought me to this state."

I shut up my shop, paid him every attention, taking him to the bath, giving him my most beautiful robes. I examined my accounts, and found that I had doubled my capital – that is, that I now possessed two thousand sequins. I gave my brother half, saying: "Now, brother, you can forget your losses." He accepted them with joy, and we lived together as we had before.

Some time afterwards my second brother wished also to sell his business and travel. My eldest brother and I did all we could to dissuade him, but it was of no use. He joined a caravan and set out. He came back at the end of a year in the same state as his elder brother. I took care of him, and as I had a thousand sequins to spare I gave them to him, and he re-opened his shop.

One day, my two brothers came to me to propose that we should make a journey and trade. At first I refused to go. "You travelled," I said, "and what did you gain?" But they came to me repeatedly, and after having held out for five years I at last gave way. But when they had made their preparation, and they began to buy the merchandise we needed, they found they had spent every piece of the thousand sequins I had given them. I did not reproach them. I divided my six thousand sequins with them, giving a thousand to each and keeping one for myself, and the other three I buried in a corner of my house. We bought merchandise, loaded a vessel with it, and set forth with a favourable wind.

After two months' sailing we arrived at a seaport, where we disembarked and did a great trade. Then we bought the merchandise of the country, and were just going to sail once more, when I was stopped on the shore by a beautiful though poorly dressed woman. She came up to me, kissed my hand, and implored me to marry her, and take her on board. At first I refused, but she begged so hard and promised to be such a good wife to me, that at last I consented. I got her some beautiful dresses, and after having married her, we embarked and set sail. During the voyage, I discovered so many good qualities in my wife that I began to love her more and more. But my brothers began to be jealous of my prosperity, and set to work to plot against my life. One night when we were sleeping they threw my wife and myself into the sea. My wife, however, was a fairy, and so she did not let me drown, but transported me to an island. When the day dawned, she said to me,

"When I saw you on the seashore I took a great fancy to you, and wished to try your good nature, so I presented myself in the disguise you saw. Now I have rewarded you by saving your life. But I am very angry with your brothers, and I shall not rest till I have taken their lives."

I thanked the fairy for all that she had done for me, but I begged her not to kill my brothers.

I appeased her wrath, and in a moment she transported me from the island where we were to the roof of my house, and she disappeared a moment afterwards. I went down, and opened the doors, and dug up the three thousand sequins which I had buried. I went to the place where my shop was, opened it, and received from my fellow-merchants congratulations on my return. When I went home, I saw two black dogs who came to meet me with sorrowful faces. I was much astonished, but the fairy who reappeared said to me,

"Do not be surprised to see these dogs; they are your two brothers. I have condemned them to remain for ten years in these shapes." Then having told me where I could hear news of her, she vanished.

The ten years are nearly passed, and I am on the road to find her. As in passing I met this merchant and the old man with the hind, I stayed with them.

This is my history, O prince of genii! Do you not think it is a most marvellous one?

"Yes, indeed," replied the genius, "and I will give up to you the third of the merchant's punishment."

Then the third old man made the genius the same request as the other two had done, and the genius promised him the last third of the merchant's punishment if his story surpassed both the others.

So he told his story to the genius, but I cannot tell you what it was, as I do not know.

But I do know that it was even more marvellous than either of the others, so that the genius was astonished, and said to the third old man, "I will give up to you the third part of the merchant's punishment. He ought to thank all three of you for having interested yourselves in his favour. But for you, he would be here no longer."

So saying, he disappeared, to the great joy of the company. The merchant did not fail to thank his friends, and then each went on his way. The merchant returned to his wife and children, and passed the rest of his days happily with them.

"But, sire," added Scheherazade, "however beautiful are the stories I have just told you, they cannot compare with the story of the Fisherman."

The Story of the Fisherman

Sire, there was once upon a time a fisherman so old and so poor that he could scarcely manage to support his wife and three children. He went every day to fish very early, and each day he made a rule not to throw his nets more than four times. He started out one morning by moonlight and came to the seashore. He undressed and threw his nets, and as he was drawing them towards the bank he felt a great weight. He thought he had caught a large fish, and he felt very pleased. But a moment afterwards, seeing that instead of a fish he only had in his nets the carcase of an ass, he was much disappointed.

Vexed with having such a bad haul, when he had mended his nets, which the carcase of the ass had broken in several places, he threw them a second time. In drawing them in he again felt a great weight, so that he thought they were full of fish. But he only found a large basket full of rubbish. He was much annoyed.

"O Fortune," he cried, "do not trifle thus with me, a poor fisherman, who can hardly support his family!"

So saying, he threw away the rubbish, and after having washed his nets clean of the dirt, he threw them for the third time. But he only drew in stones, shells, and mud. He was almost in despair.

Then he threw his nets for the fourth time. When he thought he had a fish he drew them in with a great deal of trouble. There was no fish however, but he found a yellow pot, which by its weight seemed full of something, and he noticed that it was fastened and sealed with lead, with the impression of a seal. He was delighted. "I will sell it to the founder," he said; "with the money I shall get for it I shall buy a measure of wheat."

He examined the jar on all sides; he shook it to see if it would rattle. But he heard nothing, and so, judging from the impression of the seal and the lid, he thought there must be something precious inside. To find out, he took his knife, and with a little trouble he opened it. He turned it upside down, but nothing came out, which surprised him very much. He set it in front of him, and whilst he was looking at it attentively, such a thick smoke came out that he

had to step back a pace or two. This smoke rose up to the clouds, and stretching over the sea and the shore, formed a thick mist, which caused the fisherman much astonishment. When all the smoke was out of the jar it gathered itself together, and became a thick mass in which appeared a genius, twice as large as the largest giant. When he saw such a terrible-looking monster, the fisherman would like to have run away, but he trembled so with fright that he could not move a step.

"Great king of the genii," cried the monster, "I will never again disobey you!"

At these words the fisherman took courage.

"What is this you are saying, great genius? Tell me your history and how you came to be shut up in that vase."

At this, the genius looked at the fisherman haughtily. "Speak to me more civilly," he said, "before I kill you."

"Alas! why should you kill me?" cried the fisherman. "I have just freed you; have you already forgotten that?"

"No," answered the genius; "but that will not prevent me from killing you; and I am only going to grant you one favour, and that is to choose the manner of your death."

"But what have I done to you?" asked the fisherman.

"I cannot treat you in any other way," said the genius, "and if you would know why, listen to my story.

"I rebelled against the king of the genii. To punish me, he shut me up in this vase of copper, and he put on the leaden cover his seal, which is enchantment enough to prevent my coming out. Then he had the vase thrown into the sea. During the first period of my captivity I vowed that if anyone should free me before a hundred years were passed, I would make him rich even after his death. But that century passed, and no one freed me. In the second century I vowed that I would give all the treasures in the world to my deliverer; but he never came.

"In the third, I promised to make him a king, to be always near him, and to grant him three wishes every day; but that century passed away as the other two had done, and I remained in the same plight. At last I grew angry at being captive for so long, and I vowed that if anyone would release me I would kill him at once, and would only allow him to choose in what manner he should die. So you see, as you have freed me today, choose in what way you will die."

The fisherman was very unhappy. "What an unlucky man I am to have freed you! I implore you to spare my life."

"I have told you," said the genius, "that it is impossible. Choose quickly; you are wasting time."

The fisherman began to devise a plot.

"Since I must die," he said, "before I choose the manner of my death, I conjure you on your honour to tell me if you really were in that vase?"

"Yes, I was," answered the genius.

"I really cannot believe it," said the fisherman. "That vase could not contain one of your feet even, and how could your whole body go in? I cannot believe it unless I see you do the thing."

Then the genius began to change himself into smoke, which, as before, spread over the sea and the shore, and which, then collecting itself together, began to go back into the vase slowly and evenly till there was nothing left outside. Then a voice came from the vase which said to the fisherman, "Well, unbelieving fisherman, here I am in the vase; do you believe me now?"

The fisherman instead of answering took the lid of lead and shut it down quickly on the vase.

"Now, O genius," he cried, "ask pardon of me, and choose by what death you will die! But no, it will be better if I throw you into the sea whence I drew you out, and I will build a house on the shore to warn fishermen who come to cast their nets here, against fishing up such a wicked genius as you are, who vows to kill the man who frees you."

At these words the genius did all he could to get out, but he could not, because of the enchantment of the lid.

Then he tried to get out by cunning.

"If you will take off the cover," he said, "I will repay you."

"No," answered the fisherman, "if I trust myself to you I am afraid you will treat me as a certain Greek king treated the physician Douban. Listen, and I will tell you."

The Story of the Greek King and the Physician Douban

In the country of Zouman, in Persia, there lived a Greek king. This king was a leper, and all his doctors had been unable to cure him, when a very clever physician came to his court.

He was very learned in all languages, and knew a great deal about herbs and medicines.

As soon as he was told of the king's illness he put on his best robe and presented himself before the king. "Sire," said he, "I know that no physician has been able to cure your majesty, but if you will follow my instructions, I will promise to cure you without any medicines or outward application."

The king listened to this proposal.

"If you are clever enough to do this," he said, "I promise to make you and your descendants rich for ever."

The physician went to his house and made a polo club, the handle of which he hollowed out, and put in it the drug he wished to use. Then he made a ball, and with these things he went the next day to the king.

He told him that he wished him to play at polo. Accordingly the king mounted his horse and went into the place where he played. There the physician approached him with the bat he had made, saying, "Take this, sire, and strike the ball till you feel your hand and whole body in a glow. When the remedy that is in the handle of the club is warmed by your hand it will penetrate throughout your body. The you must return to your palace, bathe, and go to sleep, and when you awake tomorrow morning you will be cured."

The king took the club and urged his horse after the ball which he had thrown. He struck it, and then it was hit back by the courtiers who were playing with him. When he felt very hot he stopped playing, and went back to the palace, went into the bath, and did all that the physician had said. The next day when he arose he found, to his great joy and astonishment, that he was completely cured. When he entered his audience-chamber all his courtiers, who were eager to see if the wonderful cure had been effected, were overwhelmed with joy.

The physician Douban entered the hall and bowed low to the ground. The king, seeing him, called him, made him sit by his side, and showed him every mark of honour.

That evening he gave him a long and rich robe of state, and presented him with two thousand sequins. The following day he continued to load him with favours.

Now the king had a grand-vizir who was avaricious, and envious, and a very bad man. He grew extremely jealous of the physician, and determined to bring about his ruin.

In order to do this he asked to speak in private with the king, saying that he had a most important communication to make.

"What is it?" asked the king.

"Sire," answered the grand-vizir, "it is most dangerous for a monarch to confide in a man whose faithfulness is not proved. You do not know that this physician is not a traitor come here to assassinate you."

"I am sure," said the king, "that this man is the most faithful and virtuous of men. If he wished to take my life, why did he cure me? Cease to speak against him. I see what it is, you are jealous of him; but do not think that I can be turned against him. I remember well what a vizir said to King Sindbad, his master, to prevent him from putting the prince, his son, to death."

What the Greek king said excited the vizir's curiosity, and he said to him, "Sire, I beg your majesty to have the condescension to tell me what the vizir said to King Sindbad."

"This vizir," he replied, "told King Sindbad that one ought not believe everything that a mother-in-law says, and told him this story."

The Story of the Husband and the Parrot

A good man had a beautiful wife, whom he loved passionately, and never left if possible. One day, when he was obliged by important business to go away from her, he went to a place where all kinds of birds are sold and bought a parrot. This parrot not only spoke well, but it had the gift of telling all that had been done before it. He brought it home in a cage, and asked his wife to put it in her room, and take great care of it while he was away. Then he departed. On his return he asked the parrot what had happened during his absence, and the parrot told him some things which made him scold his wife.

She thought that one of her slaves must have been telling tales of her, but they told her it was the parrot, and she resolved to revenge herself on him.

When her husband next went away for one day, she told one slave to turn under the bird's cage a hand-mill; another to throw water down from above the cage, and a third to take a mirror and turn it in front of its eyes, from left to right by the light of a candle. The slaves did this for part of the night, and did it very well.

The next day when the husband came back he asked the parrot what he had seen. The bird replied, "My good master, the lightning, thunder and rain disturbed me so much all night long, that I cannot tell you what I have suffered."

The husband, who knew that it had neither rained nor thundered in the night, was convinced that the parrot was not speaking the truth, so he took him out of the cage and threw him so roughly on the ground that he killed him. Nevertheless he was sorry afterwards, for he found that the parrot had spoken the truth.

"When the Greek king," said the fisherman to the genius, "had finished the story of the parrot, he added to the vizir, 'And so, vizir, I shall not listen to you, and I shall take care of the physician, in case I repent as the husband did when he had killed the parrot.' But the vizir was determined. 'Sire,' he replied, 'the death of the parrot was nothing. But when it is a question of the life of a king it is better to sacrifice the innocent than save the guilty. It is no uncertain thing, however. The physician, Douban, wishes to assassinate you. My zeal prompts me to disclose this to your Majesty. If I am wrong, I deserve to be punished as a vizir was once punished.' 'What had the vizir done,' said the Greek king, 'to merit the punishment?' 'I will tell your Majesty, if you will do me the honour to listen,' answered the vizir."

The Story of the Vizir who was Punished

There was once upon a time a king who had a son who was very fond of hunting. He often allowed him to indulge in this pastime, but he had ordered his grand-vizir always to go with him, and never to lose sight of him. One day the huntsman roused a stag, and the prince, thinking that the vizir was behind, gave chase, and rode so hard that he found himself alone. He stopped, and having lost sight of it, he turned to rejoin the vizir, who had not been careful enough to follow him. But he lost his way. Whilst he was trying to find it, he saw on the side of the road a beautiful lady who was crying bitterly. He drew his horse's rein, and asked her who she was and what she was doing in this place, and if she needed help. "I am the daughter of an Indian king," she answered, "and whilst riding in the country I fell asleep and tumbled off. My horse has run away, and I do not know what has become of him."

The young prince had pity on her, and offered to take her behind him, which he did. As they passed by a ruined building the lady dismounted and went in. The prince also dismounted and followed her. To his great surprise, he heard her saying to some one inside, "Rejoice, my children; I am bringing you a nice fat youth." And other voices replied, "Where is he, mamma, that we may eat him at once, as we are very hungry?"

The prince at once saw the danger he was in. He now knew that the lady who said she was the daughter of an Indian king was an ogress, who lived in desolate places, and who by a thousand wiles surprised and devoured passers-by. He was terrified, and threw himself on his horse. The pretended princess appeared at this moment, and seeing that she had lost her prey, she said to him, "Do not be afraid. What do you want?"

"I am lost," he answered, "and I am looking for the road."

"Keep straight on," said the ogress, "and you will find it."

The prince could hardly believe his ears, and rode off as hard as he could. He found his way, and arrived safe and sound at his father's house, where he told him of the danger he had run because of the grand-vizir's carelessness. The king was very angry, and had him strangled immediately.

H.J.FORD.

"Sire," went on the vizir to the Greek king, "to return to the physician, Douban. If you do not take care, you will repent of having trusted him. Who knows what this remedy, with which he has cured you, may not in time have a bad effect on you?"

The Greek king was naturally very weak, and did not perceive the wicked intention of his vizir, nor was he firm enough to keep to his first resolution.

"Well, vizir," he said, "you are right. Perhaps he did come to take my life. He might do it by the mere smell of one of his drugs. I must see what can be done."

"The best means, sire, to put your life in security, is to send for him at once, and to cut off his head directly he comes," said the vizir.

"I really think," replied the king, "that will be the best way."

He then ordered one of his ministers to fetch the physician, who came at once.

"I have had you sent for," said the king, "in order to free myself from you by taking your life."

The physician was beyond measure astonished when he heard he was to die.

"What crimes have I committed, your majesty?"

"I have learnt," replied the king, "that you are a spy, and intend to kill me. But I will be first, and kill you. Strike," he added to an executioner who was by, "and rid me of this assassin."

At this cruel order the physician threw himself on his knees. "Spare my life," he cried, "and yours will be spared."

The fisherman stopped here to say to the genius: "You see what passed between the Greek king and the physician has just passed between us two. The Greek king," he went on, "had no mercy on him, and the executioner bound his eyes."

All those present begged for his life, but in vain.

The physician on his knees, and bound, said to the king: "At least let me put my affairs in order, and leave my books to persons who will make good use of them. There is one which I should like to present to your majesty. It is very precious, and ought to be kept carefully in your treasury. It contains many curious things the chief being that when you cut off my head, if your majesty will turn to the sixth leaf, and read the third line of the left-hand page, my head will answer all the questions you like to ask it."

The king, eager to see such a wonderful thing, put off his execution to the next day, and sent him under a strong guard to his house. There the physician put his affairs in order, and the next day there was a great crowd assembled in the hall to see his death, and the doings after it. The physician went up to the foot of the throne with a large book in his hand. He carried a basin, on which he spread the covering of the book, and presenting it to the king, said: "Sire, take this book, and when my head is cut off, let it be placed in the basin on the covering of this book; as soon as it is there, the blood will cease to flow. Then open the book, and my head will answer your questions. But, sire, I implore your mercy, for I am innocent."

"Your prayers are useless, and if it were only to hear your head speak when you are dead, you should die."

So saying, he took the book from the physician's hands, and ordered the executioner to do his duty.

The head was so cleverly cut off that it fell into the basin, and directly the blood ceased to flow. Then, to the great astonishment of the king, the eyes opened, and the head said, "Your majesty, open the book." The king did so, and finding that the first leaf stuck against the second, he put his finger in his mouth, to turn it more easily. He did the same thing till he reached the sixth page, and not seeing any writing on it, "Physician," he said, "there is no writing."

"Turn over a few more pages," answered the head. The king went on turning, still putting his finger in his mouth, till the poison in which each page was dipped took effect. His sight failed him, and he fell at the foot of his throne.

When the physician's head saw that the poison had taken effect, and that the king had only a few more minutes to live, "Tyrant," it cried, "see how cruelty and injustice are punished."

Scarcely had it uttered these words than the king died, and the head lost also the little life that had remained in it.

That is the end of the story of the Greek king, and now let us return to the fisherman and the genius.

"If the Greek king," said the fisherman, "had spared the physician, he would not have thus died. The same thing applies to you. Now I am going to throw you into the sea."

"My friend," said the genius, "do not do such a cruel thing. Do not treat me as Imma treated Ateca."

"What did Imma do to Ateca?" asked the fisherman.

"Do you think I can tell you while I am shut up in here?" replied the genius. "Let me out, and I will make you rich."

The hope of being no longer poor made the fisherman give way.

"If you will give me your promise to do this, I will open the lid. I do not think you will dare to break your word."

The genius promised, and the fisherman lifted the lid. He came out at once in smoke, and then, having resumed his proper form, the first thing he did was to kick the vase into the sea. This frightened the fisherman, but the genius laughed and said, "Do not be afraid; I only did it to frighten you, and to show you that I intend to keep my word; take your nets and follow me."

He began to walk in front of the fisherman, who followed him with some misgivings. They passed in front of the town, and went up a mountain and then down into a great plain, where there was a large lake lying between four hills.

When they reached the lake the genius said to the fisherman, "Throw your nets and catch fish."

The fisherman did as he was told, hoping for a good catch, as he saw plenty of fish. What was his astonishment at seeing that there were four quite different kinds, some white, some red, some blue, and some yellow. He caught four, one of each colour. As he had never seen any like them he admired them very much, and he was very pleased to think how much money he would get for them.

"Take these fish and carry them to the Sultan, who will give you more money for them than you have ever had in your life. You can come every day to fish in this lake, but be careful not to throw your nets more than once every day, otherwise some harm will happen to you. If you follow my advice carefully you will find it good."

Saying these words, he struck his foot against the ground, which opened, and when he had disappeared, it closed immediately.

The fisherman resolved to obey the genius exactly, so he did not cast his nets a second time, but walked into the town to sell his fish at the palace.

When the Sultan saw the fish he was much astonished. He looked at them one after the other, and when he had admired them long enough, "Take these fish," he said to his first vizir, "and give them to the clever cook the Emperor of the Greeks sent me. I think they must be as good as they are beautiful."

The vizir took them himself to the cook, saying, "Here are four fish that have been brought to the Sultan. He wants you to cook them."

Then he went back to the Sultan, who told him to give the fisherman four hundred gold pieces. The fisherman, who had never before possessed such a large sum of money at once, could hardly believe his good fortune. He at once relieved the needs of his family, and made good use of it.

But now we must return to the kitchen, which we shall find in great confusion. The cook, when she had cleaned the fish, put them in a pan with some oil to fry them. When she thought them cooked enough on one side she turned them on the other. But scarcely had she done so when the walls of the kitchen opened, and there came out a young and beautiful damsel. She was dressed in an Egyptian dress of flowered satin, and she wore earrings, and a necklace of white pearls, and bracelets of gold set with rubies, and she held a wand of myrtle in her hand.

She went up to the pan, to the great astonishment of the cook, who stood motionless at the sight of her. She struck one of the fish with her rod, "Fish, fish," said she, "are you doing your duty?" The fish answered nothing, and then she repeated her question, whereupon they all raised their heads together and answered very distinctly, "Yes, yes. If you reckon, we reckon. If you pay your debts, we pay ours. If you fly, we conquer, and we are content."

When they had spoken the girl upset the pan, and entered the opening in the wall, which at once closed, and appeared the same as before.

When the cook had recovered from her fright she lifted up the fish which had fallen into the ashes, but she found them as black as cinders, and not fit to serve up to the Sultan. She began to cry.

"Alas! what shall I say to the Sultan? He will be so angry with me, and I know he will not believe me!"

Whilst she was crying the grand-vizir came in and asked if the fish were ready. She told him all that had happened, and he was much surprised. He sent at once for the fisherman, and when he came said to him, "Fisherman, bring me four more fish like you have brought already, for an accident has happened to them so that they cannot be served up to the Sultan."

The fisherman did not say what the genius had told him, but he excused himself from bringing them that day on account of the length of the way, and he promised to bring them next day.

In the night he went to the lake, cast his nets, and on drawing them in found four fish, which were like the others, each of a different colour.

He went back at once and carried them to the grand-vizir as he had promised.

He then took them to the kitchen and shut himself up with the cook, who began to cook them as she had done the four others on the previous day. When she was about to turn them on the other side, the wall opened, the damsel appeared, addressed the same words to the fish, received the same answer, and then overturned the pan and disappeared.

The grand-vizir was filled with astonishment. "I shall tell the Sultan all that has happened," said he. And he did so.

The Sultan was very much astounded, and wished to see this marvel for himself. So he sent for the fisherman, and asked him to procure four more fish. The fisherman asked for three days, which were granted, and he then cast his nets in the lake, and again caught four different coloured fish. The Sultan was delighted to see he had got them, and gave him again four hundred gold pieces.

As soon as the Sultan had the fish he had them carried to his room with all that was needed to cook them.

Then he shut himself up with the grand-vizir, who began to prepare them and cook them. When they were done on one side he turned them over on the other. Then the wall of the room opened, but instead of the maiden a black slave came out. He was enormously tall, and carried a large green stick with which he touched the fish, saying in a terrible voice, "Fish, fish, are you doing your duty?" To these words the fish lifting up their heads replied, "Yes, yes. If you reckon, we reckon. If you pay your debts, we pay ours. If you fly, we conquer, and are content."

The black slave overturned the pan in the middle of the room, and the fish were turned to cinders. Then he stepped proudly back into the wall, which closed round him.

"After having seen this," said the Sultan, "I cannot rest. These fish signify some mystery I must clear up."

He sent for the fisherman. "Fisherman," he said, "the fish you have brought us have caused me some anxiety. Where did you get them from?"

"Sire," he answered, "I got them from a lake which lies in the middle of four hills beyond yonder mountains."

"Do you know this lake?" asked the Sultan of the grand-vizir.

"No; though I have hunted many times round that mountain, I have never heard of it," said the vizir.

As the fisherman said it was only three hours' journey away, the Sultan ordered his whole court to mount and ride thither, and the fisherman led them.

They climbed the mountain, and then, on the other side, saw the lake as the fisherman had described. The water was so clear that they could see the four kinds of fish swimming about in it. They looked at them for some time, and then the Sultan ordered them to make a camp by the edge of the water.

When night came the Sultan called his vizir, and said to him, "I have resolved to clear up this mystery. I am going out alone, and do you stay here in my tent, and when my ministers come tomorrow, say I am not well, and cannot see them. Do this each day till I return."

The grand-vizir tried to persuade the Sultan not to go, but in vain. The Sultan took off his state robe and put on his sword, and when he saw all was quiet in the camp he set forth alone.

He climbed one of the hills, and then crossed the great plain, till, just as the sun rose, he beheld far in front of him a large building. When he came near to it he saw it was a splendid palace of beautiful black polished marble, covered with steel as smooth as a mirror.

He went to the gate, which stood half open, and went in, as nobody came when he knocked. He passed through a magnificent courtyard and still saw no one, though he called aloud several times.

He entered large halls where the carpets were of silk, the lounges and sofas covered with tapestry from Mecca, and the hangings of the most beautiful Indian stuffs of gold and silver. Then he found himself in a splendid room, with a fountain supported by golden lions. The water out of the lions' mouths turned into diamonds and pearls, and thc leaping water almost touched a most beautifully-painted dome. The palace was surrounded on three sides by magnificent gardens, little lakes, and woods. Birds sang in the trees, which were netted over to keep them always there.

Still the Sultan saw no one, till he heard a plaintive cry, and a voice which said, "Oh that I could die, for I am too unhappy to wish to live any longer!"

The Sultan looked round to discover who it was who thus bemoaned his fate, and at last saw a handsome young man, richly clothed, who was sitting on a throne raised slightly from the ground. His face was very sad.

The Sultan approached him and bowed to him. The young man bent his head very low, but did not rise.

"Sire," he said to the Sultan, "I cannot rise and do you the reverence that I am sure should be paid to your rank."

"Sir," answered the Sultan, "I am sure you have a good reason for not doing so, and having heard your cry of distress, I am come to offer you my help. Whose is this palace, and why is it thus empty?"

Instead of answering the young man lifted up his robe, and showed the Sultan that, from the waist downwards, he was a block of black marble.

The Sultan was horrified, and begged the young man to tell him his story.

"Willingly I will tell you my sad history," said the young man.

The Story of the Young King of the Black Isles

You must know, sire, that my father was Mahmoud, the king of this country, the Black Isles, so called from the four little mountains which were once islands, while the capital was the place where now the great lake lies. My story will tell you how these changes came about.

My father died when he was sixty-six, and I succeeded him. I married my cousin, whom I loved tenderly, and I thought she loved me too.

But one afternoon, when I was half asleep, and was being fanned by two of her maids, I heard one say to the other, "What a pity it is that our mistress no longer loves our master! I believe she would like to kill him if she could, for she is an enchantress."

I soon found by watching that they were right, and when I mortally wounded a favourite slave of hers for a great crime, she begged that she might build a palace in the garden, where she wept and bewailed him for two years.

At last I begged her to cease grieving for him, for although he could not speak or move, by her enchantments she just kept him alive. She turned upon me in a rage, and said over me some magic words, and I instantly became as you see me now, half man and half marble.

Then this wicked enchantress changed the capital, which was a very populous and flourishing city, into the lake and desert plain you saw. The fish of four colours which are in it are the different races who lived in the town; the four hills are the four islands which give the name to my kingdom. All this the enchantress told me to add to my troubles. And this is not all. Every day she comes and beats me with a whip of buffalo hide.

When the young king had finished his sad story he burst once more into tears, and the Sultan was much moved.

"Tell me," he cried, "where is this wicked woman, and where is the miserable object of her affection, whom she just manages to keep alive?"

H J FORD
97

"Where she lives I do not know," answered the unhappy prince, "but she goes every day at sunrise to see if the slave can yet speak to her, after she has beaten me."

"Unfortunate king," said the Sultan, "I will do what I can to avenge you."

So he consulted with the young king over the best way to bring this about, and they agreed their plan should be put in effect the next day. The Sultan then rested, and the young king gave himself up to happy hopes of release. The next day the Sultan arose, and then went to the palace in the garden where the black slave was. He drew his sword and destroyed the little life that remained in him, and then threw the body down a well. He then lay down on the couch where the slave had been, and waited for the enchantress.

She went first to the young king, whom she beat with a hundred blows.

Then she came to the room where she thought her wounded slave was, but where the Sultan really lay.

She came near his couch and said, "Are you better today, my dear slave? Speak but one word to me."

"How can I be better," answered the Sultan, imitating the language of the Ethiopians, "when I can never sleep for the cries and groans of your husband?"

"What joy to hear you speak!" answered the queen. "Do you wish him to regain his proper shape?"

"Yes," said the Sultan; "hasten to set him at liberty, so that I may no longer hear his cries."

The queen at once went out and took a cup of water, and said over it some words that made it boil as if it were on the fire. Then she threw it over the prince, who at once regained his own form. He was filled with joy, but the enchantress said, "Hasten away from this place and never come back, lest I kill you."

So he hid himself to see the end of the Sultan's plan.

The enchantress went back to the Palace of Tears and said, "Now I have done what you wished."

"What you have done," said the Sultan, "is not enough to cure me. Every day at midnight all the people whom you have changed into fish lift their heads out of the lake and cry for vengeance. Go quickly, and give them their proper shape."

The enchantress hurried away and said some words over the lake.

The fish then became men, women, and children, and the houses and shops were once more filled. The Sultan's suite, who had encamped by the lake, were not a little astonished to see themselves in the middle of a large and beautiful town.

As soon as she had disenchanted it the queen went back to the palace.

"Are you quite well now?" she said.

"Come near," said the Sultan. "Nearer still."

She obeyed. Then he sprang up, and with one blow of his sword he cut her in two.

Then he went and found the prince.

"Rejoice," he said, "your cruel enemy is dead."

The prince thanked him again and again.

"And now," said the Sultan, "I will go back to my capital, which I am glad to find is so near yours."

"So near mine!" said the King of the Black Isles.

"Do you know it is a whole year's journey from here? You came here in a few hours because it was enchanted. But I will accompany you on your journey."

"It will give me much pleasure if you will escort me," said the Sultan, "and as I have no children, I will make you my heir."

The Sultan and the prince set out together, the Sultan laden with rich presents from the King of the Black Isles.

The day after he reached his capital the Sultan assembled his court and told them all that had befallen him, and told them how he intended to adopt the young king as his heir.

Then he gave each man presents in proportion to his rank.

As for the fisherman, as he was the first cause of the deliverance of the young prince, the Sultan gave him much money, and made him and his family happy for the rest of their days.

The Story of the Three Calenders, Sons of Kings, and of Five Ladies of Bagdad

In the reign of the Caliph Haroun-al-Raschid, there lived at Bagdad a porter who, in spite of his humble calling, was an intelligent and sensible man. One morning he was sitting in his usual place with his basket before him, waiting to be hired, when a tall young lady, covered with a long muslin veil, came up to him and said, "Pick up your basket and follow me." The porter, who was greatly pleased by her appearance and voice, jumped up at once, poised his basket on his head, and accompanied the lady, saying to himself as he went, "Oh, happy day! Oh, lucky meeting!"

The lady soon stopped before a closed door, at which she knocked. It was opened by an old man with a long white beard, to whom the lady held out money without speaking. The old man, who seemed to understand what she wanted, vanished into the house, and returned bringing a large jar of wine, which the porter placed in his basket. Then the lady signed to him to follow, and they went their way.

The next place she stopped at was a fruit and flower shop, and here she bought a large quantity of apples, apricots, peaches, and other things, with lilies, jasmine, and all sorts of sweet-smelling plants. From this shop she went to a butcher's, a grocer's, and a poulterer's, till at last the porter exclaimed in despair, "My good lady, if you had only told me you were going to buy enough provisions to stock a town, I would have brought a horse, or rather a camel." The lady laughed, and told him she had not finished yet, but after choosing various kinds of scents and spices from a druggist's store, she halted before a magnificent palace, at the door of which she knocked gently. The porteress who opened it was of such beauty that the eyes of the man were quite dazzled, and he was the more astonished as he saw clearly that she was no slave. The lady who had led him hither stood watching him with amusement, till the porteress exclaimed, "Why don't you come in, my sister? This poor man is so heavily weighed down that he is ready to drop."

When they were both inside the door was fastened, and they all three entered a large court, surrounded by an open-work gallery. At one end of the court was a platform, and on the platform stood an amber throne supported by four ebony columns, garnished with pearls and diamonds. In the middle of the court stood a marble basin filled with water from the mouth of a golden lion.

The porter looked about him, noticing and admiring everything; but his attention was specially attracted by a third lady sitting on the throne, who was even more beautiful than the other two. By the respect shown to her by the others, he judged that she must be the eldest, and in this he was right. This lady's name was Zobeida, the porteress was Sadie, and the housekeeper was Amina. At a word from Zobeida, Sadie and Amina took the basket from the porter, who was glad enough to be relieved from its weight; and when it was emptied, paid him handsomely for its use. But instead of taking up his basket and going away, the man still lingered, till Zobeida inquired what he was waiting for, and if he expected more money. "Oh, madam," returned he, "you have already given me too much, and I fear I may have been guilty of rudeness in not taking my departure at once. But, if you will pardon my saying so, I was lost in astonishment at seeing such beautiful ladies by themselves. A company of women without men is, however, as dull as a company of men without women." And after telling some stories to prove his point, he ended by entreating them to let him stay and make a fourth at their dinner.

The ladies were rather amused at the man's assurances and after some discussion it was agreed that he should be allowed to stay, as his society might prove entertaining. "But listen, friend," said Zobeida, "if we grant your request, it is only on condition that you behave with the utmost politeness, and that you keep the secret of our way of living, which chance has revealed to you." Then they all sat down to table, which had been covered by Amina with the dishes she had bought.

After the first few mouthfuls Amina poured some wine into a golden cup. She first drank herself, according to the Arab custom, and then filled it for her sisters. When it came to the porter's turn he kissed Amina's hand, and sang a song, which he composed at the moment in praise of the wine. The three ladies were pleased with the song, and then sang themselves, so that the repast was a merry one, and lasted much longer than usual.

At length, seeing that the sun was about to set, Sadie said to the porter, "Rise and go; it is now time for us to separate."

"Oh, madam," replied he, "how can you desire me to quit you in the state in which I am? Between the wine I have drunk, and the pleasure of seeing you, I should never find the way to my house. Let me remain here till morning, and when I have recovered my senses I will go when you like."

"Let him stay," said Amina, who had before proved herself his friend. "It is only just, as he has given us so much amusement."

"If you wish it, my sister," replied Zobeida; "but if he does, I must make a new condition. Porter," she continued, turning to him, "if you remain, you must promise to ask no questions about anything you may see. If you do, you may perhaps hear what you don't like."

This being settled, Amina brought in supper, and lit up the hall with a number of sweet smelling tapers. They then sat down again at the table, and began with fresh appetites to eat, drink, sing, and recite verses. In fact, they were all enjoying themselves mightily when they heard a knock at the outer door, which Sadie rose to open. She soon returned saying that three Calenders, all blind in the right eye, and all with their heads, faces, and eyebrows clean shaved, begged for admittance, as they were newly arrived in Bagdad, and night had already fallen. "They seem to have pleasant manners," she added, "but you have no idea how funny they look. I am sure we should find their company diverting."

Zobeida and Amina made some difficulty about admitting the new comers, and Sadie knew the reason of their hesitation. But she urged the matter so strongly that Zobeida was at last forced to consent. "Bring them in, then," said she, "but make them understand that they are not to make remarks about what does not concern them, and be sure to make them read the inscription over the door." For on the door was written in letters of gold, "Whoso meddles in affairs that are no business of his, will hear truths that will not please him."

The three Calenders bowed low on entering, and thanked the ladies for their kindness and hospitality. The ladies replied with words of welcome, and they were all about to seat themselves when the eyes of the Calenders fell on the porter, whose dress was not so very unlike their own, though he still wore all the hair that nature had given him. "This," said one of them, "is apparently one of our Arab brothers, who has rebelled against our ruler."

The porter, although half asleep from the wine he had drunk, heard the words, and without moving cried angrily to the Calender, "Sit down and mind your own business. Did you not read the inscription over the door? Everybody is not obliged to live in the same way."

"Do not be so angry, my good man," replied the Calender; "we should be very sorry to displease you;" so the quarrel was smoothed over, and supper began in good earnest. When the Calenders had satisfied their hunger, they offered to play to their hostesses, if there were any instruments in the house. The ladies were delighted at the idea, and Sadie went to see what she could find, returning in a few moments laden with two different kinds of flutes and a tambourine. Each Calender took the one he preferred, and began to play a well-known air, while the ladies sang the words of the song. These words were the gayest and liveliest possible, and every now and then the singers had to stop to indulge the laughter which almost choked them. In the midst of all their noise, a knock was heard at the door.

Now early that evening the Caliph secretly left the palace, accompanied by his grand-vizir,

Giafar, and Mesrour, chief of the eunuchs, all three wearing the dresses of merchants. Passing down the street, the Caliph had been attracted by the music of instruments and the sound of laughter, and had ordered his vizir to go and knock at the door of the house, as he wished to enter. The vizir replied that the ladies who lived there seemed to be entertaining their friends, and he thought his master would do well not to intrude on them; but the Caliph had taken it into his head to see for himself, and insisted on being obeyed.

The knock was answered by Sadie, with a taper in her hand, and the vizir, who was surprised at her beauty, bowed low before her, and said respectfully, "Madam, we are three merchants who have lately arrived from Moussoul, and, owing to a misadventure which befell us this very night, only reached our inn to find that the doors were closed to us till tomorrow morning. Not knowing what to do, we wandered in the streets till we happened to pass your house, when, seeing lights and hearing the sound of voices, we resolved to ask you to give us shelter till the dawn. If you will grant us this favour, we will, with your permission, do all in our power to help you spend the time pleasantly."

Sadie answered the merchant that she must first consult her sisters; and after having talked over the matter with them, she returned to tell him that he and his two friends would be welcome to join their company. They entered and bowed politely to the ladies and their guests. Then Zobeida, as the mistress, came forward and said gravely, "You are welcome here, but I hope you will allow me to beg one thing of you – have as many eyes as you like, but no tongues; and ask no questions about anything you see, however strange it may appear to you."

"Madam," returned the vizir, "you shall be obeyed. We have quite enough to please and interest us without troubling ourselves about that with which we have no concern." Then they all sat down, and drank to the health of the new comers.

While the vizir, Giafar, was talking to the ladies the Caliph was occupied in wondering who they could be, and why the three Calenders had each lost his right eye. He was burning to inquire the reason of it all, but was silenced by Zobeida's request, so he tried to rouse himself and to take his part in the conversation, which was very lively, the subject of discussion being the many different sorts of pleasures that there were in the world. After some time the Calenders got up and performed some curious dances, which delighted the rest of the company.

When they had finished Zobeida rose from her seat, and, taking Amina by the hand, she said to her, "My sister, our friends will excuse us if we seem to forget their presence and fulfil our nightly task." Amina understood her sister's meaning, and collecting the dishes, glasses, and musical instruments, she carried them away, while Sadie swept the hall and put everything in order. Having done this she begged the Calenders to sit on a sofa on one side of the room, and the Caliph and his friends to place themselves opposite. As to the porter, she requested him to come and help her and her sister.

Shortly after Amina entered carrying a seat, which she put down in the middle of the empty space. She next went over to the door of a closet and signed to the porter to follow her. He did so, and soon reappeared leading two black dogs by a chain, which he brought into the centre of the hall. Zobeida then got up from her seat between the Calenders and the Caliph and walked slowly across to where the porter stood with the dogs. "We must do our duty," she said with a deep sigh, pushing back her sleeves, and, taking a whip from Sadie, she said to the man, "Take one of those dogs to my sister Amina and give me the other."

The porter did as he was bid, but as he led the dog to Zobeida it uttered piercing howls, and gazed up at her with looks of entreaty. But Zobeida took no notice, and whipped the dog till she was out of breath. She then took the chain from the porter, and, raising the dog on its hind legs, they looked into each other's eyes sorrowfully till tears began to fall from both. Then Zobeida took her handkerchief and wiped the dog's eyes tenderly, after which she kissed it, then, putting the chain into the porter's hand she said, "Take it back to the closet and bring me the other."

The same ceremony was gone through with the second dog, and all the while the whole company looked on with astonishment. The Caliph in particular could hardly contain himself, and made signs to the vizir to ask what it all meant. But the vizir pretended not to see, and turned his head away.

Zobeida remained for some time in the middle of the room, till at last Sadie went up to her and begged her to sit down, as she also had her part to play. At these words Amina fetched a lute from a case of yellow satin and gave it to Sadie, who sang several songs to its accompaniment. When she was tired she said to Amina, "My sister, I can do no more; come, I pray you, and take my place."

Amina struck a few chords and then broke into a song, which she sang with so much ardour that she was quite overcome, and sank gasping on a pile of cushions, tearing open her dress as she did so to give herself some air. To the amazement of all present, her neck, instead of being as smooth and white as her face, was a mass of scars.

The Calenders and the Caliph looked at each other, and whispered together, unheard by Zobeida and Sadie, who were tending their fainting sister.

H.J.FORD

"What does it all mean?" asked the Caliph.

"We know no more than you," said the Calender to whom he had spoken.

"What! You do not belong to the house?"

"My lord," answered all the Calenders together, "we came here for the first time an hour before you."

They then turned to the porter to see if he could explain the mystery, but the porter was no wiser than they were themselves. At length the Caliph could contain his curiosity no longer, and declared that he would compel the ladies to tell them the meaning of their strange conduct. The vizir, foreseeing what would happen, implored him to remember the condition their hostesses had imposed, and added in a whisper that if his Highness would only wait till morning he could as Caliph summon the ladies to appear before him. But the Caliph, who was not accustomed to be contradicted, rejected this advice, and it was resolved after a little more talking that the question should be put by the porter. Suddenly Zobeida turned round, and seeing their excitement she said, "What is the matter – what are you all discussing so earnestly?"

"Madam," answered the porter, "these gentlemen entreat you to explain to them why you should first whip the dogs and then cry over them, and also how it happens that the fainting lady is covered with scars. They have requested me, Madam, to be their mouthpiece."

"Is it true, gentlemen," asked Zobeida, drawing herself up, "that you have charged this man to put me that question?"

"It is," they all replied, except Giafar, who was silent.

"Is this," continued Zobeida, growing more angry every moment, "is this the return you make for the hospitality I have shown you? Have you forgotten the one condition on which you were allowed to enter the house? Come quickly," she added, clapping her hands three times, and the words were hardly uttered when seven black slaves, each armed with a sabre, burst in and stood over the seven men, throwing them on the ground, and preparing themselves, on a sign from their mistress, to cut off their heads.

The seven culprits all thought their last hour had come, and the Caliph repented bitterly that he had not taken the vizir's advice. But they made up their minds to die bravely, all except the porter, who loudly inquired of Zobeida why he was to suffer for other people's faults, and declared that these misfortunes would never have happened if it had not been for the Calenders, who always brought ill-luck. He ended by imploring Zobeida not to confound the innocent with the guilty and to spare his life.

In spite of her anger, there was something so comic in the groans of the porter that Zobeida could not refrain from laughing. But putting him aside she addressed the others a second time, saying, "Answer me; who are you? Unless you tell me truly you have not another moment to live. I can hardly think you are men of any position, whatever country you belong to. If you were, you would have had more consideration for us."

The Caliph, who was naturally very impatient, suffered far more than either of the others at feeling that his life was at the mercy of a justly offended lady, but when he heard her question he began to breathe more freely, for he was convinced that she had only to learn his name and rank for all danger to be over. So he whispered hastily to the vizir, who was next to him, to reveal their secret. But the vizir, wiser than his master, wished to conceal from the public the affront they had received, and merely answered, "After all, we have only got what we deserved."

Meanwhile Zobeida had turned to the three Calenders and inquired if, as they were all blind, they were brothers.

"No, madam," replied one, "we are no blood relations at all, only brothers by our mode of life."

"And you," she asked, addressing another, "were you born blind of one eye?"

"No, madam," returned he, "I became blind through a most surprising adventure, such as probably has never happened to anybody. After that I shaved my head and eyebrows and put on the dress in which you see me now."

Zobeida put the same question to the other two Calenders, and received the same answer.

"But," added the third, "it may interest you, madam, to know that we are not men of low birth, but are all three sons of kings, and of kings, too, whom the world holds in high esteem."

At these words Zobeida's anger cooled down, and she turned to her slaves and said, "You can give them a little more liberty, but do not leave the hall. Those that will tell us their histories and their reasons for coming here shall be allowed to leave unhurt; those who refuse—" And she paused, but in a moment the porter, who understood that he had only to relate his story to set himself free from this terrible danger, immediately broke in,

"Madam, you know already how I came here, and what I have to say will soon be told. Your sister found me this morning in the place where I always stand waiting to be hired. She bade me follow her to various shops, and when my basket was quite full we returned to this house, when you had the goodness to permit me to remain, for which I shall be eternally grateful. That is my story."

He looked anxiously to Zobeida, who nodded her head and said, "You can go; and take care we never meet again."

"Oh, madam," cried the porter, "let me stay yet a little while. It is not just that the others should have heard my story and that I should not hear theirs," and without waiting for permission he seated himself on the end of the sofa occupied by the ladies, whilst the rest crouched on the carpet, and the slaves stood against the wall.

Then one of the Calenders, addressing himself to Zobeida as the principal lady, began his story.

The Story of the First Calender, Son of a King

In order, madam, to explain how I came to lose my right eye, and to wear the dress of a Calender, you must first know that I am the son of a king. My father's only brother reigned over the neighbouring country, and had two children, a daughter and a son, who were of the same age as myself.

As I grew up, and was allowed more liberty, I went every year to pay a visit to my uncle's court, and usually stayed there about two months. In this way my cousin and I became very intimate, and were much attached to each other. The very last time I saw him he seemed more delighted to see me than ever, and gave a great feast in my honour. When we had finished eating, he said to me, "My cousin, you would never guess what I have been doing since your last visit to us! Directly after your departure I set a number of men to work on a building after my own design. It is now completed, and ready to be lived in. I should like to show it to you, but you must first swear two things: to be faithful to me, and to keep my secret."

Of course I did not dream of refusing him anything he asked, and gave the promise without the least hesitation. He then bade me wait an instant, and vanished, returning in a few moments with a richly dressed lady of great beauty, but as he did not tell me her name, I thought it was better not to inquire. We all three sat down to table and amused ourselves with talking of all sorts of indifferent things, and with drinking each other's health. Suddenly the prince said to me, "Cousin, we have no time to lose; be so kind as to conduct this lady to a certain spot, where you will find a dome-like tomb, newly built. You cannot mistake it. Go in, both of you, and wait till I come. I shall not be long."

As I had promised I prepared to do as I was told, and giving my hand to the lady, I escorted her, by the light of the moon, to the place of which the prince had spoken. We had barely reached it when he joined us himself, carrying a small vessel of water, a pickaxe, and a little bag containing plaster.

With the pickaxe he at once began to destroy the empty sepulchre in the middle of the tomb. One by one he took the stones and piled them up in a corner. When he had knocked down the whole sepulchre he proceeded to dig at the earth, and beneath where the sepulchre had been I saw a trap-door. He raised the door and I caught sight of the top of a spiral staircase; then he said, turning to the lady, "Madam, this is the way that will lead you down to the spot which I told you of."

The lady did not answer, but silently descended the staircase, the prince following her. At the top, however, he looked at me. "My cousin," he exclaimed, "I do not know how to thank you for your kindness. Farewell."

"What do you mean?" I cried. "I don't understand."

"No matter," he replied, "go back by the path that you came."

He would say no more, and, greatly puzzled, I returned to my room in the palace and went to bed. When I woke, and considered my adventure, I thought that I must have been dreaming, and sent a servant to ask if the prince was dressed and could see me. But on hearing that he had not slept at home I was much alarmed, and hastened to the cemetery, where, unluckily, the tombs were all so alike that I could not discover which was the one I was in search of, though I spent four days in looking for it.

You must know that all this time the king, my uncle, was absent on a hunting expedition, and as no one knew when he would be back, I at last decided to return home, leaving the ministers to make my excuses. I longed to tell them what had become of the prince, about whose fate they felt the most dreadful anxiety, but the oath I had sworn kept me silent.

On my arrival at my father's capital, I was astonished to find a large detachment of guards drawn up before the gate of the palace; they surrounded me directly I entered. I asked the officers in command the reason of this strange behaviour, and was horrified to learn that the army had mutinied and put to death the king, my father, and had placed the grand-vizir on the throne. Further, that by his orders I was placed under arrest.

Now this rebel vizir had hated me from my boy-hood, because once, when shooting at a bird with a bow, I had shot out his eye by accident. Of course I not only sent a servant at once to offer him my regrets and apologies, but I made them in person. It was all of no use. He cherished an undying hatred towards me, and lost no occasion of showing it. Having once got me in his power I felt he could show no mercy, and I was right. Mad with triumph and fury he came to me in my prison and tore out my right eye. That is how I lost it.

My persecutor, however, did not stop here. He shut me up in a large case and ordered his executioner to carry me into a desert place, to cut off my head, and then to abandon my body to the birds of prey. The case, with me inside it, was accordingly placed on a horse, and the executioner, accompanied by another man, rode into the country until they found a spot suitable for the purpose. But their hearts were not so hard as they seemed, and my tears and prayers made them waver.

"Forsake the kingdom instantly," said the executioner at last, "and take care never to come

back, for you will not only lose your head, but make us lose ours." I thanked him gratefully, and tried to console myself for the loss of my eye by thinking of the other misfortunes I had escaped.

After all I had gone through, and my fear of being recognised by some enemy, I could only travel very slowly and cautiously, generally resting in some out-of-the-way place by day, and walking as far as I was able by night, but at length I arrived in the kingdom of my uncle, of whose protection I was sure.

I found him in great trouble about the disappearance of his son, who had, he said, vanished without leaving a trace; but his own grief did not prevent him sharing mine. We mingled our tears, for the loss of one was the loss of the other, and then I made up my mind that it was my duty to break the solemn oath I had sworn to the prince. I therefore lost no time in telling my uncle everything I knew, and I observed that even before I had ended his sorrow appeared to be lightened a little.

"My dear nephew," he said, "your story gives me some hope. I was aware that my son was building a tomb, and I think I can find the spot. But as he wished to keep the matter secret, let us go alone and seek the place ourselves."

He then bade me disguise myself, and we both slipped out of a garden door which opened on to the cemetery. It did not take long for us to arrive at the scene of the prince's disappearance, or to discover the tomb I had sought so vainly before. We entered it, and found the trap-door which led to the staircase, but we had great difficulty in raising it, because the prince had fastened it down underneath with the plaster he had brought with him.

My uncle went first, and I followed him. When we reached the bottom of the stairs we stepped into a sort of ante-room, filled with such a dense smoke that it was hardly possible to see anything. However, we passed through the smoke into a large chamber, which at first seemed quite empty. The room was brilliantly lighted, and in another moment we perceived a sort of platform at one end, on which were the bodies of the prince and a lady, both half-burned, as if they had been dragged out of a fire before it had quite consumed them.

This horrible sight turned me faint, but, to my surprise, my uncle did not show so much surprise as anger.

"I knew," he said, "that my son was tenderly attached to this lady, whom it was impossible he should ever marry. I tried to turn his thoughts, and presented to him the most beautiful princesses, but he cared for none of them, and, as you see, they have now been united by a horrible death in an underground tomb." But, as he spoke, his anger melted into tears, and again I wept with him.

When he recovered himself he drew me to him. "My dear nephew," he said, embracing me, "you have come to me to take his place, and I will do my best to forget that I ever had a son who could act in so wicked a manner." Then he turned and went up the stairs.

We reached the palace without anyone having noticed our absence, when, shortly after, a clashing of drums, and cymbals, and the blare of trumpets burst upon our astonished ears. At the same time a thick cloud of dust on the horizon told of the approach of a great army. My heart sank when I perceived that the commander was the vizir who had dethroned my father, and was come to seize the kingdom of my uncle.

The capital was utterly unprepared to stand a siege, and seeing that resistance was useless, at once opened its gates. My uncle fought hard for his life, but was soon overpowered, and when he fell I managed to escape through a secret passage, and took refuge with an officer whom I knew I could trust.

Persecuted by ill-fortune, and stricken with grief, there seemed to be only one means of safety left to me. I shaved my beard and my eyebrows, and put on the dress of a calender, in which it was easy for me to travel without being known. I avoided the towns till I reached the kingdom of the famous and powerful Caliph, Haroun-al-Raschid, when I had no further reason to fear my enemies. It was my intention to come to Bagdad and to throw myself at the feet of his Highness, who would, I felt certain, be touched by my sad story, and would grant me, besides, his help and protection.

After a journey which lasted some months I arrived at length at the gates of this city. It was sunset, and I paused for a little to look about me, and to decide which way to turn my steps. I was still debating on this subject when I was joined by this other calender, who stopped to greet me. "You, like me, appear to be a stranger," I said. He replied that I was right, and before he could say more the third calender came up. He, also, was newly arrived in Bagdad, and being brothers in misfortune, we resolved to cast in our lots together, and to share whatever fate might have in store.

By this time it had grown late, and we did not know where to spend the night. But our lucky star having guided us to this door, we took the liberty of knocking and of asking for shelter, which was given to us at once with the best grace in the world.

This, madam, is my story.

"I am satisfied," replied Zobeida; "you can go when you like."

The calender, however, begged leave to stay and to hear the histories of his two friends and of the three other persons of the company, which he was allowed to do.

The Story of the Second Calendar, Son of a King

"Madam," said the young man, addressing Zobeida, "if you wish to know how I lost my right eye, I shall have to tell you the story of my whole life."

I was scarcely more than a baby, when the king my father, finding me unusually quick and clever for my age, turned his thoughts to my education. I was taught first to read and write, and then to learn the Koran, which is the basis of our holy religion, and the better to understand it, I read with my tutors the ablest commentators on its teaching, and committed to memory all the traditions respecting the Prophet, which have been gathered from the mouth of those who were his friends. I also learnt history, and was instructed in poetry, versification, geography, chronology, and in all the outdoor exercises in which every prince should excel. But what I liked best of all was writing Arabic characters, and in this I soon surpassed my masters, and gained a reputation in this branch of knowledge that reached as far as India itself.

Now the Sultan of the Indies, curious to see a young prince with such strange tastes, sent an ambassador to my father, laden with rich presents, and a warm invitation to visit his court. My father, who was deeply anxious to secure the friendship of so powerful a monarch, and held besides that a little travel would greatly improve my manners and open my mind, accepted gladly, and in a short time I had set out for India with the ambassador, attended only by a small suite on account of the length of the journey, and the badness of the roads. However, as was my duty, I took with me ten camels, laden with rich presents for the Sultan.

We had been travelling for about a month, when one day we saw a cloud of dust moving swiftly towards us; and as soon as it came near, we found that the dust concealed a band of fifty robbers. Our men barely numbered half, and as we were also hampered by the camels, there was no use in fighting, so we tried to overawe them by informing them who we were, and whither we were going. The robbers, however, only laughed, and declared that was none of their business, and, without more words, attacked us brutally. I defended myself to the last, wounded though I was, but at length, seeing that resistance was hopeless, and that the ambassador and all our followers were made prisoners, I put spurs to my horse and rode away as fast as I could, till the poor beast fell dead from a wound in his side. I managed to jump off without any injury, and looked about to see if I was pursued. But for the moment I was safe, for, as I imagined, the robbers were all engaged in quarrelling over their booty.

I found myself in a country that was quite new to me, and dared not return to the main road lest I should again fall into the hands of the robbers. Luckily my wound was only a slight one, and after binding it up as well as I could, I walked on for the rest of the day, till I reached a cave at the foot of a mountain, where I passed the night in peace, making my supper off some fruits I had gathered on the way.

I wandered about for a whole month without knowing where I was going, till at length I found myself on the outskirts of a beautiful city, watered by winding streams, which enjoyed an eternal spring. My delight at the prospect of mixing once more with human beings was somewhat damped at the thought of the miserable object I must seem. My face and hands had been burned nearly black; my clothes were all in rags, and my shoes were in such a state that I had been forced to abandon them altogether.

I entered the town, and stopped at a tailor's shop to inquire where I was. The man saw I was better than my condition, and begged me to sit down, and in return I told him my whole story. The tailor listened with attention, but his reply, instead of giving me consolation, only increased my trouble.

"Beware," he said, "of telling any one what you have told me, for the prince who governs the kingdom is your father's greatest enemy, and he will be rejoiced to find you in his power."

I thanked the tailor for his counsel, and said I would do whatever he advised; then, being very hungry, I gladly ate of the food he put before me, and accepted his offer of a lodging in his house.

In a few days I had quite recovered from the hardships I had undergone, and then the tailor, knowing that it was the custom for the princes of our religion to learn a trade or profession so as to provide for themselves in times of ill-fortune, inquired if there was anything I could do for my living. I replied that I had been educated as a grammarian and a poet, but that my great gift was writing.

"All that is of no use here," said the tailor. "Take my advice, put on a short coat, and as you seem hardy and strong, go into the woods and cut firewood, which you will sell in the streets.

By this means you will earn your living, and be able to wait till better times come. The hatchet and the cord shall be my present."

This counsel was very distasteful to me, but I thought I could not do otherwise than adopt it. So the next morning I set out with a company of poor wood-cutters, to whom the tailor had introduced me. Even on the first day I cut enough wood to sell for a tolerable sum, and very soon I became more expert, and had made enough money to repay the tailor all he had lent me.

I had been a wood-cutter for more than a year, when one day I wandered further into the forest than I had ever done before, and reached a delicious green glade, where I began to cut wood. I was hacking at the root of a tree, when I beheld an iron ring fastened to a trapdoor of the same metal. I soon cleared away the earth, and pulling up the door, found a staircase, which I hastily made up my mind to go down, carrying my hatchet with me by way of protection. When I reached the bottom I discovered that I was in a huge palace, as brilliantly lighted as any palace above ground that I had ever seen, with a long gallery supported by pillars of jasper, ornamented with capitals of gold. Down this gallery a lady came to meet me, of such beauty that I forgot everything else, and thought only of her.

To save her all the trouble possible, I hastened towards her, and bowed low.

"Who are you? Who are you?" she said. "A man or a genius?"

"A man, madam," I replied; "I have nothing to do with genii."

"By what accident do you come here?" she asked again with a sigh. "I have been in this place now for five and twenty years, and you are the first man who has visited me."

Emboldened by her beauty and gentleness, I ventured to reply, "Before, madam, I answer your question, allow me to say how grateful I am for this meeting, which is not only a consolation to me in my own heavy sorrow, but may perhaps enable me to render your lot happier," and then I told her who I was, and how I had come there.

"Alas, prince," she said, with a deeper sigh than before, "you have guessed rightly in supposing me an unwilling prisoner in this gorgeous place. I am the daughter of the king of the Ebony Isle, of whose fame you surely must have heard. At my father's desire I was married to a prince who was my own cousin; but on my very wedding day, I was snatched up by a genius, and brought here in a faint. For a long while I did nothing but weep, and would not suffer the genius to come near me; but time teaches us submission, and I have now got accustomed to his presence, and if clothes and jewels could content me, I have them in plenty. Every tenth day, for five and twenty years, I have received a visit from him, but in case I should need his help at any other time, I have only to touch a talisman that stands at the entrance of my chamber. It wants still five days to his next visit, and I hope that during that time you will do me the honour to be my guest."

I was too much dazzled by her beauty to dream of refusing her offer, and accordingly the princess had me conducted to the bath, and a rich dress befitting my rank was provided for me. Then a feast of the most delicate dishes was served in a room hung with embroidered Indian fabrics.

Next day, when we were at dinner, I could maintain my patience no longer, and implored the princess to break her bonds, and return with me to the world which was lighted by the sun.

"What you ask is impossible," she answered; "but stay here with me instead, and we can be happy, and all you will have to do is to betake yourself to the forest every tenth day, when I am expecting my master the genius. He is very jealous, as you know, and will not suffer a man to come near me."

"Princess," I replied, "I see it is only fear of the genius that makes you act like this. For myself, I dread him so little that I mean to break his talisman in pieces! Awful though you think him, he shall feel the weight of my arm, and I herewith take a solemn vow to stamp out the whole race."

The princess, who realized the consequences of such audacity, entreated me not to touch the talisman. "If you do, it will be the ruin of both of us," said she; "I know genii much better than you." But the wine I had drunk had confused my brain; I gave one kick to the talisman, and it fell into a thousand pieces.

Hardly had my foot touched the talisman when the air became as dark as night, a fearful noise was heard, and the palace shook to its very foundations. In an instant I was sobered, and understood what I had done. "Princess!" I cried, "what is happening?"

"Alas!" she exclaimed, forgetting all her own terrors in anxiety for me, "fly, or you are lost."

I followed her advice and dashed up the staircase, leaving my hatchet behind me. But I was too late. The palace opened and the genius appeared, who, turning angrily to the princess, asked indignantly,

"What is the matter, that you have sent for me like this?"

"A pain in my heart," she replied hastily, "obliged me to seek the aid of this little bottle. Feeling faint, I slipped and fell against the talisman, which broke. That is really all."

"You are an impudent liar!" cried the genius. "How did this hatchet and those shoes get here?"

"I never saw them before," she answered, "and you came in such a hurry that you may have picked them up on the road without knowing it." To this the genius only replied by insults and blows. I could hear the shrieks and groans of the princess, and having by this time taken off my rich garments and put on those in which I had arrived the previous day, I lifted the trap, found myself once more in the forest, and returned to my friend the tailor, with a light load of wood and a heart full of shame and sorrow.

The tailor, who had been uneasy at my long absence, was, delighted to see me; but I kept silence about my adventure, and as soon as possible retired to my room to lament in secret over my folly. While I was thus indulging my grief my host entered, and said, "There is an old man downstairs who has brought your hatchet and slippers, which he picked up on the road, and now restores to you, as he found out from one of your comrades where you lived. You had better come down and speak to him yourself." At this speech I changed colour, and my legs trembled under me. The tailor noticed my confusion, and was just going to inquire the reason when the door of the room opened, and the old man appeared, carrying with him my hatchet and shoes.

"I am a genius," he said, "the son of the daughter of Eblis, prince of the genii. Is not this hatchet yours, and these shoes?" Without waiting for an answer – which, indeed, I could hardly have given him, so great was my fright – he seized hold of me, and darted up into the air with the quickness of lightning, and then, with equal swiftness, dropped down towards the earth. When he touched the ground, he rapped it with his foot; it opened, and we found ourselves in the enchanted palace, in the presence of the beautiful princess of the Ebony Isle. But how different she looked from what she was when I had last seen her, for she was lying stretched on the ground covered with blood, and weeping bitterly.

"Traitress!" cried the genius, "is not this man your lover?"

She lifted up her eyes slowly, and looked sadly at me. "I never saw him before," she answered slowly. "I do not know who he is."

"What!" exclaimed the genius, "you owe all your sufferings to him, and yet you dare to say he is a stranger to you!"

"But if he really is a stranger to me," she replied, "why should I tell a lie and cause his death?"

"Very well," said the genius, drawing his sword, "take this, and cut off his head."

"Alas," answered the princess, "I am too weak even to hold the sabre. And supposing that I had the strength, why should I put an innocent man to death?"

"You condemn yourself by your refusal," said the genius; then turning to me, he added, "and you, do you not know her?"

"How should I?" I replied, resolved to imitate the princess in her fidelity. "How should I, when I never saw her before?"

"Cut her head off," then, "if she is a stranger to you, and I shall believe you are speaking the truth, and will set you at liberty."

"Certainly," I answered, taking the sabre in my hands, and making a sign to the princess to fear nothing, as it was my own life that I was about to sacrifice, and not hers. But the look of gratitude she gave me shook my courage, and I flung the sabre to the earth.

"I should not deserve to live," I said to the genius, "if I were such a coward as to slay a lady who is not only unknown to me, but who is at this moment half dead herself. Do with me as you will – I am in your power – but I refuse to obey your cruel command."

"I see," said the genius, "that you have both made up your minds to brave me, but I will give you a sample of what you may expect." So saying, with one sweep of his sabre he cut off a hand of the princess, who was just able to lift the other to wave me an eternal farewell. Then I lost consciousness for several minutes.

When I came to myself I implored the genius to keep me no longer in this state of suspense, but to lose no time in putting an end to my sufferings. The genius, however, paid no attention to my prayers, but said sternly, "That is the way in which a genius treats the woman who has betrayed him. If I chose, I could kill you also; but I will be merciful, and content myself with changing you into a dog, an ass, a lion, or a bird – whichever you prefer."

I caught eagerly at these words, as giving me a faint hope of softening his wrath. "O genius!" I cried, "as you wish to spare my life, be generous, and spare it altogether. Grant my prayer, and pardon my crime, as the best man in the whole world forgave his neighbour who was eaten up with envy of him." Contrary to my hopes, the genius seemed interested in my words, and said he would like to hear the story of the two neighbours; and as I think, madam, it may please you, I will tell it to you also.

The Story of the Envious Man and of Him who was Envied

In a town of moderate size, two men lived in neighbouring houses; but they had not been there very long before one man took such a hatred of the other, and envied him so bitterly, that the poor man determined to find another home, hoping that when they no longer met every day his enemy would forget all about him. So he sold his house and the little furniture it contained, and moved into the capital of the country, which was luckily at no great distance. About half a mile from this city he bought a nice little place, with a large garden and a fair-sized court, in the centre of which stood an old well.

In order to live a quieter life, the good man put on the robe of a dervish, and divided his house into a quantity of small cells, where he soon established a number of other dervishes. The fame of his virtue gradually spread abroad, and many people, including several of the highest quality, came to visit him and ask his prayers.

Of course it was not long before his reputation reached the ears of the man who envied him, and this wicked wretch resolved never to rest till he had in some way worked ill to the dervish whom he hated. So he left his house and his business to look after themselves, and betook himself to the new dervish monastery, where he was welcomed by the founder with all the warmth imaginable. The excuse he gave for his appearance was that he had come to consult the chief of the dervishes on a private matter of great importance. "What I have to say must not be overheard," he whispered; "command, I beg of you, that your dervishes retire into their cells, as night is approaching, and meet me in the court."

The dervish did as he was asked without delay, and directly they were alone together the envious man began to tell a long story, edging, as they walked to and fro, always nearer to the well, and when they were quite close, he seized the dervish and dropped him in. He then ran off triumphantly, without having been seen by anyone, and congratulating himself that the object of his hatred was dead, and would trouble him no more.

But in this he was mistaken! The old well had long been inhabited (unknown to mere human beings) by a set of fairies and genii, who caught the dervish as he fell, so that he received no hurt. The dervish himself could see nothing, but he took for granted that something strange had happened, or he must certainly have been dashed against the side of the well and been killed. He lay quite still, and in a moment he heard a voice saying, "Can you guess whom this man is that we have saved from death?"

"No," replied several other voices.

And the first speaker answered, "I will tell you. This man, from pure goodness of heart, forsook the town where he lived and came to dwell here, in the hope of curing one of his neighbours of the envy he felt towards him. But his character soon won him the esteem of all, and the envious man's hatred grew, till he came here with the deliberate intention of causing his death. And this he would have done, without our help, the very day before the Sultan has arranged to visit this holy dervish, and to entreat his prayers for the princess, his daughter."

"But what is the matter with the princess that she needs the dervish's prayers?" asked another voice.

"She has fallen into the power of the genius Maimoum, the son of Dimdim," replied the first voice. "But it would be quite simple for this holy chief of the dervishes to cure her if he only knew! In his convent there is a black cat which has a tiny white tip to its tail. Now to cure the princess the dervish must pull out seven of these white hairs, burn three, and with their smoke perfume the head of the princess. This will deliver her so completely that Maimoum, the son of Dimdim, will never dare to approach her again."

The fairies and genii ceased talking, but the dervish did not forget a word of all they had said; and when morning came he perceived a place in the side of the well which was broken, and where he could easily climb out.

The dervishes, who could not imagine what had become of him, were enchanted at his reappearance. He told them of the attempt on his life made by his guest of the previous day, and then retired into his cell. He was soon joined here by the black cat of which the voice had spoken, who came as usual to say good-morning to his master. He took him on his knee and seized the opportunity to pull seven white hairs out of his tail, and put them on one side till they were needed.

The sun had not long risen before the Sultan, who was anxious to leave nothing undone that might deliver the princess, arrived with a large suite at the gate of the monastery, and was received by the dervishes with profound respect. The Sultan lost no time in declaring the object of his visit, and leading the chief of the dervishes aside, he said to him, "Noble scheik, you have guessed perhaps what I have come to ask you?"

"Yes, sire," answered the dervish; "if I am not mistaken, it is the illness of the princess which has procured me this honour."

"You are right," returned the Sultan, "and you will give me fresh life if you can by your prayers deliver my daughter from the strange malady that has taken possession of her."

"Let your highness command her to come here, and I will see what I can do."

The Sultan, full of hope, sent orders at once that the princess was to set out as soon as possible, accompanied by her usual staff of attendants. When she arrived, she was so thickly veiled that the dervish could not see her face, but he desired a brazier to be held over her head, and laid the seven hairs on the burning coals. The instant they were consumed, terrific cries were heard, but no one could tell from whom they proceeded. Only the dervish guessed that they were uttered by Maimoum the son of Dimdim, who felt the princess escaping him.

All this time she had seemed unconscious of what she was doing, but now she raised her hand to her veil and uncovered her face. "Where am I?" she said in a bewildered manner; "and how did I get here?"

The Sultan was so delighted to hear these words that he not only embraced his daughter, but kissed the hand of the dervish. Then, turning to his attendants who stood round, he said to them, "What reward shall I give to the man who has restored me my daughter?"

They all replied with one accord that he deserved the hand of the princess.

"That is my own opinion," said he, "and from this moment I declare him to be my son-in-law."

Shortly after these events, the grand-vizir died, and his post was given to the dervish. But he did not hold it for long, for the Sultan fell a victim to an attack of illness, and as he had no sons, the soldiers and priests declared the dervish heir to the throne, to the great joy of all the people.

One day, when the dervish, who had now become Sultan, was making a royal progress with his court, he perceived the envious man standing in the crowd. He made a sign to one of his vizirs, and whispered in his ear, "Fetch me that man who is standing out there, but take great care not to frighten him." The vizir obeyed, and when the envious man was brought before the Sultan, the monarch said to him, "My friend, I am delighted to see you again." Then turning to an officer, he added, "Give him a thousand pieces of gold out of my treasury, and twenty waggon-loads of merchandise out of my private stores, and let an escort of soldiers accompany him home." He then took leave of the envious man, and went on his way.

Now when I had ended my story, I proceeded to show the genius how to apply it to himself. "O genius," I said, "you see that this Sultan was not content with merely forgiving the envious man for the attempt on his life; he heaped rewards and riches upon him."

But the genius had made up his mind, and could not be softened. "Do not imagine that you are going to escape so easily," he said. "All I can do is to give you bare life; you will have to learn what happens to people who interfere with me."

As he spoke he seized me violently by the arm; the roof of the palace opened to make way for us, and we mounted up so high into the air that the earth looked like a little cloud. Then, as before, he came down with the swiftness of lightning, and we touched the ground on a mountain top.

Then he stooped and gathered a handful of earth, and murmured some words over it, after which he threw the earth in my face, saying as he did so, "Quit the form of a man, and assume that of a monkey." This done, he vanished, and I was in the likeness of an ape, and in a country I had never seen before.

However there was no use in stopping where I was, so I came down the mountain and found myself in a flat plain which was bounded by the sea. I travelled towards it, and was pleased to see a vessel moored about half a mile from shore. There were no waves, so I broke off the branch of a tree, and dragging it down to the water's edge, sat across it, while, using two sticks for oars, I rowed myself towards the ship.

The deck was full of people, who watched my progress with interest, but when I seized a rope and swung myself on board, I found that I had only escaped death at the hands of the genius to perish by those of the sailors, lest I should bring ill-luck to the vessel and the merchants. "Throw him into the sea!" cried one. "Knock him on the head with a hammer," exclaimed another. "Let me shoot him with an arrow," said a third; and certainly somebody would have had his way if I had not flung myself at the captain's feet and grasped tight hold of his dress. He appeared touched by my action and patted my head, and declared that he would take me under his protection, and that no one should do me any harm.

At the end of about fifty days we cast anchor before a large town, and the ship was immediately surrounded by a multitude of small boats filled with people, who had come either to meet their friends or from simple curiosity. Among others, one boat contained several officials, who asked to see the merchants on board, and informed them that they had been sent by the Sultan in token of welcome, and to beg them each to write a few lines on a roll of paper. "In order to explain this strange request," continued the officers, "it is necessary that you should know that the grand-vizir, lately dead, was celebrated for his beautiful handwriting, and the Sultan is anxious to find a similar talent in his successor. Hitherto the search has been a failure, but his Highness has not yet given up hope."

One after another the merchants set down a few lines upon the roll, and when they had all finished, I came forward, and snatched the paper from the man who held it. At first they all thought I was going to throw it into the sea, but they were quieted when they saw I held it with great care, and great was their surprise when I made signs that I too wished to write something.

"Let him do it if he wants to," said the captain. "If he only makes a mess of the paper, you may be sure I will punish him for it. But if, as I hope, he really can write, for he is the cleverest monkey I ever saw, I will adopt him as my son. The one I lost had not nearly so much sense!"

No more was said, and I took the pen and wrote the six sorts of writing in use among the Arabs, and each sort contained an original verse or couplet, in praise of the Sultan. And not only did my handwriting completely eclipse that of the merchants, but it is hardly too much to say that none so beautiful had ever before been seen in that country. When I had ended the officials took the roll and returned to the Sultan.

As soon as the monarch saw my writing he did not so much as look at the samples of the merchants, but desired his officials to take the finest and most richly caparisoned horse in his stables, together with the most magnificent dress they could procure, and to put it on the person who had written those lines, and bring him to court.

The officials began to laugh when they heard the Sultan's command, but as soon as they could speak they said, "Deign, your highness, to excuse our mirth, but those lines were not written by a man but by a monkey."

"A monkey!" exclaimed the Sultan.

"Yes, sire," answered the officials. "They were written by a monkey in our presence."

"Then bring me the monkey," he replied, "as fast as you can."

The Sultan's officials returned to the ship and showed the royal order to the captain.

"He is the master," said the good man, and desired that I should be sent for.

Then they put on me the gorgeous robe and rowed me to land, where I was placed on the horse and led to the palace. Here the Sultan was awaiting me in great state surrounded by his court.

All the way along the streets I had been the object of curiosity to a vast crowd, which had filled every doorway and every window, and it was amidst their shouts and cheers that I was ushered into the presence of the Sultan.

I approached the throne on which he was seated and made him three low bows, then prostrated myself at his feet to the surprise of everyone, who could not understand how it was possible that a monkey should be able to distinguish a Sultan from other people, and to pay him the respect due to his rank. However, excepting the usual speech, I omitted none of the common forms attending a royal audience.

When it was over the Sultan dismissed all the court, keeping with him only the chief of the eunuchs and a little slave. He then passed into another room and ordered food to be brought, making signs to me to sit at table with him and eat. I rose from my seat, kissed the ground, and took my place at the table, eating, as you may suppose, with care and in moderation.

Before the dishes were removed I made signs that writing materials, which stood in one corner of the room, should be laid in front of me. I then took a peach and wrote on it some verses in praise of the Sultan, who was speechless with astonishment; but when I did the same thing on a glass from which I had drunk he murmured to himself, "Why, a man who could do as much would be cleverer than any other man, and this is only a monkey!"

Supper being over chessmen were brought, and the Sultan signed to me to know if I would play with him. I kissed the ground and laid my hand on my head to show that I was ready to show myself worthy of the honour. He beat me the first game, but I won the second and third, and seeing that this did not quite please I dashed off a verse by way of consolation.

The Sultan was so enchanted with all the talents of which I had given proof that he wished me to exhibit some of them to other people. So turning to the chief of the eunuchs he said, "Go and beg my daughter, Queen of Beauty, to come here. I will show her something she has never seen before."

The chief of the eunuchs bowed and left the room, ushering in a few moments later the princess, Queen of Beauty. Her face was uncovered, but the moment she set foot in the room she threw her veil over her head. "Sire," she said to her father, "what can you be thinking of to summon me like this into the presence of a man?"

"I do not understand you," replied the Sultan. "There is nobody here but the eunuch, who is your own servant, the little slave, and myself, yet you cover yourself with your veil and reproach me for having sent for you, as if I had committed a crime."

"Sire," answered the princess, "I am right and you are wrong. This monkey is really no monkey at all, but a young prince who has been turned into a monkey by the wicked spells of a genius, son of the daughter of Eblis."

H.J. FORD

As will be imagined, these words took the Sultan by surprise, and he looked at me to see how I should take the statement of the princess. As I was unable to speak, I placed my hand on my head to show that it was true.

"But how do you know this, my daughter?" asked he.

"Sire," replied Queen of Beauty, "the old lady who took care of me in my childhood was an accomplished magician, and she taught me seventy rules of her art, by means of which I could, in the twinkling of an eye, transplant your capital into the middle of the ocean. Her art likewise teaches me to recognise at first sight all persons who are enchanted, and tells me by whom the spell was wrought."

"My daughter," said the Sultan, "I really had no idea you were so clever."

"Sire," replied the princess, "there are many out-of-the-way things it is as well to know, but one should never boast of them."

"Well," asked the Sultan, "can you tell me what must be done to disenchant the young prince?"

"Certainly; and I can do it."

"Then restore him to his former shape," cried the Sultan. "You could give me no greater pleasure, for I wish to make him my grand-vizir, and to give him to you for your husband."

"As your Highness pleases," replied the princess.

Queen of Beauty rose and went to her chamber, from which she fetched a knife with some Hebrew words engraven on the blade. She then desired the Sultan, the chief of the eunuchs, the little slave, and myself to descend into a secret court of the palace, and placed us beneath a gallery which ran all round, she herself standing in the centre of the court. Here she traced a large circle and in it wrote several words in Arab characters.

When the circle and the writing were finished she stood in the middle of it and repeated some verses from the Koran. Slowly the air grew dark, and we felt as if the earth was about to crumble away, and our fright was by no means diminished at seeing the genius, son of the daughter of Eblis, suddenly appear under the form of a colossal lion.

"Dog," cried the princess when she first caught sight of him, "you think to strike terror into me by daring to present yourself before me in this hideous shape."

"And you," retorted the lion, "have not feared to break our treaty that engaged solemnly we should never interfere with each other."

"Accursed genius!" exclaimed the princess, "it is you by whom that treaty was first broken."

"I will teach you how to give me so much trouble," said the lion, and opening his huge

mouth he advanced to swallow her. But the princess expected something of the sort and was on her guard. She bounded on one side, and seizing one of the hairs of his mane repeated two or three words over it. In an instant it became a sword, and with a sharp blow she cut the lion's body into two pieces. These pieces vanished no one knew where, and only the lion's head remained, which was at once changed into a scorpion. Quick as thought the princess assumed the form of a serpent and gave battle to the scorpion, who, finding he was getting the worst of it, turned himself into an eagle and took flight. But in a moment the serpent had become an eagle more powerful still, who soared up in the air and after him, and then we lost sight of them both.

We all remained where we were quaking with anxiety, when the ground opened in front of us and a black and white cat leapt out, its hair standing on end, and miauing frightfully. At its heels was a wolf, who had almost seized it, when the cat changed itself into a worm, and, piercing the skin of a pomegranate which had tumbled from a tree, hid itself in the fruit. The pomegranate swelled till it grew as large as a pumpkin, and raised itself on to the roof of the gallery, from which it fell into the court and was broken into bits. While this was taking place the wolf, who had transformed himself into a cock, began to swallow the seed of the pomegranate as fast as he could. When all were gone he flew towards us, flapping his wings as if to ask if we saw any more, when suddenly his eye fell on one which lay on the bank of the little canal that flowed through the court; he hastened towards it, but before he could touch it the seed rolled into the canal and became a fish. The cock flung himself in after the fish and took the shape of a pike, and for two hours they chased each other up and down under the water, uttering horrible cries, but we could see nothing. At length they rose from the water in their proper forms, but darting such flames of fire from their mouths that we dreaded lest the palace should catch fire. Soon, however, we had much greater cause for alarm, as the genius, having shaken off the princess, flew towards us. Our fate would have been sealed if the princess, seeing our danger, had not attracted the attention of the genius to herself. As it was, the Sultan's beard was singed and his face scorched, the chief of the eunuchs was burned to a cinder, while a spark deprived me of the sight of one eye. Both I and the Sultan had given up all hope of a rescue, when there was a shout of "Victory, victory!" from the princess, and the genius lay at her feet a great heap of ashes.

Exhausted though she was, the princess at once ordered the little slave, who alone was uninjured, to bring her a cup of water, which she took in her hand. First repeating some magic words over it, she dashed it into my face saying, "If you are only a monkey by enchantment, resume the form of the man you were before." In an instant I stood before her the same man I had formerly been, though having lost the sight of one eye.

I was about to fall on my knees and thank the princess but she did not give me time. Turning to the Sultan, her father, she said, "Sire, I have gained the battle, but it has cost me dear. The fire has penetrated to my heart, and I have only a few moments to live. This would not have happened if I had only noticed the last pomegranate seed and eaten it like the rest. It was the last struggle of the genius, and up to that time I was quite safe. But having let this chance slip I was forced to resort to fire, and in spite of all his experience I showed the genius that I knew

KJP.

more than he did. He is dead and in ashes, but my own death is approaching fast."

"My daughter," cried the Sultan, "how sad is my condition! I am only surprised I am alive at all! The eunuch is consumed by the flames, and the prince whom you have delivered has lost the sight of one eye." He could say no more, for sobs choked his voice, and we all wept together.

Suddenly the princess shrieked, "I burn, I burn!" and death came to free her from her torments.

I have no words, madam, to tell you of my feelings at this terrible sight. I would rather have remained a monkey all my life than let my benefactress perish in this shocking manner. As for the Sultan, he was quite inconsolable, and his subjects, who had dearly loved the princess, shared his grief. For seven days the whole nation mourned, and then the ashes of the princess were buried with great pomp, and a superb tomb was raised over her.

As soon as the Sultan recovered from the severe illness which had seized him after the death of the princess he sent for me and plainly, though politely, informed me that my presence would always remind him of his loss, and he begged that I would instantly quit his kingdom, and on pain of death never return to it. I was, of course, bound to obey, and not knowing what was to become of me I shaved my beard and eyebrows and put on the dress of a calender. After wandering aimlessly through several countries, I resolved to come to Bagdad and request an audience of the Commander of the Faithful.

And that, madam, is my story.

The other Calender then told his story.

The Story of the Third Calender, Son of a King

My story, said the Third Calender, is quite different from those of my two friends. It was fate that deprived them of the sight of their right eyes, but mine was lost by my own folly.

My name is Agib, and I am the son of a king called Cassib, who reigned over a large kingdom, which had for its capital one of the finest seaport towns in the world.

When I succeeded to my father's throne my first care was to visit the provinces on the mainland, and then to sail to the numerous islands which lay off the shore, in order to gain the hearts of my subjects. These voyages gave me such a taste for sailing that I soon determined to explore more distant seas, and commanded a fleet of large ships to be got ready without delay. When they were properly fitted out I embarked on my expedition.

For forty days wind and weather were all in our favour, but the next night a terrific storm arose, which blew us hither and thither for ten days, till the pilot confessed that he had quite lost his bearings. Accordingly a sailor was sent up to the masthead to try to catch a sight of land, and reported that nothing was to be seen but the sea and sky, except a huge mass of blackness that lay astern.

On hearing this the pilot grew white, and, beating his breast, he cried, "Oh, sir, we are lost, lost!" till the ship's crew trembled at they knew not what. When he had recovered himself a little, and was able to explain the cause of his terror, he replied, in answer to my question, that we had drifted far out of our course, and that the following day about noon we should come near that mass of darkness, which, said he, is nothing but the famous Black Mountain. This mountain is composed of adamant, which attracts to itself all the iron and nails in your ship; and as we are helplessly drawn nearer, the force of attraction will become so great that the iron and nails will fall out of the ships and cling to the mountain, and the ships will sink to the bottom with all that are in them. This it is that causes the side of the mountain towards the sea to appear of such a dense blackness.

As may be supposed – continued the pilot – the mountain sides are very rugged, but on the summit stands a brass dome supported on pillars, and bearing on top the figure of a brass horse, with a rider on his back. This rider wears a breastplate of lead, on which strange signs and figures are engraved, and it is said that as long as this statue remains on the dome, vessels will never cease to perish at the foot of the mountain.

So saying, the pilot began to weep afresh, and the crew, fearing their last hour had come, made their wills, each one in favour of his fellow.

At noon next day, as the pilot had foretold, we were so near to the Black Mountain that we saw all the nails and iron fly out of the ships and dash themselves against the mountain with a horrible noise. A moment after the vessels fell asunder and sank, the crews with them. I alone managed to grasp a floating plank, and was driven ashore by the wind, without even a scratch. What was my joy on finding myself at the bottom of some steps which led straight up the mountain, for there was not another inch to the right or the left where a man could set his foot. And, indeed, even the steps themselves were so narrow and so steep that, if the lightest breeze had arisen, I should certainly have been blown into the sea.

When I reached the top I found the brass dome and the statue exactly as the pilot had described, but was too wearied with all I had gone through to do more than glance at them, and, flinging myself under the dome, was asleep in an instant. In my dreams an old man appeared to me and said, "Hearken, Agib! As soon as thou art awake dig up the ground underfoot, and thou shalt find a bow of brass and three arrows of lead. Shoot the arrows at the statue, and the rider shall tumble into the sea, but the horse will fall down by thy side, and thou shalt bury him in the place from which thou tookest the bow and arrows. This being done the sea will rise and cover the mountain, and on it thou wilt perceive the figure of a metal man seated in a boat, having an oar in each hand. Step on board and let him conduct thee; but if thou wouldest behold thy kingdom again, see that thou takest not the name of Allah into thy mouth."

Having uttered these words the vision left me, and I woke, much comforted. I sprang up and drew the bow and arrows out of the ground, and with the third shot the horseman fell with a great crash into the sea, which instantly began to rise, so rapidly, that I had hardly time to bury the horse before the boat approached me. I stepped silently in and sat down, and the metal man pushed off, and rowed without stopping for nine days, after which land appeared on the horizon. I was so overcome with joy at this sight that I forgot all the old man had told me, and cried out, "Allah be praised! Allah be praised!"

The words were scarcely out of my mouth when the boat and man sank from beneath me, and left me floating on the surface. All that day and the next night I swam and floated alternately, making as well as I could for the land which was nearest to me. At last my strength

HJF.

began to fail, and I gave myself up for lost, when the wind suddenly rose, and a huge wave cast me on a flat shore. Then, placing myself in safety, I hastily spread my clothes out to dry in the sun, and flung myself on the warm ground to rest.

Next morning I dressed myself and began to look about me. There seemed to be no one but myself on the island, which was covered with fruit trees and watered with streams, but seemed a long distance from the mainland which I hoped to reach. Before, however, I had time to feel cast down, I saw a ship making directly for the island, and not knowing whether it would contain friends or foes, I hid myself in the thick branches of a tree.

The sailors ran the ship into a creek, where ten slaves landed, carrying spades and pickaxes. In the middle of the island they stopped, and after digging some time, lifted up what seemed to be a trapdoor. They then returned to the vessel two or three times for furniture and provisions, and finally were accompanied by an old man, leading a handsome boy of fourteen or fifteen years of age. They all disappeared down the trapdoor, and after remaining below for a few minutes came up again, but without the boy, and let down the trapdoor, covering it with earth as before. This done, they entered the ship and set sail.

As soon as they were out of sight, I came down from my tree, and went to the place where the boy had been buried. I dug up the earth till I reached a large stone with a ring in the centre. This, when removed, disclosed a flight of stone steps which led to a large room richly furnished and lighted by tapers. On a pile of cushions, covered with tapestry, sat the boy. He looked up, startled and frightened at the sight of a stranger in such a place, and to soothe his fears, I at once spoke: "Be not alarmed, sir, whoever you may be. I am a king, and the son of a king, and will do you no hurt. On the contrary, perhaps I have been sent here to deliver you out of this tomb, where you have been buried alive."

Hearing my words, the young man recovered himself, and when I had ended, he said, "The reasons, Prince, that have caused me to be buried in this place are so strange that they cannot but surprise you. My father is a rich merchant, owning much land and many ships, and has great dealings in precious stones, but he never ceased mourning that he had no child to inherit his wealth.

"At length one day he dreamed that the following year a son would be born to him, and when this actually happened, he consulted all the wise men in the kingdom as to the future of the infant. One and all they said the same thing. I was to live happily till I was fifteen, when a terrible danger awaited me, which I should hardly escape. If, however, I should succeed in doing so, I should live to a great old age. And, they added, when the statue of the brass horse on the top of the mountain of adamant is thrown into the sea by Agib, the son of Cassib, then beware, for fifty days later your son shall fall by his hand!

"This prophecy struck the heart of my father with such woe, that he never got over it, but that did not prevent him from attending carefully to my education till I attained, a short time ago, my fifteenth birthday. It was only yesterday that the news reached him that ten days previously the statue of brass had been thrown into the sea, and he at once set about hiding me in this underground chamber, which was built for the purpose, promising to fetch me out when the forty days have passed. For myself, I have no fears, as Prince Agib is not likely to come here to look for me."

I listened to his story with an inward laugh as to the absurdity of my ever wishing to cause the death of this harmless boy, whom I hastened to assure of my friendship and even of my protection; begging him, in return, to convey me in his father's ship to my own country. I need hardly say that I took special care not to inform him that I was the Agib whom he dreaded.

The day passed in conversation on various subjects, and I found him a youth of ready wit and of some learning. I took on myself the duties of a servant, held the basin and water for him when he washed, prepared the dinner and set it on the table. He soon grew to love me, and for thirty-nine days we spent as pleasant an existence as could be expected underground.

The morning of the fortieth dawned, and the young man when he woke gave thanks in an outburst of joy that the danger was passed. "My father may be here at any moment," said he, "so make me, I pray you, a bath of hot water, that I may bathe, and change my clothes, and be ready to receive him."

So I fetched the water as he asked, and washed and rubbed him, after which he lay down again and slept a little. When he opened his eyes for the second time, he begged me to bring him a melon and some sugar, that he might eat and refresh himself.

I soon chose a fine melon out of those which remained, but could find no knife to cut it with. "Look in the cornice over my head," said he, "and I think you will see one." It was so high above me, that I had some difficulty in reaching it, and catching my foot in the covering of the bed, I slipped, and fell right upon the young man, the knife going straight into his heart.

At this awful sight I shrieked aloud in my grief and pain. I threw myself on the ground and rent my clothes and tore my hair with sorrow. Then, fearing to be punished as his murderer by the unhappy father, I raised the great stone which blocked the staircase, and quitting the underground chamber, made everything fast as before.

Scarcely had I finished when, looking out to sea, I saw the vessel heading for the island,

and, feeling that it would be useless for me to protest my innocence, I again concealed myself among the branches of a tree that grew near by.

The old man and his slaves pushed off in a boat directly the ship touched land, and walked quickly towards the entrance to the underground chamber; but when they were near enough to see that the earth had been disturbed, they paused and changed colour. In silence they all went down and called to the youth by name; then for a moment I heard no more. Suddenly a fearful scream rent the air, and the next instant the slaves came up the steps, carrying with them the body of the old man, who had fainted from sorrow! Laying him down at the foot of the tree in which I had taken shelter, they did their best to recover him, but it took a long while. When at last he revived, they left him to dig a grave, and then laying the young man's body in it, they threw in the earth.

This ended, the slaves brought up all the furniture that remained below, and put it on the vessel, and breaking some boughs to weave a litter, they laid the old man on it, and carried him to the ship, which spread its sails and stood out to sea.

So once more I was quite alone, and for a whole month I walked daily over the island, seeking for some chance of escape. At length one day it struck me that my prison had grown much larger, and that the mainland seemed to be nearer. My heart beat at this thought, which was almost too good to be true. I watched a little longer: there was no doubt about it, and soon there was only a tiny stream for me to cross.

Even when I was safe on the other side I had a long distance to go on the mud and sand before I reached dry ground, and very tired I was, when far in front of me I caught sight of a castle of red copper, which, at first sight, I took to be a fire. I made all the haste I could, and after some miles of hard walking stood before it, and gazed at it in astonishment, for it seemed to me the most wonderful building I had ever beheld. While I was still staring at it, there came towards me a tall old man, accompanied by ten young men, all handsome, and all blind of the right eye.

Now in its way, the spectacle of ten men walking together, all blind of the right eye, is as uncommon as that of a copper castle, and I was turning over in my mind what could be the meaning of this strange fact, when they greeted me warmly, and inquired what had brought me there. I replied that my story was somewhat long, but that if they would take the trouble to sit down, I should be happy to tell it them. When I had finished, the young men begged that I would go with them to the castle, and I joyfully accepted their offer. We passed through what seemed to me an endless number of rooms, and came at length into a large hall, furnished with ten small blue sofas for the ten young men, which served as beds as well as chairs, and with another sofa in the middle for the old man. As none of the sofas could hold more than one person, they bade me place myself on the carpet, and to ask no questions about anything I should see.

After a little while the old man rose and brought in supper, which I ate heartily, for I was very hungry. Then one of the young men begged me to repeat my story, which had struck them all with astonishment, and when I had ended, the old man was bidden to "do his duty", as it was late, and they wished to go to bed. At these words he rose, and went to a closet, from which he brought out ten basins, all covered with blue stuff. He set one before each of the young men, together with a lighted taper.

When the covers were taken off the basins, I saw they were filled with ashes, coal-dust, and lamp-black. The young men mixed these all together, and smeared the whole over their heads and faces. They then wept and beat their breasts, crying, "This is the fruit of idleness, and of our wicked lives."

This ceremony lasted nearly the whole night, and when it stopped they washed themselves carefully, and put on fresh clothes, and lay down to sleep.

All this while I had refrained from questions, though my curiosity almost seemed to burn a hole in me, but the following day, when we went out to walk, I said to them, "Gentlemen, I must disobey your wishes, for I can keep silence no more. You do not appear to lack wit, yet you do such actions as none but madmen could be capable of. Whatever befalls me I cannot forbear asking, 'Why you daub your faces with black, and how it is you are all blind of one eye?'" But they only answered that such questions were none of my business, and that I should do well to hold my peace.

During that day we spoke of other things, but when night came, and the same ceremony was repeated, I implored them most earnestly to let me know the meaning of it all.

"It is for your own sake," replied one of the young men, "that we have not granted your request, and to preserve you from our unfortunate fate. If, however, you wish to share our destiny we will delay no longer."

I answered that whatever might be the consequence I wished to have my curiosity satisfied, and that I would take the result on my own head. He then assured me that, even when I had lost my eye, I should be unable to remain with them, as their number was complete, and could not be added to. But to this I replied that, though I should be grieved to part company with such honest gentlemen, I would not be turned from my resolution on that account.

On hearing my determination my ten hosts then took a sheep and killed it, and handed me a knife, which they said I should by-and-by find useful. "We must sew you into this sheep-skin," said they, "and then leave you. A fowl of monstrous size, called a roc, will appear in the air, taking you to be a sheep. He will snatch you up and carry you into the sky, but be not

alarmed, for he will bring you safely down and lay you on the top of a mountain. When you are on the ground cut the skin with the knife and throw it off. As soon as the roc sees you he will fly away from fear, but you must walk on till you come to a castle covered with plates of gold, studded with jewels. Enter boldly at the gate, which always stands open, but do not ask us to tell you what we saw or what befell us there, for that you will learn for yourself. This only we may say, that it cost us each our right eye, and has imposed upon us our nightly penance."

After the young gentlemen had been at the trouble of sewing the sheep-skin on me they left me, and retired to the hall. In a few minutes the roc appeared, and bore me off to the top of the mountain in his huge claws as lightly as if I had been a feather, for this great white bird is so strong that he has been known to carry even an elephant to his nest in the hills.

The moment my feet touched the ground I took out my knife and cut the threads that bound me, and the sight of me in my proper clothes so alarmed the roc that he spread his wings and flew away. Then I set out to seek the castle.

I found it after wandering about for half a day, and never could I have imagined anything so glorious. The gate led into a square court, into which opened a hundred doors, ninety-nine of them being of rare woods and one of gold. Through each of these doors I caught glimpses of splendid gardens or of rich storehouses.

Entering one of the doors which was standing open I found myself in a vast hall where forty young ladies, magnificently dressed, and of perfect beauty, were reclining. As soon as they saw me they rose and uttered words of welcome, and even forced me to take possession of a seat that was higher than their own, though my proper place was at their feet. Not content with this, one brought me splendid garments, while another filled a basin with scented water and poured it over my hands, and the rest busied themselves with preparing refreshments. After I had eaten and drunk of the most delicate food and rarest wines, the ladies crowded round me and begged me to tell them all my adventures.

By the time I had finished night had fallen, and the ladies lighted up the castle with such a prodigious quantity of tapers that even day could hardly have been brighter. We then sat down to a supper of dried fruits and sweetmeats, after which some sang and others danced. I was so well amused that I did not notice how the time was passing, but at length one of the ladies approached and informed me it was midnight, and that, as I must be tired, she would conduct me to the room that had been prepared for me. Then, bidding me good-night, I was left to sleep.

I spent the next thirty-nine days in much the same way as the first, but at the close of that time the ladies appeared (as was their custom) in my room one morning to inquire how I had slept, and instead of looking cheerful and smiling they were in floods of tears. "Prince," said they, "we must leave you, and never was it so hard to part from any of our friends. Most likely we shall never see you again, but if you have sufficient self-command perhaps we may yet look forward to a meeting."

"Ladies," I replied, "what is the meaning of these strange words – I pray you to tell me?"

"Know then," answered one of them, "that we are all princesses – each a king's daughter. We live in this castle together, in the way that you have seen, but at the end of every year secret duties call us away for the space of forty days. The time has now come; but before we depart, we will leave you our keys, so that you may not lack entertainment during our absence. But one thing we would ask of you. The Golden Door, alone, forbear to open, as you value your own peace, and the happiness of your life. That door once unlocked, we must bid you farewell for ever."

Weeping, I assured them of my prudence, and after embracing me tenderly, they went their ways.

Every day I opened two or three fresh doors, each of which contained behind it so many

curious things that I had no chance of feeling dull, much as I regretted the absence of the ladies. Sometimes it was an orchard, whose fruit far exceeded in bigness any that grew in my father's garden. Sometimes it was a court planted with roses, jessamine, daffodils, hyacinths and anemones, and a thousand other flowers of which I did not know the names. Or again, it would be an aviary, fitted with all kinds of singing birds, or a treasury heaped up with precious stones; but whatever I might see, all was perfect of its own sort.

Thirty-nine days passed away more rapidly than I could have conceived possible, and the following morning the princesses were to return to the castle. But alas! I had explored every corner, save only the room that was shut in by the Golden Door, and I had no longer anything to amuse myself with. I stood before the forbidden place for some time, gazing at its beauty; then a happy inspiration struck me, that because I unlocked the door it was not necessary that I should enter the chamber. It would be enough for me to stand outside and view whatever hidden wonders might be therein.

Thus arguing against my own conscience, I turned the key, when a smell rushed out that, pleasant though it was, overcame me completely, and I fell fainting across the threshold. Instead of being warned by this accident, directly I came to myself I went for a few moments

H J FORD.

into the air to shake off the effects of the perfume, and then entered boldly. I found myself in a large, vaulted room, lighted by tapers, scented with aloes and ambergris, standing in golden candle-sticks, whilst gold and silver lamps hung from the ceiling.

Though objects of rare workmanship lay heaped around me, I paid them scant attention, so much was I struck by a great black horse which stood in one corner, the handsomest and best-shaped animal I had ever seen. His saddle and bridle were of massive gold, curiously wrought, one side of his trough was filled with clean barley and sesame, and the other with rose water. I led the animal into the open air, and then jumped on his back, shaking the reins as I did so, but as he never stirred, I touched him lightly with a switch I had picked up in his stable. No sooner did he feel the stroke, than he spread his wings (which I had not perceived before), and flew up with me straight into the sky. When he had reached a prodigious height, he next darted back to earth, and alighted on the terrace belonging to a castle, shaking me violently out of the saddle as he did so, and giving me such a blow with his tail, that he knocked out my right eye.

Half-stunned as I was with all that had happened to me, I rose to my feet, thinking as I did so of what had befallen the ten young men, and watching the horse which was soaring into the clouds. I left the terrace and wandered on till I came to a hall, which I knew to have been the one from which the roc had taken me, by the ten blue sofas against the wall.

The ten young men were not present when I first entered, but came in soon after, accompanied by the old man. They greeted me kindly, and bewailed my misfortune, though, indeed, they had expected nothing less. "All that has happened to you," they said, "we also have undergone, and we should be enjoying the same happiness still, had we not opened the Golden Door while the princesses were absent. You have been no wiser than we, and have suffered the same punishment. We would gladly receive you among us, to perform such penance as we do, but we have already told you that this is impossible. Depart, therefore, from hence and go to the Court of Bagdad, where you shall meet with him that can decide your destiny." They told me the way I was to travel, and I left them.

On the road I caused my beard and eyebrows to be shaved, and put on a Calender's habit. I have had a long journey, but arrived this evening in the city, where I met my brother Calenders at the gate, being strangers like myself. We wondered much at one another, to see we were all blind of the same eye, but we had no leisure to discourse at length of our common calamities. We had only so much time as to come hither to implore those favours which you have been generously pleased to grant us.

He finished, and it was Zobeida's turn to speak: "Go wherever you please," she said, addressing all three. "I pardon you all, but you must depart immediately out of this house."

The Seven Voyages of Sindbad the Sailor

In the times of the Caliph Haroun-al-Raschid there lived in Bagdad a poor porter named Hindbad, who on a very hot day was sent to carry a heavy load from one end of the city to the other. Before he had accomplished half the distance he was so tired that, finding himself in a quiet street where the pavement was sprinkled with rose water, and a cool breeze was blowing, he set his burden upon the ground, and sat down to rest in the shade of a grand house. Very soon he decided that he could not have chosen a pleasanter place; a delicious perfume of aloes wood and pastilles came from the open windows and mingled with the scent of the rose water which steamed up from the hot pavement. Within the palace he heard some music, as of many instruments cunningly played, and the melodious warble of nightingales and other birds, and by this, and the appetising smell of many dainty dishes of which he presently became aware, he judged that feasting and merry-making were going on. He wondered who lived in this magnificent house which he had never seen before, the street in which it stood being one which he seldom had occasion to pass. To satisfy his curiosity he went up to some splendidly dressed servants who stood at the door, and asked one of them the name of the master of the mansion.

"What," replied he, "do you live in Bagdad, and not know that here lives the noble Sindbad the Sailor, that famous traveller who sailed over every sea upon which the sun shines?"

The porter, who had often heard people speak of the immense wealth of Sindbad, could not help feeling envious of one whose lot seemed to be as happy as his own was miserable. Casting his eyes up to the sky he exclaimed aloud,

"Consider, Mighty Creator of all things, the differences between Sindbad's life and mine. Every day I suffer a thousand hardships and misfortunes, and have hard work to get even enough bad barley bread to keep myself and my family alive, while the lucky Sindbad spends money right and left and lives upon the fat of the land! What has he done that you should give him this pleasant life – what have I done to deserve so hard a fate?"

So saying he stamped upon the ground like one beside himself with misery and despair. Just at this moment a servant came out of the palace, and taking him by the arm said, "Come with me, the noble Sindbad, my master, wishes to speak to you."

Hindbad was not a little surprised at this summons, and feared that his unguarded words might have drawn upon him the displeasure of Sindbad, so he tried to excuse himself upon the pretext that he could not leave the burden which had been entrusted to him in the street. However the lackey promised him that it should be taken care of, and urged him to obey the call so pressingly that at last the porter was obliged to yield.

He followed the servant into a vast room, where a great company was seated round a table covered with all sorts of delicacies. In the place of honour sat a tall, grave man whose long white beard gave him a venerable air. Behind his chair stood a crowd of attendants eager to minister to his wants. This was the famous Sindbad himself. The porter, more than ever alarmed at the sight of so much magnificence, tremblingly saluted the noble company. Sindbad, making a sign to him to approach, caused him to be seated at his right hand, and himself heaped choice morsels upon his plate, and poured out for him a draught of excellent wine, and presently, when the banquet drew to a close, spoke to him familiarly, asking his name and occupation.

"My lord," replied the porter, "I am called Hindbad."

"I am glad to see you here," continued Sindbad. "And I will answer for the rest of the company that they are equally pleased, but I wish you to tell me what it was that you said just now in the street." For Sindbad, passing by the open window before the feast began, had heard his complaint and therefore had sent for him.

At this question Hindbad was covered with confusion, and hanging down his head, replied, "My lord, I confess that, overcome by weariness and ill-humour, I uttered indiscreet words, which I pray you to pardon me."

"Oh!" replied Sindbad, "do not imagine that I am so unjust as to blame you. On the contrary, I understand your situation and can pity you. Only you appear to be mistaken about me, and I wish to set you right. You doubtless imagine that I have acquired all the wealth and luxury that you see me enjoy without difficulty or danger, but this is far indeed from being the case. I have only reached this happy state after having for years suffered every possible kind of toil and danger.

"Yes, my noble friends," he continued, addressing the company, "I assure you that my adventures have been strange enough to deter even the most avaricious men from seeking wealth by traversing the seas. Since you have, perhaps, heard but confused accounts of my seven voyages, and the dangers and wonders that I have met with by sea and land, I will now give you a full and true account of them, which I think you will be well pleased to hear."

As Sindbad was relating his adventures chiefly on account of the porter, he ordered, before beginning his tale, that the burden which had been left in the street should be carried by some of his own servants to the place for which Hindbad had set out at first, while he remained to listen to the story.

First Voyage

I had inherited considerable wealth from my parents, and being young and foolish I at first squandered it recklessly upon every kind of pleasure, but presently, finding that riches speedily take to themselves wings if managed as badly as I was managing mine, and remembering also that to be old and poor is misery indeed, I began to bethink me of how I could make the best of what still remained to me. I sold all my household goods by public auction, and joined a company of merchants who traded by sea, embarking with them at Balsora in a ship which we had fitted out between us.

We set sail and took our course towards the East Indies by the Persian Gulf, having the coast of Persia upon our left hand and upon our right the shores of Arabia Felix. I was at first much troubled by the uneasy motion of the vessel, but speedily recovered my health, and since that hour have been no more plagued by sea-sickness.

From time to time we landed at various islands, where we sold or exchanged our merchandise, and one day, when the wind dropped suddenly, we found ourselves becalmed close to a small island like a green meadow, which only rose slightly above the surface of the water. Our sails were furled, and the captain gave permission to all who wished to land for a while and amuse themselves. I was among the number, but when after strolling about for some time we lighted a fire and sat down to enjoy the repast which we had brought with us, we were startled by a sudden and violent trembling of the island, while at the same moment those left upon the ship set up an outcry bidding us come on board for our lives, since what we had taken for an island was nothing but the back of a sleeping whale. Those who were nearest to the boat threw themselves into it, others sprang into the sea, but before I could save myself the whale plunged suddenly into the depths of the ocean, leaving me clinging to a piece of the wood which we had brought to make our fire. Meanwhile a breeze had sprung up, and in the confusion that ensued on board our vessel in hoisting the sails and taking up those who were in the boat and clinging to its sides, no one missed me and I was left at the mercy of the waves. All that day I floated up and down, now beaten this way, now that, and when night fell I despaired for my life; but, weary and spent as I was, I clung to my frail support, and great was my joy when the morning light showed me that I had drifted against an island.

The cliffs were high and steep, but luckily for me some tree-roots protruded in places, and by their aid I climbed up at last, and stretched myself upon the turf at the top, where I lay, more dead than alive, till the sun was high in the heavens. By that time I was very hungry, but after some searching I came upon some eatable herbs, and a spring of clear water, and much refreshed I set out to explore the island. Presently I reached a great plain where a grazing horse was tethered, and as I stood looking at it I heard voices talking apparently underground, and in a moment a man appeared who asked me how I came upon the island. I told him my adventures, and heard in return that he was one of the grooms of Mihrage, the king of the island, and that each year they came to feed their master's horses in this plain. He took me to a cave where his companions were assembled, and when I had eaten of the food they set before me, they bade me think myself fortunate to have come upon them when I did, since they were going back to their master on the morrow, and without their aid I could certainly never have found my way to the inhabited part of the island.

Early the next morning we accordingly set out, and when we reached the capital I was graciously received by the king, to whom I related my adventures, upon which he ordered that I should be well cared for and provided with such things as I needed. Being a merchant I sought out men of my own profession, and particularly those who came from foreign countries, as I hoped in this way to hear news from Bagdad, and find out some means of returning thither, for the capital was situated upon the seashore, and visited by vessels from all parts of the world. In the meantime I heard many curious things, and answered many questions concerning my own country, for I talked willingly with all who came to me. Also to while away the time of waiting I explored a little island named Cassel, which belonged to King Mihrage, and which was supposed to be inhabited by a spirit named Deggial. Indeed, the sailors assured me that often at night the playing of timbals could be heard upon it. However, I saw nothing strange upon my voyage, saving some fish that were full two hundred cubits long, but were fortunately more in dread of us than even we were of them, and fled from us if we did but strike upon a board to frighten them. Other fishes there were only a cubit long which had heads like owls.

One day after my return, as I went down to the quay, I saw a ship which had just cast anchor, and was discharging her cargo, while the merchants to whom it belonged were busily directing the removal of it to their warehouses. Drawing nearer I presently noticed that my own name was marked upon some of the packages, and after having carefully examined them, I felt sure that they were indeed those which I had put on board our ship at Balsora. I then recognised the captain of the vessel, but as I was certain that he believed me to be dead, I went up to him and asked who owned the packages that I was looking at.

"There was on board my ship," he replied, "a merchant of Bagdad named Sindbad. One day he and several of my other passengers landed upon what we supposed to be an island, but which was really an enormous whale floating asleep upon the waves. No sooner did it feel upon its back the heat of the fire which had been kindled, than it plunged into the depths of the sea. Several of the people who were upon it perished in the waters, and among others this unlucky Sindbad. This merchandise is his, but I have resolved to dispose of it for the benefit of his family if I should ever chance to meet with them."

"Captain," said I, "I am that Sindbad whom you believe to be dead, and these are my possessions!"

When the captain heard these words he cried out in amazement, "Lackaday! and what is the world coming to? In these days there is not an honest man to be met with. Did I not with my own eyes see Sindbad drown, and now you have the audacity to tell me that you are he! I should have taken you to be a just man, and yet for the sake of obtaining that which does not belong to you, you are ready to invent this horrible falsehood."

"Have patience, and do me the favour to hear my story," said I.

"Speak then," replied the captain, "I'm all attention."

So I told him of my escape and of my fortunate meeting with the king's grooms, and how kindly I had been received at the palace. Very soon I began to see that I had made some impression upon him, and after the arrival of some of the other merchants, who showed great joy at once more seeing me alive, he declared that he also recognised me.

Throwing himself upon my neck he exclaimed, "Heaven be praised that you have escaped from so great a danger. As to your goods, I pray you take them, and dispose of them as you please." I thanked him, and praised his honesty, begging him to accept several bales of merchandise in token of my gratitude, but he would take nothing. Of the choicest of my goods I prepared a present for King Mihrage, who was at first amazed, having known that I had lost my all. However, when I had explained to him how my bales had been miraculously restored to me, he graciously accepted my gifts, and in return gave me many valuable things. I then took leave of him, and exchanging my merchandise for sandal and aloes wood, camphor, nutmegs, cloves, pepper, and ginger, I embarked upon the same vessel and traded so successfully upon our homeward voyage that I arrived in Balsora with about one hundred thousand sequins. My family received me with as much joy as I felt upon seeing them once more. I bought land and slaves, and built a great house in which I resolved to live happily, and in the enjoyment of all the pleasures of life to forget my past sufferings.

Here Sindbad paused, and commanded the musicians to play again, while the feasting continued until evening. When the time came for the porter to depart, Sindbad gave him a purse containing one hundred sequins, saying, "Take this, Hindbad, and go home, but tomorrow come again and you shall hear more of my adventures."

The porter retired quite overcome by so much generosity, and you may imagine that he was well received at home, where his wife and children thanked their lucky stars that he had found such a benefactor.

The next day Hindbad, dressed in his best, returned to the voyager's house, and was received with open arms. As soon as all the guests had arrived the banquet began as before, and when they had feasted long and merrily, Sindbad addressed them thus:

"My friends, I beg that you will give me your attention while I relate the adventures of my second voyage, which you will find even more astonishing than the first."

Second Voyage

I had resolved, as you know, on my return from my first voyage, to spend the rest of my days quietly in Bagdad, but very soon I grew tired of such an idle life and longed once more to find myself upon the sea.

I procured, therefore, such goods as were suitable for the places I intended to visit, and embarked for the second time in a good ship with other merchants whom I knew to be honourable men. We went from island to island, often making excellent bargains, until one day we landed at a spot which, though covered with fruit trees and abounding in springs of excellent water, appeared to possess neither houses nor people. While my companions wandered here and there gathering flowers and fruit I sat down in a shady place, and, having heartily enjoyed the provisions and the wine I had brought with me, I fell asleep, lulled by the murmur of a clear brook which flowed close by.

How long I slept I know not, but when I opened my eyes and started to my feet I perceived with horror that I was alone and that the ship was gone. I rushed to and fro like one distracted, uttering cries of despair, and when from the shore I saw the vessel under full sail just disappearing upon the horizon, I wished bitterly enough that I had been content to stay at home in safety. But since wishes could do me no good, I presently took courage and looked about me for a means of escape. When I had climbed a tall tree I first of all directed my anxious glances towards the sea; but, finding nothing hopeful there, I turned landward, and my curiosity was excited by a huge dazzling white object, so far off that I could not make out what it might be.

Descending from the tree I hastily collected what remained of my provisions and set off as fast as I could go towards it. As I drew near it seemed to me to be a white ball of immense size and height, and when I could touch it, I found it marvellously smooth and soft. As it was impossible to climb it – for it presented no foot-hold – I walked round about it seeking some opening, but there was none. I counted, however, that it was at least fifty paces round. By this time the sun was near setting, but quite suddenly it fell dark, something like a huge black cloud came swiftly over me, and I saw with amazement that it was a bird of extraordinary size which was hovering near. Then I remembered that I had often heard the sailors speak of a wonderful bird called a roc, and it occurred to me that the white object which had so puzzled me must be its egg.

Sure enough the bird settled slowly down upon it, covering it with its wings to keep it warm, and I cowered close beside the egg in such a position that one of the bird's feet, which was as large as the trunk of a tree, was just in front of me. Taking off my turban I bound myself securely to it with the linen in the hope that the roc, when it took flight next morning, would bear me away with it from the desolate island. And this was precisely what did happen. As soon as the dawn appeared the bird rose into the air carrying me up and up till I could no longer see the earth, and then suddenly it descended so swiftly that I almost lost consciousness. When I became aware that the roc had settled and that I was once again upon solid ground, I hastily unbound my turban from its foot and freed myself, and that not a moment too soon; for the

bird, pouncing upon a huge snake, killed it with a few blows from its powerful beak, and seizing it up rose into the air once more and soon disappeared from my view. When I had looked about me I began to doubt if I had gained anything by quitting the desolate island.

The valley in which I found myself was deep and narrow, and surrounded by mountains which towered into the clouds, and were so steep and rocky that there was no way of climbing up their sides. As I wandered about, seeking anxiously for some means of escaping from this trap, I observed that the ground was strewed with diamonds, some of them of an astonishing size. This sight gave me great pleasure, but my delight was speedily damped when I saw also numbers of horrible snakes so long and so large that the smallest of them could have swallowed an elephant with ease. Fortunately for me they seemed to hide in caverns of the rocks by day, and only came out by night, probably because of their enemy the roc.

All day long I wandered up and down the valley, and when it grew dusk I crept into a little cave, and having blocked up the entrance to it with a stone, I ate part of my little store of food and lay down to sleep, but all through the night the serpents crawled to and fro, hissing horribly, so that I could scarcely close my eyes for terror. I was thankful when the morning light appeared, and when I judged by the silence that the serpents had retreated to their dens I came tremblingly out of my cave and wandered up and down the valley once more, kicking the diamonds contemptuously out of my path, for I felt that they were indeed vain things to a man in my situation. At last, overcome with weariness, I sat down upon a rock, but I had hardly closed my eyes when I was startled by something which fell to the ground with a thud close beside me.

It was a huge piece of fresh meat, and as I stared at it several more pieces rolled over the cliffs in different places. I had always thought that the stories the sailors told of the famous valley of diamonds, and of the cunning way which some merchants had devised for getting at the precious stones, were mere travellers' tales invented to give pleasure to the hearers, but now I perceived that they were surely true. These merchants came to the valley at the time when the eagles, which keep their eyries in the rocks, had hatched their young. The merchants then threw great lumps of meat into the valley. These, falling with so much force upon the diamonds, were sure to take up some of the precious stones with them, when the eagles pounced upon the meat and carried it off to their nests to feed their hungry broods. Then the merchants, scaring away the parent birds with shouts and outcries, would secure their treasures. Until this moment I had looked upon the valley as my grave, for I had seen no possibility of getting out of it alive, but now I took courage and began to devise a means of escape. I began by picking up all the largest diamonds I could find and storing them carefully in the leathern wallet which had held my provisions; this I tied securely to my belt. I then chose the piece of meat which seemed most suited to my purpose, and with the aid of my turban bound it firmly to my back; this done I laid down upon my face and awaited the coming of the eagles. I soon heard the flapping of their mighty wings above me, and had the satisfaction of feeling one of them seize upon my piece of meat, and me with it, and rise slowly towards his nest, into which he presently dropped me. Luckily for me the merchants were on the watch, and setting up their usual outcries they rushed to the nest scaring away the eagle. Their amazement was great when they discovered me, and also their disappointment, and with one accord they fell to abusing me for having robbed them of their usual profit. Addressing myself to the one who seemed most aggrieved, I said:

"I am sure, if you knew all that I have suffered, you would show more kindness towards me, and as for diamonds, I have enough here of the very best for you and me and all your company."

So saying I showed them to him. The others all crowded round me, wondering at my adventures and admiring the device by which I had escaped from the valley, and when they had led me to their camp and examined my diamonds, they assured me that in all the years that they had carried on their trade they had seen no stones to be compared with them for size and beauty.

I found that each merchant chose a particular nest, and took his chance of what he might find in it. So I begged the one who owned the nest to which I had been carried to take as much as he would of my treasure, but he contented himself with one stone, and that by no means the largest, assuring me that with such a gem his fortune was made, and he need toil no more. I stayed with the merchants several days, and then as they were journeying homewards I gladly accompanied them. Our way lay across high mountains infested with frightful serpents, but we had the good luck to escape them and came at last to the seashore. Thence we sailed to the isle of Rohat where the camphor trees grow to such a size that a hundred men could shelter under one of them with ease. The sap flows from an incision made high up in the tree into a vessel hung there to receive it, and soon hardens into the substance called camphor, but the tree itself withers up and dies when it has been so treated.

In this same island we saw the rhinoceros, an animal which is smaller than the elephant and larger than the buffalo. It has one horn about a cubit long which is solid, but has a furrow from the base to the tip. Upon it is traced in white lines the figure of a man. The rhinoceros fights with the elephant, and transfixing him with his horn carries him off upon his head, but becoming blinded with the blood of his enemy, he falls helpless to the ground, and then comes the roc, and clutches them both up in his talons and takes them to feed his young. This doubtless astonishes you, but if you do not believe my tale go to Rohat and see for yourself. For fear of wearying you I pass over in silence many other wonderful things which we saw in this island. Before we left I exchanged one of my diamonds for much goodly merchandise by which I profited greatly on our homeward way. At last we reached Balsora, whence I hastened to Bagdad, where my first action was to bestow large sums of money upon the poor, after which I settled down to enjoy tranquilly the riches I had gained with so much toil and pain.

Having thus related the adventures of his second voyage, Sindbad again bestowed a hundred sequins upon Hindbad, inviting him to come again on the following day and hear how he fared upon his third voyage. The other guests also departed to their homes, but all returned at the same hour next day, including the porter, whose former life of hard work and poverty had already begun to seem to him like a bad dream. Again after the feast was over did Sindbad claim the attention of his guests and began the account of his third voyage.

Third Voyage

After a very short time the pleasant easy life I led made me quite forget the perils of my two voyages. Moreover, as I was still in the prime of life, it pleased me better to be up and doing. So once more providing myself with the rarest and choicest merchandise of Bagdad, I conveyed it to Balsora, and set sail with other merchants of my acquaintance for distant lands. We had touched at many ports and made much profit, when one day upon the open sea we were caught by a terrible wind which blew us completely out of our reckoning, and lasting for several days finally drove us into harbour on a strange island.

"I would rather have come to anchor anywhere than here," quoth our captain. "This island and all adjoining it are inhabited by hairy savages, who are certain to attack us, and whatever these dwarfs may do we dare not resist, since they swarm like locusts, and if one of them is killed the rest will fall upon us, and speedily make an end of us."

These words caused great consternation among all the ship's company, and only too soon we were to find out that the captain spoke truly. There appeared a vast multitude of hideous savages, not more than two feet high and covered with reddish fur. Throwing themselves into the waves they surrounded our vessel. Chattering meanwhile in a language we could not understand, and clutching at ropes and gangways, they swarmed up the ship's side with such speed and agility that they almost seemed to fly.

You may imagine the rage and terror that seized us as we watched them, neither daring to hinder them nor able to speak a word to deter them from their purpose, whatever it might be. Of this we were not left long in doubt. Hoisting the sails, and cutting the cable of the anchor, they sailed our vessel to an island which lay a little further off, where they drove us ashore; then taking possession of her, they made off to the place from which they had come, leaving us helpless upon a shore avoided with horror by all mariners for a reason which you will soon learn.

Turning away from the sea we wandered miserably inland, finding as we went various herbs and fruits which we ate, feeling that we might as well live as long as possible though we had no hope of escape. Presently we saw in the far distance what seemed to us to be a splendid palace, towards which we turned our weary steps, but when we reached it we saw that it was a castle, lofty, and strongly built. Pushing back the heavy ebony doors we entered the courtyard, but upon the threshold of the great hall beyond it we paused, frozen with horror, at the sight which greeted us. On one side lay a huge pile of bones – human bones, and on the other numberless spits for roasting! Overcome with despair we sank trembling to the ground, and lay there without speech or motion. The sun was setting when a loud noise aroused us, the door of the hall was violently burst open and a horrible giant entered. He was as tall as a palm tree, and perfectly black, and had one eye, which flamed like a burning coal in the middle of his

forehead. His teeth were long and sharp and grinned horribly, while his lower lip hung down upon his chest, and he had ears like elephant's ears, which covered his shoulders, and nails like the claws of some fierce bird.

At this terrible sight our senses left us and we lay like dead men. When at last we came to ourselves the giant sat examining us attentively with his fearful eye. Presently when he had looked at us enough he came towards us, and stretching out his hand took me by the back of the neck, turning me this way and that, but feeling that I was mere skin and bone he set me down again and went on to the next, whom he treated in the same fashion; at last he came to the captain, and finding him the fattest of us all, he took him up in one hand and stuck him upon a spit and proceeded to kindle a huge fire at which he presently roasted him. After the giant had supped he lay down to sleep, snoring like the loudest thunder, while we lay shivering with horror the whole night through, and when day broke he awoke and went out, leaving us in the castle.

When we believed him to be really gone we started up bemoaning our horrible fate, until the hall echoed with our despairing cries. Though we were many and our enemy was alone it did not occur to us to kill him, and indeed we should have found that a hard task, even if we had thought of it, and no plan could we devise to deliver ourselves. So at last, submitting to our sad fate, we spent the day in wandering up and down the island eating such fruits as we could find, and when night came we returned to the castle, having sought in vain for any other place of shelter. At sunset the giant returned, supped upon one of our unhappy comrades, slept and snored till dawn, and then left us as before. Our condition seemed to us so frightful that several of my companions thought it would be better to leap from the cliffs and perish in the waves at once, rather than await so miserable an end; but I had a plan of escape which I now unfolded to them, and which they at once agreed to attempt.

"Listen, my brothers," I added. "You know that plenty of driftwood lies along the shore. Let us make several rafts, and carry them to a suitable place. If our plot succeeds, we can wait patiently for the chance of some passing ship which would rescue us from this fatal island. If it fails, we must quickly take to our rafts; frail as they are, we have more chance of saving our lives with them than we have if we remain here."

All agreed with me, and we spent the day in building rafts, each capable of carrying three persons. At nightfall we returned to the castle, and very soon in came the giant, and one more of our number was sacrificed. But the time of our vengeance was at hand! As soon as he had finished his horrible repast he lay down to sleep as before, and when we heard him begin to snore I, and nine of the boldest of my comrades, rose softly, and took each a spit, which we made red-hot in the fire, and then at a given signal we plunged it with one accord into the giant's eye, completely blinding him. Uttering a terrible cry, he sprang to his feet clutching in all directions to try to seize one of us, but we had all fled different ways as soon as the deed was done, and thrown ourselves flat upon the ground in corners where he was not likely to touch us with his feet.

After a vain search he fumbled about till he found the door, and fled out of it howling frightfully. As for us, when he was gone we made haste to leave the fatal castle, and, stationing ourselves beside our rafts, we waited to see what would happen. Our idea was that if, when the sun rose, we saw nothing of the giant, and no longer heard his howls, which still came faintly through the darkness, growing more and more distant, we should conclude that he was dead, and that we might safely stay upon the island and need not risk our lives upon the frail rafts. But alas! morning light showed us our enemy approaching us, supported on either hand by two giants nearly as large and fearful as himself, while a crowd of others followed close upon their heels. Hesitating no longer we clambered upon our rafts and rowed with all our might out to sea. The giants, seeing their prey escaping them, seized up huge pieces of rock, and wading into the water hurled them after us with such good aim that all the rafts except the one I was upon were swamped, and their luckless crews drowned, without our being able to do anything to help them. Indeed I and my two companions had all we could do to keep our own raft beyond the reach of the giants, but by dint of hard rowing we at last gained the open sea. Here we were at the mercy of the winds and waves, which tossed us to and fro all that day and night, but the next morning we found ourselves near an island, upon which we gladly landed.

There we found delicious fruits, and having satisfied our hunger we presently lay down to rest upon the shore. Suddenly we were aroused by a loud rustling noise, and starting up, saw that it was caused by an immense snake which was gliding towards us over the sand. So swiftly it came that it had seized one of my comrades before he had time to fly, and in spite of his cries and struggles speedily crushed the life out of him in its mighty coils and proceeded to swallow him. By this time my other companion and I were running for our lives to some place where we might hope to be safe from this new horror, and seeing a tall tree we climbed up into it, having first provided ourselves with a store of fruit off the surrounding bushes. When night came I fell asleep, but only to be awakened once more by the terrible snake, which after hissing horribly round the

H J FORD.

tree at last reared itself up against it, and finding my sleeping comrade who was perched just below me, it swallowed him also, and crawled away leaving me half dead with terror.

When the sun rose I crept down from the tree with hardly a hope of escaping the dreadful fate which had overtaken my comrades; but life is sweet, and I determined to do all I could to save myself. All day long I toiled with frantic haste and collected quantities of dry brushwood, reeds and thorns, which I bound with faggots, and making a circle of them under my tree I piled them firmly one upon another until I had a kind of tent in which I crouched like a mouse in a hole when she sees the cat coming. You may imagine what a fearful night I passed, for the snake returned eager to devour me, and glided round and round my frail shelter seeking an entrance. Every moment I feared that it would succeed in pushing aside some of the faggots, but happily for me they held together, and when it grew light my enemy retired, baffled and hungry, to his den. As for me I was more dead than alive! Shaking with fright and half suffocated by the poisonous breath of the monster, I came out of my tent and crawled down to the sea, feeling that it would be better to plunge from the cliffs and end my life at once than pass such another night of horror. But to my joy and relief I saw a ship sailing by, and by shouting wildly and waving my turban I managed to attract the attention of her crew.

A boat was sent to rescue me, and very soon I found myself on board surrounded by a wondering crowd of sailors and merchants eager to know by what chance I found myself in that desolate island. After I had told my story they regaled me with the choicest food the ship afforded, and the captain, seeing that I was in rags, generously bestowed upon me one of his own coats. After sailing about for some time and touching at many ports we came at last to the island of Salahat, where sandal wood grows in great abundance. Here we anchored, and as I stood watching the merchants disembarking their goods and preparing to sell or exchange them, the captain came up to me and said,

"I have here, brother, some merchandise belonging to a passenger of mine who is dead. Will you do me the favour to trade with it, and when I meet with his heirs I shall be able to give them the money, though it will be only just that you shall have a portion for your trouble."

I consented gladly, for I did not like standing by idle. Whereupon he pointed the bales out to me, and sent for the person whose duty it was to keep a list of the goods that were upon the ship. When this man came he asked in what name the merchandise was to be registered.

"In the name of Sindbad the Sailor," replied the captain.

At this I was greatly surprised, but looking carefully at him I recognised him to be the captain of the ship upon which I had made my second voyage, though he had altered much since that time. As for him, believing me to be dead it was no wonder that he had not recognised me.

"So, captain," said I, "the merchant who owned those bales was called Sindbad?"

"Yes," he replied. "He was so named. He belonged to Bagdad, and joined my ship at Balsora, but by mischance he was left behind upon a desert island where we had landed to fill up our water-casks, and it was not until four hours later that he was missed. By that time the wind had freshened, and it was impossible to put back for him."

"You suppose him to have perished then?" said I.

"Alas! yes," he answered.

"Why, captain!" I cried, "look well at me. I am that Sindbad who fell asleep upon the island and awoke to find himself abandoned!"

The captain stared at me in amazement, but was presently convinced that I was indeed speaking the truth, and rejoiced greatly at my escape.

"I am glad to have that piece of carelessness off my conscience at any rate," said he. "Now take your goods, and the profit I have made for you upon them, and may you prosper in future."

I took them gratefully, and as we went from one island to another I laid in stores of cloves, cinnamon, and other spices. In one place I saw a tortoise which was twenty cubits long and as many broad, also a fish that was like a cow and had skin so thick that it was used to make shields. Another I saw that was like a camel in shape and colour. So by degrees we came back to Balsora, and I returned to Bagdad with so much money that I could not myself count it, besides treasures without end. I gave largely to the poor, and bought much land to add to what I already possessed, and thus ended my third voyage.

When Sindbad had finished his story he gave another hundred sequins to Hindbad, who then departed with the other guests, but next day when they had all reassembled, and the banquet was ended, their host continued his adventures.

Fourth Voyage

Rich and happy as I was after my third voyage, I could not make up my mind to stay at home altogether. My love of trading, and the pleasure I took in anything that was new and strange, made me set my affairs in order, and begin my journey through some of the Persian provinces, having first sent off stores of goods to await my coming in the different places I intended to visit. I took ship at a distant seaport, and for some time all went well, but at last, being caught in a violent hurricane, our vessel became a total wreck in spite of all our worthy captain could do to save her, and many of our company perished in the waves. I, with a few others, had the good fortune to be washed ashore clinging to pieces of the wreck, for the storm had driven us near an island, and scrambling up beyond the reach of the waves we threw ourselves down quite exhausted, to wait for morning.

At daylight we wandered inland, and soon saw some huts, to which we directed our steps. As we drew near their inhabitants swarmed out in great numbers and surrounded us, and we were led to their houses, and as it were divided among our captors. I with five others was taken into a hut, where we were made to sit upon the ground, and certain herbs were given to us, which the captors made signs to us to eat. Observing that they themselves did not touch them, I was careful only to pretend to taste my portion; but my companions, being very hungry, rashly ate up all that was set before them, and very soon I had the horror of seeing them become perfectly mad. Though they chattered incessantly I could not understand a word they said, nor did they heed when I spoke to them. The savages now produced large bowls full of rice prepared with cocoanut oil, of which my crazy comrades ate eagerly, but I only tasted a few grains, understanding clearly that the object of our captors was to fatten us speedily for their own eating, and this was exactly what happened. My unlucky companions having lost their reason, felt neither anxiety nor fear, and ate greedily all that was offered them. So they were soon fat and there was an end of them, but I grew leaner day by day, for I ate but little, and even that little did me no good by reason of my fear of what lay before me. However, as I was so far from being a tempting morsel, I was allowed to wander about freely, and one day, when all the men had gone off upon some expedition leaving only an old man to guard me, I managed to escape from him and plunged into the forest, running faster the more he cried to me to come back, until I had completely distanced him.

For seven days I hurried on, resting only when the darkness stopped me, and living chiefly upon cocoanuts, which afforded me both meat and drink, and on the eighth day I reached the seashore and saw a party of white men gathering pepper, which grew abundantly all about. Reassured by the nature of their occupation, I advanced towards them and they greeted me in Arabic, asking who I was and whence I came. My delight was great on hearing this familiar speech, and I willingly satisfied their curiosity, telling them how I had been shipwrecked and captured. "But these savages devour men!" said they. "How did you escape?" I repeated to them what I have just told you, at which they were mightily astonished. I stayed with them until they had collected as much pepper as they wished, and then they took me back to their own country and presented me to their king, by whom I was hospitably received. To him also I had to relate my adventures, which surprised him much, and when I had finished he ordered that I should be supplied with food and raiment and treated with consideration.

The island on which I found myself was full of people, and abounded in all sorts of desirable things, and a great deal of traffic went on in the capital, where I soon began to feel at home and contented. Moreover, the king treated me with special favour, and in consequence of this everyone, whether at the court or in the town, sought to make life pleasant to me. One thing I remarked which I thought very strange; this was that, from the greatest to the least, all men rode their horses without bridle or stirrups. I one day presumed to ask his majesty why he did not use them, to which he replied, "You speak to me of things of which I have never before heard!" This gave me an idea. I found a clever workman, and made him cut out under my direction the foundation of a saddle, which I wadded and covered with choice leather, adorning it with rich gold embroidery. I then got a locksmith to make me a bit and a pair of spurs after a pattern that I drew for him, and when all these things were completed I presented them to the king and showed him how to use them. When I had saddled one of his horses he mounted it and rode about quite delighted with the novelty, and to show his gratitude he rewarded me with large gifts. After this I had to make saddles for all the principal officers of the king's household, and as they all gave me rich presents I soon became very wealthy and quite an important person in the city.

One day the king sent for me and said, "Sindbad, I am going to ask a favour of you. Both I and my subjects esteem you, and wish you to end your days amongst us. Therefore I desire that you will marry a rich and beautiful lady whom I will find for you, and think no more of your own country."

As the king's will was law I accepted the charming bride he presented to me, and lived happily with her. Nevertheless I had every intention of escaping at the first opportunity, and going back to Bagdad. Things were thus going prosperously with me when it happened that the wife of one of my neighbours, with whom I had struck up quite a friendship, fell ill, and presently died. I went to his house to offer my consolations, and found him in the depths of woe.

"Heaven preserve you," said I, "and send you a long life!"

"Alas!" he replied, "what is the good of saying that when I have but an hour left to live!"

"Come, come!" said I, "surely it is not so bad as all that. I trust that you may be spared to me for many years."

"I hope," answered he, "that your life may be long, but as for me, all is finished. I have set my house in order, and today I shall be buried with my wife. This has been the law upon our island from the earliest ages – the living husband goes to the grave with his dead wife, the living wife with her dead husband. So did our fathers, and so must we do. The law changes not, and all must submit to it!"

As he spoke the friends and relations of the unhappy pair began to assemble. The body, decked in rich robes and sparkling with jewels, was laid upon an open bier, and the procession started, taking its way to a high mountain at some distance from the city, the wretched husband, clothed from head to foot in a black mantle, following mournfully.

When the place of interment was reached the corpse was lowered, just as it was, into a deep pit. Then the husband, bidding farewell to all his friends, stretched himself upon another bier, upon which were laid seven little loaves of bread and a pitcher of water, and he also was let down-down-down to the depths of the horrible cavern, and then a stone was laid over the opening, and the melancholy company wended its way back to the city.

You may imagine that I was no unmoved spectator of these proceedings; to all the others it was a thing to which they had been accustomed from their youth up; but I was so horrified that I could not help telling the king how it struck me.

"Sire," I said, "I am more astonished than I can express to you at the strange custom which exists in your dominions of burying the living with the dead. In all my travels I have never before met with so cruel and horrible a law."

"What would you have, Sindbad?" he replied. "It is the law for everybody. I myself should be buried with the queen if she were the first to die."

"But, your Majesty," said I, "dare I ask if this law applies to foreigners also?"

"Why, yes," replied the king smiling, in what I could but consider a very heartless manner, "they are no exception to the rule if they have married in the country."

When I heard this I went home much cast down, and from that time forward my mind was never easy. If only my wife's little finger ached I fancied she was going to die, and sure enough before very long she fell really ill and in a few days breathed her last. My dismay was great, for it seemed to me that to be buried alive was even a worse fate than to be devoured by cannibals,

nevertheless there was no escape. The body of my wife, arrayed in her richest robes and decked with all her jewels, was laid upon the bier. I followed it, and after me came a great procession, headed by the king and all his nobles, and in this order we reached the fatal mountain, which was one of a lofty chain bordering the sea.

Here I made one more frantic effort to excite the pity of the king and those who stood by, hoping to save myself even at this last moment, but it was of no avail. No one spoke to me, they even appeared to hasten over their dreadful task, and I speedily found myself descending into the gloomy pit, with my seven loaves and pitcher of water beside me. Almost before I reached the bottom the stone was rolled into its place above my head, and I was left to my fate. A feeble ray of light shone into the cavern through some chink, and when I had the courage to look about me I could see that I was in a vast vault, bestrewn with bones and bodies of the dead. I even fancied that I heard the expiring sighs of those who, like myself, had come into this dismal place alive. All in vain did I shriek aloud with rage and despair, reproaching myself for the love of gain and adventure which had brought me to such a pass, but at length, growing calmer, I took up my bread and water, and wrapping my face in my mantle I groped my way towards the end of the cavern, where the air was fresher.

Here I lived in darkness and misery until my provisions were exhausted, but just as I was nearly dead from starvation the rock was rolled away overhead and I saw that a bier was being lowered into the cavern, and that the corpse upon it was a man. In a moment my mind was made up, the woman who followed had nothing to expect but a lingering death; I should be doing her a service if I shortened her misery. Therefore when she descended, already insensible from terror, I was ready armed with a huge bone, one blow from which left her dead, and I secured the bread and water which gave me a hope of life. Several times did I have recourse to this desperate expedient, and I know not how long I had been a prisoner when one day I fancied that I heard something near me, which breathed loudly. Turning to the place from which the sound came I dimly saw a shadowy form which fled at my movement, squeezing itself through a cranny in the wall. I pursued it as fast as I could, and found myself in a narrow crack among the rocks, along which I was just able to force my way. I followed it for what seemed to me many miles, and at last saw before me a glimmer of light which grew clearer every moment until I emerged upon the seashore with a joy which I cannot describe. When I was sure that I was not dreaming, I realised that it was doubtless some little animal which had found its way into the cavern from the sea, and when disturbed had fled, showing me a means of escape which I could never have discovered for myself. I hastily surveyed my surroundings, and saw that I was safe from all pursuit from the town.

The mountains sloped sheer down to the sea, and there was no road across them. Being assured of this I returned to the cavern, and amassed a rich treasure of diamonds, rubies, emeralds, and jewels of all kinds which strewed the ground. These I made up into bales, and stored them into a safe place upon the beach, and then waited hopefully for the passing of a ship. I had looked out for two days, however, before a single sail appeared, so it was with much delight that I at last saw a vessel not very far from the shore, and by waving my arms and uttering loud cries succeeded in attracting the attention of her crew. A boat was sent off to me, and in answer to the questions of the sailors as to how I came to be in such a plight, I replied that I had been shipwrecked two days before, but had managed to scramble ashore with the bales which I pointed out to them. Luckily for me they believed my story, and without even looking at the place where they found me, took up my bundles, and rowed me back to the ship. Once on board, I soon saw that the captain was too much occupied with the difficulties of navigation to pay much heed to me, though he generously made me welcome, and would not even accept the jewels with which I offered to pay my passage. Our voyage was prosperous, and after visiting many lands, and collecting in each place great store of goodly merchandise, I found myself at last in Bagdad once more with unheard of riches of every description. Again I gave large sums of money to the poor, and enriched all the mosques in the city, after which I gave myself up to my friends and relations, with whom I passed my time in feasting and merriment.

Here Sindbad paused, and all his hearers declared that the adventures of his fourth voyage had pleased them better than anything they had heard before. They then took their leave, followed by Hindbad, who had once more received a hundred sequins, and with the rest had been bidden to return next day for the story of the fifth voyage.

When the time came all were in their places, and when they had eaten and drunk of all that was set before them Sindbad began his tale.

Fifth Voyage

Not even all that I had gone through could make me contented with a quiet life. I soon wearied of its pleasures, and longed for change and adventure. Therefore I set out once more, but this time in a ship of my own, which I built and fitted out at the nearest seaport. I wished to be able to call at whatever port I chose, taking my own time; but as I did not intend carrying enough goods for a full cargo, I invited several merchants of different nations to join me. We set sail with the first favourable wind, and after a long voyage upon the open seas we landed upon an unknown island which proved to be uninhabited. We determined, however, to explore it, but had not gone far when we found a roc's egg, as large as the one I had seen before and evidently very nearly hatched, for the beak of the young bird had already pierced the shell. In spite of all I could say to deter them, the merchants who were with me fell upon it with their hatchets, breaking the shell, and killing the young roc. Then lighting a fire upon the ground they hacked morsels from the bird, and proceeded to roast them while I stood by aghast.

Scarcely had they finished their ill-omened repast, when the air above us was darkened by two mighty shadows. The captain of my ship, knowing by experience what this meant, cried out to us that the parent birds were coming, and urged us to get on board with all speed. This we did, and the sails were hoisted, but before we had made any way the rocs reached their despoiled nest and hovered about it, uttering frightful cries when they discovered the mangled remains of their young one. For a moment we lost sight of them, and were flattering ourselves that we had escaped, when they reappeared and soared into the air directly over our vessel, and we saw that each held in its claws an immense rock ready to crush us. There was a moment of breathless suspense, then one bird loosed its hold and the huge block of stone hurtled through the air, but thanks to the presence of mind of the helmsman, who turned our ship violently in another direction, it fell into the sea close beside us, cleaving it asunder till we could nearly see the bottom. We had hardly time to draw a breath of relief before the other rock fell with a mighty crash right in the midst of our luckless vessel, smashing it into a thousand fragments, and crushing, or hurling into the sea, passengers and crew. I myself went down with the rest, but had the good fortune to rise unhurt, and by holding on to a piece of driftwood with one hand and swimming with the other I kept myself afloat and was presently washed up by the tide on to an island. Its shores were steep and rocky, but I scrambled up safely and threw myself down to rest upon the green turf.

When I had somewhat recovered I began to examine the spot in which I found myself, and truly it seemed to me that I had reached a garden of delights. There were trees everywhere, and they were laden with flowers and fruit, while a crystal stream wandered in and out under their shadow. When night came I slept sweetly in a cosy nook, though the remembrance that I was alone in a strange land made me sometimes start up and look around me in alarm, and then I wished heartily that I had stayed at home at ease. However, the morning sunlight restored my courage, and I once more wandered among the

trees, but always with some anxiety as to what I might see next. I had penetrated some distance into the island when I saw an old man bent and feeble sitting upon the river bank, and at first I took him to be some shipwrecked mariner like myself. Going up to him I greeted him in a friendly way, but he only nodded his head at me in reply. I then asked what he did there, and he made signs to me that he wished to get across the river to gather some fruit, and seemed to beg me to carry him on my back. Pitying his age and feebleness, I took him up, and wading across the stream I bent down that he might more easily reach the bank, and bade him get down. But instead of allowing himself to be set upon his feet (even now it makes me laugh to think of it!), this creature who had seemed to me so decrepit leaped nimbly upon my shoulders, and hooking his legs round my neck gripped me so tightly that I was well-nigh choked, and so overcome with terror that I fell insensible to the ground. When I recovered my enemy was still in his place, though he had released his hold enough to allow me breathing space, and seeing me revive he prodded me adroitly first with one foot and then with the other, until I was forced to get up and stagger about with him under the trees while he gathered and ate the choicest fruits. This went on all day, and even at night, when I threw myself down half dead with weariness, the terrible old man held on tight to my neck, nor did he fail to greet the first glimmer of morning light by drumming upon me with his heels, until I perforce awoke and resumed my dreary march with rage and bitterness in my heart.

It happened one day that I passed a tree under which lay several dry gourds, and catching one up I amused myself with scooping out its contents and pressing into it the juice of several bunches of grapes which hung from every bush. When it was full I left it propped in the fork of a tree, and a few days later, carrying the hateful old man that way, I snatched at my gourd as I passed it and had the satisfaction of a draught of excellent wine so good and refreshing that I even forgot my detestable burden, and began to sing and caper.

The old monster was not slow to perceive the effect which my draught had produced and that I carried him more lightly than usual, so he stretched out his skinny hand and seizing the gourd first tasted its contents cautiously, then drained them to the very last drop. The wine was strong and the gourd capacious, so he also began to sing after a fashion, and soon I had the delight of feeling the iron grip of his goblin legs unclasp, and with one vigorous effort I threw him to the ground, from which he never moved again. I was so rejoiced to have at last got rid of this uncanny old man that I ran leaping and bounding down to the seashore, where, by the greatest good luck, I met with some mariners who had anchored off the island to enjoy the delicious fruits, and to renew their supply of water.

They heard the story of my escape with amazement, saying, "You fell into the hands of the Old Man of the Sea, and it is a mercy that he did not strangle you as he has everyone else upon whose shoulders he has managed to perch himself. This island is well known as the scene of his evil deeds, and no merchant or sailor who lands upon it cares to stray far away from his comrades." After we had talked for a while they took me back with them on board their ship, where the captain received me kindly, and we soon set sail, and after several days reached a large and prosperous-looking town where all the houses were built of stone. Here we anchored, and one of the merchants, who had been very friendly to me on the way, took me ashore with him and showed me a lodging set apart for strange merchants. He then provided me with a large sack, and pointed out to me a party of others equipped in like manner.

"Go with them," said he, "and do as they do, but beware of losing sight of them, for if you strayed your life would be in danger."

With that he supplied me with provisions, and bade me farewell, and I set out with my new companions. I soon learnt that the object of our expedition was to fill our sacks with cocoanuts, but when at length I saw the trees and noted their immense height and the slippery smoothness of their slender trunks, I did not at all understand how we were to do it. The crowns of the cocoa palms were all alive with monkeys, big and little, which skipped from one to the other with surprising agility, seeming to be curious about us and disturbed at our appearance, and I was at first surprised when my companions after collecting stones began to throw them at the lively creatures, which seemed to me quite harmless. But very soon I saw the reason of it and joined them heartily, for the monkeys, annoyed and wishing to pay us back in our own coin, began to tear the nuts from the trees and cast them at us with angry and spiteful gestures, so that after very little labour our sacks were filled with the fruit which we could not otherwise have obtained.

As soon as we had as many as we could carry we went back to the town, where my friend bought my share and advised me to continue the same occupation until I had earned money enough to carry me to my own country. This I did, and before long had amassed a considerable sum. Just then I heard that there was a trading ship ready to sail, and taking leave of my friend I went on board, carrying with me a goodly store of cocoanuts; and we sailed first to the islands where pepper grows, then to Comari where the best aloes wood is found, and where men drink no wine by an unalterable law. Here I exchanged my nuts for pepper and good aloes wood, and went a-fishing for pearls with some of the other merchants, and my divers were so lucky that very soon I had an immense number, and those very large and perfect. With all these treasures I came joyfully back to Bagdad, where I disposed of them for large sums of money, of which I did not fail as before to give the tenth part to the poor, and after that I rested from my labours and comforted myself with all the pleasures that my riches could give me.

Having thus ended his story, Sindbad ordered that one hundred sequins should be given to Hindbad, and the guests then withdrew; but after the next day's feast he began the account of his sixth voyage as follows.

Sixth Voyage

It must be a marvel to you how, after having five times met with shipwreck and unheard of perils, I could again tempt fortune and risk fresh trouble. I am even surprised myself when I look back, but evidently it was my fate to rove, and after a year of repose I prepared to make a sixth voyage, regardless of the entreaties of my friends and relations, who did all they could to keep me at home. Instead of going by the Persian Gulf, I travelled a considerable way overland, and finally embarked from a distant Indian port with a captain who meant to make a long voyage. And truly he did so, for we fell in with stormy weather which drove us completely out of our course, so that for many days neither captain nor pilot knew where we were, nor where we were going. When they did at last discover our position we had small ground for rejoicing, for the captain, casting his turban upon the deck and tearing his beard, declared that we were in the most dangerous spot upon the whole wide sea, and had been caught by a current which was at that minute sweeping us to destruction. It was too true! In spite of all the sailors could do we were driven with frightful rapidity towards the foot of a mountain, which rose sheer out of the sea, and our vessel was dashed to pieces upon the rocks at its base, not, however, until we had managed to scramble on shore, carrying with us the most precious of our possessions. When we had done this the captain said to us:

"Now we are here we may as well begin to dig our graves at once, since from this fatal spot no shipwrecked mariner has ever returned."

This speech discouraged us much, and we began to lament over our sad fate.

The mountain formed the seaward boundary of a large island, and the narrow strip of rocky shore upon which we stood was strewn with the wreckage of a thousand gallant ships, while the bones of the luckless mariners shone white in the sunshine, and we shuddered to think how soon our own would be added to the heap. All around, too, lay vast quantities of the costliest merchandise, and treasures were heaped in every cranny of the rocks, but all these things only added to the desolation of the scene. It struck me as a very strange thing that a river of clear fresh water, which gushed out from the mountain not far from where we stood, instead of flowing into the sea as rivers generally do, turned off sharply, and flowed out of sight under a natural archway of rock, and when I went to examine it more closely I found that inside the cave the walls were thick with diamonds, and rubies, and masses of crystal, and the floor was strewn with ambergris. Here, then, upon this desolate shore we abandoned ourselves to our fate, for there was no possibility of scaling the mountain, and if a ship had appeared it could only have shared our doom. The first thing our captain did was to divide equally amongst us all the food we possessed, and then the length of each man's life depended on the time he could make his portion last. I myself could live upon very little.

Nevertheless, by the time I had buried the last of my companions my stock of provisions was so small that I hardly thought I should live long enough to dig my own grave, which I set about doing, while I regretted bitterly the roving disposition which was always bringing me into such straits, and thought longingly of all the comfort and luxury that I had left. But luckily for me the fancy took me to stand once more beside the river where it plunged out of sight in the depths of the cavern, and as I did so an idea struck me. This river which hid itself underground doubtless emerged again at some distant spot. Why should I not build a raft and trust myself to its swiftly flowing waters? If I perished before I could reach the light of day once more I should be no worse off than I was now, for death stared me in the face, while there was always the possibility that, as I was born under a lucky star, I might find myself safe and sound in some desirable land. I decided at any rate to risk it, and speedily built myself a stout raft of drift-wood with strong cords, of which enough and to spare lay strewn upon the beach. I then made up many packages of rubies, emeralds, rock crystal, ambergris, and precious stuffs, and bound them upon my raft, being careful to preserve the balance, and then I seated myself upon it, having two small oars that I had fashioned laid ready to my hand, and loosed the cord which held it to the bank. Once out in the current my raft flew swiftly under the gloomy archway, and I found myself in total darkness, carried smoothly forward by the rapid river. On I went as it seemed to me for many nights and days. Once the channel became so small that I had a narrow escape of being crushed against the rocky roof, and after that I took the precaution of lying flat upon my precious bales. Though I only ate what was absolutely necessary to keep myself alive, the inevitable moment came when, after swallowing my last morsel of food, I began to wonder if I must after all die of hunger. Then, worn out with anxiety and fatigue, I fell into a deep sleep, and when I again opened my eyes I was once more in the light of day; a beautiful country lay before me, and my raft, which was tied to the river bank, was surrounded by friendly looking black men. I rose and saluted them, and they spoke to me in return, but I could not understand a word of their language. Feeling perfectly bewildered by my sudden return to life and light, I murmured to myself in Arabic, "Close thine eyes, and while thou sleepest Heaven will change thy fortune from evil to good."

One of the natives, who understood this tongue, then came forward saying:

"My brother, be not surprised to see us; this is our land, and as we came to get water from the river we noticed your raft floating down it, and one of us swam out and brought you to the shore. We have waited for your awakening; tell us now whence you come and where you were going by that dangerous way?"

I replied that nothing would please me better than to tell them, but that I was starving, and would fain eat something first. I was soon supplied with all I needed, and having satisfied my hunger I told them faithfully all that had befallen me. They were lost in wonder at my tale when it was interpreted to them, and said that adventures so surprising must be related to their king only by the man to whom they had happened. So, procuring a horse, they mounted me upon it, and we set out, followed by several strong men carrying my raft just as it was upon their shoulders. In this order we marched into the city of Serendib, where the natives presented me to their king, whom I saluted in the Indian fashion, prostrating myself at his feet and kissing the ground; but the monarch bade me rise and sit beside him, asking first what was my name.

"I am Sindbad," I replied, "whom men call 'the Sailor,' for I have voyaged much upon many seas."

"And how come you here?" asked the king.

I told my story, concealing nothing, and his surprise and delight were so great that he ordered my adventures to be written in letters of gold and laid up in the archives of his kingdom.

Presently my raft was brought in and the bales opened in his presence, and the king declared that in all his treasury there were no such rubies and emeralds as those which lay in great heaps before him. Seeing that he looked at them with interest, I ventured to say that I myself and all that I had were at his disposal, but he answered me smiling:

"Nay, Sindbad. Heaven forbid that I should covet your riches; I will rather add to them, for I desire that you shall not leave my kingdom without some tokens of my good will." He then commanded his officers to provide me with a suitable lodging at his expense, and sent slaves to wait upon me and carry my raft and my bales to my new dwelling place. You may imagine that I praised his generosity and gave him grateful thanks, nor did I fail to present myself daily in his audience chamber, and for the rest of my time I amused myself in seeing all that was most worthy of attention in the city. The island of Serendib being situated on the equinoctial line, the days and nights there are of equal length. The chief city is placed at the end of a beautiful valley, formed by the highest mountain in the world, which is in the middle of the island. I had the curiosity to ascend to its very summit, for this was the place to which Adam was banished out of Paradise. Here are found rubies and many precious things, and rare plants grow abundantly, with cedar trees and cocoa palms. On the seashore and at the mouths of the rivers the divers seek for pearls, and in some valleys diamonds are plentiful. After many days I petitioned the king that I might return to my own country, to which he graciously consented. Moreover, he loaded me with rich gifts, and when I went to take leave of him he entrusted me with a royal present and a letter to the Commander of the Faithful, our sovereign lord, saying, "I pray you give these to the Caliph Haroun-al-Raschid, and assure him of my friendship."

I accepted the charge respectfully, and soon embarked upon the vessel which the king himself had chosen for me. The king's letter was written in blue characters upon a rare and precious skin of yellowish colour, and these were the words of it: "The King of the Indies, before whom walk a thousand elephants, who lives in a palace, of which the roof blazes with a hundred thousand rubies, and whose treasure house contains twenty thousand diamond crowns, to the Caliph Haroun-al-Raschid sends greeting. Though the offering we present to you is unworthy of your notice, we pray you to accept it as a mark of the esteem and friendship which we cherish for you, and of which we gladly send you this token, and we ask of you a like regard if you deem us worthy of it. Adieu, brother."

The present consisted of a vase carved from a single ruby, six inches high and as thick as my finger; this was filled with the choicest pearls, large, and of perfect shape and lustre; secondly, a huge snake skin, with scales as large as a sequin, which would preserve from sickness those who slept upon it. Then quantities of aloes wood, camphor, and pistachio-nuts; and lastly, a beautiful slave girl, whose robes glittered with precious stones.

After a long and prosperous voyage we landed at Balsora, and I made haste to reach Bagdad, and taking the king's letter I presented myself at the palace gate, followed by the beautiful slave, and various members of my own family, bearing the treasure.

As soon as I had declared my errand I was conducted into the presence of the Caliph, to whom, after I had made my obeisance, I gave the letter and the king's gift, and when he had examined them he demanded of me whether the Prince of Serendib was really as rich and powerful as he claimed to be.

"Commander of the Faithful," I replied, again bowing humbly before him, "I can assure your Majesty that he has in no way exaggerated his wealth and grandeur. Nothing can equal the magnificence of his palace. When he goes abroad his throne is prepared upon the back of an elephant, and on either side of him ride his ministers, his favourites, and courtiers. On his elephant's neck sits an officer, his golden lance in his hand, and behind him stands another bearing a pillar of gold, at the top of which is an emerald as long as my hand. A thousand men in cloth of gold, mounted upon richly caparisoned elephants, go before him, and as the procession moves onward the officer who guides his elephant cries aloud, 'Behold the mighty monarch, the powerful and valiant Sultan of the Indies, whose palace is covered with a hundred thousand rubies, who possesses twenty thousand diamond crowns. Behold a monarch greater than Solomon and Mihrage in all their glory!'"

"Then the one who stands behind the throne answers: 'This king, so great and powerful, must die, must die, must die!'"

"And the first takes up the chant again, 'All praise to Him who lives for evermore.'"

"Further, my lord, in Serendib no judge is needed, for to the king himself his people come for justice."

The Caliph was well satisfied with my report.

"From the king's letter," said he, "I judged that he was a wise man. It seems that he is worthy of his people, and his people of him."

So saying he dismissed me with rich presents, and I returned in peace to my own house.

When Sindbad had done speaking his guests withdrew, Hindbad having first received a hundred sequins, but all returned next day to hear the story of the seventh voyage, Sindbad thus began.

Seventh and Last Voyage

After my sixth voyage I was quite determined that I would go to sea no more. I was now of an age to appreciate a quiet life, and I had run risks enough. I only wished to end my days in peace. One day, however, when I was entertaining a number of my friends, I was told that an officer of the Caliph wished to speak to me, and when he was admitted he bade me follow him into the presence of Haroun-al-Raschid, which I accordingly did. After I had saluted him, the Caliph said:

"I have sent for you, Sindbad, because I need your services. I have chosen you to bear a letter and a gift to the King of Serendib in return for his message of friendship."

The Caliph's commandment fell upon me like a thunderbolt.

"Commander of the Faithful," I answered, "I am ready to do all that your Majesty commands, but I humbly pray you to remember that I am utterly disheartened by the unheard of sufferings I have undergone. Indeed, I have made a vow never again to leave Bagdad."

With this I gave him a long account of some of my strangest adventures, to which he listened patiently.

"I admit," said he, "that you have indeed had some extraordinary experiences, but I do not see why they should hinder you from doing as I wish. You have only to go straight to Serendib and give my message, then you are free to come back and do as you will. But go you must; my honour and dignity demand it."

Seeing that there was no help for it, I declared myself willing to obey; and the Caliph, delighted at having got his own way, gave me a thousand sequins for the expenses of the voyage. I was soon ready to start, and taking the letter and the present I embarked at Balsora, and sailed quickly and safely to Serendib. Here, when I had disclosed my errand, I was well received, and brought into the presence of the king, who greeted me with joy.

"Welcome, Sindbad," he cried. "I have thought of you often, and rejoice to see you once more."

After thanking him for the honour that he did me, I displayed the Caliph's gifts. First a bed with complete hangings all cloth of gold, which cost a thousand sequins, and another like to it of crimson stuff. Fifty robes of rich embroidery, a hundred of the finest white linen from Cairo, Suez, Cufa, and Alexandria. Then more beds of different fashion, and an agate vase carved with the figure of a man aiming an arrow at a lion, and finally a costly table, which had once belonged to King Solomon. The King of Serendib received with satisfaction the assurance of the Caliph's friendliness toward him, and now my task being accomplished I was anxious to depart, but it was some time before the king would think of letting me go. At last, however, he dismissed me with many presents, and I lost no time in going on board a ship, which sailed at once, and for four days all went well. On the fifth day we had the misfortune to fall in with pirates, who seized our vessel, killing all who resisted, and making prisoners of those who were prudent enough to submit at once, of whom I was one. When they had despoiled us of all we possessed, they forced us to put on vile raiment, and sailing to a distant island there sold us for slaves. I fell into the hands of a rich merchant, who took me home with him, and clothed and fed me well, and after some days sent for me and questioned me as to what I could do.

I answered that I was a rich merchant who had been captured by pirates, and therefore I knew no trade.

"Tell me," said he, "can you shoot with a bow?"

I replied that this had been one of the pastimes of my youth, and that doubtless with practice my skill would come back to me.

Upon this he provided me with a bow and arrows, and mounting me with him upon his own elephant took the way to a vast forest which lay far from the town. When we had reached the wildest part of it we stopped, and my master said to me: "This forest swarms with elephants. Hide yourself in this great tree, and shoot at all that pass you. When you have succeeded in killing one come and tell me."

So saying he gave me a supply of food, and returned to the town, and I perched myself high up in the tree and kept watch. That night I saw nothing, but just after sunrise the next morning a large herd of elephants came crashing and trampling by. I lost no time in letting fly several arrows, and at last one of the great animals fell to the ground dead, and the others retreated, leaving me free to come down from my hiding place and run back to tell my master of my success, for which I was praised and regaled with good things. Then we went back to the forest together and dug a mighty trench in which we buried the elephant I had killed, in order that when it became a skeleton my master might return and secure its tusks.

For two months I hunted thus, and no day passed without my securing an elephant. Of course I did not always station myself in the same tree, but sometimes in one place, sometimes in another. One morning as I watched the coming of the elephants I was surprised to see that, instead of passing the tree I was in, as they usually did, they paused, and completely surrounded it, trumpeting horribly, and shaking the very ground with their heavy tread, and when I saw that their eyes were fixed upon me I was terrified, and my arrows dropped from my trembling hand. I had indeed good reason for my terror when, an instant later, the largest of the animals wound his trunk round the stem of my tree, and with one mighty effort tore it up by the roots, bringing me to the ground entangled in its branches. I thought now that my last hour was surely come; but the huge creature, picking me up gently enough, set me upon its back, where I clung more dead than alive, and followed by the whole herd turned and crashed off into the dense forest. It seemed to me a long time before I was once more set upon my feet by the elephant, and I stood as if in a dream watching the herd, which turned and trampled off in another direction, and were soon hidden in the dense underwood. Then, recovering myself, I looked about me, and found that I was standing upon the side of a great hill, strewn as far as I could see on either hand with bones and tusks of elephants. "This then must be the elephants' burying place," I said to myself, "and they must have brought me here that I might cease to persecute them, seeing that I want nothing but their tusks, and here lie more than I could carry away in a lifetime."

Whereupon I turned and made for the city as fast as I could go, not seeing a single elephant by the way, which convinced me that they had retired deeper into the forest to leave the way open to the Ivory Hill, and I did not know how sufficiently to admire their sagacity. After a day and a night I reached my master's house, and was received by him with joyful surprise.

"Ah! poor Sindbad," he cried, "I was wondering what could have become of you. When I went to the forest I found the tree newly uprooted, and the arrows lying beside it, and I feared I should never see you again. Pray tell me how you escaped death."

I soon satisfied his curiosity, and the next day we went together to the Ivory Hill, and he

HJF.

was overjoyed to find that I had told him nothing but the truth. When we had loaded our elephant with as many tusks as it could carry and were on our way back to the city, he said:

"My brother – since I can no longer treat as a slave one who has enriched me thus – take your liberty and may Heaven prosper you. I will no longer conceal from you that these wild elephants have killed numbers of our slaves every year. No matter what good advice we gave them, they were caught sooner or later. You alone have escaped the wiles of these animals, therefore you must be under the special protection of Heaven. Now through you the whole town will be enriched without further loss of life, therefore you shall not only receive your liberty, but I will also bestow a fortune upon you."

To which I replied, "Master, I thank you, and wish you all prosperity. For myself I only ask liberty to return to my own country."

"It is well," he answered, "the monsoon will soon bring the ivory ships hither, then I will send you on your way with somewhat to pay your passage."

So I stayed with him till the time of the monsoon, and every day we added to our store of ivory till all his warehouses were overflowing with it. By this time the other merchants knew the secret, but there was enough and to spare for all. When the ships at last arrived my master himself chose the one in which I was to sail, and put on board for me a great store of choice provisions, also ivory in abundance, and all the costliest curiosities of the country, for which I could not thank him enough, and so we parted. I left the ship at the first port we came to, not feeling at ease upon the sea after all that had happened to me by reason of it, and having disposed of my ivory for much gold, and bought many rare and costly presents, I loaded my pack animals, and joined a caravan of merchants. Our journey was long and tedious, but I bore it patiently, reflecting that at least I had not to fear tempests, nor pirates, nor serpents, nor any of the other perils from which I had suffered before, and at length we reached Bagdad. My first care was to present myself before the Caliph, and give him an account of my embassy. He assured me that my long absence had disquieted him much, but he had nevertheless hoped for the best. As to my adventure among the elephants he heard it with amazement, declaring that he could not have believed it had not my truthfulness been well known to him.

By his orders this story and the others I had told him were written by his scribes in letters of gold, and laid up among his treasures. I took my leave of him, well satisfied with the honours and rewards he bestowed upon me; and since that time I have rested from my labours, and given myself up wholly to my family and my friends.

Thus Sindbad ended the story of his seventh and last voyage, and turning to Hindbad he added:

"Well, my friend, and what do you think now? Have you ever heard of anyone who has suffered more, or had more narrow escapes than I have? Is it not just that I should now enjoy a life of ease and tranquillity?"

Hindbad drew near, and kissing his hand respectfully, replied, "Sir, you have indeed known fearful perils; my troubles have been nothing compared to yours. Moreover, the generous use you make of your wealth proves that you deserve it. May you live long and happily in the enjoyment in it."

Sindbad then gave him a hundred sequins, and henceforward counted him among his friends; also he caused him to give up his profession as a porter, and to eat daily at his table that he might all his life remember Sindbad the Sailor.

The Little Hunchback

In the kingdom of Kashgar, which is, as everybody knows, situated on the frontiers of Great Tartary, there lived long ago a tailor and his wife who loved each other very much. One day, when the tailor was hard at work, a little hunchback came and sat at the entrance of the shop, and began to sing and play his tambourine. The tailor was amused with the antics of the fellow, and thought he would take him home to divert his wife. The hunchback having agreed to his proposal, the tailor closed his shop and they set off together.

When they reached the house they found the table ready laid for supper, and in a very few minutes all three were sitting before a beautiful fish which the tailor's wife had cooked with her own hands. But unluckily, the hunchback happened to swallow a large bone, and, in spite of all the tailor and his wife could do to help him, died of suffocation in an instant. Besides being very sorry for the poor man, the tailor and his wife were very much frightened on their own account, for if the police came to hear of it the worthy couple ran the risk of being thrown into prison for wilful murder. In order to prevent this dreadful calamity they both set about inventing some plan which would throw suspicion on some one else, and at last they made up their minds that they could do no better than select a Jewish doctor who lived close by as the author of the crime. So the tailor picked up the hunchback by his head while his wife took his feet and carried him to the doctor's house. Then they knocked at the door, which opened straight on to a steep staircase. A servant soon appeared, feeling her way down the dark staircase and inquired what they wanted.

"Tell your master," said the tailor, "that we have brought a very sick man for him to cure; and," he added, holding out some money, "give him this in advance, so that he may not feel he is wasting his time." The servant remounted the stairs to give the message to the doctor, and the moment she was out of sight the tailor and his wife carried the body swiftly after her, propped it up at the top of the staircase, and ran home as fast as their legs could carry them.

Now the doctor was so delighted at the news of a patient (for he was young, and had not many of them), that he was transported with joy.

"Get a light," he called to the servant, "and follow me as fast as you can!" and rushing out of his room he ran towards the staircase. There he nearly fell over the body of the hunchback, and without knowing what it was gave it such a kick that it rolled right to the bottom, and very nearly dragged the doctor after it. "A light! a light!" he cried again, and when it was brought and he saw what he had done he was almost beside himself with terror.

"Holy Moses!" he exclaimed, "why did I not wait for the light? I have killed the sick man whom they brought me; and if the sacred Ass of Esdras does not come to my aid I am lost! It will not be long before I am led to jail as a murderer."

Agitated though he was, and with reason, the doctor did not forget to shut the house door, lest some passers-by might chance to see what had happened. He then took up the corpse and carried it into his wife's room, nearly driving her crazy with fright.

"It is all over with us!" she wailed, "if we cannot find some means of getting the body out of the house. Once let the sun rise and we can hide it no longer! How were you driven to commit such a terrible crime?"

"Never mind that," returned the doctor, "the thing is to find a way out of it."

For a long while the doctor and his wife continued to turn over in their minds a way of escape, but could not find any that seemed good enough. At last the doctor gave it up altogether and resigned himself to bear the penalty of his misfortune.

But his wife, who had twice his brains, suddenly exclaimed, "I have thought of something! Let us carry the body on the roof of the house and lower it down the chimney of our neighbour the Mussulman." Now this Mussulman was employed by the Sultan, and furnished his table with oil and butter. Part of his house was occupied by a great storeroom, where rats and mice held high revel.

The doctor jumped at his wife's plan, and they took up the hunchback, and passing cords under his armpits they let him down into the purveyor's bed-room so gently that he really seemed to be leaning against the wall. When they felt he was touching the ground they drew up the cords and left him.

Scarcely had they got back to their own house when the purveyor entered his room. He had spent the evening at a wedding feast, and had a lantern in his hand. In the dim light it cast he was astonished to see a man standing in his chimney, but being naturally courageous he seized a stick and made straight for the supposed thief. "Ah!" he cried, "so it is you, and not the rats and mice, who steal my butter. I'll take care that you don't want to come back!"

So saying he struck him several hard blows. The corpse fell on the floor, but the man only redoubled his blows, till at length it occurred to him it was odd that the thief should lie so still and make no resistance. Then, finding he was quite dead, a cold fear took possession of him. "Wretch that I am," said he, "I have murdered a man. Ah, my revenge has gone too far. Without the help of Allah I am undone! Cursed be the goods which have led me to my ruin." And already he felt the rope round his neck.

But when he had got over the first shock he began to think of some way out of the difficulty, and seizing the hunchback in his arms he carried him out into the street, and leaning him against the wall of a shop he stole back to his own house, without once looking behind him.

A few minutes before the sun rose, a rich Christian merchant, who supplied the palace with all sorts of necessaries, left his house, after a night of feasting, to go to the bath. Though he was very drunk, he was yet sober enough to know that the dawn was at hand, and that all good Mussulmen would shortly be going to prayer. So he hastened his steps lest he should meet some one on his way to the mosque, who, seeing his condition, would send him to prison as a drunkard. In his haste he jostled against the hunchback, who fell heavily upon him, and the merchant, thinking he was being attacked by a thief, knocked him down with one blow of his fist. He then called loudly for help, beating the fallen man all the while.

The chief policeman of the quarter came running up, and found a Christian ill-treating a Mussulman. "What are you doing?" he asked indignantly.

"He tried to rob me," replied the merchant, "and very nearly choked me."

"Well, you have had your revenge," said the man, catching hold of his arm. "Come, be off with you!"

As he spoke he held out his hand to the hunchback to help him up, but the hunchback never moved. "Oho!" he went on, looking closer, "so this is the way a Christian has the impudence to treat a Mussulman!" and seizing the merchant in a firm grasp he took him to the inspector of police, who threw him into prison till the judge should be out of bed and ready to attend to his case. All this brought the merchant to his senses, but the more he thought of it the less he could understand how the hunchback could have died merely from the blows he had received.

The merchant was still pondering on this subject when he was summoned before the chief of police and questioned about his crime, which he could not deny. As the hunchback was one of the Sultan's private jesters, the chief of police resolved to defer sentence of death until he had consulted his master. He went to the palace to demand an audience, and told his story to the Sultan, who only answered,

"There is no pardon for a Christian who kills a Mussulman. Do your duty."

So the chief of police ordered a gallows to be erected, and sent criers to proclaim in every street in the city that a Christian was to be hanged that day for having killed a Mussulman.

When all was ready the merchant was brought from prison and led to the foot of the gallows. The executioner knotted the cord firmly round the unfortunate man's neck and was just about to swing him into the air, when the Sultan's purveyor dashed through the crowd, and cried, panting, to the hangman,

"Stop, stop, don't be in such a hurry. It was not he who did the murder, it was I."

The chief of police, who was present to see that everything was in order, put several questions to the purveyor, who told him the whole story of the death of the hunchback, and how he had carried the body to the place where it had been found by the Christian merchant.

"You are going," he said to the chief of police, "to kill an innocent man, for it is impossible that he should have murdered a creature who was dead already. It is bad enough for me to have slain a Mussulman without having it on my conscience that a Christian who is guiltless should suffer through my fault."

Now the purveyor's speech had been made in a loud voice, and was heard by all the crowd, and even if he had wished it, the chief of police could not have escaped setting the merchant free.

"Loose the cords from the Christian's neck," he commanded, turning to the executioner, "and hang this man in his place, seeing that by his own confession he is the murderer."

The hangman did as he was bid, and was tying the cord firmly, when he was stopped by the voice of the Jewish doctor beseeching him to pause, for he had something very important to say. When he had fought his way through the crowd and reached the chief of police,

"Worshipful sir," he began, "this Mussulman whom you desire to hang is unworthy of death; I alone am guilty. Last night a man and a woman who were strangers to me knocked at my door, bringing with them a patient for me to cure. The servant opened it, but having no light was hardly able to make out their faces, though she readily agreed to wake me and to hand me the fee for my services. While she was telling me her story they seem to have carried the sick man to the top of the staircase and then left him there. I jumped up in a hurry without waiting for a lantern, and in the darkness I fell against something, which tumbled headlong down the stairs and never stopped till it reached the bottom. When I examined the body I found it was quite dead, and the corpse was that of a hunchback Mussulman. Terrified at what we had done, my wife and I took the body on the roof and let it down the chimney of our neighbour the purveyor, whom you were just about to hang. The purveyor, finding him in his room, naturally thought he was a thief, and struck him such a blow that the man fell down and lay motionless on the floor. Stooping to examine him, and finding him stone dead, the purveyor supposed that the man had died from the blow he had received; but of course this was a mistake, as you will see from my account, and I only am the murderer; and although I am innocent of any wish to commit a crime, I must suffer for it all the same, or else have the blood of two Musselmans on my conscience. Therefore send away this man, I pray you, and let me take his place, as it is I who am guilty."

On hearing the declaration of the Jewish doctor, the chief of police commanded that he should be led to the gallows, and the Sultan's purveyor go free. The cord was placed round the

Jew's neck, and his feet had already ceased to touch the ground when the voice of the tailor was heard beseeching the executioner to pause one moment and to listen to what he had to say.

"Oh, my lord," he cried, turning to the chief of police, "how nearly have you caused the death of three innocent people! But if you will only have the patience to listen to my tale, you shall know who is the real culprit. If some one has to suffer, it must be me! Yesterday, at dusk, I was working in my shop with a light heart when the little hunchback, who was more than half drunk, came and sat in the doorway. He sang me several songs, and then I invited him to finish the evening at my house. He accepted my invitation, and we went away together. At supper I helped him to a slice of fish, but in eating it a bone stuck in his throat, and in spite of all we could do he died in a few minutes. We felt deeply sorry for his death, but fearing lest we should be held responsible, we carried the corpse to the house of the Jewish doctor. I knocked, and desired the servant to beg her master to come down as fast as possible and see a sick man whom we had brought for him to cure; and in order to hasten his movements I placed a piece of money in her hand as the doctor's fee. Directly she had disappeared I dragged the body to the top of the stairs, and then hurried away with my wife back to our house. In descending the stairs the doctor accidentally knocked over the corpse, and finding him dead believed that he himself was the murderer. But now you know the truth set him free, and let me die in his stead."

The chief of police and the crowd of spectators were lost in astonishment at the strange events to which the death of the hunchback had given rise.

"Loosen the Jewish doctor," said he to the hangman, "and string up the tailor instead, since he has made confession of his crime. Really, one cannot deny that this is a very singular story, and it deserves to be written in letters of gold."

The executioner speedily untied the knots which confined the doctor, and was passing the cord round the neck of the tailor, when the Sultan of Kashgar, who had missed his jester, happened to make inquiry of his officers as to what had become of him.

"Sire," replied they, "the hunchback having drunk more than was good for him, escaped from the palace and was seen wandering about the town, where this morning he was found dead. A man was arrested for having caused his death, and held in custody till a gallows was erected. At the moment that he was about to suffer punishment, first one man arrived, and then another, each accusing themselves of the murder, and this went on for a long time, and at the present instant the chief of police is engaged in questioning a man who declares that he alone is the true assassin."

The Sultan of Kashgar no sooner heard these words than he ordered an usher to go to the chief of police and to bring all the persons concerned in the hunchback's death, together with the corpse, that he wished to see once again. The usher hastened on his errand, but was only just in time, for the tailor was positively swinging in the air, when his voice fell upon the silence of the crowd, commanding the hangman to cut down the body. The hangman, recognising the usher as one of the king's servants, cut down the tailor, and the usher, seeing the man was safe, sought the chief of police and gave him the Sultan's message. Accordingly, the chief of police at once set out for the palace, taking with him the tailor, the doctor, the purveyor, and the merchant, who bore the dead hunchback on their shoulders.

When the procession reached the palace the chief of police prostrated himself at the feet of the Sultan, and related all that he knew of the matter. The Sultan was so much struck by the circumstances that he ordered his private historian to write down an exact account of what had passed, so that in the years to come the miraculous escape of the four men who had thought themselves murderers might never be forgotten.

The Sultan asked everybody concerned in the hunchback's affair to tell him their stories. Among others was a prating barber, whose tale of one of his brothers follows.

The Story of the Barber's Fifth Brother

As long as our father lived Alnaschar was very idle. Instead of working for his bread he was not ashamed to ask for it every evening, and to support himself next day on what he had received the night before. When our father died, worn out by age, he only left seven hundred silver drachmas to be divided amongst us, which made one hundred for each son. Alnaschar, who had never possessed so much money in his life, was quite puzzled to know what to do with it. After reflecting upon the matter for some time he decided to lay it out on glasses, bottles, and things of that sort, which he would buy from a wholesale merchant. Having bought his stock he next proceeded to look out for a small shop in a good position, where he sat down at the open door, his wares being piled up in an uncovered basket in front of him, waiting for a customer among the passers-by.

In this attitude he remained seated, his eyes fixed on the basket, but his thoughts far away. Unknown to himself he began to talk out loud, and a tailor, whose shop was next door to his, heard quite plainly what he was saying.

"This basket," said Alnaschar to himself, "has cost me a hundred drachmas – all that I possess in the world. Now in selling the contents piece by piece I shall turn two hundred, and these hundreds I shall again lay out in glass, which will produce four hundred. By this means I shall in course of time make four thousand drachmas, which will easily double themselves. When I have got ten thousand I will give up the glass trade and become a jeweller, and devote all my time to trading in pearls, diamonds, and other precious stones. At last, having all the wealth that heart can desire, I will buy a beautiful country house, with horses and slaves, and then I will lead a merry life and entertain my friends. At my feasts I will send for musicians and dancers from the neighbouring town to amuse my guests. In spite of my riches I shall not, however, give up trade till I have amassed a capital of a hundred thousand drachmas, when, having become a man of much consideration, I shall request the hand of the grand-vizir's daughter, taking care to inform the worthy father that I have heard favourable reports of her beauty and wit, and that I will pay down on our wedding day a thousand gold pieces. Should the vizir refuse my proposal, which after all is hardly to be expected, I will seize him by the beard and drag him to my house."

When I shall have married his daughter I will give her ten of the best eunuchs that can be found for her service. Then I shall put on my most gorgeous robes, and mounted on a horse with a saddle of fine gold, and its trappings blazing with diamonds, followed by a train of slaves, I shall present myself at the house of the grand-vizir, the people casting down their eyes and bowing low as I pass along. At the foot of the grand-vizir's staircase I shall dismount, and while my servants stand in a row to right and left I shall ascend the stairs, at the head of which the grand-vizir will be waiting to receive me. He will then embrace me as his son-in-law, and giving me his seat will place himself below me. This being done (as I have every reason to expect), two of my servants will enter, each bearing a purse containing a thousand pieces of gold. One of these I shall present to him saying, "Here are the thousand gold pieces that I offered for your daughter's hand, and here," I shall continue, holding out the second purse, "are another thousand to show you that I am a man who is better than his word." After hearing of such generosity the world will talk of nothing else.

I shall return home with the same pomp as I set out, and my wife will send an officer to compliment me on my visit to her father, and I shall confer on the officer the honour of a rich dress and a handsome gift. Should she send one to me I shall refuse it and dismiss the bearer. I shall never allow my wife to leave her rooms on any pretext whatever without my permission, and my visits to her will be marked by all the ceremony calculated to inspire respect. No establishment will be better ordered than mine, and I shall take care always to be dressed in a manner suitable to my position. In the evening, when we retire to our apartments, I shall sit in the place of honour, where I shall assume a grand demeanour and speak little, gazing straight before me, and when my wife, lovely as the full moon, stands humbly in front of my chair I shall pretend not to see her. Then her women will say to me, "Respected lord and master, your wife and slave is before you waiting to be noticed. She is mortified that you never deign to look her way; she is tired of standing so long. Beg her, we pray you, to be seated." Of course I shall give no signs of even hearing this speech, which will vex them mightily. They will throw themselves at my feet with lamentations, and at length I will raise my head and throw a careless glance at her, then I shall go back to my former attitude. The women will think that I am displeased at my wife's dress and will lead her away to put on a finer one, and I on my side shall replace the one I am wearing with another yet more splendid. They will then return to the charge, but this time it will take much longer before they persuade me even to look at my wife. It is as well to begin on my wedding day as I mean to go on for the rest of our lives.

The next day she will complain to her mother of the way she has been treated, which will fill my heart with joy. Her mother will come to seek me, and, kissing my hands with respect, will say, "My lord" (for she could not dare to risk my anger by using the familiar title of "son-in-law"), "My lord, do not, I implore you, refuse to look upon my daughter or to approach her. She only lives to please you, and loves you with all her soul." But I shall pay no more heed to my mother-in-law's words than I did to those of the women. Again she will beseech me to listen to

her entreaties, throwing herself this time at my feet, but all to no purpose. Then, putting a glass of wine into my wife's hand, she will say to her, "There, present that to him yourself, he cannot have the cruelty to reject anything offered by so beautiful a hand," and my wife will take it and offer it to me tremblingly with tears in her eyes, but I shall look in the other direction. This will cause her to weep still more, and she will hold out the glass crying, "Adorable husband, never shall I cease my prayers till you have done me the favour to drink." Sick of her importunities, these words will goad me to fury. I shall dart an angry look at her and give her a sharp blow on the cheek, at the same time giving her a kick so violent that she will stagger across the room and fall on to the sofa.

"My brother," pursued the barber, "was so much absorbed in his dreams that he actually did give a kick with his foot, which unluckily hit the basket of glass. It fell into the street and was instantly broken into a thousand pieces."

His neighbour the tailor, who had been listening to his visions, broke into a loud fit of laughter as he saw this sight.

"Wretched man!" he cried, "you ought to die of shame at behaving so to a young wife who has done nothing to you. You must be a brute for her tears and prayers not to touch your heart. If I were the grand-vizir I would order you a hundred blows from a bullock whip, and would have you led round the town accompanied by a herald who should proclaim your crimes."

The accident, so fatal to all his profits, had restored my brother to his senses, and seeing that the mischief had been caused by his own insufferable pride, he rent his clothes and tore his hair, and lamented himself so loudly that the passers-by stopped to listen. It was a Friday, so these were more numerous than usual. Some pitied Alnaschar, others only laughed at him, but the vanity which had gone to his head had disappeared with his basket of glass, and he was loudly bewailing his folly when a lady, evidently a person of consideration, rode by on a mule. She stopped and inquired what was the matter, and why the man wept. They told her that he was a poor man who had laid out all his money on this basket of glass, which was now broken. On hearing the cause of these loud wails the lady turned to her attendant and said to him, "Give him whatever you have got with you." The man obeyed, and placed in my brother's hands a purse containing five hundred pieces of gold. Alnaschar almost died of joy on receiving it. He blessed the lady a thousand times, and, shutting up his shop where he had no longer anything to do, he returned home.

He was still absorbed in contemplating his good fortune, when a knock came to his door, and on opening it he found an old woman standing outside.

"My son," she said, "I have a favour to ask of you. It is the hour of prayer and I have not yet washed myself. Let me, I beg you, enter your house, and give me water."

My brother, although the old woman was a stranger to him, did not hesitate to do as she wished. He gave her a vessel of water and then went back to his place and his thoughts, and with his mind busy over his last adventure, he put his gold into a long and narrow purse, which he could easily carry in his belt. During this time the old woman was busy over her prayers, and when she had finished she came and prostrated herself twice before my brother, and then rising called down endless blessings on his head. Observing her shabby clothes, my brother thought that her gratitude was in reality a hint that he should give her some money to buy some new ones, so he held out two pieces of gold. The old woman started back in surprise as if she had received an insult. "Good heavens!" she exclaimed, "what is the meaning of this? Is it possible that you take me, my lord, for one of those miserable creatures who force their way into houses to beg for alms? Take back your money. I am thankful to say I do not need it, for I belong to a beautiful lady who is very rich and gives me everything I want."

My brother was not clever enough to detect that the old woman had merely refused the two pieces of money he had offered her in order to get more, but he inquired if she could procure him the pleasure of seeing this lady.

"Willingly," she replied; "and she will be charmed to marry you, and to make you the master of all her wealth. So pick up your money and follow me."

Delighted at the thought that he had found so easily both a fortune and a beautiful wife, my brother asked no more questions, but concealing his purse, with the money the lady had given him, in the folds of his dress, he set out joyfully with his guide.

They walked for some distance till the old woman stopped at a large house, where she knocked. The door was opened by a young Greek slave, and the old woman led my brother across a well-paved court into a well-furnished hall. Here she left him to inform her mistress of his presence, and as the day was hot he flung himself on a pile of cushions and took off his heavy turban. In a few minutes there entered a lady, and my brother perceived at the first glance that she was even more beautiful and more richly dressed than he had expected. He rose from his seat, but the lady signed to him to sit down again and placed herself beside him. After the usual compliments had passed between them she said, "We are not comfortable here, let us go into another room," and passing into a smaller chamber, apparently communicating with no other, she continued to talk to him for some time. Then rising hastily she left him, saying, "Stay where you are, I will come back in a moment."

He waited as he was told, but instead of the lady there entered a huge black slave with a sword in his hand. Approaching my brother with an angry countenance, he exclaimed, "What business have you here?" His voice and manner were so terrific that Alnaschar had not strength to reply, and allowed his gold to be taken from him, and even sabre cuts to be inflicted on him without making any resistance. As soon as he was let go, he sank on the ground powerless to move, though he still had possession of his senses. Thinking he was dead, the black slave ordered the Greek slave to bring him some salt, and between them they rubbed it into his wounds, thus giving him acute agony, though he had the presence of mind to give no sign of life. They then left him, and their place was taken by the old woman, who dragged him to a trapdoor and threw him down into a vault filled with the bodies of murdered men.

At first the violence of his fall caused him to lose consciousness, but luckily the salt which had been rubbed into his wounds had by its smarting preserved his life, and little by little he regained his strength. At the end of two days he lifted the trapdoor during the night and hid himself in the courtyard till daybreak, when he saw the old woman leave the house in search of more prey. Luckily she did not observe him, and when she was out of sight he stole from this nest of assassins and took refuge in my house.

I dressed his wounds and tended him carefully, and when a month had passed he was as well as ever. His one thought was how to be revenged on that wicked old hag, and for this purpose he had a purse made large enough to contain five hundred gold pieces, but filled it instead with bits of glass. This he tied round him with his sash, and, disguising himself as an old woman, he took a sabre, which he hid under his dress.

One morning as he was hobbling through the streets he met his old enemy prowling to see if she could find anyone to decoy. He went up to her and, imitating the voice of a woman, he said, "Do you happen to have a pair of scales you could lend me? I have just come from Persia and have brought with me five hundred gold pieces, and I am anxious to see if they are the proper weight."

"Good woman," replied the old hag, "you could not have asked anyone better. My son is a money-changer, and if you will follow me he will weigh them for you himself. Only we must be quick or he will have gone to his shop." So saying she led the way to the same house as before, and the door was opened by the same Greek slave.

Again my brother was left in the hall, and the pretended son appeared under the form of the black slave. "Miserable crone," he said to my brother, "get up and come with me," and turned to lead the way to the place of murder. Alnaschar rose too, and drawing the sabre from under his dress dealt the black slave such a blow on his neck that his head was severed from his body. My brother picked up the head with one hand, and seizing the body with the other dragged it to the vault, when he threw it in and sent the head after it. The Greek slave, supposing that all had passed as usual, shortly arrived with the basin of salt, but when she beheld Alnaschar with the sabre in his hand she let the basin fall and turned to fly. My brother, however, was too quick for her, and in another instant her head was rolling from her shoulders. The noise brought the old woman running to see what was the matter, and he seized her before she had time to escape. "Wretch!" he cried, "do you know me?"

"Who are you, my lord?" she replied trembling all over. "I have never seen you before."

"I am he whose house you entered to offer your hypocritical prayers. Don't you remember now?"

She flung herself on her knees to implore mercy, but he cut her into four pieces.

There remained only the lady, who was quite ignorant of all that was taking place around her. He sought her through the house, and when at last he found her, she nearly fainted with terror at the sight of him. She begged hard for life, which he was generous enough to give her, but he bade her to tell him how she had got into partnership with the abominable creatures he had just put to death.

"I was once," replied she, "the wife of an honest merchant, and that old woman, whose wickedness I did not know, used occasionally to visit me. 'Madam,' she said to me one day, 'we have a grand wedding at our house today. If you would do us the honour to be present, I am sure you would enjoy yourself.' I allowed myself to be persuaded, put on my richest dress, and took a purse with a hundred pieces of gold. Once inside the doors I was kept by force by that dreadful man, and it is now three years that I have been here, to my great grief."

"That horrible man must have amassed great wealth," remarked my brother.

"Such wealth," returned she, "that if you succeed in carrying it all away it will make you rich for ever. Come and let us see how much there is."

She led Alnaschar into a chamber filled with coffers packed with gold, which he gazed at with an admiration he was powerless to conceal. "Go," she said, "and bring men to carry them away."

My brother did not wait to be told twice, and hurried out into the streets, where he soon collected ten men. They all came back to the house, but what was his surprise to find the

door open, and the room with the chests of gold quite empty. The lady had been cleverer than himself, and had made the best use of her time. However, he tried to console himself by removing all the beautiful furniture, which more than made up for the five hundred gold pieces he had lost.

Unluckily, on leaving the house, he forgot to lock the door, and the neighbours, finding the place empty, informed the police, who next morning arrested Alnaschar as a thief. My brother tried to bribe them to let him off, but far from listening to him they tied his hands, and forced him to walk between them to the presence of the judge. When they had explained to the official the cause of complaint, he asked Alnaschar where he had obtained all the furniture that he had taken to his house the day before.

"Sir," replied Alnaschar, "I am ready to tell you the whole story, but give, I pray you, your word, that I shall run no risk of punishment."

"That I promise," said the judge. So my brother began at the beginning and related all his adventures, and how he had avenged himself on those who had betrayed him. As to the furniture, he entreated the judge at least to allow him to keep part to make up for the five hundred pieces of gold which had been stolen from him.

The judge, however, would say nothing about this, and lost no time in sending men to fetch away all that Alnaschar had taken from the house. When everything had been moved and placed under his roof he ordered my brother to leave the town and never more to enter it on peril of his life, fearing that if he returned he might seek justice from the Caliph. Alnaschar obeyed, and was on his way to a neighbouring city when he fell in with a band of robbers, who stripped him of his clothes and left him naked by the roadside. Hearing of his plight, I hurried after him to console him for his misfortunes, and to dress him in my best robe. I then brought him back disguised, under cover of night, to my house, where I have since given him all the care I bestow on my other brothers.

The Story of the Barber's Sixth Brother

There now remains for me to relate to you the story of my sixth brother, whose name was Schacabac. Like the rest of us, he inherited a hundred silver drachmas from our father, which he thought was a large fortune, but through ill-luck, he soon lost it all, and was driven to beg. As he had a smooth tongue and good manners, he really did very well in his new profession, and he devoted himself specially to making friends with the servants in big houses, so as to gain access to their masters.

One day he was passing a splendid mansion, with a crowd of servants lounging in the courtyard. He thought that from the appearance of the house it might yield him a rich harvest, so he entered and inquired to whom it belonged.

"My good man, where do you come from?" replied the servant. "Can't you see for yourself that it can belong to nobody but a Barmecide?" for the Barmecides were famed for their liberality and generosity. My brother, hearing this, asked the porters, of whom there were several, if they would give him alms. They did not refuse, but told him politely to go in, and speak to the master himself.

My brother thanked them for their courtesy and entered the building which was so large that it took him some time to reach the apartments of the Barmecide. At last, in a room richly decorated with paintings, he saw an old man with a long white beard, sitting on a sofa, who received him with such kindness that my brother was emboldened to make his petition.

"My lord," he said, "you behold in me a poor man who only lives by the help of persons as rich and as generous as you."

Before he could proceed further, he was stopped by the astonishment shown by the Barmecide. "Is it possible," he cried, "that while I am in Bagdad, a man like you should be starving? That is a state of things that must at once be put an end to! Never shall it be said that I have abandoned you, and I am sure that you, on your part, will never abandon me."

"My lord," answered my brother, "I swear that I have not broken my fast this whole day."

"What, you are dying of hunger?" exclaimed the Barmecide. "Here, slave; bring water, that we may wash our hands before meat!" No slave appeared, but my brother remarked that the Barmecide did not fail to rub his hands as if the water had been poured over them.

Then he said to my brother, "Why don't you wash your hands too?" and Schacabac, supposing that it was a joke on the part of the Barmecide (though he could see none himself), drew near, and imitated his motion.

When the Barmecide had done rubbing his hands, he raised his voice, and cried, "Set food before us at once, we are very hungry." No food was brought, but the Barmecide pretended to help himself from a dish, and carry a morsel to his mouth, saying as he did so, "Eat, my friend, eat, I entreat. Help yourself as freely as if you were at home! For a starving man, you seem to have a very small appetite."

"Excuse me, my lord," replied Schacabac, imitating his gestures as before, "I really am not losing time, and I do full justice to the repast."

"How do you like this bread?" asked the Barmecide. "I find it particularly good myself."

"Oh, my lord," answered my brother, who beheld neither meat nor bread, "never have I tasted anything so delicious."

"Eat as much as you want," said the Barmecide. "I bought the woman who makes it for five hundred pieces of gold, so that I might never be without it."

After ordering a variety of dishes (which never came) to be placed on the table, and discussing the merits of each one, the Barmecide declared that having dined so well, they would now proceed to take their wine. To this my brother at first objected, declaring that it was forbidden; but on the Barmecide insisting that it was out of the question that he should drink by himself, he consented to take a little. The Barmecide, however, pretended to fill their glasses so often, that my brother feigned that the wine had gone into his head, and struck the Barmecide such a blow on the head, that he fell to the ground. Indeed, he raised his hand to strike him a second time, when the Barmecide cried out that he was mad, upon which my brother controlled himself, and apologised and protested that it was all the fault of the wine he had drunk. At this the Barmecide, instead of being angry, began to laugh, and embraced him heartily. "I have long been seeking," he exclaimed, "a man of your description, and henceforth my house shall be yours. You have had the good grace to fall in with my humour, and to pretend to eat and to drink when nothing was there. Now you shall be rewarded by a really good supper."

HJFORD

Then he clapped his hands, and all the dishes were brought that they had tasted in imagination before and during the repast, slaves sang and played on various instruments. All the while Schacabac was treated by the Barmecide as a familiar friend, and dressed in a garment out of his own wardrobe.

Twenty years passed by, and my brother was still living with the Barmecide, looking after his house, and managing his affairs. At the end of that time his generous benefactor died without heirs, so all his possessions went to the prince. They even despoiled my brother of those that rightly belonged to him, and he, now as poor as he had ever been in his life, decided to cast in his lot with a caravan of pilgrims who were on their way to Mecca. Unluckily, the caravan was attacked and pillaged by the Bedouins, and the pilgrims were taken prisoners. My brother became the slave of a man who beat him daily, hoping to drive him to offer a ransom, although, as Schacabac pointed out, it was quite useless trouble, as his relations were as poor as himself. At length the Bedouin grew tired of tormenting, and sent him on a camel to the top of a high barren mountain, where he left him to take his chance. A passing caravan, on its way to Bagdad, told me where he was to be found, and I hurried to his rescue, and brought him in a deplorable condition back to the town.

"This," continued the barber, "is the tale I related to the Caliph, who, when I had finished, burst into fits of laughter.

"Well were you called 'the Silent'," said he; "no name was ever better deserved. But for reasons of my own, which it is not necessary to mention, I desire you to leave the town, and never to come back."

"I had of course no choice but to obey, and travelled about for several years until I heard of the death of the Caliph, when I hastily returned to Bagdad, only to find that all my brothers were dead. It was at this time that I rendered to the young cripple the important service of which you have heard, and for which, as you know, he showed such profound ingratitude, that he preferred rather to leave Bagdad than to run the risk of seeing me. I sought him long from place to place, but it was only today, when I expected it least, that I came across him, as much irritated with me as ever" – So saying the tailor went on to relate the story of the lame man and the barber, which has already been told.

"When the barber," he continued, "had finished his tale, we came to the conclusion that the young man had been right, when he had accused him of being a great chatter-box. However, we wished to keep him with us, and share our feast, and we remained at table till the hour of afternoon prayer. Then the company broke up, and I went back to work in my shop.

"It was during this interval that the little hunchback, half drunk already, presented himself before me, singing and playing on his drum. I took him home, to amuse my wife, and she invited him to supper. While eating some fish, a bone got into his throat, and in spite of all we could do, he died shortly. It was all so sudden that we lost our heads, and in order to divert suspicion from ourselves, we carried the body to the house of a Jewish physician. He placed it in the chamber of the purveyor, and the purveyor propped it up in the street, where it was thought to have been killed by the merchant.

"This, Sire, is the story which I was obliged to tell to satisfy your Highness. It is now for you to say if we deserve mercy or punishment; life or death?"

The Sultan of Kashgar listened with an air of pleasure which filled the tailor and his friends with hope. "I must confess," he exclaimed, "that I am much more interested in the stories of the barber and his brothers, and of the lame man, than in that of my own jester. But before I allow you all four to return to your own homes, and have the corpse of the hunchback properly buried, I should like to see this barber who has earned your pardon. And as he is in this town, let an usher go with you at once in search of him."

The usher and the tailor soon returned, bringing with them an old man who must have been at least ninety years of age. "O Silent One," said the Sultan, "I am told that you know many strange stories. Will you tell some of them to me?"

"Never mind my stories for the present," replied the barber, "but will your Highness graciously be pleased to explain why this Jew, this Christian, and this Mussulman, as well as this dead body, are all here?"

"What business is that of yours?" asked the Sultan with a smile; but seeing that the barber had some reasons for his question, he commanded that the tale of the hunchback should be told him.

"It is certainly most surprising," cried he, when he had heard it all, "but I should like to examine the body." He then knelt down, and took the head on his knees, looking at it attentively. Suddenly he burst into such loud laughter that he fell right backwards, and when he had recovered himself enough to speak, he turned to the Sultan. "The man is no more dead than I am," he said; "watch me." As he spoke he drew a small case of medicines from his pocket and rubbed the neck of the hunchback with some ointment made of balsam. Next he opened the dead man's mouth, and by the help of a pair of pincers drew the bone from his throat. At this the hunchback sneezed, stretched himself and opened his eyes.

The Sultan and all those who saw this operation did not know which to admire most, the constitution of the hunchback who had apparently been dead for a whole night and most of one day, or the skill of the barber, whom everyone now began to look upon as a great man. His Highness desired that the history of the hunchback should be written down, and placed in the archives beside that of the barber, so that they might be associated in people's minds to the end of time. And he did not stop there; for in order to wipe out the memory of what they had undergone, he commanded that the tailor, the doctor, the purveyor and the merchant, should each be clothed in his presence with a robe from his own wardrobe before they returned home. As for the barber, he bestowed on him a large pension, and kept him near his own person.

The Adventures of Prince Camaralzaman and the Princess Badoura

Some twenty days' sail from the coast of Persia lies the isle of the children of Khaledan. The island is divided into several provinces, in each of which are large flourishing towns, and the whole forms an important kingdom. It was governed in former days by a king named Schahzaman, who, with good right, considered himself one of the most peaceful, prosperous, and fortunate monarchs on the earth. In fact, he had but one grievance, which was that none of his four wives had given him an heir.

This distressed him so greatly that one day he confided his grief to the grand-vizir, who, being a wise counsellor, said: "Such matters are indeed beyond human aid. Allah alone can grant your desire, and I should advise you, sire, to send large gifts to those holy men who spend their lives in prayer, and to beg for their intercessions. Who knows whether their petitions may not be answered!"

The king took his vizir's advice, and the result of so many prayers for an heir to the throne was that a son was born to him the following year.

Schahzaman sent noble gifts as thank-offerings to all the mosques and religious houses, and great rejoicings were celebrated in honour of the birth of the little prince, who was so beautiful that he was named Camaralzaman, or "Moon of the Century".

Prince Camaralzaman was brought up with extreme care by an excellent governor and all the cleverest teachers, and he did such credit to them that when he was grown up, a more charming and accomplished young man was not to be found. Whilst he was still a youth the king, his father, who loved him dearly, had some thoughts of abdicating in his favour. As usual he talked over his plans with his grand-vizir, who, though he did not approve the idea, would not state all his objections.

"Sire," he replied, "the prince is still very young for the cares of state. Your Majesty fears his growing idle and careless, and doubtless you are right. But how would it be if he were first to marry? This would attach him to his home, and your Majesty might give him a share in your counsels, so that he might gradually learn how to wear a crown, which you can give up to him whenever you find him capable of wearing it."

The vizir's advice once more struck the king as being good, and he sent for his son, who lost no time in obeying the summons, and standing respectfully with downcast eyes before the king asked for his commands.

"I have sent for you," said the king, "to say that I wish you to marry. What do you think about it?"

The prince was so much overcome by these words that he remained silent for some time. At length he said: "Sire, I beg you to pardon me if I am unable to reply as you might wish. I certainly did not expect such a proposal as I am still so young, and I confess that the idea of marrying is very distasteful to me. Possibly I may not always be in this mind, but I certainly feel that it will require some time to induce me to take the step which your Majesty desires."

This answer greatly distressed the king, who was sincerely grieved by his objection to marriage. However he would not have recourse to extreme measures, so he said: "I do not wish to force you; I will give you time to reflect, but remember that such a step is necessary for a prince such as you who will some day be called to rule over a great kingdom."

From this time Prince Camaralzaman was admitted to the royal council, and the king showed him every mark of favour.

At the end of a year the king took his son aside, and said: "Well, my son, have you changed your mind on the subject of marriage, or do you still refuse to obey my wish?"

The prince was less surprised but no less firm than on the former occasion, and begged his father not to press the subject, adding that it was quite useless to urge him any longer.

This answer much distressed the king, who again confided his trouble to his vizir.

"I have followed your advice," he said; "but Camaralzaman declines to marry, and is more obstinate than ever."

"Sire," replied the vizir, "much is gained by patience, and your Majesty might regret any violence. Why not wait another year and then inform the prince in the midst of the assembled council that the good of the state demands his marriage? He cannot possibly refuse again before so distinguished an assemblage, and in our immediate presence."

The Sultan ardently desired to see his son married at once, but he yielded to the vizir's arguments and decided to wait. He then visited the prince's mother, and after telling her of his disappointment and of the further respite he had given his son, he added: "I know that Camaralzaman confides more in you than he does in me. Pray speak very seriously to him on this subject, and make him realise that he will most seriously displease me if he remains obstinate, and that he will certainly regret the measures I shall be obliged to take to enforce my will."

So the first time the Sultana Fatima saw her son she told him she had heard of his refusal to marry, adding how distressed she felt that he should have vexed his father so much. She asked what reasons he could have for his objections to obey.

"Madam," replied the prince, "I make no doubt that there are as many good, virtuous, sweet, and amiable women as there are others very much the reverse. Would that all were like you! But what revolts me is the idea of marrying a woman without knowing anything at all about her. My father will ask the hand of the daughter of some neighbouring sovereign, who will give his consent to our union. Be she fair or frightful, clever or stupid, good or bad, I must marry her, and am left no choice in the matter. How am I to know that she will not be proud, passionate, contemptuous, and recklessly extravagant, or that her disposition will in any way suit mine?"

"But, my son," urged Fatima, "you surely do not wish to be the last of a race which has reigned so long and so gloriously over this kingdom?"

"Madam," said the prince, "I have no wish to survive the king, my father, but should I do so I will try to reign in such a manner as may be considered worthy of my predecessors."

These and similar conversations proved to the Sultan how useless it was to argue with his son, and the year elapsed without bringing any change in the prince's ideas.

At length a day came when the Sultan summoned him before the council, and there informed him that not only his own wishes but the good of the empire demanded his marriage, and desired him to give his answer before the assembled ministers.

At this Camaralzaman grew so angry and spoke with so much heat that the king, naturally irritated at being opposed by his son in full council, ordered the prince to be arrested and locked up in an old tower, where he had nothing but a very little furniture, a few books, and a single slave to wait on him.

Camaralzaman, pleased to be free to enjoy his books, showed himself very indifferent to his sentence.

When night came he washed himself, performed his devotions, and, having read some pages of the Koran, lay down on a couch, without putting out the light near him, and was soon asleep.

Now there was a deep well in the tower in which Prince Camaralzaman was imprisoned, and this well was a favourite resort of the fairy Maimoune, daughter of Damriat, chief of a legion of genii. Towards midnight Maimoune floated lightly up from the well, intending, according to her usual habit, to roam about the upper world as curiosity or accident might prompt.

The light in the prince's room surprised her, and without disturbing the slave, who slept across the threshold, she entered the room, and approaching the bed was still more astonished to find it occupied.

The prince lay with his face half hidden by the coverlet. Maimoune lifted it a little and beheld the most beautiful youth she had ever seen.

"What a marvel of beauty he must be when his eyes are open!" she thought. "What can he have done to deserve to be treated like this?"

She could not weary gazing at Camaralzaman, but at length, having softly kissed his brow and each cheek, she replaced the coverlet and resumed her flight through the air.

As she entered the middle region she heard the sound of great wings coming towards her, and shortly met one of the race of bad genii. This genie, whose name was Danhasch, recognised Maimoune with terror, for he knew the supremacy which her goodness gave her over him. He would gladly have avoided her altogether, but they were so near that he must either be prepared to fight or yield to her, so he at once addressed her in a conciliatory tone:

"Good Maimoune, swear to me by Allah to do me no harm, and on my side I will promise not to injure you."

"Accursed genie!" replied Maimoune, "what harm can you do me? But I will grant your power and give the promise you ask. And now tell me what you have seen and done to-night."

"Fair lady," said Danhasch, "you meet me at the right moment to hear something really interesting. I must tell you that I come from the furthest end of China, which is one of the largest and most powerful kingdoms in the world. The present king has one only daughter, who is so perfectly lovely that neither you, nor I, nor any other creature could find adequate terms in which to describe her marvellous charms. You must therefore picture to yourself the most perfect features, joined to a brilliant and delicate complexion, and an enchanting expression, and even then imagination will fall short of the reality.

"The king, her father, has carefully shielded this treasure from the vulgar gaze, and has taken every precaution to keep her from the sight of everyone except the happy mortal he may choose to be her husband. But in order to give her variety in her confinement he has built her

seven palaces such as have never been seen before. The first palace is entirely composed of rock crystal, the second of bronze, the third of fine steel, the fourth of another and more precious species of bronze, the fifth of touchstone, the sixth of silver, and the seventh of solid gold. They are all most sumptuously furnished, whilst the gardens surrounding them are laid out with exquisite taste. In fact, neither trouble nor cost has been spared to make this retreat agreeable to the princess. The report of her wonderful beauty has spread far and wide, and many powerful kings have sent embassies to ask her hand in marriage. The king has always received these embassies graciously, but says that he will never oblige the princess to marry against her will, and as she regularly declines each fresh proposal, the envoys have had to leave as disappointed in the result of their missions as they were gratified by their magnificent receptions.

"'Sire,' said the princess to her father, 'you wish me to marry, and I know you desire to please me, for which I am very grateful. But, indeed, I have no inclination to change my state, for where could I find so happy a life amidst so many beautiful and delightful surroundings? I feel that I could never be as happy with any husband as I am here, and I beg you not to press one on me.'

"At last an embassy came from a king so rich and powerful that the King of China felt constrained to urge this suit on his daughter. He told her how important such an alliance would be, and pressed her to consent. In fact, he pressed her so persistingly that the princess at length lost her temper and quite forgot the respect due to her father. 'Sire,' cried she angrily, 'do not speak further of this or any other marriage or I will plunge this dagger in my breast and so escape from all these importunities.'

"The king of China was extremely indignant with his daughter and replied: 'You have lost your senses and you must be treated accordingly.' So he had her shut in one set of rooms in one of her palaces, and only allowed her ten old women, of whom her nurse was the head, to wait on her and keep her company. He next sent letters to all the kings who had sued for the princess's hand, begging they would think of her no longer, as she was quite insane, and he desired his various envoys to make it known that anyone who could cure her should have her to wife.

"Fair Maimoune," continued Danhasch, "this is the present state of affairs. I never pass a day without going to gaze on this incomparable beauty, and I am sure that if you would only accompany me you would think the sight well worth the trouble, and own that you never saw such loveliness before."

The fairy only answered with a peal of laughter, and when at length she had control of her voice she cried, "Oh, come, you are making game of me! I thought you had something really interesting to tell me instead of raving about some unknown damsel. What would you say if you could see the prince I have just been looking at and whose beauty is really transcendent? That is something worth talking about, you would certainly quite lose your head."

"Charming Maimoune," asked Danhasch, "may I inquire who and what is the prince of whom you speak?"

"Know," replied Maimoune, "that he is in much the same case as your princess. The king, his father, wanted to force him to marry, and on the prince's refusal to obey he has been imprisoned in an old tower where I have just seen him."

"I don't like to contradict a lady," said Danhasch, "but you must really permit me to doubt any mortal being as beautiful as my princess."

"Hold your tongue," cried Maimoune. "I repeat that is impossible."

"Well, I don't wish to seem obstinate," replied Danhasch, "the best plan to test the truth of what I say will be for you to let me take you to see the princess for yourself."

"There is no need for that," retorted Maimoune; "we can satisfy ourselves in another way. Bring your princess here and lay her down beside my prince. We can then compare them at leisure, and decide which is in the right."

Danhasch readily consented, and after having the tower where the prince was confined pointed out to him, and making a wager with Maimoune as to the result of the comparison, he flew off to China to fetch the princess.

In an incredibly short time Danhasch returned, bearing the sleeping princess. Maimoune led him to the prince's room, and the rival beauty was placed beside him.

When the prince and princess lay thus side by side, an animated dispute as to their respective charms arose between the fairy and the genius. Danhasch began by saying:

"Now you see that my princess is more beautiful than your prince. Can you doubt any longer?"

"Doubt! Of course I do!" exclaimed Maimoune. "Why, you must be blind not to see how much my prince excels your princess. I do not deny that your princess is very handsome, but only look and you must own that I am in the right."

"There is no need for me to look longer," said Danhasch, "my first impression will remain the same; but of course, charming Maimoune, I am ready to yield to you if you insist on it."

"By no means," replied Maimoune. "I have no idea of being under any obligation to an accursed genius like you. I refer the matter to an umpire, and shall expect you to submit to his verdict."

Danhasch readily agreed, and on Maimoune striking the floor with her foot it opened, and a hideous, hump-backed, lame, squinting genius, with six horns on his head and hands like claws, emerged. As soon as he beheld Maimoune he threw himself at her feet and asked her commands.

"Rise, Caschcasch," said she. "I summoned you to judge between me and Danhasch. Glance at that couch, and say without any partiality whether you think the youth or the maiden lying there the more beautiful."

Caschcasch looked at the prince and princess with every token of surprise and admiration. At length, having gazed long without being able to come to a decision, he said.

"Madam, I must confess that I should deceive you were I to declare one to be handsomer than the other. There seems to me only one way in which to decide the matter, and that is to wake one after the other and judge which of them expresses the greater admiration for the other."

This advice pleased Maimoune and Danhasch, and the fairy at once transformed herself into the shape of a gnat and settling on Camaralzaman's throat stung him so sharply that he awoke. As he did so his eyes fell on the Princess of China. Surprised at finding a lady so near him, he raised himself on one arm to look at her. The youth and beauty of the princess at once awoke a feeling to which his heart had as yet been a stranger, and he could not restrain his delight.

"What loveliness! What charms! Oh, my heart, my soul!" he exclaimed, as he kissed her forehead, her eyes and mouth in a way which would certainly have roused her had not the genie's enchantments kept her asleep.

"How, fair lady!" he cried, "you do not wake at the signs of Camaralzaman's love? Be you who you may, he is not unworthy of you."

It then suddenly occurred to him, that perhaps this was the bride his father had destined for him, and that the king had probably had her placed in this room in order to see how far Camaralzaman's aversion to marriage would withstand her charms.

"At all events," he thought, "I will take this ring as a remembrance of her."

So saying he drew off a fine ring which the princess wore on her finger, and replaced it by one of his own. After which he lay down again and was soon fast asleep.

Then Danhasch, in his turn, took the form of a gnat and bit the princess on her lip.

She started up, and was not a little amazed at seeing a young man beside her. From surprise she soon passed to admiration, and then to delight on perceiving how handsome and fascinating he was.

"Why," cried she, "was it you my father wished me to marry? How unlucky that I did not know sooner! I should not have made him so angry. But wake up! wake up! for I know I shall love you with all my heart."

So saying she shook Camaralzaman so violently that nothing but the spells of Maimoune could have prevented his waking.

"Oh!" cried the princess. "Why are you so drowsy?" So saying she took his hand and noticed her own ring on his finger, which made her wonder still more. But as he still remained in a profound slumber she pressed a kiss on his cheek and soon fell fast asleep too.

Then Maimoune turning to the genie said: "Well, are you satisfied that my prince surpasses your princess? Another time pray believe me when I assert anything."

Then turning to Caschcasch: "My thanks to you, and now do you and Danhasch bear the princess back to her own home."

The two genii hastened to obey, and Maimoune returned to her well.

On waking next morning the first thing Prince Camaralzaman did was to look round for the lovely lady he had seen at night, and the next to question the slave who waited on him about her. But the slave persisted so strongly that he knew nothing of any lady, and still less of how she got into the tower, that the prince lost all patience, and after giving him a good beating tied a rope round him and ducked him in the well till the unfortunate man cried out that he would tell everything. Then the prince drew him up all dripping wet, but the slave begged leave to change his clothes first, and as soon as the prince consented hurried off just as he was to the palace. Here he found the king talking to the grand-vizir of all the anxiety his son had caused him. The slave was admitted at once and cried:

"Alas, Sire! I bring sad news to your Majesty. There can be no doubt that the prince has completely lost his senses. He declares that he saw a lady sleeping on his couch last night, and the state you see me in proves how violent contradiction makes him." He then gave a minute account of all the prince had said and done.

The king, much moved, begged the vizir to examine into this new misfortune, and the latter at once went to the tower, where he found the prince quietly reading a book. After the first exchange of greetings the vizir said:

"I feel really very angry with your slave for alarming his Majesty by the news he brought him."

"What news?" asked the prince.

"Ah!" replied the vizir, "something absurd, I feel sure, seeing how I find you."

"Most likely," said the prince; "but now that you are here I am glad of the opportunity to ask you where is the lady who slept in this room last night?"

The grand-vizir felt beside himself at this question.

"Prince!" he exclaimed, "how would it be possible for any man, much less a woman, to enter this room at night without walking over your slave on the threshold? Pray consider the matter, and you will realise that you have been deeply impressed by some dream."

But the prince angrily insisted on knowing who and where the lady was, and was not to be persuaded by all the vizir's protestations to the contrary that the plot had not been one of his making. At last, losing patience, he seized the vizir by the beard and loaded him with blows.

"Stop, Prince," cried the unhappy vizir, "stay and hear what I have to say."

The prince, whose arm was getting tired, paused.

"I confess, Prince," said the vizir, "that there is some foundation for what you say. But you know well that a minister has to carry out his master's orders. Allow me to go and to take to the king any message you may choose to send."

"Very well," said the prince; "then go and tell him that I consent to marry the lady whom he sent or brought here last night. Be quick and bring me back his answer."

The vizir bowed to the ground and hastened to leave the room and tower.

"Well," asked the king as soon as he appeared, "and how did you find my son?"

"Alas, sire," was the reply, "the slave's report is only too true!"

He then gave an exact account of his interview with Camaralzaman and of the prince's fury when told that it was not possible for any lady to have entered his room, and of the treatment he himself had received. The king, much distressed, determined to clear up the matter himself, and, ordering the vizir to follow him, set out to visit his son.

The prince received his father with profound respect, and the king, making him sit beside him, asked him several questions, to which Camaralzaman replied with much good sense. At last the king said: "My son, pray tell me about the lady who, it is said, was in your room last night."

"Sire," replied the prince, "pray do not increase my distress in this matter, but rather make me happy by giving her to me in marriage. However much I may have objected to matrimony formerly, the sight of this lovely girl has overcome all my prejudices, and I will gratefully receive her from your hands."

The king was almost speechless on hearing his son, but after a time assured him most solemnly that he knew nothing whatever about the lady in question, and had not connived at her appearance. He then desired the prince to relate the whole story to him.

Camaralzaman did so at great length, showed the ring, and implored his father to help to find the bride he so ardently desired.

"After all you tell me," remarked the king, "I can no longer doubt your word; but how and whence the lady came, or why she should have stayed so short a time I cannot imagine. The whole affair is indeed mysterious. Come, my dear son, let us wait together for happier days."

So saying the king took Camaralzaman by the hand and led him back to the palace, where the prince took to his bed and gave himself up to despair, and the king shutting himself up with his son entirely neglected the affairs of state.

The prime minister, who was the only person admitted, felt it his duty at last to tell the king

H.J.F

how much the court and all the people complained of his seclusion, and how bad it was for the nation. He urged the Sultan to remove with the prince to a lovely little island close by, whence he could easily attend public audiences, and where the charming scenery and fine air would do the invalid so much good as to enable him to bear his father's occasional absence.

The king approved the plan, and as soon as the castle on the island could be prepared for their reception he and the prince arrived there, Schahzaman never leaving his son except for the prescribed public audiences twice a week.

Whilst all this was happening in the capital of Schahzaman the two genii had carefully borne the Princess of China back to her own palace and replaced her in bed. On waking next morning she first turned from one side to another and then, finding herself alone, called loudly for her women.

"Tell me," she cried, "where is the young man I love so dearly, and who slept near me last night?"

"Princess," exclaimed the nurse, "we cannot tell what you allude to without more explanation."

"Why," continued the princess, "the most charming and beautiful young man lay sleeping beside me last night. I did my utmost to wake him, but in vain."

"Your Royal Highness wishes to make game of us," said the nurse. "Is it your pleasure to rise?"

"I am quite in earnest," persisted the princess, "and I want to know where he is."

"But, Princess," expostulated the nurse, "we left you quite alone last night, and we have seen no one enter your room since then."

At this the princess lost all patience, and taking the nurse by her hair she boxed her ears soundly, crying out: "You *shall* tell me, you old witch, or I'll kill you."

The nurse had no little trouble in escaping, and hurried off to the queen, to whom she related the whole story with tears in her eyes.

"You see, madam," she concluded, "that the princess must be out of her mind. If only you will come and see her, you will be able to judge for yourself."

The queen hurried to her daughter's apartments, and after tenderly embracing her, asked her why she had treated her nurse so badly.

"Madam," said the princess, "I perceive that your Majesty wishes to make game of me, but I can assure you that I will never marry anyone except the charming young man whom I saw last night. You must know where he is, so pray send for him."

The queen was much surprised by these words, but when she declared that she knew nothing whatever of the matter the princess lost all respect, and answered that if she were not allowed to marry as she wished she should kill herself, and it was in vain that the queen tried to pacify her and bring her to reason.

The king himself came to hear the rights of the matter, but the princess only persisted in her story, and as a proof showed the ring on her finger. The king hardly knew what to make of it all, but ended by thinking that his daughter was more crazy than ever, and without further argument he had her placed in still closer confinement, with only her nurse to wait on her and a powerful guard to keep the door.

Then he assembled his council, and having told them the sad state of things, added: "If any of you can succeed in curing the princess, I will give her to him in marriage, and he shall be my heir."

An elderly emir present, fired with the desire to possess a young and lovely wife and to rule over a great kingdom, offered to try the magic arts with which he was acquainted.

"You are welcome to try," said the king, "but I make one condition, which is, that should you fail you will lose your life."

The emir accepted the condition, and the king led him to the princess, who, veiling her face, remarked, "I am surprised, sire, that you should bring an unknown man into my presence."

"You need not be shocked," said the king; "this is one of my emirs who asks your hand in marriage."

"Sire," replied the princess, "this is not the one you gave me before and whose ring I wear. Permit me to say that I can accept no other."

The emir, who had expected to hear the princess talk nonsense, finding how calm and reasonable she was, assured the king that he could not venture to undertake a cure, but placed his head at his Majesty's disposal, on which the justly irritated monarch promptly had it cut off.

This was the first of many suitors for the princess whose inability to cure her cost them their lives.

Now it happened that after things had been going on in this way for some time the nurse's son Marzavan returned from his travels. He had been in many countries and learnt many things, including astrology. Needless to say that one of the first things his mother told him was the sad condition of the princess, his foster-sister. Marzavan asked if she could not manage to let him see the princess without the king's knowledge.

After some consideration his mother consented, and even persuaded the eunuch on guard to make no objection to Marzavan's entering the royal apartment.

The princess was delighted to see her foster-brother again, and after some conversation she confided to him all her history and the cause of her imprisonment.

Marzavan listened with downcast eyes and the utmost attention. When she had finished speaking he said,

"If what you tell me, Princess, is indeed the case, I do not despair of finding comfort for you. Take patience yet a little longer. I will set out at once to explore other countries, and when you hear of my return be sure that he for whom you sigh is not far off." So saying, he took his leave and started next morning on his travels.

Marzavan journeyed from city to city and from one island and province to another, and wherever he went he heard people talk of the strange story of the Princess Badoura, as the Princess of China was named.

After four months he reached a large populous seaport town named Torf, and here he heard no more of the Princess Badoura but a great deal of Prince Camaralzaman, who was reported ill, and whose story sounded very similar to that of the Princess Badoura.

Marzavan was rejoiced, and set out at once for Prince Camaralzaman's residence. The ship on which he embarked had a prosperous voyage till she got within sight of the capital of King Schahzaman, but when just about to enter the harbour she suddenly struck on a rock, and foundered within sight of the palace where the prince was living with his father and the grand-vizir.

Marzavan, who swam well, threw himself into the sea and managed to land close to the palace, where he was kindly received, and after having a change of clothing given him was brought before the grand-vizir. The vizir was at once attracted by the young man's superior air and intelligent conversation, and perceiving that he had gained much experience in the course of his travels, he said, "Ah, how I wish you had learnt some secret which might enable you to cure a malady which has plunged this court into affliction for some time past!"

Marzavan replied that if he knew what the illness was he might possibly be able to suggest a remedy, on which the vizir related to him the whole history of Prince Camaralzaman.

On hearing this Marzavan rejoiced inwardly, for he felt sure that he had at last discovered the object of the Princess Badoura's infatuation. However, he said nothing, but begged to be allowed to see the prince.

On entering the royal apartment the first thing which struck him was the prince himself, who lay stretched out on his bed with his eyes closed. The king sat near him, but, without paying any regard to his presence, Marzavan exclaimed, "Heavens! what a striking likeness!" And, indeed, there was a good deal of resemblance between the features of Camaralzaman and those of the Princess of China.

These words caused the prince to open his eyes with languid curiosity, and Marzavan seized this moment to pay him his compliments, contriving at the same time to express the condition of the Princess of China in terms unintelligible, indeed, to the Sultan and his vizir, but which left the prince in no doubt that his visitor could give him some welcome information.

The prince begged his father to allow him the favour of a private interview with Marzavan, and the king was only too pleased to find his son taking an interest in anyone or anything. As soon as they were left alone Marzavan told the prince the story of the Princess Badoura and her sufferings, adding, "I am convinced that you alone can cure her; but before starting on so long a journey you must be well and strong, so do your best to recover as quickly as may be."

These words produced a great effect on the prince, who was so much cheered by the hopes held out that he declared he felt able to get up and be dressed. The king was overjoyed at the result of Marzavan's interview, and ordered public rejoicings in honour of the prince's recovery.

Before long the prince was quite restored to his original state of health, and as soon as he felt himself really strong he took Marzavan aside and said:

"Now is the time to perform your promise. I am so impatient to see my beloved princess once more that I am sure I shall fall ill again if we do not start soon. The one obstacle is my father's tender care of me, for, as you may have noticed, he cannot bear me out of his sight."

"Prince," replied Marzavan, "I have already thought over the matter, and this is what seems to me the best plan. You have not been out of doors since my arrival. Ask the king's permission to go with me for two or three days' hunting, and when he has given leave order two good horses to be held ready for each of us. Leave all the rest to me."

Next day the prince seized a favourable opportunity for making his request, and the king gladly granted it on condition that only one night should be spent out for fear of too great fatigue after such a long illness.

Next morning Prince Camaralzaman and Marzavan were off betimes, attended by two grooms leading the two extra horses. They hunted a little by the way, but took care to get as far from the towns as possible. At nightfall they reached an inn, where they supped and slept till midnight. Then Marzavan awoke and roused the prince without disturbing anyone else. He begged the prince to give him the coat he had been wearing and to put on another which they had brought with them. They mounted their second horses, and Marzavan led one of the grooms' horses by the bridle.

By daybreak our travellers found themselves where four cross roads met in the middle of the forest. Here Marzavan begged the prince to wait for him, and leading the groom's horse into a dense part of the wood he cut its throat, dipped the prince's coat in its blood, and having rejoined the prince threw the coat on the ground where the roads parted.

In answer to Camaralzaman's inquiries as to the reason for this, Marzavan replied that the only chance they had of continuing their journey was to divert attention by creating the idea of the prince's death. "Your father will doubtless be plunged in the deepest grief," he went on, "but his joy at your return will be all the greater."

The prince and his companion now continued their journey by land and sea, and as they had brought plenty of money to defray their expenses they met with no needless delays. At length they reached the capital of China, where they spent three days in a suitable lodging to recover from their fatigues.

During this time Marzavan had an astrologer's dress prepared for the prince. They then went to the baths, after which the prince put on the astrologer's robe and was conducted within sight of the king's palace by Marzavan, who left him there and went to consult his mother, the princess's nurse.

Meantime the prince, according to Marzavan's instructions, advanced close to the palace gates and there proclaimed aloud:

"I am an astrologer and I come to restore health to the Princess Badoura, daughter of the high and mighty King of China, on the conditions laid down by His Majesty of marrying her should I succeed, or of losing my life if I fail."

It was some little time since anyone had presented himself to run the terrible risk involved in attempting to cure the princess, and a crowd soon gathered round the prince. On perceiving his youth, good looks, and distinguished bearing, everyone felt pity for him.

"What are you thinking of, sir," exclaimed some; "why expose yourself to certain death? Are not the heads you see exposed on the town wall sufficient warning? For mercy's sake give up this mad idea and retire whilst you can."

But the prince remained firm, and only repeated his cry with greater assurance, to the horror of the crowd.

"He is resolved to die!" they cried; "may heaven have pity on him!"

Camaralzaman now called out for the third time, and at last the grand-vizir himself came out and fetched him in.

The prime minister led the prince to the king, who was much struck by the noble air of this new adventurer, and felt such pity for the fate so evidently in store for him, that he tried to persuade the young man to renounce his project.

But Camaralzaman politely yet firmly persisted in his intentions, and at length the king desired the eunuch who had the guard of the princess's apartments to conduct the astrologer to her presence.

The eunuch led the way through long passages, and Camaralzaman followed rapidly, in haste to reach the object of his desires. At last they came to a large hall which was the ante-room to the princess's chamber, and here Camaralzaman said to the eunuch:

"Now you shall choose. Shall I cure the princess in her own presence, or shall I do it from here without seeing her?"

The eunuch, who had expressed many contemptuous doubts as they came along of the newcomer's powers, was much surprised and said:

"If you really can cure, it is immaterial when you do it. Your fame will be equally great."

"Very well," replied the prince: "then, impatient though I am to see the princess, I will effect the cure where I stand, the better to convince you of my power." He accordingly drew out his writing case and wrote as follows:

"Adorable princess! The enamoured Camaralzaman has never forgotten the moment when, contemplating your sleeping beauty, he gave you his heart. As he was at that time deprived of the happiness of conversing with you, he ventured to give you his ring as a token of his love, and to take yours in exchange, which he now encloses in this letter. Should you deign to return it to him he will be the happiest of mortals, if not he will cheerfully resign himself to death, seeing he does so for love of you. He awaits your reply in your ante-room."

Having finished this note the prince carefully enclosed the ring in it without letting the eunuch see it, and gave him the letter, saying:

"Take this to your mistress, my friend, and if on reading it and seeing its contents she is not instantly cured, you may call me an impudent impostor."

The eunuch at once passed into the princess's room, and handing her the letter said:

"Madam, a new astrologer has arrived, who declares that you will be cured as soon as you have read this letter and seen what it contains."

The princess took the note and opened it with languid indifference. But no sooner did she see her ring than, barely glancing at the writing, she rose hastily and with one bound reached the doorway and pushed back the hangings. Here she and the prince recognised each other, and in a moment they were locked in each other's arms, where they tenderly embraced, wondering how they came to meet at last after so long a separation. The nurse, who had hastened after her charge, drew them back to the inner room, where the princess restored her ring to Camaralzaman.

"Take it back," she said, "I could not keep it without returning yours to you, and I am resolved to wear that as long as I live."

Meantime the eunuch had hastened back to the king. "Sire," he cried, "all the former doctors and astrologers were mere quacks. This man has cured the princess without even seeing her." He then told all to the king, who, overjoyed, hastened to his daughter's apartments, where, after embracing her, he placed her hand in that of the prince, saying:

"Happy stranger, I keep my promise, and give you my daughter to wife, be you who you may. But, if I am not much mistaken, your condition is above what you appear to be."

The prince thanked the king in the warmest and most respectful terms, and added: "As regards my person, your Majesty has rightly guessed that I am not an astrologer. It is but a

disguise which I assumed in order to merit your illustrious alliance. I am myself a prince, my name is Camaralzaman, and my father is Schahzaman, King of the Isles of the Children of Khaledan." He then told his whole history, including the extraordinary manner of his first seeing and loving the Princess Badoura.

When he had finished the king exclaimed: "So remarkable a story must not be lost to posterity. It shall be inscribed in the archives of my kingdom and published everywhere abroad."

The wedding took place next day amidst great pomp and rejoicings. Marzavan was not forgotten, but was given a lucrative post at court, with a promise of further advancement.

The prince and princess were now entirely happy, and months slipped by unconsciously in the enjoyment of each other's society.

One night, however, Prince Camaralzaman dreamt that he saw his father lying at the point of death, and saying: "Alas! my son whom I loved so tenderly, has deserted me and is now causing my death."

The prince woke with such a groan as to startle the princess, who asked what was the matter.

"Ah!" cried the prince, "at this very moment my father is perhaps no more!" and he told his dream.

The princess said but little at the time, but next morning she went to the king, and kissing his hand said:

"I have a favour to ask of your Majesty, and I beg you to believe that it is in no way prompted by my husband. It is that you will allow us both to visit my father-in-law King Schahzaman."

Sorry though the king felt at the idea of parting with his daughter, he felt her request to be so reasonable that he could not refuse it, and made but one condition, which was that she should only spend one year at the court of King Schahzaman, suggesting that in future the young couple should visit their respective parents alternately.

The princess brought this good news to her husband, who thanked her tenderly for this fresh proof of her affection.

All preparations for the journey were now pressed forwards, and when all was ready the king accompanied the travellers for some days, after which he took an affectionate leave of his daughter, and charging the prince to take every care of her, returned to his capital.

The prince and princess journeyed on, and at the end of a month reached a huge meadow interspersed with clumps of big trees which cast a most pleasant shade. As the heat was great, Camaralzaman thought it well to encamp in this cool spot. Accordingly the tents were pitched, and the princess entering hers whilst the prince was giving his further orders, removed her girdle, which she placed beside her, and desiring her women to leave her, lay down and was soon asleep.

When the camp was all in order the prince entered the tent and, seeing the princess asleep, he sat down near her without speaking. His eyes fell on the girdle which, he took up, and whilst inspecting the precious stones set in it he noticed a little pouch sewn to the girdle and fastened by a loop. He touched it and felt something hard within. Curious as to what this might be, he opened the pouch and found a cornelian engraved with various figures and strange characters.

"This cornelian must be something very precious," thought he, "or my wife would not wear it on her person with so much care."

In truth it was a talisman which the Queen of China had given her daughter, telling her it would ensure her happiness as long as she carried it about her.

The better to examine the stone the prince stepped to the open doorway of the tent. As he stood there holding it in the open palm of his hand, a bird suddenly swooped down, picked the stone up in its beak and flew away with it.

Imagine the prince's dismay at losing a thing by which his wife evidently set such store!

The bird having secured its prey flew off some yards and alighted on the ground, holding the talisman it its beak. Prince Camaralzaman advanced, hoping the bird would drop it, but as soon as he approached the thief fluttered on a little further still. He continued his pursuit till the bird suddenly swallowed the stone and took a longer flight than before. The prince then hoped to kill it with a stone, but the more hotly he pursued the further flew the bird.

In this fashion he was led on by hill and dale through the entire day, and when night came the tiresome creature roosted on the top of a very high tree where it could rest in safety.

The prince in despair at all his useless trouble began to think whether he had better return to the camp. "But," thought he, "how shall I find my way back? Must I go up hill or down? I should certainly lose my way in the dark, even if my strength held out." Overwhelmed by hunger, thirst, fatigue and sleep, he ended by spending the night at the foot of the tree.

Next morning Camaralzaman woke up before the bird left its perch, and no sooner did it take flight than he followed it again with as little success as the previous day, only stopping to eat some herbs and fruit he found by the way. In this fashion he spent ten days, following the bird all day and spending the night at the foot of a tree, whilst it roosted on the topmost bough. On the eleventh day the bird and the prince reached a large town, and as soon as they were close to its walls the bird took a sudden and higher flight and was shortly completely out of sight, whilst Camaralzaman felt

in despair at having to give up all hopes of ever recovering the talisman of the Princess Badoura.

Much cast down, he entered the town, which was built near the sea and had a fine harbour. He walked about the streets for a long time, not knowing where to go, but at length as he walked near the seashore he found a garden door open and walked in.

The gardener, a good old man, who was at work, happened to look up, and, seeing a stranger, whom he recognised by his dress as a Mussulman, he told him to come in at once and to shut the door.

Camaralzaman did as he was bid, and inquired why this precaution was taken.

"Because," said the gardener, "I see that you are a stranger and a Mussulman, and this town is almost entirely inhabited by idolaters, who hate and persecute all of our faith. It seems almost a miracle that has led you to this house, and I am indeed glad that you have found a place of safety."

Camaralzaman warmly thanked the kind old man for offering him shelter, and was about to say more, but the gardener interrupted him with:

"Leave compliments alone. You are weary and must be hungry. Come in, eat, and rest." So saying he led the prince into his cottage, and after satisfying his hunger begged to learn the cause of his arrival.

Camaralzaman told him all without disguise, and ended by inquiring the shortest way to his father's capital. "For," added he, "if I tried to rejoin the princess, how should I find her after eleven days' separation? Perhaps, indeed, she may be no longer alive!" At this terrible thought he burst into tears.

The gardener informed Camaralzaman that they were quite a year's land journey to any Mahomedan country, but that there was a much shorter route by sea to the Ebony Island, from whence the Isles of the Children of Khaledan could be easily reached, and that a ship sailed once a year for the Ebony Island by which he might get so far as his very home.

"If only you had arrived a few days sooner," he said, "you might have embarked at once. As it is you must now wait till next year, but if you care to stay with me I offer you my house, such as it is, with all my heart."

Prince Camaralzaman thought himself lucky to find some place of refuge, and gladly accepted the gardener's offer. He spent his days working in the garden, and his nights thinking of and sighing for his beloved wife.

Let us now see what had become during this time of the Princess Badoura.

On first waking she was much surprised not to find the prince near her. She called her women and asked if they knew where he was, and whilst they were telling her that they had seen him enter the tent, but had not noticed his leaving it, she took up her belt and perceived that the little pouch was open and the talisman gone.

She at once concluded that her husband had taken it and would shortly bring it back. She waited for him till evening rather impatiently, and wondering what could have kept him from her so long. When night came without him she felt in despair and abused the talisman and its maker roundly. In spite of her grief and anxiety however, she did not lose her presence of mind, but decided on a courageous, though very unusual step.

Only the princess and her women knew of Camaralzaman's disappearance, for the rest of the party were sleeping or resting in their tents. Fearing some treason should the truth be known, she ordered her women not to say a word which would give rise to any suspicion, and proceeded to change her dress for one of her husband's, to whom, as has been already said, she bore a strong likeness.

In this disguise she looked so like the prince that when she gave orders next morning to break up the camp and continue the journey no one suspected the change. She made one of her women enter her litter, whilst she herself mounted on horseback and the march began.

After a protracted journey by land and sea the princess, still under the name and disguise of Prince Camaralzaman, arrived at the capital of the Ebony Island whose king was named Armanos.

No sooner did the king hear that the ship which was just in port had on board the son of his old friend and ally than he hurried to meet the supposed prince, and had him and his retinue brought to the palace, where they were lodged and entertained sumptuously.

After three days, finding that his guest, to whom he had taken a great fancy, talked of continuing his journey, King Armanos said to him:

"Prince, I am now an old man, and unfortunately I have no son to whom to leave my kingdom. It has pleased Heaven to give me only one daughter, who possesses such great beauty and charm that I could only give her to a prince as highly born and as accomplished as yourself. Instead, therefore, of returning to your own country, take my daughter and my crown and stay with us. I shall feel that I have a worthy successor, and shall cheerfully retire from the fatigues of government."

The king's offer was naturally rather embarrassing to the Princess Badoura. She felt that it was equally impossible to confess that she had deceived him, or to refuse the marriage on which he had set his heart; a refusal which might turn all his kindness to hatred and persecution.

All things considered, she decided to accept, and after a few moments' silence said with a blush, which the king attributed to modesty:

"Sire, I feel so great an obligation for the good opinion your Majesty has expressed for my person and of the honour you do me, that, though I am quite unworthy of it, I dare not refuse. But, sire, I can only accept such an alliance if you give me your promise to assist me with your counsels."

The marriage being thus arranged, the ceremony was fixed for the following day, and the princess employed the intervening time in informing the officers of her suite of what had happened, assuring them that the Princess Badoura had given her full consent to the marriage. She also told her women, and bade them keep her secret well.

King Armanos, delighted with the success of his plans, lost no time in assembling his court and council, to whom he presented his successor, and placing his future son-in-law on the throne made everyone do homage and take oaths of allegiance to the new king.

At night the whole town was filled with rejoicings, and with much pomp the Princess Haiatelnefous (this was the name of the king's daughter) was conducted to the palace of the Princess Badoura.

Now Badoura had thought much of the difficulties of her first interview with King Armanos' daughter, and she felt the only thing to do was at once to take her into her confidence.

Accordingly, as soon as they were alone she took Haiatelnefous by the hand and said:

"Princess, I have a secret to tell you, and must throw myself on your mercy. I am not Prince Camaralzaman, but a princess like yourself and his wife, and I beg you to listen to my story, then I am sure you will forgive my imposture, in consideration of my sufferings."

She then related her whole history, and at its close Haiatelnefous embraced her warmly, and assured her of her entire sympathy and affection.

The two princesses now planned out their future action, and agreed to combine to keep up the deception and to let Badoura continue to play a man's part until such time as there might be news of the real Camaralzaman.

Whilst these things were passing in the Ebony Island Prince Camaralzaman continued to find shelter in the gardener's cottage in the town of the idolaters.

Early one morning the gardener said to the prince:

"Today is a public holiday, and the people of the town not only do not work themselves but forbid others to do so. You had better therefore take a good rest whilst I go to see some friends, and as the time is near for the arrival of the ship of which I told you I will make inquiries about it, and try to bespeak a passage for you." He then put on his best clothes and went out, leaving the prince, who strolled into the garden and was soon lost in thoughts of his dear wife and their sad separation.

As he walked up and down he was suddenly disturbed in his reverie by the noise two large birds were making in a tree.

Camaralzaman stood still and looked up, and saw that the birds were fighting so savagely with beaks and claws that before long one fell dead to the ground, whilst the conqueror spread his wings and flew away. Almost immediately two other larger birds, who had been watching the duel, flew up and alighted, one at the head and the other at the feet of the dead bird. They stood there some time sadly shaking their heads, and then dug up a grave with their claws in which they buried him.

As soon as they had filled in the grave the two flew off, and ere long returned, bringing with them the murderer, whom they held, one by a wing and the other by a leg, with their beaks, screaming and struggling with rage and terror. But they held tight, and having brought him to his victim's grave, they proceeded to kill him, after which they tore open his body, scattered the inside and once more flew away.

The prince, who had watched the whole scene with much interest, now drew near the spot where it happened, and glancing at the dead bird he noticed something red lying near which had evidently fallen out of its inside. He picked it up, and what was his surprise when he recognised the Princess Badoura's talisman which had been the cause of many misfortunes. It would be impossible to describe his joy; he kissed the talisman repeatedly, wrapped it up, and carefully tied it round his arm. For the first time since his separation from the princess he had a good night, and next morning he was up at daybreak and went cheerfully to ask what work he should do.

The gardener told him to cut down an old fruit tree which had quite died away, and Camaralzaman took an axe and fell to vigorously. As he was hacking at one of the roots the axe struck on something hard. On pushing away the earth he discovered a large slab of bronze, under which was disclosed a staircase with ten steps. He went down them and found himself in a roomy kind of cave in which stood fifty large bronze jars, each with a cover on it. The prince uncovered one after another, and found them all filled with gold dust. Delighted with his discovery he left the cave, replaced the slab, and having finished cutting down the tree waited for the gardener's return.

The gardener had heard the night before that the ship about which he was inquiring would start ere long, but the exact date not being yet known he had been told to return next day for further information. He had gone therefore to inquire, and came back with good news beaming in his face.

"My son," said he, "rejoice and hold yourself ready to start in three days' time. The ship is to set sail, and I have arranged all about your passage with the captain."

"You could not bring me better news," replied Camaralzaman, "and in return I have something pleasant to tell you. Follow me and see the good fortune which has be-fallen you."

He then led the gardener to the cave, and having shown him the treasure stored up there, said how happy it made him that Heaven should in this way reward his kind host's many virtues and compensate him for the privations of many years.

"What do you mean?" asked the gardener. "Do you imagine that I should appropriate this treasure? It is yours, and I have no right whatever to it. For the last eighty years I have dug up the ground here without discovering anything. It is clear that these riches are intended for you, and they are much more needed by a prince like yourself than by an old man like me, who am near my end and require nothing. This treasure comes just at the right time, when you are about to return to your own country, where you will make good use of it."

But the prince would not hear of this suggestion, and finally after much discussion they agreed to divide the gold. When this was done the gardener said:

"My son, the great thing now is to arrange how you can best carry off this treasure as secretly as possible for fear of losing it. There are no olives in the Ebony Island, and those imported

from here fetch a high price. As you know, I have a good stock of the olives which grew in this garden. Now you must take fifty jars, fill each half full of gold dust and fill them up with the olives. We will then have them taken on board ship when you embark."

The prince took this advice, and spent the rest of the day filling the fifty jars, and fearing lest the precious talisman might slip from his arm and be lost again, he took the precaution of putting it in one of the jars, on which he made a mark so as to be able to recognise it. When night came the jars were all ready, and the prince and his host went to bed.

Whether in consequence of his great age, or of the fatigues and excitement of the previous day, I do not know, but the gardener passed a very bad night. He was worse next day, and by the morning of the third day was dangerously ill. At daybreak the ship's captain and some of his sailors knocked at the garden door and asked for the passenger who was to embark.

"I am he," said Camaralzaman, who had opened the door. "The gardener who took my passage is ill and cannot see you, but please come in and take these jars of olives and my bag, and I will follow as soon as I have taken leave of him."

The sailors did as he asked, and the captain before leaving charged Camaralzaman to lose no time, as the wind was fair, and he wished to set sail at once.

As soon as they were gone the prince returned to the cottage to bid farewell to his old friend, and to thank him once more for all his kindness. But the old man was at his last gasp, and had barely murmured his confession of faith when he expired.

Camaralzaman was obliged to stay and pay him the last offices, so having dug a grave in the garden he wrapped the kind old man up and buried him. He then locked the door, gave up the key to the owner of the garden, and hurried to the quay only to hear that the ship had sailed long ago, after waiting three hours for him.

It may well be believed that the prince felt in despair at this fresh misfortune, which obliged him to spend another year in a strange and distasteful country. Moreover, he had once more lost the Princess Badoura's talisman, which he feared he might never see again. There was nothing left for him but to hire the garden as the old man had done, and to live on in the cottage. As he could not well cultivate the garden by himself, he engaged a lad to help him, and to secure the rest of the treasure he put the remaining gold dust into fifty more jars, filling them up with olives so as to have them ready for transport.

Whilst the prince was settling down to this second year of toil and privation, the ship made a rapid voyage and arrived safely at the Ebony Island.

As the palace of the new king, or rather of the Princess Badoura, overlooked the harbour, she saw the ship entering it and asked what vessel it was coming in so gaily decked with flags, and was told that it was a ship from the Island of the Idolaters which yearly brought rich merchandise.

The princess, ever on the look out for any chance of news of her beloved husband, went down to the harbour attended by some officers of the court, and arrived just as the captain was landing. She sent for him and asked many questions as to his country, voyage, what passengers he had, and what his vessel was laden with. The captain answered all her questions, and said that his passengers consisted entirely of traders who brought rich stuffs from various countries, fine muslins, precious stones, musk, amber, spices, drugs, olives, and many other things.

As soon as he mentioned olives, the princess, who was very partial to them, exclaimed:

"I will take all you have on board. Have them unloaded and we will make our bargain at once, and tell the other merchants to let me see all their best wares before showing them to other people."

"Sire," replied the captain, "I have on board fifty very large pots of olives. They belong to a merchant who was left behind, as in spite of waiting for him he delayed so long that I was obliged to set sail without him."

"Never mind," said the princess, "unload them all the same, and we will arrange the price."

The captain accordingly sent his boat off to the ship and it soon returned laden with the fifty pots of olives. The princess asked what they might be worth.

"Sire," replied the captain, "the merchant is very poor. Your Majesty will not overpay him if you give him a thousand pieces of silver."

"In order to satisfy him and as he is so poor," said the princess, "I will order a thousand pieces of gold to be given you, which you will be sure to remit to him."

So saying she gave orders for the payment and returned to the palace, having the jars carried before her. When evening came the Princess Badoura retired to the inner part of the palace, and going to the apartments of the Princess Haiatelnefous she had the fifty jars of olives brought to her. She opened one to let her friend taste the olives and to taste them herself, but great was her surprise when, on pouring some into a dish, she found them all powdered with gold dust. "What an adventure! how extraordinary!" she cried. Then she had the other jars opened, and was more and more surprised to find the olives in each jar mixed with gold dust.

But when at length her talisman was discovered in one of the jars her emotion was so great that she fainted away. The Princess Haiatelnefous and her women hastened to restore her, and as soon as she recovered consciousness she covered the precious talisman with kisses.

Then, dismissing the attendants, she said to her friend:

"You will have guessed, my dear, that it was the sight of this talisman which has moved me so deeply. This was the cause of my separation from my dear husband, and now, I am convinced, it will be the means of our reunion."

As soon as it was light next day the Princess Badoura sent for the captain, and made further inquiries about the merchant who owned the olive jars she had bought.

In reply the captain told her all he knew of the place where the young man lived, and how, after engaging his passage, he came to be left behind.

"If that is the case," said the princess, "you must set sail at once and go back for him. He is a debtor of mine and must be brought here at once, or I will confiscate all your merchandise. I shall now give orders to have all the warehouses where your cargo is placed under the royal seal, and they will only be opened when you have brought me the man I ask for. Go at once and obey my orders."

H.J. FORD.

The captain had no choice but to do as he was bid, so hastily provisioning his ship he started that same evening on his return voyage.

When, after a rapid passage, he gained sight of the Island of Idolaters, he judged it better not to enter the harbour, but casting anchor at some distance he embarked at night in a small boat with six active sailors and landed near Camaralzaman's cottage.

The prince was not asleep, and as he lay awake moaning over all the sad events which had separated him from his wife, he thought he heard a knock at the garden door. He went to open it, and was immediately seized by the captain and sailors, who without a word of explanation forcibly bore him off to the boat, which took them back to the ship without loss of time. No sooner were they on board than they weighed anchor and set sail.

Camaralzaman, who had kept silence till then, now asked the captain (whom he had recognised) the reason for this abduction.

"Are you not a debtor of the King of the Ebony Island?" asked the captain.

"I? Why, I never even heard of him before, and never set foot in his kingdom!" was the answer.

"Well, you must know better than I," said the captain. "You will soon see him now, and meantime be content where you are and have patience."

The return voyage was as prosperous as the former one, and though it was night when the ship entered the harbour, the captain lost no time in landing with his passenger, whom he conducted to the palace, where he begged an audience with the king.

Directly the Princess Badoura saw the prince she recognised him in spite of his shabby clothes. She longed to throw herself on his neck, but restrained herself, feeling it was better for them both that she should play her part a little longer. She therefore desired one of her officers to take care of him and to treat him well. Next she ordered another officer to remove the seals from the warehouse, whilst she presented the captain with a costly diamond, and told him to keep the thousand pieces of gold paid for the olives, as she would arrange matters with the merchant himself.

She then returned to her private apartments, where she told the Princess Haiatelnefous all that had happened, as well as her plans for the future, and begged her assistance, which her friend readily promised.

Next morning she ordered the prince to be taken to the bath and clothed in a manner suitable to an emir or governor of a province. He was then introduced to the council, where his good looks and grand air drew the attention of all on him.

Princess Badoura, delighted to see him looking himself once more, turned to the other emirs, saying:

"My lords, I introduce to you a new colleague, Camaralzaman, whom I have known on my travels and who, I can assure you, you will find well deserves your regard and admiration."

Camaralzaman was much surprised at hearing the king – whom he never suspected of being a woman in disguise – asserting their acquaintance, for he felt sure he had never seen her before. However he received all the praises bestowed on him with becoming modesty, and prostrating himself, said:

"Sire, I cannot find words in which to thank your Majesty for the great honour conferred on me. I can but assure you that I will do all in my power to prove myself worthy of it."

On leaving the council the prince was conducted to a splendid house which had been prepared for him, where he found a full establishment and well-filled stables at his orders. On entering his study his steward presented him with a coffer filled with gold pieces for his current expenses. He felt more and more puzzled by such good fortune, and little guessed that the Princess of China was the cause of it.

After a few days the Princess Badoura promoted Camaralzaman to the post of grand treasurer, an office which he filled with so much integrity and benevolence as to win universal esteem.

He would now have thought himself the happiest of men had it not been for that separation which he never ceased to bewail. He had no clue to the mystery of his present position, for the princess, out of compliment to the old king, had taken his name, and was generally known as King Armanos the younger, few people remembering that on her first arrival she went by another name.

At length the princess felt that the time had come to put an end to her own and the prince's suspense, and having arranged all her plans with the Princess Haiatelnefous, she informed Camaralzaman that she wished his advice on some important business, and, to avoid being disturbed, desired him to come to the palace that evening.

The prince was punctual, and was received in the private apartment, when, having ordered her attendants to withdraw, the princess took from a small box the talisman, and, handing it to Camaralzaman, said: "Not long ago an astrologer gave me this talisman. As you are universally well informed, you can perhaps tell me what is its use."

Camaralzaman took the talisman and, holding it to the light, cried with surprise, "Sire, you ask me the use of this talisman. Alas! Hitherto it has been only a source of misfortune to me, being the cause of my separation from the one I love best on earth. The story is so sad and strange that I am sure your Majesty will be touched by it if you will permit me to tell it you."

"I will hear it some other time," replied the princess. "Meanwhile I fancy it is not quite unknown to me. Wait here for me. I will return shortly."

So saying she retired to another room, where she hastily changed her masculine attire for that of a woman, and, after putting on the girdle she wore the day they parted, returned to Camaralzaman.

The prince recognised her at once, and, embracing her with the utmost tenderness, cried, "Ah, how can I thank the king for this delightful surprise?"

"Do not expect ever to see the king again," said the princess, as she wiped the tears of joy from her eyes, "in me you see the king. Let us sit down, and I will tell you all about it."

She then gave a full account of all her adventures since their parting, and dwelt much on the charms and noble disposition of the Princess Haiatelnefous, to whose friendly assistance she owed so much. When she had done she asked to hear the prince's story, and in this manner they spent most of the night.

Next morning the princess resumed her woman's clothes, and as soon as she was ready she desired the chief eunuch to beg King Armanos to come to her apartments.

When the king arrived great was his surprise at finding a strange lady in company of the grand treasurer who had no actual right to enter the private apartment. Seating himself he asked for the king.

"Sire," said the princess, "yesterday I was the king, today I am only the Princess of China and wife to the real Prince Camaralzaman, son of King Schahzaman, and I trust that when your Majesty shall have heard our story you will not condemn the innocent deception I have been obliged to practise."

The king consented to listen, and did so with marked surprise.

At the close of her narrative the princess said, "Sire, as our religion allows a man to have more than one wife, I would beg your Majesty to give your daughter, the Princess Haiatelnefous, in marriage to Prince Camaralzaman. I gladly yield to her the precedence and title of queen in recognition of the debt of gratitude which I owe her."

King Armanos heard the princess with surprise and admiration, then, turning to Camaralzaman, he said, "My son, as your wife, the Princess Badoura (whom I have hitherto looked on as my son-in-law), consents to share your hand and affections with my daughter, I have only to ask if this marriage is agreeable to you, and if you will consent to accept the crown which the Princess Badoura deserves to wear all her life, but which she prefers to resign for love of you."

"Sire," replied Camaralzaman, "I can refuse your Majesty nothing."

Accordingly Camaralzaman was duly proclaimed king, and as duly married with all pomp to the Princess Haiatelnefous, with whose beauty, talents, and affections he had every reason to be pleased.

The two queens lived in true sisterly harmony together, and after a time each presented King Camaralzaman with a son, whose births were celebrated throughout the kingdom with the utmost rejoicing.

Noureddin and the Fair Persian

Balsora was the capital of a kingdom long tributary to the Caliph. During the time of the Caliph Haroun-al-Raschid the king of Balsora, who was his cousin, was called Zinebi. Not thinking one vizir enough for the administration of his estates he had two, named Khacan and Saouy.

Khacan was kind, generous, and liberal, and took pleasure in obliging, as far as in him lay, those who had business with him. Throughout the entire kingdom there was no one who did not esteem and praise him as he deserved.

Saouy was quite a different character, and repelled everyone with whom he came in contact; he was always gloomy, and, in spite of his great riches, so miserly that he denied himself even the necessaries of life. What made him particularly detested was the great aversion he had to Khacan, of whom he never ceased to speak evil to the king.

One day, while the king amused himself talking with his two vizirs and other members of the council, the conversation turned on female slaves. While some declared that it sufficed for a slave to be beautiful, others, and Khacan was among the number, maintained that beauty alone was not enough, but that it must be accompanied by wit, wisdom, modesty, and, if possible, knowledge.

The king not only declared himself to be of this opinion, but charged Khacan to procure him a slave who should fulfil all these conditions. Saouy, who had been of the opposite side, and was jealous of the honour done to Khacan, said, "Sire, it will be very difficult to find a slave as accomplished as your Majesty desires, and, if she is to be found, she will be cheap if she cost less than 10,000 gold pieces."

"Saouy," answered the king, "you seem to find that a very great sum. For you it may be so, but not for me."

And forthwith he ordered his grand treasurer, who was present, to send 10,000 gold pieces to Khacan for the purchase of the slave.

As soon, then, as Khacan returned home he sent for the dealers in female slaves, and charged them directly they had found such a one as he described to inform him. They promised to do their utmost, and no day passed that they did not bring a slave for his inspection but none was found without some defect.

At length, early one morning, while Khacan was on his way to the king's palace, a dealer, throwing himself in his way, announced eagerly that a Persian merchant, arrived late the previous evening, had a slave to sell whose wit and wisdom were equal to her incomparable beauty.

Khacan, overjoyed at this news, gave orders that the slave should be brought for his inspection on his return from the palace. The dealer appearing at the appointed hour, Khacan found the slave beautiful beyond his expectations, and immediately gave her the name of "The Fair Persian".

Being a man of great wisdom and learning, he perceived in the short conversation he had with her that he would seek in vain another slave to surpass her in any of the qualities required by the king, and therefore asked the dealer what price the merchant put upon her.

"Sir," was the answer, "for less than 10,000 gold pieces he will not let her go; he declares that, what with masters for her instruction, and for bodily exercises, not to speak of clothing and nourishment, he has already spent that sum upon her. She is in every way fit to be the slave of a king; she plays every musical instrument, she sings, she dances, she makes verses, in fact there is no accomplishment in which she does not excel."

Khacan, who was better able to judge of her merits than the dealer, wishing to bring the matter to a conclusion, sent for the merchant, and said to him, "It is not for myself that I wish to buy your slave, but for the king. Her price, however, is too high."

"Sir," replied the merchant, "I should esteem it an honour to present her to his Majesty, did it become a merchant to do such a thing. I ask no more than the sum it has cost me to make her such as she is."

Khacan, not wishing to bargain, immediately had the sum counted out, and given to the merchant, who before withdrawing said:

"Sir, as she is destined for the king, I would have you observe that she is extremely tired with the long journey, and before presenting her to his Majesty you would do well to keep her a fortnight in your own house, and to see that a little care is bestowed upon her. The sun has tanned her complexion, but when she has been two or three times to the bath, and is fittingly dressed, you will see how much her beauty will be increased."

Khacan thanked the merchant for his advice, and determined to follow it. He gave the

beautiful Persian an apartment near to that of his wife, whom he charged to treat her as befitting a lady destined for the king, and to order for her the most magnificent garments.

Before bidding adieu to the fair Persian, he said to her: "No happiness can be greater than what I have procured for you; judge for yourself, you now belong to the king. I have, however, to warn you of one thing. I have a son, who, though not wanting in sense, is young, foolish, and headstrong, and I charge you to keep him at a distance."

The Persian thanked him for his advice, and promised to profit by it.

Noureddin – for so the vizir's son was named – went freely in and out of his mother's apartments. He was young, well-made and agreeable, and had the gift of charming all with whom he came in contact. As soon as he saw the beautiful Persian, though aware that she was destined for the king, he let himself be carried away by her charms, and determined at once to use every means in his power to retain her for himself. The Persian was equally captivated by Noureddin, and said to herself: "The vizir does me too great honour in buying me for the king. I should esteem myself very happy if he would give me to his son."

Noureddin availed himself of every opportunity to gaze upon her beauty, to talk and laugh with her, and never would have left her side if his mother had not forced him.

Some time having elapsed, on account of the long journey, since the beautiful Persian had been to the bath, five or six days after her purchase the vizir's wife gave orders that the bath should be heated for her, and that her own female slaves should attend her there, and afterwards should array her in a magnificent dress that had been prepared for her.

Her toilet completed, the beautiful Persian came to present herself to the vizir's wife, who hardly recognised her, so greatly was her beauty increased. Kissing her hand, the beautiful slave said: "Madam, I do not know how you find me in this dress that you have had prepared for me; your women assure me that it suits me so well that they hardly knew me. If it is the truth they tell me, and not flattery, it is to you I owe the transformation."

"My daughter," answered the vizir's wife, "they do not flatter you. I myself hardly recognised you. The improvement is not due to the dress alone, but largely to the beautifying effects of the bath. I am so struck by its results, that I would try it on myself."

Acting forthwith on this decision she ordered two little slaves during her absence to watch over the beautiful Persian, and not to allow Noureddin to enter should he come.

She had no sooner gone than he arrived, and not finding his mother in her apartment, would have sought her in that of the Persian. The two little slaves barred the entrance, saying that his mother had given orders that he was not to be admitted. Taking each by an arm, he put them out of the ante-room, and shut the door. Then they rushed to the bath, informing their mistress with shrieks and tears that Noureddin had driven them away by force and gone in.

This news caused great consternation to the lady, who, dressing herself as quickly as possible, hastened to the apartment of the fair Persian, to find that Noureddin had already gone out. Much astonished to see the vizir's wife enter in tears, the Persian asked what misfortune had happened.

"What!" exclaimed the lady, "you ask me that, knowing that my son Noureddin has been alone with you?"

"But, madam," inquired the Persian, "what harm is there in that?"

"How! Has my husband not told you that you are destined for the king?"

"Certainly, but Noureddin has just been to tell me that his father has changed his mind and has bestowed me upon him. I believed him, and so great is my affection for Noureddin that I would willingly pass my life with him."

"Would to heaven," exclaimed the wife of the vizir, "that what you say were true; but Noureddin has deceived you, and his father will sacrifice him in vengeance for the wrong he has done."

So saying, she wept bitterly, and all her slaves wept with her.

Khacan, entering shortly after this, was much astonished to find his wife and her slaves in tears, and the beautiful Persian greatly perturbed. He inquired the cause, but for some time no answer was forthcoming. When his wife was at length sufficiently calm to inform him of what had happened, his rage and mortification knew no bounds. Wringing his hands and rending his beard, he exclaimed:

"Wretched son! thou destroyest not only thyself but thy father. The king will shed not only thy blood but mine."

His wife tried to console him, saying:

"Do not torment thyself. With the sale of my jewels I will obtain 10,000 gold pieces, and with this sum you will buy another slave."

"Do not suppose," replied her husband, "that it is the loss of the money that affects me. My honour is at stake, and that is more precious to me than all my wealth. You know that Saouy is my mortal enemy. He will relate all this to the king, and you will see the consequences that will ensue."

HJ
FORD

"My lord," said his wife, "I am quite aware of Saouy's baseness, and that he is capable of playing you this malicious trick. But how can he or anyone else know what takes place in this house? Even if you are suspected and the king accuses you, you have only to say that, after examining the slave, you did not find her worthy of his Majesty. Reassure yourself, and send to the dealers, saying that you are not satisfied, and wish them to find you another slave."

This advice appearing reasonable, Khacan decided to follow it, but his wrath against his son did not abate. Noureddin dared not appear all that day, and fearing to take refuge with his usual associates in case his father should seek him there, he spent the day in a secluded garden where he was not known. He did not return home till after his father had gone to bed, and went out early next morning before the vizir awoke, and these precautions he kept up during an entire month.

His mother, though knowing very well that he returned to the house every evening, dare not ask her husband to pardon him. At length she took courage and said:

"My lord, I know that a son could not act more basely towards his father than Noureddin has done towards you, but after all will you now pardon him? Do you not consider the harm you may be doing yourself, and fear that malicious people, seeking the cause of your estrangement, may guess the real one?"

"Madam," replied the vizir, "what you say is very just, but I cannot pardon Noureddin before I have mortified him as he deserves."

"He will be sufficiently punished," answered the lady, "if you do as I suggest. In the evening, when he returns home, lie in wait for him and pretend that you will slay him. I will come to his aid, and while pointing out that you only yield his life at my supplications, you can force him to take the beautiful Persian on any conditions you please." Khacan agreed to follow this plan, and everything took place as arranged. On Noureddin's return Khacan pretended to be about to slay him, but yielding to his wife's intercession, said to his son:

"You owe your life to your mother. I pardon you on her intercession, and on the conditions that you take the beautiful Persian for your wife, and not your slave, that you never sell her, nor put her away."

Noureddin, not hoping for so great indulgence, thanked his father, and vowed to do as he desired. Khacan was at great pains frequently to speak to the king of the difficulties attending the commission he had given him, but some whispers of what had actually taken place did reach Saouy's ears.

More than a year after these events the minister took a chill, leaving the bath while still heated to go out on important business. This resulted in inflammation of the lungs, which rapidly increased. The vizir, feeling that his end was at hand, sent for Noureddin, and charged him with his dying breath never to part with the beautiful Persian.

Shortly afterwards he expired, leaving universal regret throughout the kingdom; rich and poor alike followed him to the grave. Noureddin showed every mark of the deepest grief at his father's death, and for long refused to see anyone. At length a day came when, one of his friends being admitted, urged him strongly to be consoled, and to resume his former place in society. This advice Noureddin was not slow to follow, and soon he formed a little society of ten young men all about his own age, with whom he spent all his time in continual feasting and merry-making.

Sometimes the fair Persian consented to appear at these festivities, but she disapproved of this lavish expenditure, and did not scruple to warn Noureddin of the probable consequences. He, however, only laughed at her advice, saying that his father had always kept him in too great constraint, and that now he rejoiced at his new-found liberty.

What added to the confusion in his affairs was that he refused to look into his accounts with his steward, sending him away every time he appeared with his book.

"See only that I live well," he said, "and do not disturb me about anything else."

Not only did Noureddin's friends constantly partake of his hospitality, but in every way they took advantage of his generosity; everything of his that they admired, whether land, houses, baths, or any other source of his revenue, he immediately bestowed on them. In vain the Persian protested against the wrong he did himself; he continued to scatter with the same lavish hand.

Throughout one entire year Noureddin did nothing but amuse himself, and dissipate the wealth his father had taken such pains to acquire. The year had barely elapsed, when one day, as they sat at table, there came a knock at the door. The slaves having been sent away, Noureddin went to open it himself. One of his friends had risen at the same time, but Noureddin was before him, and finding the intruder to be the steward, he went out and closed the door. The friend, curious to hear what passed between them, hid himself behind the hangings, and heard the following words:

"My lord," said the steward, "I beg a thousand pardons for interrupting you, but what I have long foreseen has taken place. Nothing remains of the sums you gave me for your expenses, and all other sources of income are also at end, having been transferred by you to others. If you wish me to remain in your service, furnish me with the necessary funds, else I must withdraw."

So great was Noureddin's consternation that he had not a word to say in reply.

The friend, who had been listening behind the curtain, immediately hastened to communicate the news to the rest of the company.

"If this is so," they said, "we must cease to come here."

Noureddin re-entering at that moment, they plainly saw, in spite of his efforts to dissemble, that what they had heard was the truth. One by one they rose, and each with a different excuse left the room, till presently he found himself alone, though little suspecting the resolution his friends had taken. Then, seeing the beautiful Persian, he confided to her the statement of the steward, with many expressions of regret for his own carelessness.

"Had I but followed your advice, beautiful Persian," he said, "all this would not have happened, but at least I have this consolation, that I have spent my fortune in the company of friends who will not desert me in an hour of need. Tomorrow I will go to them, and amongst them they will lend me a sum sufficient to start in some business."

Accordingly next morning early Noureddin went to seek his ten friends, who all lived in the same street. Knocking at the door of the first and chief, the slave who opened it left him to wait in a hall while he announced his visit to his master. "Noureddin!" he heard him exclaim quite audibly. "Tell him, every time he calls, that I am not at home." The same thing happened at the second door, and also at the third, and so on with all the ten. Noureddin, much mortified, recognised too late that he had confided in false friends, who abandoned him in his hour of need. Overwhelmed with grief, he sought consolation from the beautiful Persian.

"Alas, my lord," she said, "at last you are convinced of the truth of what I foretold. There is now no other resource left but to sell your slaves and your furniture."

First then he sold the slaves, and subsisted for a time on the proceeds, after that the furniture was sold, and as much of it was valuable it sufficed for some time. Finally this resource also came to an end, and again he sought counsel from the beautiful Persian.

"My lord," she said, "I know that the late vizir, your father, bought me for 10,000 gold pieces, and though I have diminished in value since, I should still fetch a large sum. Do not therefore hesitate to sell me, and with the money you obtain go and establish yourself in business in some distant town."

"Charming Persian," answered Noureddin, "how could I be guilty of such baseness? I would die rather than part from you whom I love better than my life."

"My lord," she replied, "I am well aware of your love for me, which is only equalled by mine for you, but a cruel necessity obliges us to seek the only remedy."

Noureddin, convinced at length of the truth of her words, yielded, and reluctantly led her to the slave market, where, showing her to a dealer named Hagi Hassan, he inquired her value.

Taking them into a room apart, Hagi Hassan exclaimed as soon as she had unveiled, "My lord, is not this the slave your father bought for 10,000 pieces?"

On learning that it was so, he promised to obtain the highest possible price for her. Leaving the beautiful Persian shut up in the room alone, he went out to seek the slave merchants, announcing to them that he had found the pearl among slaves, and asking them to come and put a value upon her. As soon as they saw her they agreed that less than 4,000 gold pieces could not be asked. Hagi Hassan, then closing the door upon her, began to offer her for sale – calling out: "Who will bid 4,000 gold pieces for the Persian slave?"

Before any of the merchants had bid, Saouy happened to pass that way, and judging that it must be a slave of extraordinary beauty, rode up to Hagi Hassan and desired to see her. Now it was not the custom to show a slave to a private bidder, but as no one dared to disobey the vizir his request was granted.

As soon as Saouy saw the Persian he was so struck by her beauty, that he immediately wished to possess her, and not knowing that she belonged to Noureddin, he desired Hagi Hassan to send for the owner and to conclude the bargain at once.

Hagi Hassan then sought Noureddin, and told him that his slave was going far below her value, and that if Saouy bought her he was capable of not paying the money. "What you must do," he said, "is to pretend that you had no real intention of selling your slave, and only swore you would in a fit of anger against her. When I present her to Saouy as if with your consent you must step in, and with blows begin to lead her away."

Noureddin did as Hagi Hassan advised, to the great wrath of Saouy, who riding straight at him endeavoured to take the beautiful Persian from him by force. Noureddin letting her go, seized Saouy's horse by the bridle, and, encouraged by the applause of the bystanders, dragged him to the ground, beat him severely, and left him in the gutter streaming with blood. Then, taking the beautiful Persian, he returned home amidst the acclamations of the people, who detested Saouy so much that they would neither interfere in his behalf nor allow his slaves to protect him.

Covered from head to foot with mire and streaming with blood he rose, and leaning on two of his slaves went straight to the palace, where he demanded an audience of the king, to whom he related what had taken place in these words:

"May it please your Majesty, I had gone to the slave market to buy myself a cook. While

there I heard a slave being offered for 4,000 pieces. Asking to see her, I found she was of incomparable beauty, and was being sold by Noureddin, the son of your late vizir, to whom your Majesty will remember giving a sum of 10,000 gold pieces for the purchase of a slave. This is the identical slave, whom instead of bringing to your Majesty he gave to his own son. Since the death of his father this Noureddin has run through his entire fortune, has sold all his possessions, and is now reduced to selling the slave. Calling him to me, I said: 'Noureddin, I will give you 10,000 gold pieces for your slave, whom I will present to the king. I will interest him at the same time in your behalf, and this will be worth much more to you than what extra money you might obtain from the merchants.' 'Bad old man,' he exclaimed, 'rather than sell my slave to you I would give her to a Jew.' 'But, Noureddin,' I remonstrated, 'you do not consider that in speaking thus you wrong the king, to whom your father owed everything.' This remonstrance only irritated him the more. Throwing himself on me like a madman, he tore me from my horse, beat me to his heart's content, and left me in the state your Majesty sees."

So saying Saouy turned aside his head and wept bitterly.

The king's wrath was kindled against Noureddin. He ordered the captain of the guard to take with him forty men, to pillage Noureddin's house, to raze it to the ground, and to bring Noureddin and the slave to him. A doorkeeper, named Sangiar, who had been a slave of Khacan's, hearing this order given, slipped out of the king's apartment, and hastened to warn Noureddin to take flight instantly with the beautiful Persian. Then, presenting him with forty gold pieces, he disappeared before Noureddin had time to thank him.

As soon, then, as the fair Persian had put on her veil they fled together, and had the good fortune to get out of the town without being observed. At the mouth of the Euphrates they found a ship just about to start for Bagdad. They embarked, and immediately the anchor was raised and they set sail.

When the captain of the guard reached Noureddin's house he caused his soldiers to burst open the door and to enter by force, but no trace was to be found of Noureddin and his slave, nor could the neighbours give any information about them. When the king heard that they had escaped, he issued a proclamation that a reward of 1,000 gold pieces would be given to whoever would bring him Noureddin and the slave, but that, on the contrary, whoever hid them would be severely punished. Meanwhile Noureddin and the fair Persian had safely reached Bagdad. When the vessel had come to an anchor they paid five gold pieces for their passage and went ashore. Never having been in Bagdad before, they did not know where to seek a lodging. Wandering along the banks of the Tigris, they skirted a garden enclosed by a high wall. The gate was shut, but in front of it was an open vestibule with a sofa on either side. "Here," said Noureddin, "let us pass the night," and reclining on the sofas they soon fell asleep.

Now this garden belonged to the Caliph. In the middle of it was a vast pavilion, whose superb saloon had eighty windows, each window having a lustre, lit solely when the Caliph spent the evening there. Only the doorkeeper lived there, an old soldier named Scheih Ibrahim, who had strict orders to be very careful whom he admitted, and never to allow anyone to sit on the sofas by the door. It happened that evening that he had gone out on an errand. When he came back and saw two persons asleep on the sofas he was about to drive them out with blows, but drawing nearer he perceived that they were a handsome young man and beautiful young woman, and decided to awake them by gentler means. Noureddin, on being awoke, told the old man that they were strangers, and merely wished to pass the night there. "Come with me," said Scheih Ibrahim, "I will lodge you better, and will show you a magnificent garden belonging to me." So saying the doorkeeper led the way into the Caliph's garden, the beauties of which filled them with wonder and amazement. Noureddin took out two gold pieces, and giving them to Scheih Ibrahim said, "I beg you to get us something to eat that we may make merry together." Being very avaricious, Scheih Ibrahim determined to spend only the tenth part of the money and to keep the rest to himself. While he was gone Noureddin and the Persian wandered through the gardens and went up the white marble staircase of the pavilion as far as the locked door of the saloon. On the return of Scheih Ibrahim they begged him to open it, and to allow them to enter and admire the magnificence within. Consenting, he brought not only the key, but a light, and immediately unlocked the door. Noureddin and the Persian entering, were dazzled with the magnificence they beheld. The paintings and furniture were of astonishing beauty, and between each window was a silver arm holding a candle.

Scheih Ibrahim spread the table in front of a sofa, and all three ate together. When they had finished eating Noureddin asked the old man to bring them a bottle of wine.

"Heaven forbid," said Scheih Ibrahim, "that I should come in contact with wine! I who have four times made the pilgrimage to Mecca, and have renounced wine for ever."

"You would, however, do us a great service in procuring us some," said Noureddin. "You need not touch it yourself. Take the ass which is tied to the gate, lead it to the nearest wine-shop, and ask some passer-by to order two jars of wine; have them put in the ass's panniers, and drive him before you. Here are two pieces of gold for the expenses."

At sight of the gold, Scheih Ibrahim set off at once to execute the commission. On his return, Noureddin said: "We have still need of cups to drink from, and of fruit, if you can procure us some." Scheih Ibrahim disappeared again, and soon returned with a table spread with cups of gold and silver, and every sort of beautiful fruit. Then he withdrew, in spite of repeated invitations to remain.

Noureddin and the beautiful Persian, finding the wine excellent, drank of it freely, and while drinking they sang. Both had fine voices, and Scheih Ibrahim listened to them with great pleasure – first from a distance, then he drew nearer, and finally put his head in at the door. Noureddin, seeing him, called to him to come in and keep them company. At first the old man declined, but was persuaded to enter the room, to sit down on the edge of the sofa nearest the door, and at last to draw closer and to seat himself by the beautiful Persian, who urged him so persistently to drink her health that at length he yielded, and took the cup she offered.

Now the old man only made a pretence of renouncing wine; he frequented wine-shops like other people, and had taken none of the precautions Noureddin had proposed. Having once yielded, he was easily persuaded to take a second cup, and a third, and so on till he no longer knew what he was doing. Till near midnight they continued drinking, laughing, and singing together.

About that time the Persian, perceiving that the room was lit by only one miserable tallow candle, asked Scheih Ibrahim to light some of the beautiful candles in the silver arms.

"Light them yourself," answered the old man; "you are younger than I, but let five or six be enough."

She did not stop, however, till she had lit all the eighty, but Scheih Ibrahim was not conscious of this, and when, soon after that, Noureddin proposed to have some of the lustres lit, he answered:

"You are more capable of lighting them than I, but not more than three."

Noureddin, far from contenting himself with three, lit all, and opened all the eighty windows.

The Caliph Haroun-al-Raschid, chancing at that moment to open a window in the saloon of his palace looking on the garden, was surprised to see the pavilion brilliantly illuminated. Calling the grand-vizir, Giafar, he said to him:

"Negligent vizir, look at the pavilion, and tell me why it is lit up when I am not there."

When the vizir saw that it was as the Caliph said, he trembled with fear, and immediately invented an excuse.

"Commander of the Faithful," he said, "I must tell you that four or five days ago Scheih Ibrahim told me that he wished to have an assembly of the ministers of his mosque, and asked permission to hold it in the pavilion. I granted his request, but forgot since to mention it to your Majesty."

"Giafar," replied the Caliph, "you have committed three faults – first, in giving the permission; second, in not mentioning it to me; and third, in not investigating the matter more closely. For punishment I condemn you to spend the rest of the night with me in company of these worthy people. While I dress myself as a citizen, go and disguise yourself, and then come with me."

When they reached the garden gate they found it open, to the great indignation of the Caliph. The door of the pavilion being also open, he went softly upstairs, and looked in at the half-

H J Ford.

closed door of the saloon. Great was his surprise to see Scheih Ibrahim, whose sobriety he had never doubted, drinking and singing with a young man and a beautiful lady. The Caliph, before giving way to his anger, determined to watch and see who the people were and what they did.

Presently Scheih Ibrahim asked the beautiful Persian if anything were wanting to complete her enjoyment of the evening.

"If only," she said, "I had an instrument upon which I might play."

Scheih Ibrahim immediately took a lute from a cupboard and gave it to the Persian, who began to play on it, singing the while with such skill and taste that the Caliph was enchanted. When she ceased he went softly downstairs and said to the vizir:

"Never have I heard a finer voice, nor the lute better played. I am determined to go in and make her play to me."

"Commander of the Faithful," said the vizir, "if Scheih Ibrahim recognises you he will die of fright."

"I should be sorry for that," answered the Caliph, "and I am going to take steps to prevent it. Wait here till I return."

Now the Caliph had caused a bend in the river to form a lake in his garden. There the finest fish in the Tigris were to be found, but fishing was strictly forbidden. It happened that night, however, that a fisherman had taken advantage of the gate being open to go in and cast his nets. He was just about to draw them when he saw the Caliph approaching. Recognising him at once in spite of his disguise, he threw himself at his feet imploring forgiveness.

"Fear nothing," said the Caliph, "only rise up and draw thy nets."

The fisherman did as he was told, and produced five or six fine fish, of which the Caliph took the two largest. Then he desired the fisherman to change clothes with him, and in a few minutes the Caliph was transformed into a fisherman, even to the shoes and the turban. Taking the two fish in his hand, he returned to the vizir, who, not recognising him, would have sent him about his business. Leaving the vizir at the foot of the stairs, the Caliph went up and knocked at the door of the saloon. Noureddin opened it, and the Caliph, standing on the threshold, said:

"Scheih Ibrahim, I am the fisher Kerim. Seeing that you are feasting with your friends, I bring you these fish."

Noureddin and the Persian said that when the fishes were properly cooked and dressed they would gladly eat of them. The Caliph then returned to the vizir, and they set to work in Scheih Ibrahim's house to cook the fish, of which they made so tempting a dish that Noureddin and the fair Persian ate of it with great relish. When they had finished Noureddin took thirty gold pieces (all that remained of what Sangiar had given him) and presented them to the Caliph, who, thanking him, asked as a further favour if the lady would play him one piece on the lute. The Persian gladly consented, and sang and played so as to delight the Caliph.

Noureddin, in the habit of giving to others whatever they admired, said, "Fisherman, as she pleases you so much, take her; she is yours."

The fair Persian, astounded that he should wish to part from her, took her lute, and with tears in her eyes sang her reproaches to its music.

The Caliph (still in the character of fisherman) said to him, "Sir, I perceive that this fair lady is your slave. Oblige me, I beg you, by relating your history."

Noureddin willingly granted this request, and recounted everything from the purchase of the slave down to the present moment.

"And where do you go now?" asked the Caliph.

"Wherever the hand of Allah leads me," said Noureddin.

"Then, if you will listen to me," said the Caliph, "you will immediately return to Balsora. I will give you a letter to the king, which will ensure you a good reception from him."

"It is an unheard-of thing," said Noureddin, "that a fisherman should be in correspondence with a king."

"Let not that astonish you," answered the Caliph; "we studied together, and have always remained the best of friends, though fortune, while making him a king, left me a humble fisherman."

The Caliph then took a sheet of paper, and wrote the following letter, at the top of which he put in very small characters this formula to show that he must be implicitly obeyed:

"*In the Name of the Most Merciful God.*

"Letter of the Caliph Haroun-al-Raschid to the King of Balsora.

"Haroun-al-Raschid, son of Mahdi, sends this letter to Mohammed Zinebi, his cousin. As soon as Noureddin, son of the Vizir Khacan, bearer of this letter, has given it to thee, and thou hast read it, take off thy royal mantle, put it on his shoulders, and seat him in thy place without fail. Farewell."

The Caliph then gave this letter to Noureddin, who immediately set off, with only what little money he possessed when Sangiar came to his assistance. The beautiful Persian, inconsolable at his departure, sank on a sofa bathed in tears.

When Noureddin had left the room, Scheih Ibrahim, who had hitherto kept silence, said:

"Kerim, for two miserable fish thou hast received a purse and a slave. I tell thee I will take the slave, and as to the purse, if it contains silver thou mayst keep one piece, if gold then I will take all and give thee what copper pieces I have in my purse."

Now here it must be related that when the Caliph went upstairs with the plate of fish he ordered the vizir to hasten to the palace and bring back four slaves bearing a change of raiment, who should wait outside the pavilion till the Caliph should clap his hands.

Still personating the fisherman, the Caliph answered: "Scheih Ibrahim, whatever is in the purse I will share equally with you, but as to the slave I will keep her for myself. If you do not agree to these conditions you shall have nothing."

The old man, furious at this insolence as he considered it, took a cup and threw it at the Caliph, who easily avoided a missile from the hand of a drunken man. It hit against the wall, and broke into a thousand pieces. Scheih Ibrahim, still more enraged, then went out to fetch a stick. The Caliph at that moment clapped his hands, and the vizir and the four slaves entering took off the fisherman's dress and put on him that which they had brought.

When Scheih Ibrahim returned, a thick stick in his hand, the Caliph was seated on his throne, and nothing remained of the fisherman but his clothes in the middle of the room. Throwing himself on the ground at the Caliph's feet, he said: "Commander of the Faithful, your miserable slave has offended you, and craves forgiveness."

The Caliph came down from his throne, and said: "Rise, I forgive thee." Then turning to the Persian he said: "Fair lady, now you know who I am; learn also that I have sent Noureddin to Balsora to be king, and as soon as all necessary preparations are made I will send you there to be queen. Meanwhile I will give you an apartment in my palace, where you will be treated with all honour."

At this the beautiful Persian took courage, and the Caliph was as good as his word, recommending her to the care of his wife Zobeida.

Noureddin made all haste on his journey to Balsora, and on his arrival there went straight to the palace of the king, of whom he demanded an audience. It was immediately granted, and holding the letter high above his head he forced his way through the crowd. While the king read the letter he changed colour. He would instantly have executed the Caliph's order, but first he showed the letter to Saouy, whose interests were equally at stake with his own. Pretending that he wished to read it a second time, Saouy turned aside as if to seek a better light; unperceived by anyone he tore off the formula from the top of the letter, put it to his mouth, and swallowed it. Then, turning to the king, he said:

"Your majesty has no need to obey this letter. The writing is indeed that of the Caliph, but the formula is absent. Besides, he has not sent an express with the patent, without which the letter is useless. Leave all to me, and I will take the consequences."

The king not only listened to the persuasions of Saouy, but gave Noureddin into his hands. Such a severe bastinado was first administered to him, that he was left more dead than alive; then Saouy threw him into the darkest and deepest dungeon, and fed him only on bread and water. After ten days Saouy determined to put an end to Noureddin's life, but dared not without the king's authority. To gain this end, he loaded several of his own slaves with rich gifts, and presented himself at their head to the king, saying that they were from the new king on his coronation.

"What!" said the king; "is that wretch still alive? Go and behead him at once. I authorise you."

"Sire," said Saouy, "I thank your Majesty for the justice you do me. I would further beg, as Noureddin publicly affronted me, that the execution might be in front of the palace, and that it might be proclaimed throughout the city, so that no one may be ignorant of it."

The king granted these requests, and the announcement caused universal grief, for the memory of Noureddin's father was still fresh in the hearts of his people. Saouy, accompanied by twenty of his own slaves, went to the prison to fetch Noureddin, whom he mounted on a wretched horse without a saddle. Arrived at the palace, Saouy went in to the king, leaving Noureddin in the square, hemmed in not only by Saouy's slaves but by the royal guard, who had great difficulty in preventing the people from rushing in and rescuing Noureddin. So great was the indignation against Saouy that if anyone had set the example he would have been stoned on his way through the streets. Saouy, who witnessed the agitation of the people from the windows of the king's privy chambers, called to the executioner to strike at once. The king, however, ordered him to delay; not only was he jealous of Saouy's interference, but he had another reason. A troop of horsemen was seen at that moment riding at full gallop towards the square. Saouy suspected who they might be, and urged the king to give the signal for the execution without delay, but this the king refused to do till he knew who the horsemen were.

Now, they were the vizir Giafar and his suite arriving at full speed from Bagdad. For several days after Noureddin's departure with the letter the Caliph had forgotten to send the express with the patent, without which the letter was useless. Hearing a beautiful voice one day in the women's part of the palace uttering lamentations, he was informed that it was the voice of the fair Persian, and suddenly calling to mind the patent, he sent for Giafar, and ordered him to

HJ FORD

make for Balsora with the utmost speed – if Noureddin were dead, to hang Saouy; if he were still alive, to bring him at once to Bagdad along with the king and Saouy.

Giafar rode at full speed through the square, and alighted at the steps of the palace, where the king came to greet him. The vizir's first question was whether Noureddin were still alive. The king replied that he was, and he was immediately led forth, though bound hand and foot. By the vizir's orders his bonds were immediately undone, and Saouy was tied with the same cords. Next day Giafar returned to Bagdad, bearing with him the king, Saouy, and Noureddin.

When the Caliph heard what treatment Noureddin had received, he authorised him to behead Saouy with his own hands, but he declined to shed the blood of his enemy, who was forthwith handed over to the executioner. The Caliph also desired Noureddin to reign over Balsora, but this, too, he declined, saying that after what had passed there he preferred never to return, but to enter the service of the Caliph. He became one of his most intimate courtiers, and lived long in great happiness with the fair Persian. As to the king, the Caliph contented himself with sending him back to Balsora, with the recommendation to be more careful in future in the choice of his vizir.

Aladdin and the Wonderful Lamp

There once lived a poor tailor, who had a son called Aladdin, a careless, idle boy who would do nothing but play all day long in the streets with little idle boys like himself. This so grieved the father that he died; yet, in spite of his mother's tears and prayers, Aladdin did not mend his ways. One day, when he was playing in the streets as usual, a stranger asked him his age, and if he were not the son of Mustapha the tailor.

"I am, sir," replied Aladdin; "but he died a long while ago."

On this the stranger, who was a famous African magician, fell on his neck and kissed him, saying: "I am your uncle, and knew you from your likeness to my brother. Go to your mother and tell her I am coming."

Aladdin ran home, and told his mother of his newly found uncle.

"Indeed, child," she said, "your father had a brother, but I always thought he was dead."

However, she prepared supper, and bade Aladdin seek his uncle, who came laden with wine and fruit. He presently fell down and kissed the place where Mustapha used to sit, bidding Aladdin's mother not to be surprised at not having seen him before, as he had been forty years out of the country. He then turned to Aladdin, and asked him his trade, at which the boy hung his head, while his mother burst into tears. On learning that Aladdin was idle and would learn no trade, he offered to take a shop for him and stock it with merchandise. Next day he bought Aladdin a fine suit of clothes, and took him all over the city, showing him the sights, and brought him home at nightfall to his mother, who was overjoyed to see her son so fine.

Next day the magician led Aladdin into some beautiful gardens a long way outside the city gates. They sat down by a fountain, and the magician pulled a cake from his girdle, which he divided between them. They then journeyed onwards till they almost reached the mountains. Aladdin was so tired that he begged to go back, but the magician beguiled him with pleasant stories, and led him on in spite of himself.

At last they came to two mountains divided by a narrow valley.

"We will go no farther," said the false uncle. "I will show you something wonderful; only do you gather up sticks while I kindle a fire."

When it was lit the magician threw on it a powder he had about him, at the same time saying some magical words. The earth trembled a little and opened in front of them, disclosing a square flat stone with a brass ring in the middle to raise it by. Aladdin tried to run away, but the magician caught him and gave him a blow that knocked him down.

"What have I done, uncle?" he said piteously; whereupon the magician said more kindly: "Fear nothing, but obey me. Beneath this stone lies a treasure which is to be yours, and no one else may touch it, so you must do exactly as I tell you."

At the word treasure, Aladdin forgot his fears, and grasped the ring as he was told, saying the names of his father and grandfather. The stone came up quite easily and some steps appeared.

"Go down," said the magician; "at the foot of those steps you will find an open door leading into three large halls. Tuck up your gown and go through them without touching anything, or you will die instantly. These halls lead into a garden of fine fruit trees. Walk on till you come to a niche in a terrace where stands a lighted lamp. Pour out the oil it contains and bring it to me."

He drew a ring from his finger and gave it to Aladdin, bidding him prosper.

Aladdin found everything as the magician had said, gathered some fruit off the trees, and, having got the lamp, arrived at the mouth of the cave. The magician cried out in a great hurry:

"Make haste and give me the lamp." This Aladdin refused to do until he was out of the cave. The magician flew into a terrible passion, and throwing some more powder on the fire, he said something, and the stone rolled back into its place.

The magician left Persia for ever, which plainly showed that he was no uncle of Aladdin's, but a cunning magician who had read in his magic books of a wonderful lamp, which would make him the most powerful man in the world. Though he alone knew where to find it, he could only receive it from the hand of another. He had picked out the foolish Aladdin for this purpose, intending to get the lamp and kill him afterwards.

For two days Aladdin remained in the dark, crying and lamenting. At last he clasped his hands in prayer, and in so doing rubbed the ring, which the magician had forgotten to take from him. Immediately an enormous and frightful genie rose out of the earth, saying:

"What wouldst thou with me? I am the Slave of the Ring, and will obey thee in all things."

Aladdin fearlessly replied: "Deliver me from this place!" whereupon the earth opened, and

HJF

he found himself outside. As soon as his eyes could bear the light he went home, but fainted on the threshold. When he came to himself he told his mother what had passed, and showed her the lamp and the fruits he had gathered in the garden, which were in reality precious stones. He then asked for some food.

"Alas! child," she said, "I have nothing in the house, but I have spun a little cotton and will go and sell it."

Aladdin bade her keep her cotton, for he would sell the lamp instead. As it was very dirty she began to rub it, that it might fetch a higher price. Instantly a hideous genie appeared, and asked what she would have. She fainted away, but Aladdin, snatching the lamp, said boldly:

"Fetch me something to eat!"

The genie returned with a silver bowl, twelve silver plates containing rich meats, two silver cups, and two bottles of wine. Aladdin's mother, when she came to herself, said:

"Whence comes this splendid feast?"

"Ask not, but eat," replied Aladdin.

So they sat at breakfast till it was dinner-time, and Aladdin told his mother about the lamp. She begged him to sell it, and have nothing to do with devils.

"No," said Aladdin, "since chance has made us aware of its virtues, we will use it and the ring likewise, which I shall always wear on my finger." When they had eaten all the genie had brought, Aladdin sold one of the silver plates, and so on till none were left. He then had recourse to the genie, who gave him another set of plates, and thus they lived for many years.

One day Aladdin heard an order from the Sultan proclaimed that everyone was to stay at home and close his shutters while the princess, his daughter, went to and from the bath. Aladdin was seized by a desire to see her face, which was very difficult, as she always went veiled. He hid himself behind the door of the bath, and peeped through a chink. The princess lifted her veil as she went in, and looked so beautiful that Aladdin fell in love with her at first sight. He went home so changed that his mother was frightened. He told her he loved the princess so deeply that he could not live without her, and meant to ask her in marriage of her father. His mother, on hearing this, burst out laughing, but Aladdin at last prevailed upon her to go before the Sultan and carry his request. She fetched a napkin and laid in it the magic fruits from the enchanted garden, which sparkled and shone like the most beautiful jewels. She took these with her to please the Sultan, and set out, trusting in the lamp. The grand-vizir and the lords of council had just gone in as she entered the hall and placed herself in front of the Sultan. He, however, took no notice of her. She went every day for a week, and stood in the same place.

When the council broke up on the sixth day the Sultan said to his vizir: "I see a certain woman in the audience-chamber every day carrying something in a napkin. Call her next time, that I may find out what she wants."

Next day, at a sign from the vizir, she went up to the foot of the throne, and remained kneeling till the Sultan said to her: "Rise, good woman, and tell me what you want."

She hesitated, so the Sultan sent away all but the vizir, and bade her speak freely, promising to forgive her beforehand for anything she might say. She then told him of her son's violent love for the princess.

"I prayed him to forget her," she said, "but in vain; he threatened to do some desperate deed if I refused to go and ask your Majesty for the hand of the princess. Now I pray you to forgive not me alone, but my son Aladdin."

The Sultan asked her kindly what she had in the napkin, whereupon she unfolded the jewels and presented them.

He was thunderstruck, and turning to the vizir said: "What sayest thou? Ought I not to bestow the princess on one who values her at such a price?"

The vizir, who wanted her for his own son, begged the Sultan to withhold her for three months, in the course of which he hoped his son would contrive to make him a richer present. The Sultan granted this, and told Aladdin's mother that, though he consented to the marriage, she must not appear before him again for three months.

Aladdin waited patiently for nearly three months, but after two had elapsed his mother, going into the city to buy oil, found everyone rejoicing, and asked what was going on.

"Do you not know," was the answer, "that the son of the grand-vizir is to marry the Sultan's daughter tonight?"

Breathless, she ran and told Aladdin, who was overwhelmed at first, but presently bethought him of the lamp. He rubbed it, and the genie appeared, saying: "What is thy will?"

Aladdin replied: "The Sultan, as thou knowest, has broken his promise to me, and the vizir's son is to have the princess. My command is that to-night you bring hither the bride and bridegroom."

"Master, I obey," said the genie.

Aladdin then went to his chamber, where, sure enough at midnight the genie transported the bed containing the vizir's son and the princess.

"Take this new-married man," he said, "and put him outside in the cold, and return at daybreak."

Whereupon the genie took the vizir's son out of bed, leaving Aladdin with the princess.

"Fear nothing," Aladdin said to her; "you are my wife, promised to me by your unjust father, and no harm shall come to you."

The princess was too frightened to speak, and passed the most miserable night of her life, while Aladdin lay down beside her and slept soundly. At the appointed hour the genie fetched in the shivering bridegroom, laid him in his place, and transported the bed back to the palace.

Presently the Sultan came to wish his daughter good-morning. The unhappy vizir's son jumped up and hid himself, while the princess would not say a word, and was very sorrowful.

The Sultan sent her mother to her, who said: "How comes it, child, that you will not speak to your father? What has happened?"

The princess sighed deeply, and at last told her mother how, during the night, the bed had been carried into some strange house, and what had passed there. Her mother did not believe her in the least, but bade her rise and consider it an idle dream.

The following night exactly the same thing happened, and next morning, on the princess's refusing to speak, the Sultan threatened to cut off her head. She then confessed all, bidding him ask the vizir's son if it were not so. The Sultan told the vizir to ask his son, who owned the truth, adding that, dearly as he loved the princess, he had rather die than go through another such fearful night, and wished to be separated from her. His wish was granted, and there was an end of feasting and rejoicing.

When the three months were over, Aladdin sent his mother to remind the Sultan of his promise. She stood in the same place as before, and the Sultan, who had forgotten Aladdin, at once remembered him, and sent for her. On seeing her poverty the Sultan felt less inclined than ever to keep his word, and asked the vizir's advice, who counselled him to set so high a value on the princess that no man living could come up to it.

The Sultan then turned to Aladdin's mother, saying: "Good woman, a Sultan must remember his promises, and I will remember mine, but your son must first send me forty basins of gold brimful of jewels, carried by forty black slaves, led by as many white ones, splendidly dressed. Tell him that I await his answer." The mother of Aladdin bowed low and went home, thinking all was lost.

She gave Aladdin the message, adding: "He may wait long enough for your answer!"

"Not so long, mother, as you think," her son replied. "I would do a great deal more than that for the princess."

He summoned the genie, and in a few moments the eighty slaves arrived, and filled up the small house and garden.

Aladdin made them set out to the palace, two and two, followed by his mother. They were so richly dressed, with such splendid jewels in their girdles, that everyone crowded to see them and the basins of gold they carried on their heads.

They entered the palace, and, after kneeling before the Sultan, stood in a half-circle round the throne with their arms crossed, while Aladdin's mother presented them to the Sultan.

He hesitated no longer, but said: "Good woman, return and tell your son that I wait for him with open arms."

She lost no time in telling Aladdin, bidding him make haste. But Aladdin first called the genie.

"I want a scented bath," he said, "a richly embroidered habit, a horse surpassing the Sultan's, and twenty slaves to attend me. Besides this, six slaves, beautifully dressed, to wait on my mother; and lastly, ten thousand pieces of gold in ten purses."

No sooner said than done. Aladdin mounted his horse and passed through the streets, the slaves strewing gold as they went. Those who had played with him in his childhood knew him not, he had grown so handsome.

When the Sultan saw him he came down from his throne, embraced him, and led him into a hall where a feast was spread, intending to marry him to the princess that very day.

But Aladdin refused, saying, "I must build a palace fit for her," and took his leave.

Once home he said to the genie: "Build me a palace of the finest marble, set with jasper, agate, and other precious stones. In the middle you shall build me a large hall with a dome, its four walls of massy gold and silver, each side having six windows, whose lattices, all except one, which is to be left unfinished, must be set with diamonds and rubies. There must be stables and horses and grooms and slaves; go and see about it!"

The palace was finished by next day, and the genie carried him there and showed him all his orders faithfully carried out, even to the laying of a velvet carpet from Aladdin's palace to the Sultan's. Aladdin's mother then dressed herself carefully, and walked to the palace with her slaves, while he followed her on horseback. The Sultan sent musicians with trumpets and cymbals to meet them, so that the air resounded with music and cheers. She was taken to the princess, who

saluted her and treated her with great honour. At night the princess said good-bye to her father, and set out on the carpet for Aladdin's palace, with his mother at her side, and followed by the hundred slaves. She was charmed at the sight of Aladdin, who ran to receive her.

"Princess," he said, "blame your beauty for my boldness if I have displeased you."

She told him that, having seen him, she willingly obeyed her father in this matter. After the wedding had taken place Aladdin led her into the hall, where a feast was spread, and she supped with him, after which they danced till midnight.

Next day Aladdin invited the Sultan to see the palace. On entering the hall with the four-and-twenty windows, with their rubies, diamonds, and emeralds, he cried:

"It is a world's wonder! There is only one thing that surprises me. Was it by accident that one window was left unfinished?"

"No, sir, by design," returned Aladdin. "I wished your Majesty to have the glory of finishing this palace."

The Sultan was pleased, and sent for the best jewellers in the city. He showed them the unfinished window, and bade them fit it up like the others.

"Sir," replied their spokesman, "we cannot find jewels enough."

The Sultan had his own fetched, which they soon used, but to no purpose, for in a month's time the work was not half done. Aladdin, knowing that their task was vain, bade them undo their work and carry the jewels back, and the genie finished the window at his command. The Sultan was surprised to receive his jewels again and visited Aladdin, who showed him the window finished. The Sultan embraced him, the envious vizir meanwhile hinting that it was the work of enchantment.

Aladdin had won the hearts of the people by his gentle bearing. He was made captain of the Sultan's armies, and won several battles for him, but remained modest and courteous as before, and lived thus in peace and content for several years.

But far away in Africa the magician remembered Aladdin, and by his magic arts discovered that Aladdin, instead of perishing miserably in the cave, had escaped, and had married a princess, with whom he was living in great honour and wealth. He knew that the poor tailor's son could only have accomplished this by means of the lamp, and travelled night and day till he reached the capital of China, bent on Aladdin's ruin. As he passed through the town he heard people talking everywhere about a marvellous palace.

"Forgive my ignorance," he asked, "what is this palace you speak of?"

"Have you not heard of Prince Aladdin's palace," was the reply, "the greatest wonder of the world? I will direct you if you have a mind to see it."

The magician thanked him who spoke, and having seen the palace knew that it had been raised by the genie of the lamp, and became half mad with rage. He determined to get hold of the lamp, and again plunge Aladdin into the deepest poverty.

Unluckily, Aladdin had gone a-hunting for eight days, which gave the magician plenty of time. He bought a dozen copper lamps, put them into a basket, and went to the palace, crying: "New lamps for old!" followed by a jeering crowd.

The princess, sitting in the hall of four-and-twenty windows, sent a slave to find out what the noise was about, who came back laughing, so that the princess scolded her.

"Madam," replied the slave, "who can help laughing to see an old fool offering to exchange fine new lamps for old ones?"

Another slave, hearing this, said: "There is an old one on the cornice there which he can have."

Now this was the magic lamp, which Aladdin had left there, as he could not take it out hunting with him. The princess, not knowing its value, laughingly bade the slave take it and make the exchange.

She went and said to the magician: "Give me a new lamp for this."

He snatched it and bade the slave take her choice, amid the jeers of the crowd. Little he cared, but left off crying his lamps, and went out of the city gates to a lonely place, where he remained till nightfall, when he pulled out the lamp and rubbed it. The genie appeared, and at the magician's command carried him, together with the palace and the princess in it, to a lonely place in Africa.

Next morning the Sultan looked out of the window towards Aladdin's palace and rubbed his eyes, for it was gone. He sent for the vizir, and asked what had become of the palace. The vizir looked out too, and was lost in astonishment. He again put it down to enchantment, and this time the Sultan believed him, and sent thirty men on horseback to fetch Aladdin in chains. They met him riding home, bound him, and forced him to go with them on foot. The people, however, who loved him, followed, armed, to see that he came to no harm. He was carried before the Sultan, who ordered the executioner to cut off his head. The executioner made Aladdin kneel down, bandaged his eyes, and raised his scimitar to strike.

At that instant the vizir, who saw that the crowd had forced their way into the courtyard and were scaling the walls to rescue Aladdin, called to the executioner to stay his hand. The

H.J. FORD

people, indeed, looked so threatening that the Sultan gave way and ordered Aladdin to be unbound, and pardoned him in the sight of the crowd.

Aladdin now begged to know what he had done.

"False wretch!" said the Sultan, "come hither," and showed him from the window the place where his palace had stood.

Aladdin was so amazed that he could not say a word.

"Where is my palace and my daughter?" demanded the Sultan. "For the first I am not so deeply concerned, but my daughter I must have, and you must find her or lose your head."

Aladdin begged for forty days in which to find her, promising if he failed to return and suffer death at the Sultan's pleasure. His prayer was granted, and he went forth sadly from the Sultan's presence. For three days he wandered about like a madman, asking everyone what had become of his palace, but they only laughed and pitied him. He came to the banks of a river, and knelt down to say his prayers before throwing himself in. In so doing he rubbed the magic ring he still wore.

The genie he had seen in the cave appeared, and asked his will.

"Save my life, genie," said Aladdin, "and bring my palace back."

"That is not in my power," said the genie; "I am only the slave of the ring; you must ask the slave of the lamp."

"Even so," said Aladdin, "but thou canst take me to the palace, and set me down under my dear wife's window." He at once found himself in Africa, under the window of the princess, and fell asleep out of sheer weariness.

He was awakened by the singing of the birds, and his heart was lighter. He saw plainly that all his misfortunes were owing to the loss of the lamp, and vainly wondered who had robbed him of it.

That morning the princess rose earlier than she had done since she had been carried into Africa by the magician, whose company she was forced to endure once a day. She, however, treated him so harshly that he dared not live there altogether. As she was dressing, one of her women looked out and saw Aladdin. The princess ran and opened the window, and at the noise she made Aladdin looked up. She called to him to come to her, and great was the joy of these lovers at seeing each other again.

After he had kissed her Aladdin said: "I beg of you, Princess, in God's name, before we speak of anything else, for your own sake and mine, tell me what has become of an old lamp I left on the cornice in the hall of four-and-twenty windows, when I went a-hunting."

"Alas!" she said, "I am the innocent cause of our sorrows," and told him of the exchange of the lamp.

"Now I know," cried Aladdin, "that we have to thank the African magician for this! Where is the lamp?"

"He carries it about with him," said the princess, "I know, for he pulled it out of his breast to show me. He wishes me to break my faith with you and marry him, saying that you were beheaded by my father's command. He is forever speaking ill of you, but I only reply by my tears. If I persist, I doubt not that he will use violence."

Aladdin comforted her, and left her for a while. He changed clothes with the first person he met in the town, and having bought a certain powder returned to the princess, who let him in by a little side door.

"Put on your most beautiful dress," he said to her, "and receive the magician with smiles, leading him to believe that you have forgotten me. Invite him to sup with you, and say you wish to taste the wine of his country. He will go for some, and while he is gone I will tell you what to do."

She listened carefully to Aladdin, and when he left her arrayed herself gaily for the first time since she left China. She put on a girdle and head-dress of diamonds, and seeing in a glass that she looked more beautiful than ever, received the magician, saying to his great amazement: "I have made up my mind that Aladdin is dead, and that all my tears will not bring him back to me, so I am resolved to mourn no more, and have therefore invited you to sup with me; but I am tired of the wines of China, and would fain taste those of Africa."

The magician flew to his cellar, and the princess put the powder Aladdin had given her in her cup. When he returned she asked him to drink her health in the wine of Africa, handing him her cup in exchange for his as a sign she was reconciled to him.

Before drinking the magician made her a speech in praise of her beauty, but the princess cut him short, saying:

"Let me drink first, and you shall say what you will afterwards." She set her cup to her lips and kept it there, while the magician drained his to the dregs and fell back lifeless.

The princess then opened the door to Aladdin, and flung her arms round his neck, but Aladdin put her away, bidding her to leave him, as he had more to do. He then went to the dead magician, took the lamp out of his vest, and bade the genie carry the palace and all in it back to China. This was done, and the princess in her chamber only felt two little shocks, and little thought she was at home again.

The Sultan, who was sitting in his closet, mourning for his lost daughter, happened to look up, and rubbed his eyes, for there stood the palace as before! He hastened thither, and Aladdin received him in the hall of the four-and-twenty windows, with the princess at his side. Aladdin told him what had happened, and showed him the dead body of the magician, that he might believe. A ten days' feast was proclaimed, and it seemed as if Aladdin might now live the rest of his life in peace; but it was not to be.

The African magician had a younger brother, who was, if possible, more wicked and more cunning than himself. He travelled to China to avenge his brother's death, and went to visit a pious woman called Fatima, thinking she might be of use to him. He entered her cell and clapped a dagger to her breast, telling her to rise and do his bidding on pain of death. He changed clothes with her, coloured his face like hers, put on her veil and murdered her, that she might tell no tales. Then he went towards the palace of Aladdin, and all the people thinking he was the holy woman, gathered round him, kissing his hands and begging his blessing. When he got to the palace there was such a noise going on round him that the princess bade her slave look out of the window and ask what was the matter. The slave said it was the holy woman, curing people by her touch of their ailments, whereupon the princess, who had long desired to see Fatima, sent for her. On coming to the princess the magician offered up a prayer for her health and prosperity. When he had done the princess made him sit by her, and begged him to stay with her always. The false Fatima, who wished for nothing better, consented, but kept his veil down for fear of discovery. The princess showed him the hall, and asked him what he thought of it.

"It is truly beautiful," said the false Fatima. "In my mind it wants but one thing."

"And what is that?" said the princess.

"If only a roc's egg," replied he, "were hung up from the middle of this dome, it would be the wonder of the world."

After this the princess could think of nothing but a roc's egg, and when Aladdin returned from hunting he found her in a very ill humour. He begged to know what was amiss, and she told him that all her pleasure in the hall was spoilt for the want of a roc's egg hanging from the dome.

"If that is all," replied Aladdin, "you shall soon be happy."

He left her and rubbed the lamp, and when the genie appeared commanded him to bring a roc's egg. The genie gave such a loud and terrible shriek that the hall shook.

"Wretch!" he cried, "is it not enough that I have done everything for you, but you must command me to bring my master and hang him up in the midst of this dome? You and your

wife and your palace deserve to be burnt to ashes; but this request does not come from you, but from the brother of the African magician whom you destroyed. He is now in your palace disguised as the holy woman – whom he murdered. He it was who put that wish into your wife's head. Take care of yourself, for he means to kill you." So saying the genie disappeared.

Aladdin went back to the princess, saying his head ached, and requesting that the holy Fatima should be fetched to lay her hands on it. But when the magician came near, Aladdin, seizing his dagger, pierced him to the heart.

"What have you done?" cried the princess. "You have killed the holy woman!"

"Not so," replied Aladdin, "but a wicked magician," and told her of how she had been deceived.

After this Aladdin and his wife lived in peace. He succeeded the Sultan when he died, and reigned for many years, leaving behind him a long line of kings.

The Adventures of Haroun-al-Raschid, Caliph of Bagdad

The Caliph Haroun-al-Raschid sat in his palace, wondering if there was anything left in the world that could possibly give him a few hours' amusement, when Giafar the grand-vizir, his old and tried friend, suddenly appeared before him. Bowing low, he waited, as was his duty, till his master spoke, but Haroun-al-Raschid merely turned his head and looked at him, and sank back into his former weary posture.

Now Giafar had something of importance to say to the Caliph, and had no intention of being put off by mere silence, so with another low bow in front of the throne, he began to speak.

"Commander of the Faithful," said he, "I have taken on myself to remind your Highness that you have undertaken secretly to observe for yourself the manner in which justice is done and order is kept throughout the city. This is the day you have set apart to devote to this object, and perhaps in fulfilling this duty you may find some distraction from the melancholy to which, as I see to my sorrow, you are a prey."

"You are right," returned the Caliph, "I had forgotten all about it. Go and change your coat, and I will change mine."

A few moments later they both re-entered the hall, disguised as foreign merchants, and passed through a secret door, out into the open country. Here they turned towards the Euphrates, and crossing the river in a small boat, walked through that part of the town which lay along the further bank, without seeing anything to call for their interference. Much pleased with the peace and good order of the city, the Caliph and his vizir made their way to a bridge, which led straight back to the palace, and had already crossed it, when they were stopped by an old and blind man, who begged for alms.

The Caliph gave him a piece of money, and was passing on, but the blind man seized his hand, and held him fast.

"Charitable person," he said, "whoever you may be grant me yet another prayer. Strike me, I beg of you, one blow. I have deserved it richly, and even a more severe penalty."

The Caliph, much surprised at this request, replied gently: "My good man, that which you ask is impossible. Of what use would my alms be if I treated you so ill?" And as he spoke he tried to loosen the grasp of the blind beggar.

"My lord," answered the man, "pardon my boldness and my persistence. Take back your money, or give me the blow which I crave. I have sworn a solemn oath that I will receive nothing without receiving chastisement, and if you knew all, you would feel that the punishment is not a tenth part of what I deserve."

Moved by these words, and perhaps still more by the fact that he had other business to attend to, the Caliph yielded, and struck him lightly on the shoulder. Then he continued his road, followed by the blessing of the blind man. When they were out of earshot, he said to the vizir, "There must be something very odd to make that man act so – I should like to find out what is the reason. Go back to him; tell him who I am, and order him to come without fail to the palace tomorrow, after the hour of evening prayer."

So the grand-vizir went back to the bridge; gave the blind beggar first a piece of money and then a blow, delivered the Caliph's message, and rejoined his master.

They passed on towards the palace, but walking through a square, they came upon a crowd watching a young and well-dressed man who was urging a horse at full speed round the open space, using at the same time his spurs and whip so unmercifully that the animal was all covered with foam and blood. The Caliph, astonished at this proceeding, inquired of a passer-by what it all meant, but no one could tell him anything, except that every day at the same hour the same thing took place.

Still wondering, he passed on, and for the moment had to content himself with telling the vizir to command the horseman also to appear before him at the same time as the blind man.

The next day, after evening prayer, the Caliph entered the hall, and was followed by the vizir bringing with him the two men of whom we have spoken, and a third, with whom we have nothing to do. They all bowed themselves low before the throne and then the Caliph bade them rise, and ask the blind man his name.

"Baba-Abdalla, your Highness," said he.

"Baba-Abdalla," returned the Caliph, "your way of asking alms yesterday seemed to me so strange, that I almost commanded you then and there to cease from causing such a public scandal. But I have sent for you to inquire what was your motive in making such a curious vow. When I know the reason I shall be able to judge whether you can be permitted to continue to practise it, for I cannot help thinking that it sets a very bad example to others. Tell me therefore the whole truth, and conceal nothing."

These words troubled the heart of Baba-Abdalla, who prostrated himself at the feet of the Caliph. Then rising, he answered: "Commander of the Faithful, I crave your pardon humbly, for my persistence in beseeching your Highness to do an action which appears on the face of it to be without any meaning. No doubt, in the eyes of men, it has none; but I look on it as a slight expiation for a fearful sin of which I have been guilty, and if your Highness will deign to listen to my tale, you will see that no punishment could atone for the crime."

The Story of the Blind Baba-Abdalla

I was born, Commander of the Faithful, in Bagdad, and was left an orphan while I was yet a very young man, for my parents died within a few days of each other. I had inherited from them a small fortune, which I worked hard night and day to increase, till at last I found myself the owner of eighty camels. These I hired out to travelling merchants, whom I frequently accompanied on their various journeys, and always returned with large profits.

One day I was coming back from Balsora, whither I had taken a supply of goods, intended for India, and halted at noon in a lonely place, which promised rich pasture for my camels. I was resting in the shade under a tree, when a dervish, going on foot towards Balsora, sat down by my side, and I inquired whence he had come and to what place he was going. We soon made friends, and after we had asked each other the usual questions, we produced the food we had with us, and satisfied our hunger.

While we were eating, the dervish happened to mention that in a spot only a little way off from where we were sitting, there was hidden a treasure so great that if my eighty camels were loaded till they could carry no more, the hiding place would seem as full as if it had never been touched.

At this news I became almost beside myself with joy and greed, and I flung my arms round the neck of the dervish, exclaiming: "Good dervish, I see plainly that the riches of this world are nothing to you, therefore of what use is the knowledge of this treasure to you? Alone and on foot, you could carry away a mere handful. But tell me where it is, and I will load my eighty camels with it, and give you one of them as a token of my gratitude."

Certainly my offer does not sound very magnificent, but it was great to me, for at his words a wave of covetousness had swept over my heart, and I almost felt as if the seventy-nine camels that were left were nothing in comparison.

The dervish saw quite well what was passing in my mind, but he did not show what he thought of my proposal.

"My brother," he answered quietly, "you know as well as I do, that you are behaving unjustly. It was open to me to keep my secret, and to reserve the treasure for myself. But the fact that I have told you of its existence shows that I had confidence in you, and that I hoped to earn your gratitude for ever, by making your fortune as well as mine. But before I reveal to you the secret of the treasure, you must swear that, after we have loaded the camels with as much as they can carry, you will give half to me, and let us go our own ways. I think you will see that this is fair, for if you present me with forty camels, I on my side will give you the means of buying a thousand more."

I could not of course deny that what the dervish said was perfectly reasonable, but, in spite of that, the thought that the dervish would be as rich as I was unbearable to me. Still there was no use in discussing the matter, and I had to accept his conditions or bewail to the end of my life the loss of immense wealth. So I collected my camels and we set out together under the guidance of the dervish. After walking some time, we reached what looked like a valley, but with such a narrow entrance that my camels could only pass one by one. The little valley, or open space, was shut up by two mountains, whose sides were formed of straight cliffs, which no human being could climb.

When we were exactly between these mountains the dervish stopped.

"Make your camels lie down in this open space," he said, "so that we can easily load them; then we will go to the treasure."

I did what I was bid, and rejoined the dervish, whom I found trying to kindle a fire out of some dry wood. As soon as it was alight, he threw on it a handful of perfumes, and pronounced a few words that I did not understand, and immediately a thick column of smoke rose high into the air. He separated the smoke into two columns, and then I saw a rock, which stood like a pillar between the two mountains, slowly open, and a splendid palace appear within.

But, Commander of the Faithful, the love of gold had taken such possession of my heart, that I could not even stop to examine the riches, but fell upon the first pile of gold within my reach and began to heap it into a sack that I had brought with me.

The dervish likewise set to work, but I soon noticed that he confined himself to collecting precious stones, and I felt I should be wise to follow his example. At length the camels were loaded with as much as they could carry, and nothing remained but to seal up the treasure, and go our ways.

Before, however, this was done, the dervish went up to a great golden vase, beautifully chased, and took from it a small wooden box, which he hid in the bosom of his dress, merely saying that it contained a special kind of ointment. Then he once more kindled the fire, threw on the perfume, and murmured the unknown spell, and the rock closed, and stood whole as before.

The next thing was to divide the camels, and to charge them with the treasure, after which we each took command of our own and marched out of the valley, till we reached the place in the high road where the routes diverge, and then we parted, the dervish going towards Balsora, and I to Bagdad. We embraced each other tenderly, and I poured out my gratitude for the honour he had done me, in singling me out for this great wealth, and having said a hearty farewell we turned our backs, and hastened after our camels.

I had hardly come up with mine when the demon of envy filled my soul. "What does a dervish want with riches like that?" I said to myself. "He alone has the secret of the treasure, and can always get as much as he wants," and I halted my camels by the roadside, and ran back after him.

I was a quick runner, and it did not take me very long to come up with him. "My brother," I exclaimed, as soon as I could speak, "almost at the moment of our leave-taking, a reflection occurred to me, which is perhaps new to you. You are a dervish by profession, and live a very quiet life, only caring to do good, and careless of the things of this world. You do not realise the burden that you lay upon yourself, when you gather into your hands such great wealth, besides the fact that no one, who is not accustomed to camels from his birth, can ever manage the stubborn beasts. If you are wise, you will not encumber yourself with more than thirty, and you will find those trouble enough."

"You are right," replied the dervish, who understood me quite well, but did not wish to fight the matter. "I confess I had not thought about it. Choose any ten you like, and drive them before you."

I selected ten of the best camels, and we proceeded along the road, to rejoin those I had left behind. I had got what I wanted, but I had found the dervish so easy to deal with, that I rather regretted I had not asked for ten more. I looked back. He had only gone a few paces, and I called after him.

"My brother," I said, "I am unwilling to part from you without pointing out what I think you scarcely grasp, that large experience of camel-driving is necessary to anybody who intends to keep together a troop of thirty. In your own interest, I feel sure you would be much happier if you entrusted ten more of them to me, for with my practice it is all one to me if I take two or a hundred."

H J FORD

As before, the dervish made no difficulties, and I drove off my ten camels in triumph, only leaving him with twenty for his share. I had now sixty, and anyone might have imagined that I should be content.

But, Commander of the Faithful, there is a proverb that says, "the more one has, the more one wants". So it was with me. I could not rest as long as one solitary camel remained to the dervish; and returning to him I redoubled my prayers and embraces, and promises of eternal gratitude, till the last twenty were in my hands.

"Make a good use of them, my brother," said the holy man. "Remember riches sometimes have wings if we keep them for ourselves, and the poor are at our gates expressly that we may help them."

My eyes were so blinded by gold, that I paid no heed to his wise counsel, and only looked about for something else to grasp. Suddenly I remembered the little box of ointment that the dervish had hidden, and which most likely contained a treasure more precious than all the rest. Giving him one last embrace, I observed accidentally, "What are you going to do with that little box of ointment? It seems hardly worth taking with you; you might as well let me have it. And really, a dervish who has given up the world has no need of ointment!"

Oh, if he had only refused my request! But then, supposing he had, I should have got possession of it by force, so great was the madness that had laid hold upon me. However, far from refusing it, the dervish at once held it out, saying gracefully, "Take it, my friend, and if there is anything else I can do to make you happy you must let me know."

Directly the box was in my hands I wrenched off the cover. "As you are so kind," I said, "tell me, I pray you, what are the virtues of this ointment?"

"They are most curious and interesting," replied the dervish. "If you apply a little of it to your left eye you will behold in an instant all the treasures hidden in the bowels of the earth. But beware lest you touch your right eye with it, or your sight will be destroyed for ever."

His words excited my curiosity to the highest pitch. "Make trial on me, I implore you," I cried, holding out the box to the dervish. "You will know how to do it better than I! I am burning with impatience to test its charms."

The dervish took the box I had extended to him, and, bidding me shut my left eye, touched it gently with the ointment. When I opened it again I saw spread out, as it were before me, treasures of every kind and without number. But as all this time I had been obliged to keep my right eye closed, which was very fatiguing, I begged the dervish to apply the ointment to that eye also.

"If you insist upon it I will do it," answered the dervish, "but you must remember what I told you just now – that if it touches your right eye you will become blind on the spot."

Unluckily, in spite of my having proved the truth of the dervish's words in so many instances, I was firmly convinced that he was now keeping concealed from me some hidden and precious virtue of the ointment. So I turned a deaf ear to all he said.

"My brother," I replied smiling, "I see you are joking. It is not natural that the same ointment should have two such exactly opposite effects."

"It is true all the same," answered the dervish, "and it would be well for you if you believed my word."

But I would not believe, and, dazzled by the greed of avarice, I thought that if one eye could show me riches, the other might teach me how to get possession of them. And I continued to press the dervish to anoint my right eye, but this he resolutely declined to do.

"After having conferred such benefits on you," said he, "I am loth indeed to work you such evil. Think what it is to be blind, and do not force me to do what you will repent as long as you live."

It was of no use. "My brother," I said firmly, "pray say no more, but do what I ask. You have most generously responded to my wishes up to this time, do not spoil my recollection of you for a thing of such little consequence. Let what will happen I take it on my own head, and will never reproach you."

"Since you are determined upon it," he answered with a sigh, "there is no use talking," and taking the ointment he laid some on my right eye, which was tight shut. When I tried to open it heavy clouds of darkness floated before me. I was as blind as you see me now!

"Miserable dervish!" I shrieked, "so it is true after all! Into what a bottomless pit has my lust after gold plunged me. Ah, now that my eyes are closed they are really opened. I know that all my sufferings are caused by myself alone! But, good brother, you, who are so kind and charitable, and know the secrets of such vast learning, have you nothing that will give me back my sight?"

"Unhappy man," replied the dervish, "it is not my fault that this has befallen you, but it is a just chastisement. The blindness of your heart has wrought the blindness of your body. Yes, I have secrets; that you have seen in the short time that we have known each other. But I have none that will give you back your sight. You have proved yourself unworthy of the riches that were given you. Now they have passed into my hands, whence they will flow into the hands of others less greedy and ungrateful than you."

The dervish said no more and left me, speechless with shame and confusion, and so wretched that I stood rooted to the spot, while he collected the eighty camels and proceeded on his way to Balsora. It was in vain that I entreated him not to leave me, but at least to take me within reach of the first passing caravan. He was deaf to my prayers and cries, and I should soon have been dead of hunger and misery if some merchants had not come along the track the following day and kindly brought me back to Bagdad.

From a rich man I had in one moment become a beggar; and up to this time I have lived solely on the alms that have been bestowed on me. But, in order to expiate the sin of avarice, which was my undoing, I oblige each passer-by to give me a blow.

This, Commander of the Faithful, is my story.

When the blind man had ended the Caliph addressed him: "Baba-Abdalla, truly your sin is great, but you have suffered enough. Henceforth repent in private, for I will see that enough money is given you day by day for all your wants."

At these words Baba-Abdalla flung himself at the Caliph's feet, and prayed that honour and happiness might be his portion for ever.

HJFORD

The Story of Sidi-Nouman

The Caliph, Haroun-al-Raschid, was much pleased with the tale of the blind man and the dervish, and when it was finished he turned to the young man who had ill-treated his horse, and inquired his name also. The young man replied that he was called Sidi-Nouman.

"Sidi-Nouman," observed the Caliph, "I have seen horses broken all my life long, and have even broken them myself, but I have never seen any horse broken in such a barbarous manner as by you yesterday. Everyone who looked on was indignant, and blamed you loudly. As for myself, I was so angry that I was very nearly disclosing who I was, and putting a stop to it at once. Still, you have not the air of a cruel man, and I would gladly believe that you did not act in this way without some reason. As I am told that it was not the first time, and indeed that every day you are to be seen flogging and spurring your horse, I wish to come to the bottom of the matter. But tell me the whole truth, and conceal nothing."

Sidi-Nouman changed colour as he heard these words, and his manner grew confused; but he saw plainly that there was no help for it. So he prostrated himself before the throne of the Caliph and tried to obey, but the words stuck in his throat, and he remained silent.

The Caliph, accustomed though he was to instant obedience, guessed something of what was passing in the young man's mind, and sought to put him at his ease. "Sidi-Nouman," he said, "do not think of me as the Caliph, but merely as a friend who would like to hear your story. If there is anything in it that you are afraid may offend me, take courage, for I pardon you beforehand. Speak then openly and without fear, as to one who knows and loves you."

Reassured by the kindness of the Caliph, Sidi-Nouman at length began his tale:

Commander of the Faithful, dazzled though I am by the lustre of your Highness' presence, I will do my best to satisfy your wishes. I am by no means perfect, but I am not naturally cruel, neither do I take pleasure in breaking the law. I admit that the treatment of my horse is calculated to give your Highness a bad opinion of me, and to set an evil example to others; yet I have not chastised it without reason, and I have hopes that I shall be judged more worthy of pity than punishment.

Commander of the Faithful, I will not trouble to describe my birth; it is not of sufficient distinction to deserve your Highness' attention. My ancestors were careful people, and I inherited enough money to enable me to live comfortably, though without show.

Having therefore a modest fortune, the only thing wanting to my happiness was a wife who could return my affection, but this blessing I was not destined to get; for on the very day after my marriage, my bride began to try my patience in every way that was most hard to bear.

Now, seeing that the customs of our land oblige us to marry without ever beholding the person with whom we are to pass our lives, a man has of course no right to complain as long as his wife is not absolutely repulsive, or is not positively deformed. And whatever defects her body may have, pleasant ways and good behaviour will go far to remedy them.

The first time I saw my wife unveiled, when she had been brought to my house with the usual ceremonies, I was enchanted to find that I had not been deceived in regard to the account that had been given me of her beauty. I began my married life in high spirits, and the best hopes of happiness.

The following day a grand dinner was served to us but as my wife did not appear, I ordered a servant to call her. Still she did not come, and I waited impatiently for some time. At last she entered the room, and we took our places at the table, and plates of rice were set before us.

I ate mine, as was natural, with a spoon, but great was my surprise to notice that my wife, instead of doing the same, drew from her pocket a little case, from which she selected a long pin, and by the help of this pin conveyed her rice grain by grain to her mouth.

"Amina," I exclaimed in astonishment, "is that the way you eat rice at home? And did you do it because your appetite was so small, or did you wish to count the grains so that you might never eat more than a certain number? If it was from economy, and you are anxious to teach me not to be wasteful, you have no cause for alarm. We shall never ruin ourselves in that way! Our fortune is large enough for all our needs, therefore, dear Amina, do not seek to check yourself, but eat as much as you desire, as I do!"

In reply to my affectionate words, I expected a cheerful answer; yet Amina said nothing at all, but continued to pick her rice as before, only at longer and longer intervals. And, instead of trying the other dishes, all she did was to put every now and then a crumb, of bread into her mouth, that would not have made a meal for a sparrow.

I felt provoked by her obstinacy, but to excuse her to myself as far as I could, I suggested that perhaps she had never been used to eat in the company of men, and that her family might have taught her that she ought to behave prudently and discreetly in the presence of her husband. Likewise that she might either have dined already or intend to do so in her own apartments. So I took no further notice, and when I had finished left the room, secretly much vexed at her strange conduct.

The same thing occurred at supper, and all through the next day, whenever we ate together. It was quite clear that no woman could live upon two or three bread-crumbs and a few grains of rice, and I determined to find out how and when she got food. I pretended not to pay attention to anything she did, in the hope that little by little she would get accustomed to me, and become more friendly; but I soon saw that my expectations were quite vain.

One night I was lying with my eyes closed, and to all appearance sound asleep, when Amina arose softly, and dressed herself without making the slightest sound. I could not imagine what she was going to do, and as my curiosity was great I made up my mind to follow her.

When she was fully dressed, she stole quietly from the room.

The instant she had let the curtain fall behind her, I flung a garment on my shoulders and a pair of slippers on my feet. Looking from a lattice which opened into the court, I saw her in the act of passing through the street door, which she carefully left open.

It was bright moonlight, so I easily managed to keep her in sight, till she entered a cemetery not far from the house. There I hid myself under the shadow of the wall, and crouched down cautiously; and hardly was I concealed, when I saw my wife approaching in company with a ghoul – one of those demons which, as your Highness is aware, wander about the country making their lairs in deserted buildings and springing out upon unwary travellers whose flesh they eat. If no live being goes their way, they then betake themselves to the cemeteries, and feed upon the dead bodies.

I was nearly struck dumb with horror on seeing my wife with this hideous female ghoul. They passed by me without noticing me, began to dig up a corpse which had been buried that day, and then sat down on the edge of the grave, to enjoy their frightful repast, talking quietly and cheerfully all the while, though I was too far off to hear what they said. When they had finished, they threw back the body into the grave, and heaped back the earth upon it. I made no effort to disturb them, and returned quickly to the house, when I took care to leave the door open, as I had previously found it. Then I got back into bed, and pretended to sleep soundly.

A short time after Amina entered as quietly as she had gone out. She undressed and stole into bed, congratulating herself apparently on the cleverness with which she had managed her expedition.

As may be guessed, after such a scene it was long before I could close my eyes, and at the first sound which called the faithful to prayer, I put on my clothes and went to the mosque. But even prayer did not restore peace to my troubled spirit, and I could not face my wife until I had made up my mind what future course I should pursue in regard to her. I therefore spent the morning roaming about from one garden to another, turning over various plans for compelling my wife to give up her horrible ways; I thought of using violence to make her submit, but felt reluctant to be unkind to her. Besides, I had an instinct that gentle means had the best chance of success; so, a little soothed, I turned towards home, which I reached about the hour of dinner.

As soon as I appeared, Amina ordered dinner to be served, and we sat down together. As usual, she persisted in only picking a few grains of rice, and I resolved to speak to her at once of what lay so heavily on my heart.

"Amina," I said, as quietly as possible, "you must have guessed the surprise I felt, when the day after our marriage you declined to eat anything but a few morsels of rice, and altogether behaved in such a manner that most husbands would have been deeply wounded. However I had patience with you, and only tried to tempt your appetite by the choicest dishes I could invent, but all to no purpose. Still, Amina, it seems to me that there be some among them as sweet to the taste as the flesh of a corpse?"

I had no sooner uttered these words than Amina, who instantly understood that I had followed her to the graveyard, was seized with a passion beyond any that I have ever witnessed. Her face became purple, her eyes looked as if they would start from her head, and she positively foamed with rage.

I watched her with terror, wondering what would happen next, but little thinking what would be the end of her fury. She seized a vessel of water that stood at hand, and plunging her hand in it, murmured some words I failed to catch. Then, sprinkling it on my face, she cried madly:

"Wretch, receive the reward of your prying, and become a dog."

The words were not out of her mouth when, without feeling conscious that any change was passing over me, I suddenly knew that I had ceased to be a man. In the greatness of the shock and surprise – for I had no idea that Amina was a magician – I never dreamed of running away, and stood rooted to the spot, while Amina grasped a stick and began to beat me. Indeed her blows were so heavy, that I only wonder they did not kill me at once. However they succeeded in rousing me from my stupor, and I dashed into the courtyard, followed closely by Amina, who made frantic dives at me, which I was not quick enough to dodge. At last she got tired of pursuing me, or else a new trick entered into her head, which would give me speedy and painful death; she opened the gate leading into the street, intending to crush me as I passed through. Dog though I was, I saw through her design, and stung into presence of mind by the greatness of the danger, I timed my movements so well that I contrived to rush through, and only the tip of my tail received a squeeze as she banged the gate.

I was safe, but my tail hurt me horribly, and I yelped and howled so loud all along the streets, that the other dogs came and attacked me, which made matters no better. In order to avoid them, I took refuge in a cookshop, where tongues and sheep's heads were sold.

At first the owner showed me great kindness, and drove away the other dogs that were still at my heels, while I crept into the darkest corner. But though I was safe for the moment, I was not destined to remain long under his protection, for he was one of those who hold all dogs

to be unclean, and that all the washing in the world will hardly purify you from their contact. So after my enemies had gone to seek other prey, he tried to lure me from my corner in order to force me into the street. But I refused to come out of my hole, and spent the night in sleep, which I sorely needed, after the pain inflicted on me by Amina.

I have no wish to weary your Highness by dwelling on the sad thoughts which accompanied my change of shape, but it may interest you to hear that the next morning my host went out early to do his marketing, and returned laden with the sheep's heads, and tongues and trotters that formed his stock in trade for the day. The smell of meat attracted various hungry dogs in the neighbourhood, and they gathered round the door begging for some bits. I stole out of my corner, and stood with them.

In spite of his objection to dogs, as unclean animals, my protector was a kind-hearted man, and knowing I had eaten nothing since yesterday, he threw me bigger and better bits than those which fell to the share of the other dogs. When I had finished, I tried to go back into the shop, but this he would not allow, and stood so firmly at the entrance with a stout stick, that I was forced to give it up, and seek some other home.

A few paces further on was a baker's shop, which seemed to have a gay and merry man for a master. At that moment he was having his breakfast, and though I gave no signs of hunger, he at once threw me a piece of bread. Before gobbling it up, as most dogs are in the habit of doing, I bowed my head and wagged my tail, in token of thanks, and he understood, and smiled pleasantly. I really did not want the bread at all, but felt it would be ungracious to refuse, so I ate it slowly, in order that he might see that I only did it out of politeness. He understood this also, and seemed quite willing to let me stay in his shop, so I sat down, with my face to the door, to show that I only asked his protection. This he gave me, and indeed encouraged me to come into the house itself, giving me a corner where I might sleep, without being in anybody's way.

The kindness heaped on me by this excellent man was far greater than I could ever have expected. He was always affectionate in his manner of treating me, and I shared his breakfast, dinner and supper, while, on my side, I gave him all the gratitude and attachment to which he had a right.

I sat with my eyes fixed on him, and he never left the house without having me at his heels; and if it ever happened that when he was preparing to go out I was asleep, and did not notice, he would call "Rufus, Rufus," for that was the name he gave me.

Some weeks passed in this way, when one day a woman came in to buy bread. In paying for it, she laid down several pieces of money, one of which was bad. The baker perceived this, and declined to take it, demanding another in its place. The woman, for her part, refused to take it back, declaring it was perfectly good, but the baker would have nothing to do with it. "It is really such a bad imitation," he exclaimed at last, "that even my dog would not be taken in. Here Rufus! Rufus!" and hearing his voice, I jumped on to the counter. The baker threw down the money before me, and said, "Find out if there is a bad coin." I looked at each in turn, and then laid my paw on the false one, glancing at the same time at my master, so as to point it out.

The baker, who had of course been only in joke, was exceedingly surprised at my cleverness, and the woman, who was at last convinced that the man spoke the truth, produced another piece of money in its place. When she had gone, my master was so pleased that he told all the neighbours what I had done, and made a great deal more of it than there really was.

The neighbours, very naturally, declined to believe his story, and tried me several times with all the bad money they could collect together, but I never failed to stand the test triumphantly.

Soon, the shop was filled from morning till night, with people who on the pretence of buying bread came to see if I was as clever as I was reported to be. The baker drove a roaring trade, and admitted that I was worth my weight in gold to him.

Of course there were plenty who envied him his large custom, and many was the pitfall set for me, so that he never dared to let me out of his sight. One day a woman, who had not been in the shop before, came to ask for bread, like the rest. As usual, I was lying on the counter, and she threw down six coins before me, one of which was false. I detected it at once, and put my paw on it, looking as I did so at the woman. "Yes," she said, nodding her head. "You are quite right, that is the one." She stood gazing at me attentively for some time, then paid for the bread, and left the shop, making a sign for me to follow her secretly.

Now my thoughts were always running on some means of shaking off the spell laid on me, and noticing the way in which this woman had looked at me, the idea entered my head that perhaps she might have guessed what had happened, and in this I was not deceived. However I let her go on a little way, and merely stood at the door watching her. She turned, and seeing that I was quite still, she again beckoned to me.

The baker all this while was busy with his oven, and had forgotten all about me, so I stole out softly, and ran after the woman.

When we came to her house, which was some distance off, she opened the door and then said to me, "Come in, come in; you will never be sorry that you followed me." When I had entered she fastened the door, and took me into a large room, where a beautiful girl was working at a piece of embroidery. "My daughter," exclaimed my guide, "I have brought you the famous dog belonging to the baker which can tell good money from bad. You know that when I first heard of him, I told you I was sure he must be really a man, changed into a dog by magic. Today I went to the baker's, to prove for myself the truth of the story, and persuaded the dog to follow me here. Now what do you say?"

"You are right, mother," replied the girl, and rising she dipped her hand into a vessel of water. Then sprinkling it over me she said, "If you were born dog, remain dog; but if you were born man, by virtue of this water resume your proper form." In one moment the spell was broken. The dog's shape vanished as if it had never been, and it was a man who stood before her.

Overcome with gratitude at my deliverance, I flung myself at her feet, and kissed the hem of her garment. "How can I thank you for your goodness towards a stranger, and for what you have done? Henceforth I am your slave. Deal with me as you will!"

Then, in order to explain how I came to be changed into a dog, I told her my whole story, and finished with rendering the mother the thanks due to her for the happiness she had brought me.

"Sidi-Nouman," returned the daughter, "say no more about the obligation you are under to us. The knowledge that we have been of service to you is ample payment. Let us speak of Amina, your wife, with whom I was acquainted before her marriage. I was aware that she was a magician, and she knew too that I had studied the same art, under the same mistress. We met often going to the same baths, but we did not like each other, and never sought to become friends. As to what concerns you, it is not enough to have broken your spell, she must be punished for her wickedness. Remain for a moment with my mother, I beg," she added hastily, "I will return shortly."

Left alone with the mother, I again expressed the gratitude I felt, to her as well as to her daughter.

"My daughter," she answered, "is, as you see, as accomplished a magician as Amina herself, but you would be astonished at the amount of good she does by her knowledge. That is why I have never interfered, otherwise I should have put a stop to it long ago." As she spoke, her daughter entered with a small bottle in her hand.

"Sidi-Nouman," she said, "the books I have just consulted tell me that Amina is not home at present, but she should return at any moment. I have likewise found out by their means, that she pretends before the servants great uneasiness as to your absence. She has circulated a

story that, while at dinner with her, you remembered some important business that had to be done at once, and left the house without shutting the door. By this means a dog had strayed in, which she was forced to get rid of by a stick. Go home then without delay, and await Amina's return in your room. When she comes in, go down to meet her, and in her surprise, she will try to run away. Then have this bottle ready, and dash the water it contains over her, saying boldly, 'Receive the reward of your crimes.' That is all I have to tell you."

Everything happened exactly as the young magician had foretold. I had not been in my house many minutes before Amina returned, and as she approached I stepped in front of her, with the water in my hand. She gave one loud cry, and turned to the door, but she was too late. I had already dashed the water in her face and spoken the magic words. Amina disappeared, and in her place stood the horse you saw me beating yesterday.

This, Commander of the Faithful, is my story, and may I venture to hope that, now you have heard the reason of my conduct, your Highness will not think this wicked woman too harshly treated?

"Sidi-Nouman," replied the Caliph, "your story is indeed a strange one, and there is no excuse to be offered for your wife. But, without condemning your treatment of her, I wish you to reflect how much she must suffer from being changed into an animal, and I hope you will let that punishment be enough. I do not order you to insist upon the young magician finding the means to restore your wife to her human shape, because I know that when once women such as she begin to work evil they never leave off, and I should only bring down on your head a vengeance far worse than the one you have undergone already."

The Story of Ali Cogia, Merchant of Bagdad

In the reign of Haroun-al-Raschid, there lived in Bagdad a merchant named Ali Cogia, who, having neither wife nor child, contented himself with the modest profits produced by his trade. He had spent some years quite happily in the house his father had left him, when three nights running he dreamed that an old man had appeared to him, and reproached him for having neglected the duty of a good Mussulman, in delaying so long his pilgrimage to Mecca.

Ali Cogia was much troubled by this dream, as he was unwilling to give up his shop, and lose all his customers. He had shut his eyes for some time to the necessity of performing this pilgrimage, and tried to atone to his conscience by an extra number of good works, but the dream seemed to him a direct warning, and he resolved to put the journey off no longer.

The first thing he did was to sell his furniture and the wares he had in his shop, only reserving to himself such goods as he might trade with on the road. The shop itself he sold also, and easily found a tenant for his private house. The only matter he could not settle satisfactorily was the safe custody of a thousand pieces of gold which he wished to leave behind him.

After some thought, Ali Cogia hit upon a plan which seemed a safe one. He took a large vase, and placing the money in the bottom of it, filled up the rest with olives. After corking the vase tightly down, he carried it to one of his friends, a merchant like himself, and said to him:

"My brother, you have probably heard that I am staffing with a caravan in a few days for Mecca. I have come to ask whether you would do me the favour to keep this vase of olives for me till I come back?"

The merchant replied readily, "Look, this is the key of my shop: take it, and put the vase wherever you like. I promise that you shall find it in the same place on your return."

A few days later, Ali Cogia mounted the camel that he had laden with merchandise, joined the caravan, and arrived in due time at Mecca. Like the other pilgrims he visited the sacred Mosque, and after all his religious duties were performed, he set out his goods to the best advantage, hoping to gain some customers among the passers-by.

Very soon two merchants stopped before the pile, and when they had turned it over, one said to the other:

"If this man was wise he would take these things to Cairo, where he would get a much better price than he is likely to do here."

Ali Cogia heard the words, and lost no time in following the advice. He packed up his wares, and instead of returning to Bagdad, joined a caravan that was going to Cairo. The results of the journey gladdened his heart. He sold off everything almost directly, and bought a stock of Egyptian curiosities, which he intended selling at Damascus; but as the caravan with which he would have to travel would not be starting for another six weeks, he took advantage of the delay to visit the Pyramids, and some of the cities along the banks of the Nile.

Now the attractions of Damascus so fascinated the worthy Ali, that he could hardly tear himself away, but at length he remembered that he had a home in Bagdad, meaning to return by way of Aleppo, and after he had crossed the Euphrates, to follow the course of the Tigris.

But when he reached Mossoul, Ali had made such friends with some Persian merchants, that they persuaded him to accompany them to their native land, and even as far as India, and so it came to pass that seven years had slipped by since he had left Bagdad, and during all that time the friend with whom he had left the vase of olives had never once thought of him or of it. In fact, it was only a month before Ali Cogia's actual return that the affair came into his head at all, owing to his wife's remarking one day, that it was a long time since she had eaten any olives, and would like some.

"That reminds me," said the husband, "that before Ali Cogia went to Mecca seven years ago, he left a vase of olives in my care. But really by this time he must be dead, and there is no reason we should not eat the olives if we like. Give me a light, and I will fetch them and see how they taste."

"My husband," answered the wife, "beware, I pray, of your doing anything so base! Supposing seven years have passed without news of Ali Cogia, he need not be dead for all that, and may come back any day. How shameful it would be to have to confess that you had betrayed your trust and broken the seal of the vase! Pay no attention to my idle words, I really have no desire for olives now. And probably after all this while they are no longer good. I have a presentiment that Ali Cogia will return, and what will he think of you? Give it up, I entreat."

The merchant, however, refused to listen to her advice, sensible though it was. He took a light and a dish and went into his shop.

"If you will be so obstinate," said his wife, "I cannot help it; but do not blame me if it turns out ill."

When the merchant opened the vase he found the topmost olives were rotten, and in order to see if the under ones were in better condition he shook some out into the dish. As they fell out a few of the gold pieces fell out too.

The sight of the money roused all the merchant's greed. He looked into the vase, and saw that all the bottom was filled with gold. He then replaced the olives and returned to his wife.

"My wife," he said, as he entered the room, "you were quite right; the olives are rotten, and I have recorked the vase so well that Ali Cogia will never know it has been touched."

"You would have done better to believe me," replied the wife. "I trust that no harm will come of it."

These words made no more impression on the merchant than the others had done; and he spent the whole night in wondering how he could manage to keep the gold if Ali Cogia should come back and claim his vase. Very early next morning he went out and bought fresh new olives; he then threw away the old ones, took out the gold and hid it, and filled up the vase with the olives he had bought. This done he recorked the vase and put it in the same place where it had been left by Ali Cogia.

A month later Ali Cogia re-entered Bagdad, and as his house was still let he went to an inn; and the following day set out to see his friend the merchant, who received him with open arms and many expressions of surprise. After a few moments given to inquiries Ali Cogia begged the merchant to hand him over the vase that he had taken care of for so long.

"Oh certainly," said he, "I am only glad I could be of use to you in the matter. Here is the key of my shop; you will find the vase in the place where you put it."

Ali Cogia fetched his vase and carried it to his room at the inn, where he opened it. He thrust down his hand but could feel no money, but still was persuaded it must be there. So he got some plates and vessels from his travelling kit and emptied out the olives. To no purpose. The gold was not there. The poor man was dumb with horror, then, lifting up his hands, he exclaimed, "Can my old friend really have committed such a crime?"

In great haste he went back to the house of the merchant. "My friend," he cried, "you will be astonished to see me again, but I can find nowhere in this vase a thousand pieces of gold that I placed in the bottom under the olives. Perhaps you may have taken a loan of them for your business purposes; if that is so you are most welcome. I will only ask you to give me a receipt, and you can pay the money at your leisure."

The merchant, who had expected something of the sort, had his reply all ready. "Ali Cogia," he said, "when you brought me the vase of olives did I ever touch it? I gave you the key of my

shop and you put it yourself where you liked, and did you not find it in exactly the same spot and in the same state? If you placed any gold in it, it must be there still. I know nothing about that; you only told me there were olives. You can believe me or not, but I have not laid a finger on the vase."

Ali Cogia still tried every means to persuade the merchant to admit the truth. "I love peace," he said, "and shall deeply regret having to resort to harsh measures. Once more, think of your reputation. I shall be in despair if you oblige me to call in the aid of the law."

"Ali Cogia," answered the merchant, "you allow that it was a vase of olives you placed in my charge. You fetched it and removed it yourself, and now you tell me it contained a thousand pieces of gold, and that I must restore them to you! Did you ever say anything about them before? Why, I did not even know that the vase had olives in it! You never showed them to me. I wonder you have not demanded pearls or diamonds. Retire, I pray you, lest a crowd should gather in front of my shop."

By this time not only the casual passers-by, but also the neighbouring merchants, were standing round, listening to the dispute, and trying every now and then to smooth matters between them. But at the merchant's last words Ali Cogia resolved to lay the cause of the quarrel before them, and told them the whole story. They heard him to the end, and inquired of the merchant what he had to say.

The accused man admitted that he had kept Ali Cogia's vase in his shop; but he denied having touched it, and swore that as to what it contained he only knew what Ali Cogia had told him, and called them all to witness the insult that had been put upon him.

"You have brought it on yourself," said Ali Cogia, taking him by the arm, "and as you appeal to the law, the law you shall have! Let us see if you will dare to repeat your story before the Cadi."

Now as a good Mussulman the merchant was forbidden to refuse this choice of a judge, so he accepted the test, and said to Ali Cogia, "Very well; I should like nothing better. We shall soon see which of us is in the right."

So the two men presented themselves before the Cadi, and Ali Cogia again repeated his tale. The Cadi asked what witnesses he had. Ali Cogia replied that he had not taken this precaution, as he had considered the man his friend, and up to that time had always found him honest.

The merchant, on his side, stuck to his story, and offered to swear solemnly that not only had he never stolen the thousand gold pieces, but that he did not even know they were there. The Cadi allowed him to take the oath, and pronounced him innocent.

Ali Cogia, furious at having to suffer such a loss, protested against the verdict, declaring that he would appeal to the Caliph, Haroun-al-Raschid, himself. But the Cadi paid no attention to his threats, and was quite satisfied that he had done what was right.

Judgment being given the merchant returned home triumphant, and Ali Cogia went back to his inn to draw up a petition to the Caliph. The next morning he placed himself on the road along which the Caliph must pass after mid-day prayer, and stretched out his petition to the officer who walked before the Caliph, whose duty it was to collect such things, and on entering the palace to hand them to his master. There Haroun-al-Raschid studied them carefully.

Knowing this custom, Ali Cogia followed the Caliph into the public hall of the palace, and waited the result. After some time the officer appeared, and told him that the Caliph had read his petition, and had appointed an hour the next morning to give him audience. He then inquired the merchant's address, so that he might be summoned to attend also.

That very evening, the Caliph, with his grand-vizir Giafar, and Mesrour, chief of the eunuchs, all three disguised, as was their habit, went out to take a stroll through the town.

Going down one street, the Caliph's attention was attracted by a noise, and looking through a door which opened into a court he perceived ten or twelve children playing in the moonlight. He hid himself in a dark corner, and watched them.

"Let us play at being the Cadi," said the brightest and quickest of them all; "I will be the Cadi. Bring before me Ali Cogia, and the merchant who robbed him of the thousand pieces of gold."

The boy's words recalled to the Caliph the petition he had read that morning, and he waited with interest to see what the children would do.

The proposal was hailed with joy by the other children, who had heard a great deal of talk about the matter, and they quickly settled the part each one was to play. The Cadi took his seat gravely, and an officer introduced first Ali Cogia, the plaintiff, and then the merchant who was the defendant.

Ali Cogia made a low bow, and pleaded his cause point by point; concluding by imploring the Cadi not to inflict on him such a heavy loss.

The Cadi having heard his case, turned to the merchant, and inquired why he had not repaid Ali Cogia the sum in question.

The false merchant repeated the reasons that the real merchant had given to the Cadi of Bagdad, and also offered to swear that he had told the truth.

"Stop a moment!" said the little Cadi, "before we come to oaths, I should like to examine the vase with the olives. Ali Cogia," he added, "have you got the vase with you?" and finding he had not, the Cadi continued, "Go and get it, and bring it to me."

So Ali Cogia disappeared for an instant, and then pretended to lay a vase at the feet of the Cadi, declaring it was his vase, which he had given to the accused for safe custody; and in order to be quite correct, the Cadi asked the merchant if he recognised it as the same vase. By his silence the merchant admitted the fact, and the Cadi then commanded to have the vase opened. Ali Cogia made a movement as if he was taking off the lid, and the little Cadi on his part made a pretence of peering into a vase.

"What beautiful olives!" he said, "I should like to taste one," and pretending to put one in his mouth, he added, "they are really excellent!

"But," he went on, "it seems to me odd that olives seven years old should be as good as that! Send for some dealers in olives, and let us hear what they say!"

Two children were presented to him as olive merchants, and the Cadi addressed them. "Tell me," he said, "how long can olives be kept so as to be pleasant eating?"

"My lord," replied the merchants, "however much care is taken to preserve them, they never last beyond the third year. They lose both taste and colour, and are only fit to be thrown away."

"If that is so," answered the little Cadi, "examine this vase, and tell me how long the olives have been in it."

The olive merchants pretended to examine the olives and taste them; then reported to the Cadi that they were fresh and good.

"You are mistaken," said he, "Ali Cogia declares he put them in that vase seven years ago."

"My lord," returned the olive merchants, "we can assure you that the olives are those of the present year. And if you consult all the merchants in Bagdad you will not find one to give a contrary opinion."

The accused merchant opened his mouth as if to protest, but the Cadi gave him no time. "Be silent," he said, "you are a thief. Take him away and hang him." So the game ended, the children clapping their hands in applause, and leading the criminal away to be hanged.

Haroun-al-Raschid was lost in astonishment at the wisdom of the child, who had given so wise a verdict on the case which he himself was to hear on the morrow. "Is there any other verdict possible?" he asked the grand-vizir, who was as much impressed as himself. "I can imagine no better judgment."

"If the circumstances are really such as we have heard," replied the grand-vizir, "it seems to me your Highness could only follow the example of this boy, in the method of reasoning, and also in your conclusions."

"Then take careful note of this house," said the Caliph, "and bring me the boy tomorrow, so that the affair may be tried by him in my presence. Summon also the Cadi, to learn his duty from the mouth of a child. Bid Ali Cogia bring his vase of olives, and see that two dealers in olives are present." So saying the Caliph returned to the palace.

The next morning early, the grand-vizir went back to the house where they had seen the children playing, and asked for the mistress and her children. Three boys appeared, and the grand-vizir inquired which had represented the Cadi in their game of the previous evening. The eldest and tallest, changing colour, confessed that it was he, and to his mother's great alarm, the grand-vizir said that he had strict orders to bring him into the presence of the Caliph.

"Does he want to take my son from me?" cried the poor woman; but the grand-vizir hastened to calm her, by assuring her that she should have the boy again in an hour, and she would be quite satisfied when she knew the reason of the summons. So she dressed the boy in his best clothes, and the two left the house.

When the grand-vizir presented the child to the Caliph, he was a little awed and confused, and the Caliph proceeded to explain why he had sent for him. "Approach, my son," he said kindly. "I think it was you who judged the case of Ali Cogia and the merchant last night? I overheard you by chance, and was very pleased with the way you conducted it. Today you will see the real Ali Cogia and the real merchant. Seat yourself at once next to me."

The Caliph being seated on his throne with the boy next him, the parties to the suit were ushered in. One by one they prostrated themselves, and touched the carpet at the foot of the throne with their foreheads. When they rose up, the Caliph said: "Now speak. This child will give you justice, and if more should be wanted I will see to it myself."

Ali Cogia and the merchant pleaded one after the other, but when the merchant offered to swear the same oath that he had taken before the Cadi, he was stopped by the child, who said that before this was done he must first see the vase of olives.

At these words, Ali Cogia presented the vase to the Caliph, and uncovered it. The Caliph took one of the olives, tasted it, and ordered the expert merchants to do the same. They pronounced the olives good, and fresh that year. The boy informed them that Ali Cogia declared it was seven years since he had placed them in the vase; to which they returned the same answer as the children had done.

The accused merchant saw by this time that his condemnation was certain, and tried to allege something in his defence. The boy had too much sense to order him to be hanged, and looked at the Caliph, saying, "Commander of the Faithful, this is not a game now; it is for your Highness to condemn him to death and not for me."

Then the Caliph, convinced that the man was a thief, bade them take him away and hang him, which was done, but not before he had confessed his guilt and the place in which he had hidden Ali Cogia's money. The Caliph ordered the Cadi to learn how to deal out justice from the mouth of a child, and sent the boy home, with a purse containing a hundred pieces of gold as a mark of his favour.

The Enchanted Horse

It was the Feast of the New Year, the oldest and most splendid of all the feasts in the Kingdom of Persia, and the day had been spent by the king in the city of Schiraz, taking part in the magnificent spectacles prepared by his subjects to do honour to the festival. The sun was setting, and the monarch was about to give his court the signal to retire, when suddenly an Indian appeared before his throne, leading a horse richly harnessed, and looking in every respect exactly like a real one.

"Sire," said he, prostrating himself as he spoke, "although I make my appearance so late before your Highness, I can confidently assure you that none of the wonders you have seen during the day can be compared to this horse, if you will deign to cast your eyes upon him."

"I see nothing in it," replied the king, "except a clever imitation of a real one; and any skilled workman might do as much."

"Sire," returned the Indian, "it is not of his outward form that I would speak, but of the use that I can make of him. I have only to mount him, and to wish myself in some special place, and no matter how distant it may be, in a very few moments I shall find myself there. It is this, Sire, that makes the horse so marvellous, and if your Highness will allow me, you can prove it for yourself."

The King of Persia, who was interested in everything out of the common, and had never before come across a horse with such qualities, bade the Indian mount the animal, and show what he could do. In an instant the man had vaulted on his back, and inquired where the monarch wished to send him.

"Do you see that mountain?" asked the king, pointing to a huge mass that towered into the sky about three leagues from Schiraz; "go and bring me the leaf of a palm that grows at the foot."

The words were hardly out of the king's mouth when the Indian turned a screw placed in the horse's neck, close to the saddle, and the animal bounded like lightning up into the air, and was soon beyond the sight even of the sharpest eyes. In a quarter of an hour the Indian was seen returning, bearing in his hand the palm, and, guiding his horse to the foot of the throne, he dismounted, and laid the leaf before the king.

Now the monarch had no sooner proved the astonishing speed of which the horse was capable than he longed to possess it himself, and indeed, so sure was he that the Indian would be quite ready to sell it, that he looked upon it as his own already.

"I never guessed from his mere outside how valuable an animal he was," he remarked to the Indian, "and I am grateful to you for having shown me my error," said he. "If you will sell it, name your own price."

"Sire," replied the Indian, "I never doubted that a sovereign so wise and accomplished as your Highness would do justice to my horse, when he once knew its power; and I even went so far as to think it probable that you might wish to possess it. Greatly as I prize it, I will yield it up to your Highness on one condition. The horse was not constructed by me, but it was given me by the inventor, in exchange for my only daughter, who made me take a solemn oath that I would never part with it, except for some object of equal value."

"Name anything you like," cried the monarch, interrupting him. "My kingdom is large, and filled with fair cities. You have only to choose which you would prefer, to become its ruler to the end of your life."

"Sire," answered the Indian, to whom the proposal did not seem nearly so generous as it appeared to the king, "I am most grateful to your Highness for your princely offer, and beseech you not to be offended with me if I say that I can only deliver up my horse in exchange for the hand of the princess your daughter."

A shout of laughter burst from the courtiers as they heard these words, and Prince Firouz Schah, the heir apparent, was filled with anger at the Indian's presumption. The king, however, thought that it would not cost him much to part from the princess in order to gain such a delightful toy, and while he was hesitating as to his answer the prince broke in.

"Sire," he said, "it is not possible that you can doubt for an instant what reply you should give to such an insolent bargain. Consider what you owe to yourself, and to the blood of your ancestors."

"My son," replied the king, "you speak nobly, but you do not realise either the value of the horse, or the fact that if I reject the proposal of the Indian, he will only make the same to some other monarch, and I should be filled with despair at the thought that anyone but myself should own this Seventh Wonder of the World. Of course I do not say that I shall accept his conditions, and perhaps he may be brought to reason, but meanwhile I should like you to examine the horse, and, with the owner's permission, to make trial of its powers."

The Indian, who had overheard the king's speech, thought that he saw in it signs of yielding to his proposal, so he joyfully agreed to the monarch's wishes, and came forward to help the prince to mount the horse, and show him how to guide it: but, before he had finished, the young man turned the screw, and was soon out of sight.

They waited some time, expecting that every moment he might be seen returning in the distance, but at length the Indian grew frightened, and prostrating himself before the throne, he said to the king, "Sire, your Highness must have noticed that the prince, in his impatience, did not allow me to tell him what it was necessary to do in order to return to the place from which he started. I implore you not to punish me for what was not my fault, and not to visit on me any misfortune that may occur."

"But why," cried the king in a burst of fear and anger, "why did you not call him back when you saw him disappearing?"

"Sire," replied the Indian, "the rapidity of his movements took me so by surprise that he was out of hearing before I recovered my speech. But we must hope that he will perceive and turn a second screw, which will have the effect of bringing the horse back to earth."

"But supposing he does!" answered the king, "what is to hinder the horse from descending straight into the sea, or dashing him to pieces on the rocks?"

"Have no fears, your Highness," said the Indian; "the horse has the gift of passing over seas, and of carrying his rider wherever he wishes to go."

"Well, your head shall answer for it," returned the monarch, "and if in three months he is not safe back with me, or at any rate does not send me news of his safety, your life shall pay the penalty." So saying, he ordered his guards to seize the Indian and throw him into prison.

Meanwhile, Prince Firouz Schah had gone gaily up into the air, and for the space of an hour continued to ascend higher and higher, till the very mountains were not distinguishable from the plains. Then he began to think it was time to come down, and took for granted that, in order to do this, it was only needful to turn the screw the reverse way; but, to his surprise and horror, he found that, turn as he might, he did not make the smallest impression. He then remembered that he had never waited to ask how he was to get back to earth again, and understood the danger in which he stood. Luckily, he did not lose his head, and set about examining the horse's neck with great care, till at last, to his intense joy, he discovered a tiny little peg, much smaller than the other, close to the right ear. This he turned, and found himself dropping to the earth, though more slowly than he had left it.

It was now dark, and as the prince could see nothing, he was obliged, not without some feeling of disquiet, to allow the horse to direct his own course, and midnight was already passed before Prince Firouz Schah again touched the ground, faint and weary from his long ride, and from the fact that he had eaten nothing since early morning.

The first thing he did on dismounting was to try to find out where he was, and, as far as he could discover in the thick darkness, he found himself on the terraced roof of a huge palace, with a balustrade of marble running round. In one corner of the terrace stood a small door, opening on to a staircase which led down into the palace.

Some people might have hesitated before exploring further, but not so the prince. "I am doing no harm," he said, "and whoever the owner may be, he will not touch me when he sees I am unarmed," and in dread of making a false step, he went cautiously down the staircase. On a landing, he noticed an open door, beyond which was a faintly lighted hall.

Before entering, the prince paused and listened, but he heard nothing except the sound of men snoring. By the light of a lantern suspended from the roof, he perceived a row of guards sleeping, each with a naked sword lying by him, and he understood that the hall must form the ante-room to the chamber of some queen or princess.

Standing quite still, Prince Firouz Schah looked about him, till his eyes grew accustomed to the gloom, and he noticed a bright light shining through a curtain in one corner. He then made his way softly towards it, and, drawing aside its folds, passed into a magnificent chamber full of sleeping women, all lying on low couches, except one, who was on a sofa; and this one, he knew, must be the princess.

Gently stealing up to the side of her bed he looked at her, and saw that she was more beautiful than any woman he had ever beheld. But, fascinated though he was, he was well aware of the danger of his position, as one cry of surprise would awake the guards, and cause his certain death.

So sinking quietly on his knees, he took hold of the sleeve of the princess and drew her arm lightly towards him. The princess opened her eyes, and seeing before her a handsome well-dressed man, she remained speechless with astonishment.

This favourable moment was seized by the prince, who bowing low while he knelt, thus addressed her:

"You behold, madame, a prince in distress, son to the King of Persia, who, owing to an adventure so strange that you will scarcely believe it, finds himself here, a suppliant for your protection. But yesterday, I was in my father's court, engaged in the celebration of our most solemn festival; today, I am in an unknown land, in danger of my life."

Now the princess whose mercy Prince Firouz Schah implored was the eldest daughter of the King of Bengal, who was enjoying rest and change in the palace her father had built her, at a little distance from the capital. She listened kindly to what he had to say, and then answered:

"Prince, be not uneasy; hospitality and humanity are practised as widely in Bengal as they are in Persia. The protection you ask will be given you by all. You have my word for it." And as the prince was about to thank her for her goodness, she added quickly, "However great may be my curiosity to learn by what means you have travelled here so speedily, I know that you must be faint for want of food, so I shall give orders to my women to take you to one of my chambers, where you will be provided with supper, and left to repose."

By this time the princess's attendants were all awake, and listening to the conversation. At a sign from their mistress they rose, dressed themselves hastily, and snatching up some of the tapers which lighted the room, conducted the prince to a large and lofty room, where two of the number prepared his bed, and the rest went down to the kitchen, from which they soon returned with all sorts of dishes. Then, showing him cupboards filled with dresses and linen, they quitted the room.

During their absence the Princess of Bengal, who had been greatly struck by the beauty of the prince, tried in vain to go to sleep again. It was of no use: she felt broad awake, and when her women entered the room, she inquired eagerly if the prince had all he wanted, and what they thought of him.

"Madame," they replied, "it is of course impossible for us to tell what impression this young man has made on you. For ourselves, we think you would be fortunate if the king your father should allow you to marry anyone so amiable. Certainly there is no one in the Court of Bengal who can be compared with him."

These flattering observations were by no means displeasing to the princess, but as she did not wish to betray her own feelings she merely said, "You are all a set of chatterboxes; go back to bed, and let me sleep."

When she dressed the following morning, her maids noticed that, contrary to her usual habit, the princess was very particular about her toilette, and insisted on her hair being dressed two or three times over. "For," she said to herself, "if my appearance was not displeasing to the prince when he saw me in the condition I was, how much more will he be struck with me when he beholds me with all my charms."

Then she placed in her hair the largest and most brilliant diamonds she could find, with a necklace, bracelets and girdle, all of precious stones. And over her shoulders her ladies put a robe of the richest stuff in all the Indies, that no one was allowed to wear except members of the royal family. When she was fully dressed according to her wishes, she sent to know if the Prince of Persia was awake and ready to receive her, as she desired to present herself before him.

When the princess's messenger entered his room, Prince Firouz Schah was in the act of leaving it, to inquire if he might be allowed to pay his homage to her mistress: but on hearing the princess's wishes, he at once gave way. "Her will is my law," he said, "I am only here to obey her orders."

In a few moments the princess herself appeared, and after the usual compliments had passed between them, the princess sat down on a sofa, and began to explain to the prince her reasons for not giving him an audience in her own apartments. "Had I done so," she said, "we might have been interrupted at any hour by the chief of the eunuchs, who has the right to enter whenever it pleases him, whereas this is forbidden ground. I am all impatience to learn the wonderful accident which has procured the pleasure of your arrival, and that is why I have come to you here, where no one can intrude upon us. Begin then, I entreat you, without delay."

So the prince began at the beginning, and told all the story of the festival of Nedrouz held yearly in Persia, and of the splendid spectacles celebrated in its honour. But when he came to the enchanted horse, the princess declared that she could never have imagined anything half so surprising. "Well then," continued the prince, "you can easily understand how the king my father, who has a passion for all curious things, was seized with a violent desire to possess this horse, and asked the Indian what sum he would take for it.

"The man's answer was absolutely absurd, as you will agree, when I tell you that it was nothing less than the hand of the princess my sister; but though all the bystanders laughed and mocked, and I was beside myself with rage, I saw to my despair that my father could not make up his mind to treat the insolent proposal as it deserved. I tried to argue with him, but in vain. He only begged me to examine the horse with a view (as I quite understood) of making me more sensible of its value.

"To please my father, I mounted the horse, and, without waiting for any instructions from the Indian, turned the peg as I had seen him do. In an instant I was soaring upwards, much quicker than an arrow could fly, and I felt as if I must be getting so near the sky that I should soon hit my head against it! I could see nothing beneath me, and for some time was so confused that I did not even know in what direction I was travelling. At last, when it was growing dark, I found another screw, and on turning it, the horse began slowly to sink towards the earth. I was forced to trust to chance, and to see what fate had in store, and it was already past midnight when I found myself on the roof of this palace. I crept down the little staircase, and made directly for a light which I perceived through an open door – I peeped cautiously in, and saw, as you will guess, the eunuchs lying asleep on the floor. I knew the risks I ran, but my need was so great that I paid no attention to them, and stole safely past your guards, to the curtain which concealed your doorway.

"The rest, Princess, you know; and it only remains for me to thank you for the kindness you have shown me, and to assure you of my gratitude. By the law of nations, I am already your slave, and I have only my heart, that is my own, to offer you. But what am I saying? My own? Alas, madame, it was yours from the first moment I beheld you!"

The air with which he said these words could have left no doubt on the mind of the princess as to the effect of her charms, and the blush which mounted to her face only increased her beauty.

"Prince," returned she as soon as her confusion permitted her to speak, "you have given me the greatest pleasure, and I have followed you closely in all your adventures, and though you are positively sitting before me, I even trembled at your danger in the upper regions of the air!

Let me say what a debt I owe to the chance that has led you to my house; you could have entered none which would have given you a warmer welcome. As to your being a slave, of course that is merely a joke, and my reception must itself have assured you that you are as free here as at your father's court. As to your heart," continued she in tones of encouragement, "I am quite sure *that* must have been disposed of long ago, to some princess who is well worthy of it, and I could not think of being the cause of your unfaithfulness to her."

Prince Firouz Schah was about to protest that there was no lady with any prior claims, but he was stopped by the entrance of one of the princess's attendants, who announced that dinner was served, and, after all, neither was sorry for the interruption.

Dinner was laid in a magnificent apartment, and the table was covered with delicious fruits; while during the repast richly dressed girls sang softly and sweetly to stringed instruments. After the prince and princess had finished, they passed into a small room hung with blue and gold, looking out into a garden stocked with flowers and arbutus trees, quite different from any that were to be found in Persia.

"Princess," observed the young man, "till now I had always believed that Persia could boast finer palaces and more lovely gardens than any kingdom upon earth. But my eyes have been opened, and I begin to perceive that, wherever there is a great king he will surround himself with buildings worthy of him."

"Prince," replied the Princess of Bengal, "I have no idea what a Persian palace is like, so I am unable to make comparisons. I do not wish to depreciate my own palace, but I can assure you that it is very poor beside that of the king my father, as you will agree when you have been there to greet him, as I hope you will shortly do."

Now the princess hoped that, by bringing about a meeting between the prince and her father, the king would be so struck with the young man's distinguished air and fine manners, that he would offer him his daughter to wife. But the reply of the Prince of Persia to her suggestion was not quite what she wished.

"Madame," he said, "by taking advantage of your proposal to visit the palace of the King of Bengal, I should satisfy not merely my curiosity, but also the sentiments of respect with which I regard him. But, Princess, I am persuaded that you will feel with me, that I cannot possibly present myself before so great a sovereign without the attendants suitable to my rank. He would think me an adventurer."

"If that is all," she answered, "you can get as many attendants here as you please. There are plenty of Persian merchants, and as for money, my treasury is always open to you. Take what you please."

Prince Firouz Schah guessed what prompted so much kindness on the part of the princess, and was much touched by it. Still his passion, which increased every moment, did not make him forget his duty. So he replied without hesitation:

"I do not know, Princess, how to express my gratitude for your obliging offer, which I would accept at once if it were not for the recollection of all the uneasiness the king my father must be suffering on my account. I should be unworthy indeed of all the love he showers upon me, if I did not return to him at the first possible moment. For, while I am enjoying the society of the most amiable of all princesses, he is, I am quite convinced, plunged in the deepest grief, having lost all hope of seeing me again. I am sure you will understand my position, and will feel that to remain away one instant longer than is necessary would not only be ungrateful on my part, but perhaps even a crime, for how do I know if my absence may not break his heart?

"But," continued the prince, "having obeyed the voice of my conscience, I shall count the moments when, with your gracious permission, I may present myself before the King of Bengal, not as a wanderer, but as a prince, to implore the favour of your hand. My father has always informed me that in my marriage I shall be left quite free, but I am persuaded that I have only to describe your generosity, for my wishes to become his own."

The Princess of Bengal was too reasonable not to accept the explanation offered by Prince Firouz Schah, but she was much disturbed at his intention of departing at once, for she feared that, no sooner had he left her, than the impression she had made on him would fade away. So she made one more effort to keep him, and after assuring him that she entirely approved of his anxiety to see his father, begged him to give her a day or two more of his company.

In common politeness the prince could hardly refuse this request, and the princess set about inventing every kind of amusement for him, and succeeded so well that two months slipped by almost unnoticed, in balls, spectacles and in hunting, of which, when unattended by danger, the princess was passionately fond. But at last, one day, he declared seriously that he could neglect his duty no longer, and entreated her to put no further obstacles in his way, promising at the same time to return, as soon as he could, with all the magnificence due both to her and to himself.

"Princess," he added, "it may be that in your heart you class me with those false lovers whose devotion cannot stand the test of absence. If you do, you wrong me; and were it not for fear of offending you, I would beseech you to come with me, for my life can only be happy when passed with you. As for your reception at the Persian Court, it will be as warm as your merits deserve; and as for what concerns the King of Bengal, he must be much more indifferent to your welfare than you have led me to believe if he does not give his consent to our marriage."

The princess could not find words in which to reply to the arguments of the Prince of Persia, but her silence and her downcast eyes spoke for her, and declared that she had no objection to accompanying him on his travels.

The only difficulty that occurred to her was that Prince Firouz Schah did not know how to manage the horse, and she dreaded lest they might find themselves in the same plight as before. But the prince soothed her fears so successfully, that she soon had no other thought than to arrange for their flight so secretly, that no one in the palace should suspect it.

This was done, and early the following morning, when the whole palace was wrapped in sleep, she stole up on to the roof, where the prince was already awaiting her, with his horse's head towards Persia. He mounted first and helped the princess up behind; then, when she was firmly seated, with her hands holding tightly to his belt, he touched the screw, and the horse began to leave the earth quickly behind him.

He travelled with his accustomed speed, and Prince Firouz Schah guided him so well that in two hours and a half from the time of starting, he saw the capital of Persia lying beneath him. He determined to alight neither in the great square from which he had started, nor in the Sultan's palace, but in a country house at a little distance from the town. Here he showed the princess a beautiful suite of rooms, and begged her to rest, while he informed his father of their arrival, and prepared a public reception worthy of her rank. Then he ordered a horse to be saddled, and set out.

All the way through the streets he was welcomed with shouts of joy by the people, who had long lost all hope of seeing him again. On reaching the palace, he found the Sultan surrounded by his ministers, all clad in the deepest mourning, and his father almost went out of his mind with surprise and delight at the mere sound of his son's voice. When he had calmed down a little, he begged the prince to relate his adventures.

The prince at once seized the opening thus given him, and told the whole story of his treatment by the Princess of Bengal, not even concealing the fact that she had fallen in love with him. "And, Sire," ended the prince, "having given my royal word that you would not refuse your consent to our marriage, I persuaded her to return with me on the Indian's horse. I have left her in one of your Highness's country houses, where she is waiting anxiously to be assured that I have not promised in vain."

As he said this the prince was about to throw himself at the feet of the Sultan, but his father prevented him, and embracing him again, said eagerly:

"My son, not only do I gladly consent to your marriage with the Princess of Bengal, but I will hasten to pay my respects to her, and to thank her in my own person for the benefits she has conferred on you. I will then bring her back with me, and make all arrangements for the wedding to be celebrated today."

So the Sultan gave orders that the habits of mourning worn by the people should be thrown off and that there should be a concert of drums, trumpets and cymbals. Also that the Indian should be taken from prison, and brought before him.

His commands were obeyed, and the Indian was led into his presence, surrounded by guards. "I have kept you locked up," said the Sultan, "so that in case my son was lost, your life should pay the penalty. He has now returned; so take your horse, and begone for ever."

The Indian hastily quitted the presence of the Sultan, and when he was outside, he inquired of the man who had taken him out of prison where the prince had really been all this time, and what he had been doing. They told him the whole story, and how the Princess of Bengal was even then awaiting in the country palace the consent of the Sultan, which at once put into the Indian's head a plan of revenge for the treatment he had experienced. Going straight to the country house, he informed the doorkeeper who was left in charge that he had been sent by the Sultan and by the Prince of Persia to fetch the princess on the enchanted horse, and to bring her to the palace.

The doorkeeper knew the Indian by sight, and was of course aware that nearly three months before he had been thrown into prison by the Sultan; and seeing him at liberty, the man took for granted that he was speaking the truth, and made no difficulty about leading him before the Princess of Bengal; while on her side, hearing that he had come from the prince, the lady gladly consented to do what he wished.

The Indian, delighted with the success of his scheme, mounted the horse, assisted the princess to mount behind him, and turned the peg at the very moment that the prince was leaving the palace in Schiraz for the country house, followed closely by the Sultan and all the court. Knowing this, the Indian deliberately steered the horse right above the city, in order that his revenge for his unjust imprisonment might be all the quicker and sweeter.

When the Sultan of Persia saw the horse and its riders, he stopped short with astonishment and horror, and broke out into oaths and curses, which the Indian heard quite unmoved, knowing that he was perfectly safe from pursuit. But mortified and furious as the Sultan was, his feelings were nothing to those of Prince Firouz Schah, when he saw the object of his passionate devotion being borne rapidly away. And while he was struck speechless with grief and remorse at not having guarded her better, she vanished swiftly out of his sight. What was he to do? Should he follow his father into the palace, and there give reins to his despair? Both his love and his courage alike forbade it; and he continued his way to the palace.

The sight of the prince showed the doorkeeper of what folly he had been guilty, and flinging himself at his master's feet, implored his pardon. "Rise," said the prince, "I am the cause of this misfortune, and not you. Go and find me the dress of a dervish, but beware of saying it is for me."

At a short distance from the country house, a convent of dervishes was situated, and the superior, or scheih, was the doorkeeper's friend. So by means of a false story made up on the spur of the moment, it was easy enough to get hold of a dervish's dress, which the prince at once put on, instead of his own. Disguised like this and concealing about him a box of pearls and diamonds he had intended as a present to the princess, he left the house at nightfall, uncertain where he should go, but firmly resolved not to return without her.

Meanwhile the Indian had turned the horse in such a direction that, before many hours had passed, it had entered a wood close to the capital of the kingdom of Cashmere. Feeling very hungry, and supposing that the princess also might be in want of food, he brought his steed down to the earth, and left the princess in a shady place, on the banks of a clear stream.

At first, when the princess had found herself alone, the idea had occurred to her of trying to escape and hide herself. But as she had eaten scarcely anything since she had left Bengal, she felt she was too weak to venture far, and was obliged to abandon her design. On the return of the Indian with meats of various kinds, she began to eat voraciously, and soon had regained sufficient courage to reply with spirit to his insolent remarks. Goaded by his threats she sprang to her feet, calling loudly for help, and luckily her cries were heard by a troop of horsemen, who rode up to inquire what was the matter.

Now the leader of these horsemen was the Sultan of Cashmere, returning from the chase, and he instantly turned to the Indian to inquire who he was, and whom he had with him. The Indian rudely answered that it was his wife, and there was no occasion for anyone else to interfere between them.

The princess, who, of course, was ignorant of the rank of her deliverer, denied altogether the Indian's story. "My lord," she cried, "whoever you may be, put no faith in this impostor. He is an abominable magician, who has this day torn me from the Prince of Persia, my destined husband, and has brought me here on this enchanted horse." She would have continued, but her tears choked her, and the Sultan of Cashmere, convinced by her beauty and her distinguished air of the truth of her tale, ordered his followers to cut off the Indian's head, which was done immediately.

But rescued though she was from one peril, it seemed as if she had only fallen into another. The Sultan commanded a horse to be given her, and conducted her to his own palace, where he led her to a beautiful apartment, and selected female slaves to wait on her, and eunuchs to be her guard. Then, without allowing her time to thank him for all he had done, he bade her repose, saying she should tell him her adventures on the following day.

The princess fell asleep, flattering herself that she had only to relate her story for the Sultan to be touched by compassion, and to restore her to the prince without delay. But a few hours were to undeceive her.

When the King of Cashmere had quitted her presence the evening before, he had resolved that the sun should not set again without the princess becoming his wife, and at daybreak proclamation of his intention was made throughout the town, by the sound of drums, trumpets, cymbals, and other instruments calculated to fill the heart with joy. The Princess of Bengal was early awakened by the noise, but she did not for one moment imagine that it had anything to do with her, till the Sultan, arriving as soon as she was dressed to inquire after her health, informed her that the trumpet blasts she heard were part of the solemn marriage ceremonies, for which he begged her to prepare. This unexpected announcement caused the princess such terror that she sank down in a dead faint.

The slaves that were in waiting ran to her aid, and the Sultan himself did his best to bring her back to consciousness, but for a long while it was all to no purpose. At length her senses began slowly to come back to her, and then, rather than break faith with the Prince of Persia by consenting to such a marriage, she determined to feign madness. So she began by saying all sorts of absurdities, and using all kinds of strange gestures, while the Sultan stood watching her with sorrow and surprise. But as this sudden seizure showed no sign of abating, he left her to her women, ordering them to take the greatest care of her. Still, as the day went on, the malady seemed to become worse, and by night it was almost violent.

Days passed in this manner, till at last the Sultan of Cashmere decided to summon all the doctors of his court to consult together over her sad state. Their answer was that madness is of so many different kinds that it was impossible to give an opinion on the case without seeing the princess, so the Sultan gave orders that they were to be introduced into her chamber, one by one, every man according to his rank.

This decision had been foreseen by the princess, who knew quite well that if once she allowed the physicians to feel her pulse, the most ignorant of them would discover that she was in perfectly good health, and that her madness was feigned, so as each man approached, she broke out into such violent paroxysms, that not one dared to lay a finger on her. A few, who pretended to be cleverer than the rest, declared that they could diagnose sick people only from sight, ordered her certain potions, which she made no difficulty about taking, as she was persuaded they were all harmless.

When the Sultan of Cashmere saw that the court doctors could do nothing towards curing the princess, he called in those of the city, who fared no better. Then he had recourse to the most celebrated physicians in the other large towns, but finding that the task was beyond their science, he finally sent messengers into the other neighbouring states, with a memorandum containing full particulars of the princess's madness, offering at the same time to pay the expenses of any physician who would come and see for himself, and a handsome reward to the one who should cure her. In answer to this proclamation many foreign professors flocked into Cashmere, but they naturally were not more successful than the rest had been, as the cure depended neither on them nor their skill, but only on the princess herself.

It was during this time that Prince Firouz Schah, wandering sadly and hopelessly from place to place, arrived in a large city of India, where he heard a great deal of talk about the Princess of Bengal who had gone out of her senses, on the very day that she was to have been married to the Sultan of Cashmere. This was quite enough to induce him to take the road to Cashmere, and to inquire at the first inn at which he lodged in the capital the full particulars of the story. When he knew that he had at last found the princess whom he had so long lost, he set about devising a plan for her rescue.

The first thing he did was to procure a doctor's robe, so that his dress, added to the long beard he had allowed to grow on his travels, might unmistakably proclaim his profession. He then lost no time in going to the palace, where he obtained an audience of the chief usher, and while apologising for his boldness in presuming to think that he could cure the princess, where so many others had failed, declared that he had the secret of certain remedies, which had hitherto never failed of their effect.

The chief usher assured him that he was heartily welcome, and that the Sultan would receive him with pleasure; and in case of success, he would gain a magnificent reward.

When the Prince of Persia, in the disguise of a physician, was brought before him, the Sultan wasted no time in talking, beyond remarking that the mere sight of a doctor threw the princess into transports of rage. He then led the prince up to a room under the roof, which had an opening through which he might observe the princess, without himself being seen.

The prince looked, and beheld the princess reclining on a sofa with tears in her eyes, singing softly to herself a song bewailing her sad destiny, which had deprived her, perhaps for ever, of a being she so tenderly loved. The young man's heart beat fast as he listened, for he needed no further proof that her madness was feigned, and that it was love of him which had caused her to resort to this species of trick. He softly left his hiding-place, and returned to the Sultan, to whom he reported that he was sure from certain signs that the princess's malady was not incurable, but that he must see her and speak with her alone.

The Sultan made no difficulty in consenting to this, and commanded that he should be ushered in to the princess's apartment. The moment she caught sight of his physician's robe, she sprang from her seat in a fury, and heaped insults upon him. The prince took no notice of her behaviour, and approaching quite close, so that his words might be heard by her alone, he said in a low whisper, "Look at me, princess, and you will see that I am no doctor, but the Prince of Persia, who has come to set you free."

At the sound of his voice, the Princess of Bengal suddenly grew calm, and an expression of joy overspread her face, such as only comes when what we wish for most and expect the least suddenly happens to us. For some time she was too enchanted to speak, and Prince Firouz Schah took advantage of her silence to explain to her all that had occurred, his despair at watching her disappear before his very eyes, the oath he had sworn to follow her over the world, and his rapture at finally discovering her in the palace at Cashmere. When he had finished, he begged in his turn that the princess would tell him how she had come there, so that he might the better devise some means of rescuing her from the tyranny of the Sultan.

It needed but a few words from the princess to make him acquainted with the whole situation, and how she had been forced to play the part of a mad woman in order to escape from a marriage with the Sultan, who had not had sufficient politeness even to ask her consent. If necessary, she added, she had resolved to die sooner than permit herself to be forced into such a union, and break faith with a prince whom she loved.

The prince then inquired if she knew what had become of the enchanted horse since the Indian's death, but the princess could only reply that she had heard nothing about it. Still she did not suppose that the horse could have been forgotten by the Sultan, after all she had told him of its value.

To this the prince agreed, and they consulted together over a plan by which she might be able to make her escape and return with him into Persia. And as the first step, she was to dress herself with care, and receive the Sultan with civility when he visited her next morning.

The Sultan was transported with delight on learning the result of the interview, and his opinion of the doctor's skill was raised still higher when, on the following day, the princess behaved towards him in such a way as to persuade him that her complete cure would not be long delayed. However he contented himself with assuring her how happy he was to see her health so much improved, and exhorted her to make every use of so clever a physician, and to repose entire confidence in him. Then he retired, without awaiting any reply from the princess.

The Prince of Persia left the room at the same time, and asked if he might be allowed humbly to inquire by what means the Princess of Bengal had reached Cashmere, which was so far distant from her father's kingdom, and how she came to be there alone. The Sultan thought the question very natural, and told him the same story that the Princess of Bengal had done, adding that he had ordered the enchanted horse to be taken to his treasury as a curiosity, though he was quite ignorant how it could be used.

"Sire," replied the physician, "your Highness's tale has supplied me with the clue I needed to complete the recovery of the princess. During her voyage hither on an enchanted horse, a portion of its enchantment has by some means been communicated to her person, and it can only be dissipated by certain perfumes of which I possess the secret. If your Highness will deign to consent, and to give the court and the people one of the most astonishing spectacles they have ever witnessed, command the horse to be brought into the big square outside the palace, and leave the rest to me. I promise that in a very few moments, in presence of all the assembled multitude, you shall see the princess as healthy both in mind and body as ever she was in her life. And in order to make the spectacle as impressive as possible, I would suggest that she should be richly dressed and covered with the noblest jewels of the crown."

The Sultan readily agreed to all that the prince proposed, and the following morning he desired that the enchanted horse should be taken from the treasury, and brought into the great square of the palace. Soon the rumour began to spread through the town, that something extraordinary was about to happen, and such a crowd began to collect that the guards had to be called out to keep order, and to make a way for the enchanted horse.

When all was ready, the Sultan appeared, and took his place on a platform, surrounded by the chief nobles and officers of his court. When they were seated, the Princess of Bengal was seen leaving the palace, accompanied by the ladies who had been assigned to her by the Sultan. She slowly approached the enchanted horse, and with the help of her ladies, she mounted on its back. Directly she was in the saddle, with her feet in the stirrups and the bridle in her hand, the physician placed around the horse some large braziers full of burning coals, into each of which he threw a perfume composed of all sorts of delicious scents. Then he crossed his hands

over his breast, and with lowered eyes walked three times round the horse, muttering the while certain words. Soon there arose from the burning braziers a thick smoke which almost concealed both the horse and princess, and this was the moment for which he had been waiting. Springing lightly up behind the lady, he leaned forward and turned the peg, and as the horse darted up into the air, he cried aloud so that his words were heard by all present, "Sultan of Cashmere, when you wish to marry princesses who have sought your protection, learn first to gain their consent."

It was in this way that the Prince of Persia rescued the Princess of Bengal, and returned with her to Persia, where they descended this time before the palace of the king himself. The marriage was only delayed just long enough to make the ceremony as brilliant as possible, and, as soon as the rejoicings were over, an ambassador was sent to the King of Bengal, to inform him of what had passed, and to ask his approbation of the alliance between the two countries, which he heartily gave.

The Story of Two Sisters who were Jealous of their Younger Sister

Once upon a time there reigned over Persia a Sultan named Kosrouschah, who from his boyhood had been fond of putting on a disguise and seeking adventures in all parts of the city, accompanied by one of his officers, disguised like himself. And no sooner was his father buried and the ceremonies over that marked his accession to the throne, than the young man hastened to throw off his robes of state, and calling to his vizir to make ready likewise, stole out in the simple dress of a private citizen into the less known streets of the capital.

Passing down a lonely street, the Sultan heard women's voices in loud discussion; and peeping through a crack in the door, he saw three sisters, sitting on a sofa in a large hall, talking in a very lively and earnest manner. Judging from the few words that reached his ear, they were each explaining what sort of men they wished to marry.

"I ask nothing better," cried the eldest, "than to have the Sultan's baker for a husband. Think of being able to eat as much as one wanted, of that delicious bread that is baked for his Highness alone! Let us see if your wish is as good as mine."

"I," replied the second sister, "should be quite content with the Sultan's head cook. What delicate stews I should feast upon! And, as I am persuaded that the Sultan's bread is used all through the palace, I should have that into the bargain. You see, my dear sister, my taste is as good as yours."

It was now the turn of the youngest sister, who was by far the most beautiful of the three, and had, besides, more sense than the other two. "As for me," she said, "I should take a higher flight; and if we are to wish for husbands, nothing less than the Sultan himself will do for me."

The Sultan was so much amused by the conversation he had overheard, that he made up his mind to gratify their wishes, and turning to the grand-vizir, he bade him note the house, and on the following morning to bring the ladies into his presence.

The grand-vizir fulfilled his commission, and hardly giving them time to change their dresses, desired the three sisters to follow him to the palace. Here they were presented one by one, and when they had bowed before the Sultan, the sovereign abruptly put the question to them:

"Tell me, do you remember what you wished for last night, when you were making merry? Fear nothing, but answer me the truth."

These words, which were so unexpected, threw the sisters into great confusion, their eyes fell, and the blushes of the youngest did not fail to make an impression on the heart of the Sultan. All three remained silent, and he hastened to continue: "Do not be afraid, I have not the slightest intention of giving you pain, and let me tell you at once, that I know the wishes formed by each one. You," he said, turning to the youngest, "who desired to have me for a husband, shall be satisfied this very day. And you," he added, addressing himself to the other two, "shall be married at the same moment to my baker and to my chief cook."

When the Sultan had finished speaking the three sisters flung themselves at his feet, and the youngest faltered out, "Oh, sire, since you know my foolish words, believe, I pray you, that they were only said in joke. I am unworthy of the honour you propose to do me, and I can only ask pardon for my boldness."

The other sisters also tried to excuse themselves, but the Sultan would hear nothing.

"No, no," he said, "my mind is made up. Your wishes shall be accomplished."

So the three weddings were celebrated that same day, but with a great difference. That of the youngest was marked by all the magnificence that was customary at the marriage of the Shah of Persia, while the festivities attending the nuptials of the Sultan's baker and his chief cook were only such as were suitable to their conditions.

This, though quite natural, was highly displeasing to the elder sisters, who fell into a passion of jealousy, which in the end caused a great deal of trouble and pain to several people. And the first time that they had the opportunity of speaking to each other, which was not till several days later at a public bath, they did not attempt to disguise their feelings.

"Can you possibly understand what the Sultan saw in that little cat," said one to the other, "for him to be so fascinated by her?"

"He must be quite blind," returned the wife of the chief cook. "As for her looking a little younger than we do, what does that matter? You would have made a far better Sultana than she."

"Oh, I say nothing of myself," replied the elder, "and if the Sultan had chosen you it would have been all very well; but it really grieves me that he should have selected a wretched little creature like that. However, I will be revenged on her somehow, and I beg you will give me your help in the matter, and to tell me anything that you can think of that is likely to mortify her."

In order to carry out their wicked scheme the two sisters met constantly to talk over their ideas, though all the while they pretended to be as friendly as ever towards the Sultana, who, on her part, invariably treated them with kindness. For a long time no plan occurred to the two plotters that seemed in the least likely to meet with success, but at length the expected birth of an heir gave them the chance for which they had been hoping.

They obtained permission of the Sultan to take up their abode in the palace for some weeks, and never left their sister night or day. When at last a little boy, beautiful as the sun, was born, they laid him in his cradle and carried it down to a canal which passed through the grounds of the palace. Then, leaving it to its fate, they informed the Sultan that instead of the son he had so fondly desired the Sultana had given birth to a puppy. At this dreadful news the Sultan was so overcome with rage and grief that it was with great difficulty that the grand-vizir managed to save the Sultana from his wrath.

Meanwhile the cradle continued to float peacefully along the canal till, on the outskirts of the royal gardens, it was suddenly perceived by the intendant, one of the highest and most respected officials in the kingdom.

"Go," he said to a gardener who was working near, "and get that cradle out for me."

The gardener did as he was bid, and soon placed the cradle in the hands of the intendant.

The official was much astonished to see that the cradle, which he had supposed to be empty, contained a baby, which, young though it was, already gave promise of great beauty. Having no children himself, although he had been married some years, it at once occurred to him that here was a child which he could take and bring up as his own. And, bidding the man pick up the cradle and follow him, he turned towards home.

"My wife," he exclaimed as he entered the room, "heaven has denied us any children, but here is one that has been sent in their place. Send for a nurse, and I will do what is needful publicly to recognise it as my son."

The wife accepted the baby with joy, and though the intendant saw quite well that it must have come from the royal palace, he did not think it was his business to inquire further into the mystery.

HJFORD.

The following year another prince was born and sent adrift, but happily for the baby, the intendant of the gardens again was walking by the canal, and carried it home as before.

The Sultan, naturally enough, was still more furious the second time than the first, but when the same curious accident was repeated in the third year he could control himself no longer, and, to the great joy of the jealous sisters, commanded that the Sultana should be executed. But the poor lady was so much beloved at court that not even the dread of sharing her fate could prevent the grand-vizir and the courtiers from throwing themselves at the Sultan's feet and imploring him not to inflict so cruel a punishment for what, after all, was not her fault.

"Let her live," entreated the grand-vizir, "and banish her from your presence for the rest of her days. That in itself will be punishment enough."

His first passion spent, the Sultan had regained his self-command. "Let her live then," he said, "since you have it so much at heart. But if I grant her life it shall only be on one condition, which shall make her daily pray for death. Let a box be built for her at the door of the principal mosque, and let the window of the box be always open. There she shall sit, in the coarsest clothes, and every Mussulman who enters the mosque shall spit in her face in passing. Anyone that refuses to obey shall be exposed to the same punishment himself. You, vizir, will see that my orders are carried out."

The grand-vizir saw that it was useless to say more, and, full of triumph, the sisters watched the building of the box, and then listened to the jeers of the people at the helpless Sultana sitting inside. But the poor lady bore herself with so much dignity and meekness that it was not long before she had won the sympathy of those that were best among the crowd.

But it is now time to return to the fate of the third baby, this time a princess. Like its brothers, it was found by the intendant of the gardens, and adopted by him and his wife, and all three were brought up with the greatest care and tenderness.

As the children grew older their beauty and air of distinction became more and more marked, and their manners had all the grace and ease that is proper to people of high birth. The princes had been named by their foster-father Bahman and Perviz, after two of the ancient kings of Persia, while the princess was called Parizade, or the child of the genii.

The intendant was careful to bring them up as befitted their real rank, and soon appointed a tutor to teach the young princes how to read and write. And the princess, determined not to be left behind, showed herself so anxious to learn with her brothers, that the intendant consented to her joining in their lessons, and it was not long before she knew as much as they did.

From that time all their studies were done in common. They had the best masters for the fine arts, geography, poetry, history and science, and even for sciences which are learned by few, and every branch seemed so easy to them, that their teachers were astonished at the progress they made. The princess had a passion for music, and could sing and play upon all sorts of instruments. She could also ride and drive as well as her brothers, shoot with a bow and arrow, and throw a javelin with the same skill as they, and sometimes even better.

In order to set off these accomplishments, the intendant resolved that his foster children should not be pent up any longer in the narrow borders of the palace gardens, where he had always lived, so he bought a splendid country house a few miles from the capital, surrounded by an immense park. This park he filled with wild beasts of various sorts, so that the princes and princess might hunt as much as they pleased.

When everything was ready, the intendant threw himself at the Sultan's feet, and after referring to his age and his long services, begged his Highness's permission to resign his post. This was granted by the Sultan in a few gracious words, and he then inquired what reward he could give to his faithful servant. But the intendant declared that he wished for nothing except the continuance of his Highness's favour, and prostrating himself once more, he retired from the Sultan's presence.

Five or six months passed away in the pleasures of the country, when death attacked the intendant so suddenly that he had no time to reveal the secret of their birth to his adopted children, and as his wife had long been dead also, it seemed as if the princes and the princess would never know that they had been born to a higher station than the one they filled. Their sorrow for their father was very deep, and they lived quietly on in their new home, without feeling any desire to leave it for court gaieties or intrigues.

One day the princes as usual went out to hunt, but their sister remained alone in her apartments. While they were gone an old Mussulman devotee appeared at the door, and asked leave to enter, as it was the hour of prayer. The princess sent orders at once that the old woman was to be taken to the private oratory in the grounds, and when she had finished her prayers was to be shown the house and gardens, and then to be brought before her.

Although the old woman was very pious, she was not at all indifferent to the magnificence of all around her, which she seemed to understand as well as to admire, and when she had seen it all she was led by the servants before the princess, who was seated in a room which surpassed in splendour all the rest.

"My good woman," said the princess pointing to a sofa, "come and sit beside me. I am delighted at the opportunity of speaking for a few moments with so holy a person." The old woman made some objections to so much honour being done her, but the princess refused to listen, and insisted that her guest should take the best seat, and as she thought she must be tired ordered refreshments.

While the old woman was eating, the princess put several questions to her as to her mode of life, and the pious exercises she practised, and then inquired what she thought of the house now that she had seen it.

"Madam," replied the pilgrim, "one must be hard indeed to please to find any fault. It is beautiful, comfortable and well ordered, and it is impossible to imagine anything more lovely than the garden. But since you ask me, I must confess that it lacks three things to make it absolutely perfect."

"And what can they be?" cried the princess. "Only tell me, and I will lose no time in getting them."

"The three things, madam," replied the old woman, "are, first, the Talking Bird, whose voice draws all other singing birds to it, to join in chorus. And second, the Singing Tree, where every leaf is a song that is never silent. And lastly the Golden Water, of which it is only needful to pour a single drop into a basin for it to shoot up into a fountain, which will never be exhausted, nor will the basin ever overflow."

"Oh, how can I thank you," cried the princess, "for telling me of such treasures! But add, I pray you, to your goodness by further informing me where I can find them."

"Madam," replied the pilgrim, "I should ill repay the hospitality you have shown me if I refused to answer your question. The three things of which I have spoken are all to be found in one place, on the borders of this kingdom, towards India. Your messenger has only to follow the road that passes by your house, for twenty days, and at the end of that time, he is to ask the first person he meets for the Talking Bird, the Singing Tree, and the Golden Water." She then rose, and bidding farewell to the princess, went her way.

The old woman had taken her departure so abruptly that the Princess Parizade did not perceive till she was really gone that the directions were hardly clear enough to enable the search to be successful. And she was still thinking of the subject, and how delightful it would be to possess such rarities, when the princes, her brothers, returned from the chase.

"What is the matter, my sister?" asked Prince Bahman; "why are you so grave? Are you ill? Or has anything happened?"

Princess Parizade did not answer directly, but at length she raised her eyes, and replied that there was nothing wrong.

"But there *must* be something," persisted Prince Bahman, "for you to have changed so much during the short time we have been absent. Hide nothing from us, I beseech you, unless you wish us to believe that the confidence we have always had in one another is now to cease."

"When I said that it was nothing," said the princess, moved by his words, "I meant that it was nothing that affected you, although I admit that it is certainly of some importance to me. Like myself, you have always thought this house that our father built for us was perfect in every respect, but only today I have learned that three things are still lacking to complete it. These are the Talking Bird, the Singing Tree, and the Golden Water." After explaining the peculiar qualities of each, the princess continued: "It was a Mussulman devotee who told me all this, and where they might all be found. Perhaps you will think that the house is beautiful enough as it is, and that we can do quite well without them; but in this I cannot agree with you, and I shall never be content until I have got them. So counsel me, I pray, whom to send on the undertaking."

"My dear sister," replied Prince Bahman, "that you should care about the matter is quite enough, even if we took no interest in it ourselves. But we both feel with you, and I claim, as the elder, the right to make the first attempt, if you will tell me where I am to go, and what steps I am to take."

Prince Perviz at first objected that, being the head of the family, his brother ought not to be allowed to expose himself to danger; but Prince Bahman would hear nothing, and retired to make the needful preparations for his journey.

The next morning Prince Bahman got up very early, and after bidding farewell to his brother and sister, mounted his horse. But just as he was about to touch it with his whip, he was stopped by a cry from the princess.

"Oh, perhaps after all you may never come back; one never can tell what accidents may happen. Give it up, I implore you, for I would a thousand times rather lose the Talking Bird, and the Singing Tree and the Golden Water, than that you should run into danger."

"My dear sister," answered the prince, "accidents only happen to unlucky people, and I hope that I am not one of them. But as everything is uncertain, I promise you to be very careful. Take this knife," he continued, handing her one that hung sheathed from his belt, "and every now and then draw it out and look at it. As long as it keeps bright and clean as it is today, you will know that I am living; but if the blade is spotted with blood, it will be a sign that I am dead, and you shall weep for me."

So saying, Prince Bahman bade them farewell once more, and started on the high road, well mounted and fully armed. For twenty days he rode straight on, turning neither to the right hand nor to the left, till he found himself drawing near the frontiers of Persia. Seated under a tree by the wayside he noticed a hideous old man, with a long white moustache, and beard that almost fell to his feet. His nails had grown to an enormous length, and on his head he wore a huge hat, which served him for an umbrella.

Prince Bahman, who, remembering the directions of the old woman, had been since sunrise on the look-out for some one, recognised the old man at once to be a dervish. He dismounted from his horse, and bowed low before the holy man, saying by way of greeting, "My father, may your days be long in the land, and may all your wishes be fulfilled!"

The dervish did his best to reply, but his moustache was so thick that his words were hardly intelligible, and the prince, perceiving what was the matter, took a pair of scissors from his saddle pockets, and requested permission to cut off some of the moustache, as he had a question of great importance to ask the dervish. The dervish made a sign that he might do as he liked, and when a few inches of his hair and beard had been pruned all round the prince assured the holy man that he would hardly believe how much younger he looked. The dervish smiled at his compliments, and thanked him for what he had done.

"Let me," he said, "show you my gratitude for making me more comfortable by telling me what I can do for you."

"Gentle dervish," replied Prince Bahman, "I come from far, and I seek the Talking Bird, the Singing Tree, and the Golden Water. I know that they are to be found somewhere in these parts, but I am ignorant of the exact spot. Tell me, I pray you, if you can, so that I may not have travelled on a useless quest." While he was speaking, the prince observed a change in the countenance of the dervish, who waited for some time before he made reply.

"My lord," he said at last, "I do know the road for which you ask, but your kindness and the friendship I have conceived for you make me loth to point it out."

"But why not?" inquired the prince. "What danger can there be?"

"The very greatest danger," answered the dervish. "Other men, as brave as you, have ridden down this road, and have put me that question. I did my best to turn them also from their

HJFORD

purpose, but it was of no use. Not one of them would listen to my words, and not one of them came back. Be warned in time, and seek to go no further."

"I am grateful to you for your interest in me," said Prince Bahman, "and for the advice you have given, though I cannot follow it. But what dangers can there be in the adventure which courage and a good sword cannot meet?"

"And suppose," answered the dervish, "that your enemies are invisible, how then?"

"Nothing will make me give it up," replied the prince, "and for the last time I ask you to tell me where I am to go."

When the dervish saw that the prince's mind was made up, he drew a ball from a bag that lay near him, and held it out. "If it must be so," he said, with a sigh, "take this, and when you have mounted your horse throw the ball in front of you. It will roll on till it reaches the foot of a mountain, and when it stops you will stop also. You will then throw the bridle on your horse's neck without any fear of his straying, and will dismount. On each side you will see vast heaps of big black stones, and will hear a multitude of insulting voices, but pay no heed to them, and, above all, beware of ever turning your head. If you do, you will instantly become a black stone like the rest. For those stones are in reality men like yourself, who have been on the same quest, and have failed, as I fear that you may fail also. If you manage to avoid this pitfall, and to reach the top of the mountain, you will find there the Talking Bird in a splendid cage, and you can ask of him where you are to seek the Singing Tree and the Golden Water. That is all I have to say. You know what you have to do, and what to avoid, but if you are wise you will think of it no more, but return whence you have come."

The prince smilingly shook his head, and thanking the dervish once more, he sprang on his horse and threw the ball before him.

The ball rolled along the road so fast that Prince Bahman had much difficulty in keeping up with it, and it never relaxed its speed till the foot of the mountain was reached. Then it came to a sudden halt, and the prince at once got down and flung the bridle on his horse's neck. He paused for a moment and looked round him at the masses of black stones with which the sides of the mountain were covered, and then began resolutely to ascend. He had hardly gone four steps when he heard the sound of voices around him, although not another creature was in sight.

"Who is this imbecile?" cried some, "stop him at once." "Kill him," shrieked others, "Help! robbers! murderers! help! help!" "Oh, let him alone," sneered another, and this was the most trying of all, "he is such a beautiful young man; I am sure the bird and the cage must have been kept for him."

At first the prince took no heed to all this clamour, but continued to press forward on his way. Unfortunately this conduct, instead of silencing the voices, only seemed to irritate them the more, and they arose with redoubled fury, in front as well as behind. After some time he grew bewildered, his knees began to tremble, and finding himself in the act of falling, he forgot altogether the advice of the dervish. He turned to fly down the mountain, and in one moment became a black stone.

As may be imagined, Prince Perviz and his sister were all this time in the greatest anxiety, and consulted the magic knife, not once but many times a day. Hitherto the blade had remained bright and spotless, but on the fatal hour on which Prince Bahman and his horse were changed into black stones, large drops of blood appeared on the surface. "Ah! my beloved brother," cried the princess in horror, throwing the knife from her, "I shall never see you again, and it is I who have killed you. Fool that I was to listen to the voice of that temptress, who probably was not speaking the truth. What are the Talking Bird and the Singing Tree to me in comparison with you, passionately though I long for them!"

Prince Perviz's grief at his brother's loss was not less than that of Princess Parizade, but he did not waste his time on useless lamentations.

"My sister," he said, "why should you think the old woman was deceiving you about these treasures, and what would have been her object in doing so? No, no, our brother must have met his death by some accident, or want of precaution, and tomorrow I will start on the same quest."

Terrified at the thought that she might lose her only remaining brother, the princess entreated him to give up his project, but he remained firm. Before setting out, however, he gave her a chaplet of a hundred pearls, and said, "When I am absent, tell this over daily for me. But if you should find that the beads stick, so that they will not slip one after the other, you will know that my brother's fate has befallen me. Still, we must hope for better luck."

Then he departed, and on the twentieth day of his journey fell in with the dervish on the same spot as Prince Bahman had met him, and began to question him as to the place where the Talking Bird, the Singing Tree and the Golden Water were to be found. As in the case of his brother, the dervish tried to make him give up his project, and even told him that only a few weeks since a young man, bearing a strong resemblance to himself, had passed that way, but had never come back again.

"That, holy dervish," replied Prince Perviz, "was my elder brother, who is now dead, though how he died I cannot say."

"He is changed into a black stone," answered the dervish, "like all the rest who have gone on the same errand, and you will become one likewise if you are not more careful in following my directions." Then he charged the prince, as he valued his life, to take no heed of the clamour of voices that would pursue him up the mountain, and handing him a ball from the bag, which still seemed to be half full, he sent him on his way.

When Prince Perviz reached the foot of the mountain he jumped from his horse, and paused for a moment to recall the instructions the dervish had given him. Then he strode boldly on, but had scarcely gone five or six paces when he was startled by a man's voice that seemed close to his ear, exclaiming: "Stop, rash fellow, and let me punish your audacity." This outrage entirely put the dervish's advice out of the prince's head. He drew his sword, and turned to avenge himself, but almost before he had realised that there was nobody there, he and his horse were two black stones.

Not a morning had passed since Prince Perviz had ridden away without Princess Parizade telling her beads, and at night she even hung them round her neck, so that if she woke she could assure herself at once of her brother's safety. She was in the very act of moving them through her fingers at the moment that the prince fell a victim to his impatience, and her heart sank when the first pearl remained fixed in its place. However she had long made up her mind what she would do in such a case, and the following morning the princess, disguised as a man, set out for the mountain.

As she had been accustomed to riding from her childhood, she managed to travel as many miles daily as her brothers had done, and it was, as before, on the twentieth day that she arrived at the place where the dervish was sitting. "Good dervish," she said politely, "will you allow me to rest by you for a few moments, and perhaps you will be so kind as to tell me if you have ever heard of a Talking Bird, a Singing Tree, and some Golden Water that are to be found somewhere near this?"

"Madam," replied the dervish, "for in spite of your manly dress your voice betrays you, I shall be proud to serve you in any way I can. But may I ask the purpose of your question?"

"Good dervish," answered the princess, "I have heard such glowing descriptions of these three things, that I cannot rest till I possess them."

"Madam," said the dervish, "they are far more beautiful than any description, but you seem ignorant of all the difficulties that stand in your way, or you would hardly have undertaken such an adventure. Give it up, I pray you, and return home, and do not ask me to help you to a cruel death."

"Holy father," answered the princess, "I come from far, and I should be in despair if I turned back without having attained my object. You have spoken of difficulties; tell me, I entreat you, what they are, so that I may know if I can overcome them, or see if they are beyond my strength."

So the dervish repeated his tale, and dwelt more firmly than before on the clamour of the voices, the horrors of the black stones, which were once living men, and the difficulties of climbing the mountain; and pointed out that the chief means of success was never to look behind till you had the cage in your grasp.

"As far as I can see," said the princess, "the first thing is not to mind the tumult of the voices that follow you till you reach the cage, and then never to look behind. As to this, I think I have enough self-control to look straight before me; but as it is quite possible that I might be frightened by the voices, as even the boldest men have been, I will stop up my ears with cotton, so that, let them make as much noise as they like, I shall hear nothing."

"Madam," cried the dervish, "out of all the number who have asked me the way to the mountain, you are the first who has ever suggested such a means of escaping the danger! It is possible that you may succeed, but all the same, the risk is great."

"Good dervish," answered the princess, "I feel in my heart that I shall succeed, and it only remains for me to ask you the way I am to go."

Then the dervish said that it was useless to say more, and he gave her the ball, which she flung before her.

The first thing the princess did on arriving at the mountain was to stop her ears with cotton, and then, making up her mind which was the best way to go, she began her ascent. In spite of the cotton, some echoes of the voices reached her ears, but not so as to trouble her. Indeed, though they grew louder and more insulting the higher she climbed, the princess only laughed, and said to herself that she certainly would not let a few rough words stand between her and the goal. At last she perceived in the distance the cage and the bird, whose voice joined itself in tones of thunder to those of the rest: "Return, return! never dare to come near me."

At the sight of the bird, the princess hastened her steps, and without vexing herself at the noise which by this time had grown deafening, she walked straight up to the cage, and seizing it, she said: "Now, my bird, I have got you, and I shall take good care that you do not escape." As she spoke she took the cotton from her ears, for it was needed no longer.

"Brave lady," answered the bird, "do not blame me for having joined my voice to those who did their best to preserve my freedom. Although confined in a cage, I was content with my lot, but if I must become a slave, I could not wish for a nobler mistress than one who has shown so much constancy, and from this moment I swear to serve you faithfully. Some day you will put me to the proof, for I know who you are better than you do yourself. Meanwhile, tell me what I can do, and I will obey you."

"Bird," replied the princess, who was filled with a joy that seemed strange to herself when she thought that the bird had cost her the lives of both her brothers, "bird, let me first thank you for your good will, and then let me ask you where the Golden Water is to be found."

The bird described the place, which was not far distant, and the princess filled a small silver flask that she had brought with her for the purpose. She then returned to the cage, and said: "Bird, there is still something else, where shall I find the Singing Tree?"

"Behind you, in that wood," replied the bird, and the princess wandered through the wood, till a sound of the sweetest voices told her she had found what she sought. But the tree was tall and strong, and it was hopeless to think of uprooting it.

"You need not do that," said the bird, when she had returned to ask counsel. "Break off a twig, and plant it in your garden, and it will take root, and grow into a magnificent tree."

When the Princess Parizade held in her hands the three wonders promised her by the old woman, she said to the bird: "All that is not enough. It was owing to you that my brothers became black stones. I cannot tell them from the mass of others, but you must know, and point them out to me, I beg you, for I wish to carry them away."

For some reason that the princess could not guess these words seemed to displease the bird, and he did not answer. The princess waited a moment, and then continued in severe tones, "Have you forgotten that you yourself said that you are my slave to do my bidding, and also that your life is in my power?"

"No, I have not forgotten," replied the bird, "but what you ask is very difficult. However, I will do my best. If you look round," he went on, "you will see a pitcher standing near. Take it, and, as you go down the mountain, scatter a little of the water it contains over every black stone and you will soon find your two brothers."

Princess Parizade took the pitcher, and, carrying with her besides the cage, the twig and the flask, returned down the mountain side. At every black stone she stopped and sprinkled it with water, and as the water touched it the stone instantly became a man. When she suddenly saw her brothers before her her delight was mixed with astonishment.

"Why, what are you doing here?" she cried.

"We have been asleep," they said.

"Yes," returned the princess, "but without me your sleep would probably have lasted till the day of judgment. Have you forgotten that you came here in search of the Talking Bird, the Singing Tree, and the Golden Water, and the black stones that were heaped up along the road?

Look round and see if there is one left. These gentlemen, and yourselves, and all your horses were changed into these stones, and I have delivered you by sprinkling you with the water from this pitcher. As I could not return home without you, even though I had gained the prizes on which I had set my heart, I forced the Talking Bird to tell me how to break the spell."

On hearing these words Prince Bahman and Prince Perviz understood all they owed their sister, and the knights who stood by declared themselves her slaves and ready to carry out her wishes. But the princess, while thanking them for their politeness, explained that she wished for no company but that of her brothers, and that the rest were free to go where they would.

So saying the princess mounted her horse, and, declining to allow even Prince Bahman to carry the cage with the Talking Bird, she entrusted him with the branch of the Singing Tree, while Prince Perviz took care of the flask containing the Golden Water.

Then they rode away, followed by the knights and gentlemen, who begged to be permitted to escort them.

It had been the intention of the party to stop and tell their adventures to the dervish, but they found to their sorrow that he was dead, whether from old age, or whether from the feeling that his task was done, they never knew.

As they continued their road their numbers grew daily smaller, for the knights turned off one by one to their own homes, and only the brothers and sister finally drew up at the gate of the palace.

The princess carried the cage straight into the garden, and, as soon as the bird began to sing, nightingales, larks, thrushes, finches, and all sorts of other birds mingled their voices in chorus. The branch she planted in a corner near the house, and in a few days it had grown into a great tree. As for the Golden Water it was poured into a great marble basin specially prepared for it, and it swelled and bubbled and then shot up into the air in a fountain twenty feet high.

The fame of these wonders soon spread abroad, and people came from far and near to see and admire.

After a few days Prince Bahman and Prince Perviz fell back into their ordinary way of life, and passed most of their time hunting. One day it happened that the Sultan of Persia was also hunting in the same direction, and, not wishing to interfere with his sport, the young men, on hearing the noise of the hunt approaching, prepared to retire, but, as luck would have it, they turned into the very path down which the Sultan was coming. They threw themselves from their horses and prostrated themselves to the earth, but the Sultan was curious to see their faces, and commanded them to rise.

The princes stood up respectfully, but quite at their ease, and the Sultan looked at them for a few moments without speaking, then he asked who they were and where they lived.

"Sire," replied Prince Bahman, "we are sons of your Highness's late intendant of the gardens, and we live in a house that he built a short time before his death, waiting till an occasion should offer itself to serve your Highness."

"You seem fond of hunting," answered the Sultan.

"Sire," replied Prince Bahman, "it is our usual exercise, and one that should be neglected by no man who expects to comply with the ancient customs of the kingdom and bear arms."

The Sultan was delighted with this remark, and said at once, "In that case I shall take great pleasure in watching you. Come, choose what sort of beasts you would like to hunt."

The princes jumped on their horses and followed the Sultan at a little distance. They had not gone very far before they saw a number of wild animals appear at once, and Prince Bahman started to give chase to a lion and Prince Perviz to a bear. Both used their javelins with such skill that, directly they arrived within striking range, the lion and the bear fell, pierced through and through. Then Prince Perviz pursued a lion and Prince Bahman a bear, and in a very few minutes they, too, lay dead. As they were making ready for a third assault the Sultan interfered, and, sending one of his officials to summon them, he said smiling, "If I let you go on, there will soon be no beasts left to hunt. Besides, your courage and manners have so won my heart that I will not have you expose yourselves to further danger. I am convinced that some day or other I shall find you useful as well as agreeable."

He then gave them a warm invitation to stay with him altogether, but with many thanks for the honour done them, they begged to be excused, and to be suffered to remain at home.

The Sultan who was not accustomed to see his offers rejected inquired their reasons, and Prince Bahman explained that they did not wish to leave their sister, and were accustomed to do nothing without consulting all three together.

"Ask her advice, then," replied the Sultan, "and tomorrow come and hunt with me, and give me your answer."

The two princes returned home, but their adventure made so little impression on them that they quite forgot to speak to their sister on the subject. The next morning when they went to hunt they met the Sultan in the same place, and he inquired what advice their sister had given. The young men looked at each other and blushed. At last Prince Bahman said, "Sire, we must throw ourselves on your Highness's mercy. Neither my brother nor myself remembered anything about it."

"Then be sure you do not forget today," answered the Sultan, "and bring me back your reply tomorrow."

When, however, the same thing happened a second time, they feared that the Sultan might be angry with them for their carelessness. But he took it in good part, and, drawing three little golden balls from his purse, he held them out to Prince Bahman, saying, "Put these in your bosom and you will not forget a third time, for when you remove your girdle to-night the noise they will make in falling will remind you of my wishes."

It all happened as the Sultan had foreseen, and the two brothers appeared in their sister's apartments just as she was in the act of stepping into bed, and told their tale.

The Princess Parizade was much disturbed at the news, and did not conceal her feelings. "Your meeting with the Sultan is very honourable to you," she said, "and will, I dare say, be of service to you, but it places me in a very awkward position. It is on my account, I know, that you have resisted the Sultan's wishes, and I am very grateful to you for it. But kings do not like to have their offers refused, and in time he would bear a grudge against you, which would render me very unhappy. Consult the Talking Bird, who is wise and far-seeing, and let me hear what he says."

So the bird was sent for and the case laid before him.

"The princes must on no account refuse the Sultan's proposal," said he, "and they must even invite him to come and see your house."

"But, bird," objected the princess, "you know how dearly we love each other; will not all this spoil our friendship?"

"Not at all," replied the bird, "it will make it all the closer."

"Then the Sultan will have to see me," said the princess.

The bird answered that it was necessary that he should see her, and everything would turn out for the best.

The following morning, when the Sultan inquired if they had spoken to their sister and what advice she had given them, Prince Bahman replied that they were ready to agree to his Highness's wishes, and that their sister had reproved them for their hesitation about the matter. The Sultan received their excuses with great kindness, and told them that he was sure they would be equally faithful to him, and kept them by his side for the rest of the day, to the vexation of the grand-vizir and the rest of the court.

When the procession entered in this order the gates of the capital, the eyes of the people who crowded the streets were fixed on the two young men, strangers to every one.

"Oh, if only the Sultan had had sons like that!" they murmured, "they look so distinguished and are about the same age that his sons would have been!"

The Sultan commanded that splendid apartments should be prepared for the two brothers, and even insisted that they should sit at table with him. During dinner he led the conversation to various scientific subjects, and also to history, of which he was especially fond, but whatever topic they might be discussing he found that the views of the young men were always worth listening to. "If they were my own sons," he said to himself, "they could not be better educated!" and aloud he complimented them on their learning and taste for knowledge.

At the end of the evening the princes once more prostrated themselves before the throne and asked leave to return home; and then, encouraged by the gracious words of farewell uttered by the Sultan, Prince Bahman said: "Sire, may we dare to take the liberty of asking whether you would do us and our sister the honour of resting for a few minutes at our house the first time the hunt passes that way?"

"With the utmost pleasure," replied the Sultan; "and as I am all impatience to see the sister of such accomplished young men you may expect me the day after tomorrow."

The princess was of course most anxious to entertain the Sultan in a fitting way, but as she had no experience in court customs she ran to the Talking Bird, and begged he would advise her as to what dishes should be served.

"My dear mistress," replied the bird, "your cooks are very good and you can safely leave all to them, except that you must be careful to have a dish of cucumbers, stuffed with pearl sauce, served with the first course."

"Cucumbers stuffed with pearls!" exclaimed the princess. "Why, bird, who ever heard of such a dish? The Sultan will expect a dinner he can eat, and not one he can only admire! Besides, if I were to use all the pearls I possess, they would not be half enough."

"Mistress," replied the bird, "do what I tell you and nothing but good will come of it. And as to the pearls, if you go at dawn tomorrow and dig at the foot of the first tree in the park, on the right hand, you will find as many as you want."

The princess had faith in the bird, who generally proved to be right, and taking the gardener with her early next morning followed out his directions carefully. After digging for some time they came upon a golden box fastened with little clasps.

These were easily undone, and the box was found to be full of pearls, not very large ones, but well-shaped and of a good colour. So leaving the gardener to fill up the hole he had made under the tree, the princess took up the box and returned to the house.

The two princes had seen her go out, and had wondered what could have made her rise so early. Full of curiosity they got up and dressed, and met their sister as she was returning with the box under her arm.

"What have you been doing?" they asked, "and did the gardener come to tell you he had found a treasure?"

"On the contrary," replied the princess, "it is I who have found one," and opening the box she showed her astonished brothers the pearls inside. Then, on the way back to the palace, she told them of her consultation with the bird, and the advice it had given her. All three tried to guess the meaning of the singular counsel, but they were forced at last to admit the explanation was beyond them, and they must be content blindly to obey.

The first thing the princess did on entering the palace was to send for the head cook and to order the repast for the Sultan. When she had finished she suddenly added, "Besides the dishes I have mentioned there is one that you must prepare expressly for the Sultan, and that no one must touch but yourself. It consists of a stuffed cucumber, and the stuffing is to be made of these pearls."

The head cook, who had never in all his experience heard of such a dish, stepped back in amazement.

"You think I am mad," answered the princess, who perceived what was in his mind. "But I know quite well what I am doing. Go, and do your best, and take the pearls with you."

The next morning the princes started for the forest, and were soon joined by the Sultan. The hunt began and continued till mid-day, when the heat became so great that they were obliged to leave off. Then, as arranged, they turned their horses' heads towards the palace, and while Prince Bahman remained by the side of the Sultan, Prince Perviz rode on to warn his sister of their approach.

The moment his Highness entered the courtyard, the princess flung herself at his feet, but he bent and raised her, and gazed at her for some time, struck with her grace and beauty, and also with the indefinable air of courts that seemed to hang round this country girl. "They are all worthy one of the other," he said to himself, "and I am not surprised that they think so much of her opinions. I must know more of them."

By this time the princess had recovered from the first embarrassment of meeting, and proceeded to make her speech of welcome.

"This is only a simple country house, sire," she said, "suitable to people like ourselves, who live a quiet life. It cannot compare with the great city mansions, much less, of course, with the smallest of the Sultan's palaces."

"I cannot quite agree with you," he replied; "even the little that I have seen I admire greatly, and I will reserve my judgment until you have shown me the whole."

The princess then led the way from room to room, and the Sultan examined everything carefully. "Do you call this a simple country house?" he said at last. "Why, if every country house was like this, the towns would soon be deserted. I am no longer astonished that you do not wish to leave it. Let us go into the gardens, which I am sure are no less beautiful than the rooms."

A small door opened straight into the garden, and the first object that met the Sultan's eyes was the Golden Water.

"What lovely coloured water!" he exclaimed; "where is the spring, and how do you make the fountain rise so high? I do not believe there is anything like it in the world." He went forward to examine it, and when he had satisfied his curiosity, the princess conducted him towards the Singing Tree.

As they drew near, the Sultan was startled by the sound of strange voices, but could see nothing. "Where have you hidden your musicians?" he asked the princess; "are they up in the air, or under the earth? Surely the owners of such charming voices ought not to conceal themselves!"

"Sire," answered the princess, "the voices all come from the tree which is straight in front of us; and if you will deign to advance a few steps, you will see that they become clearer."

The Sultan did as he was told, and was so wrapt in delight at what he heard that he stood some time in silence.

"Tell me, madam, I pray you," he said at last, "how this marvellous tree came into your garden? It must have been brought from a great distance, or else, fond as I am of all curiosities, I could not have missed hearing of it! What is its name?"

"The only name it has, sire," replied she, "is the Singing Tree, and it is not a native of this country. Its history is mixed up with those of the Golden Water and the Talking Bird, which you have not yet seen. If your Highness wishes I will tell you the whole story, when you have recovered from your fatigue."

"Indeed, madam," returned he, "you show me so many wonders that it is impossible to feel any fatigue. Let us go once more and look at the Golden Water; and I am dying to see the Talking Bird."

The Sultan could hardly tear himself away from the Golden Water, which puzzled him more and more. "You say," he observed to the princess, "that this water does not come from any spring, neither is brought by pipes. All I understand is, that neither it nor the Singing Tree is a native of this country."

"It is as you say, sire," answered the princess, "and if you examine the basin, you will see that it is all in one piece, and therefore the water could not have been brought through it. What is more astonishing is, that I only emptied a small flaskful into the basin, and it increased to the quantity you now see."

"Well, I will look at it no more today," said the Sultan. "Take me to the Talking Bird."

On approaching the house, the Sultan noticed a vast quantity of birds, whose voices filled the air, and he inquired why they were so much more numerous here than in any other part of the garden.

"Sire," answered the princess, "do you see that cage hanging in one of the windows of the saloon? that is the Talking Bird, whose voice you can hear above them all, even above that of the nightingale. And the birds crowd to this spot, to add their songs to his."

The Sultan stepped through the window, but the bird took no notice, continuing his song as before.

"My slave," said the princess, "this is the Sultan; make him a pretty speech."

The bird stopped singing at once, and all the other birds stopped too.

"The Sultan is welcome," he said. "I wish him long life and all prosperity."

"I thank you, good bird," answered the Sultan, seating himself before the repast, which was spread at a table near the window, "and I am enchanted to see in you the Sultan and King of the Birds."

The Sultan, noticing that his favourite dish of cucumber was placed before him, proceeded to help himself to it, and was amazed to find that the stuffing was of pearls. "A novelty, indeed!" cried he, "but I do not understand the reason of it; one cannot eat pearls!"

"Sire," replied the bird, before either the princes or the princess could speak, "surely your Highness cannot be so surprised at beholding a cucumber stuffed with pearls, when you believed without any difficulty that the Sultana had presented you, instead of children, with a dog, a cat, and a log of wood."

"I believed it," answered the Sultan, "because the women attending on her told me so."

"The women, sire," said the bird, "were the sisters of the Sultana, who were devoured with jealousy at the honour you had done her, and in order to revenge themselves invented this story. Have them examined, and they will confess their crime. These are your children, who were saved from death by the intendant of your gardens, and brought up by him as if they were his own."

Like a flash the truth came to the mind of the Sultan. "Bird," he cried, "my heart tells me that what you say is true. My children," he added, "let me embrace you, and embrace each other, not only as brothers and sister, but as having in you the blood royal of Persia which could flow in no nobler veins."

When the first moments of emotion were over, the Sultan hastened to finish his repast, and then turning to his children he exclaimed: "Today you have made acquaintance with your father. Tomorrow I will bring you the Sultana your mother. Be ready to receive her."

The Sultan then mounted his horse and rode quickly back to the capital. Without an instant's delay he sent for the grand-vizir, and ordered him to seize and question the Sultana's sisters that very day. This was done. They were confronted with each other and proved guilty, and were executed in less than an hour.

But the Sultan did not wait to hear that his orders had been carried out before going on foot, followed by his whole court to the door of the great mosque, and drawing the Sultana with his own hand out of the narrow prison where she had spent so many years, "Madam," he cried, embracing her with tears in his eyes, "I have come to ask your pardon for the injustice I have done you, and to repair it as far as I may. I have already begun by punishing the authors of this abominable crime, and I hope you will forgive me when I introduce you to our children, who are the most charming and accomplished creatures in the whole world. Come with me, and take back your position and all the honour that is due to you."

This speech was delivered in the presence of a vast multitude of people, who had gathered from all parts on the first hint of what was happening, and the news was passed from mouth to mouth in a few seconds.

Early next day the Sultan and Sultana, dressed in robes of state and followed by all the court, set out for the country house of their children. Here the Sultan presented them to the Sultana one by one, and for some time there was nothing but embraces and tears and tender words. Then they ate of the magnificent dinner which had been prepared for them, and after they were all refreshed they went into the garden, where the Sultan pointed out to his wife the Golden Water and the Singing Tree. As to the Talking Bird, she had already made acquaintance with him.

In the evening they rode together back to the capital, the princes on each side of their father, and the princess with her mother. Long before they reached the gates the way was lined with people, and the air filled with shouts of welcome, with which were mingled the songs of the Talking Bird, sitting in its cage on the lap of the princess, and of the birds who followed it.

And in this manner they came back to their father's palace.